Girls Are
Not Smiling

WOL-VRIEY

Burning Bulb
PUBLISHING

Other Books By Wol-vriey:

The Bizarro Story of I

Meat Suitcase

Chainsaw Cop Corpse

Vegan Zombie Apocalypse

Boston Posh (Bud Malone #1)

Vegan Vampire Vaginas

Vagina Mundi

Melanie Nemesis Catchpole

Bizarro 101: A Basic Primer

Boston Corpse (Bud Malone #2)

Dr. Orgasm

Boston Lust (Bud Malone #3)

Pussy Transmission

Hell Dancer

Novellas and Short Stories By Wol-vriey

Big Trouble in Little Ass
A novella featured in
Westward Hoes

Forever Ago Sunshine
A short story featured in
The Big Book of Bizarro

Girls Are
Not Smiling

WOL-VRIEY

Burning Bulb
PUBLISHING

Girls Are Not Smiling
By **Wol-vriey**

Burning Bulb Publishing
P.O. Box 4721
Bridgeport, WV 26330-4721
United States of America
www.BurningBulbPublishing.com

Cover image of strict young woman licensed from Fotolia #78314710 © gromovataya.
Author Photo: Lolade Akinsowon © 2014.

First Edition.

Paperback Edition ISBN: 978-0997773033

Printed in the United States of America

FRIDAY NIGHT

CHAPTER 1

Pagan / Joker

They were gathered in the basement of the Hole Faith, a nightclub in the lower Boston suburb of West Roxbury.

The club basement was a wide stone enclosure well outfitted for activities like this—bloodletting and human sacrifice.

For one thing, it was soundproof—the screams of the dying had nowhere to go but around and around until they—tragedy-laden audio ghosts—expired like their makers. For another, the basement was mess-proof too: its walls, floor, and pillars were of polished red stone, and a black altar stood in its exact middle, which was also the center of the black pentagram etched in the red floor with chips of black stone. The altar's sides were decorated with reversed crosses. The ground right beside the altar was riddled with holes to drain away the blood falling from its gutters, drain the redness down to pipes that in turn ferried it away into the building's waste disposal system.

The basement of the Hole Faith was designed with the same utilitarian planning used for morgues. All in all, the place was perfect for bloodshed and murder with arcane purpose.

There were six members of the Abyss Club present at the ritual in the basement: a priestess, five acolytes, and the sacrifice—a little boy a week old who lay naked on the black altar gurgling happily amidst the warmth.

The heat and light came from torches fixed to the red walls, torches that also threw shadows which if considered closely, looked less human than they should. In these ambient flickers, the upside-down crosses hung in the room's four corners all seemed alive, wooden creatures of deep malefic intent. Occasionally—when one of the witches present looked their way—the crosses did move, their forms turning suddenly limbed and scaly, and then they were merely blasphemous wooden totems again.

Pagan, priestess of this Abyss coven, stood by the baby's head. A tall and attractive young woman, she was as naked as the day she was born. Her black hair hung free to halfway down her back. Her blue eyes—made up in black—were pools of concentration. Her black-painted lips parted and shut continually as she recited the ritual of invocation. Tattooed on her left breast (on the outside of her left nipple) was the Abyss Club's logo—an upside down 'A.'

The five acolytes—three men and two women—stood solemn-faced around the altar in their black robes, though one of the men clearly had an erection. This was permitted in Satanic ritual. Both acolyte women had flushed faces, their nipples pressed hard as penises against their vestments, their breasts rising and falling with their intense and excited breathing.

Pagan chanted on. Her voice ebbed and flowed, tumultuous yet soothing like the waves off the Massachusetts coastline.

On the altar, the little boy gurgled away, blissfully unaware that his life expectancy could be measured in seconds.

Suddenly Pagan fell silent. A shadow had appeared in the air over the sacrificial child. It was black and razor-thin.

A man gasped on seeing it; Pagan froze him with a cold look. This wasn't the time to wimp out, fear could ruin the summoning. In addition to being a bloodthirsty son-of-a-bitch, the demon Avex was known to be capricious as hell. Despite their protecting pentagrams, it might turn on them in an instant if it thought them easy prey.

Pagan lifted the black knife over her head. Her muscles corded with tension, she held it there, awaiting the right moment to strike the child.

But . . .

The slice of shadow slowly thickened, becoming a floating wisp, like cigarette smoke uncertain of which way to drift. The baby's eyes seemed to catch it; the child raised its hands as if impatient to be possessed by the summoned evil.

Suddenly Pagan felt much less sure of herself. *Is this ritual really the right thing to do?*

She had no permission whatever from the Abyss Club's Overseer Council to do what she was about to. Nor would they have granted it had she asked. In fact, this summoning was simply a plot of hers for self-advancement within the Abyss organization: trapping one of the pit's most powerful demons in a human body couldn't be overlooked, and the witch who performed that feat was only steps away from a place on the council herself. Similarly, those who helped her accomplish it were themselves assured of accelerated promotion through the ranks.

Black blade poised overhead, she looked around at her helpers.

Directly opposite her by the baby's feet was its mother Sarah, her body still plump from her pregnancy; her breasts swollen with nourishing milk which even now wet the front of her robe. Pagan wondered how Sarah felt about what they were doing. She wondered what it felt like to carry a child in your body for nine months, then a week later watch it being butchered . . .

She met Sarah's eyes. They were flushed with lust, like she couldn't wait for the ritual to be over already so she could drag her husband Joe off to fuck and make another child for Pagan to sacrifice. Sarah licked her lips. No, she clearly didn't care about the kid on the altar. Her gaze said maternal instinct could go screw itself.

Pagan looked away from her, at Joe. He was the one with the erection. She understood that—evil was seductive, it had a sexual charge. The greater the evil, the greater the erotic charge. And what evil could ever be greater than handing over your own child to be killed?

(Pagan herself felt little arousal, just the slightest of warmths between her thighs which might even be attributed to the heat in the room. But that was because she was controlling the action, her concentration so focused on getting this right that it was almost giving her a headache. Had she been a mere participant, it would be all she could do to keep from fingering herself here by the blasphemous altar.)

Her eyes roved left, then right, to the other two men. Both stood stony faced, hands clutched in front of their robes, their gazes riveted on the mass of smoke now swirling above the child, a mass that now had a recognizable head and limbs.

It's almost time, Pagan thought. Now the knife felt clammy in her grasp, and her arms seemed to tire. But no, she was going through with this. She wasn't prepared to remain a nobody in Abyss, like so many others she'd seen. That was easy—being *nobody* was easy—you just did nothing, existed, were one of the devil's black sheep.

Pagan wanted the top spot in Abyss. She willed the weariness from her arms, clutched her knife tighter. Pentagrams flickered in its ebonite metal. Her black hair was damp with the sweat from her scalp and her back, and her back itched, but she forced her mind off her discomfort and onto the last person involved in this ritual.

Joker.

Joker, a young six-foot-tall redhead as slim as a snake, stood on Sarah's left, near the foot of the altar. Her face too was flushed with lust, her green eyes gleaming like she'd happily screw a goat now if given the chance. Pagan grimaced on seeing her nipples so stiff against her silk robe.

Her expression neutral, she locked eyes with Joker.

(Above the table, the smoke kept thickening. It looked like someone was pouring in darkness from somewhere and filling up an invisible inkwell. The temperature in the basement amped up a notch.

Despite the increased heat, Pagan felt chilled, chilled by her fears of what might still go wrong. If this ritual failed . . . the repercussions could be disastrous for her. Particularly if news of her doings here reached the ears of the coven supervisors.

A disobedience of this magnitude without a success to justify it would fetch her the severest of punishments. A mutilation possibly, losing a breast or a limb, or even an eye. At the very least, she faced half a year spent making degrading animal porn flicks, or serving time in one of the organization's private hells, where she'd beg for a merciful death that would never come.

Joker nodded back at Pagan as coolly as she could manage through her arousal.

Pagan couldn't stand the 22-year-old, with her pretty face and leaf-green eyes. She just knew that Joker was out to oust her as coven priestess. Joker was simply too magic-savvy to be content to remain in her shadow.

Worse still, Pagan suspected Joker knew more magic than she did.

And, she also had almost iron self-control. Pagan had been at her initiation a year earlier. Joker hadn't flinched an inch even at that most extreme of pain tests: inserting a cattle prod into her sex and triggering it. (The test was to ensure that the new member wouldn't crack under torture: male initiates had electrodes stuck into their testicles and a specially modified electric prod inserted into their rectums where it rested perfectly against their prostate glands. Any man who could withstand that level of agony was to be treasured—most successful new acolytes couldn't walk for two days afterwards.) Joker had frozen solid when the electric shock hit her vagina; she'd twitched and streams of tears had run from her bulging eyes; but no, she'd not even whimpered once, never given voice to her obvious agony.

"Damn, I got a real charge out of that," she'd moaned weakly after the prod was removed. An impressive statement considering the kind of pain she was in.

Pagan had taken note of her that day. A woman like that was someone to watch out for. Someone to fear even.

And, yes, Pagan feared Joker. For a witch, she was simply too perfect, too bad to be true.

And now it was almost time. Pagan forced her mind off her companions. Her skin ran with sweat from the heat, her breasts and sex felt swollen, her nipples felt incredibly fat.

The infant she was about sacrificing seemed frozen though: his little body was rigid, his gaze was locked on the black 'thing' in the air over the altar.

It's glorious, she thought, watching the airborne oil-spill develop a face, one that grimaced evilly at them all.

Time to do this, she decided.

And then, about to stab the knife into the child's belly and slice its torso in two to grant the hanging demon access to its flesh, Pagan was distracted by unwelcome noise.

She stiffened and listened. The noise recurred and grew louder; it was coming from outside the basement. (She could sense the demon's impatience to possess its vessel of flesh, but this sounded serious.) She wasn't the only one who'd heard the loud sounds, all the others were also looking over at the basement door.

Oh fuck, she thought a moment later, when Boston's finest broke down the door and crashed through into the basement. Six cops carrying large guns like this was a terrorist cell bust.

"Freeze, you're all under arrest for attempted murder!"

The six witches stood there looking confused. Pagan felt like crying. *Oh, no, this can't be happening.* She wasn't supposed to get caught holding a knife above a newborn with clear intent to murder it. There was no other legal interpretation. She was in deep shit now.

The only member of their group who seemed unfazed by the raid was Joker. She looked calm. Pagan wondered if *she'd* sold them out to the cops.

Gun poised ready to shoot, the foremost policeman pushed through the group to the black altar. A burly man with hard gray eyes, he frowned coldly at Pagan. "Now if I were you, lady, I'd lower that knife . . . and slowly, alright?" He waved his gun at her. "Hey, I ain't frigging joking. That knife touches down anywhere near that baby and you'll be shopping for a new head."

Behind him, the other cops were brandishing handcuffs at the club members, Sarah was already manacled and weeping and flinging glances at her unsacrificed baby, clearly wondering how she'd let Pagan talk her into something that'd likely see her locked in a stone motel for the next twenty years on a 'conspiracy to commit murder' charge.

"I'm Lt. Bradley, BPD," the burly officer informed Pagan. "We've been keeping an eye on you lot for a while. Looks like our tipoff paid off big time this time—now we're shutting you assholes down for good." Behind him, Joe was protesting loudly while being manhandled to the floor and his hands cuffed behind him.

Lt. Bradley tuned to scowl at Joe. "Hey, shut the fuck up, punk."

He returned his attention to Pagan. "What the hell do you need a little kid for? Can't you sacrifice its mother?"

Then, while she slowly lowered the black knife like he'd ordered, Lt. Bradley got a good look at the swirling black midair mass for the first time. (He'd previously mistaken it for a decoration, a satanic chandelier.)

"What in God's holy name is that?"

"Welcome to my world, lieutenant," Pagan said. "There's no frigging way I'm letting you lock me up."

And that was true. It suddenly seemed to her an utterly pathetic way to fizzle out: to be arrested by the BPD while you had a very powerful demon floating in midair.

Lt. Bradley still hadn't gotten over his shock. "I said, what the motherfucking shit is that damn thing?" The other cops too were now staring at the strange apparition in the room, which was grinning at them with black lips like bicycle tires, blinking eyes like huge black clams.

Taking advantage of the lawmen's confusion, Pagan burst into desperate motion. Maybe she could still salvage this fucked-up situation. She was definitely going to try. Following the cop's instructions to do it slowly, she'd so far lowered her knife to breast level. Now she yanked it high overhead again and stabbed down with all her might at the baby boy. Once she completed the ritual, Avex would be strong enough to save them all. It could easily destroy the policemen, maybe even reduce this entire building to rubble too; whatever it would take. Given the slightest chance, the supernatural generally kicked the natural's ass.

She'd however not counted on the lieutenant's fast reflexes. Realizing she was about sacrificing the baby, he grabbed it by an arm and leg and yanked it sideways off the stone.

With no infant flesh cushioning its fall, Pagan slammed the knife hard into the altar. The force of the blow slipped her right hand off the knife's hilt and down over its blade so it sliced her palm open. She yelped with pain as her blood poured onto the black stone, then yelped again as she realized that something had gone wrong.

Feeling a dark descending presence overhead, she looked up. *Oh, no, fuck!* The black swirl—the demon Avex—was falling towards her. *Shit, my spilled blood's given the damn thing access to me!*

She wasn't the only one scared either. Joker, usually the picture of calm, now had an utterly horrified look on her face.

The flailing oil slick that was Avex hit Pagan smack in the face. For an instant she was blinded, then the dark ectoplasm sank through the membrane of her eyes and she could see again. The room looked the same, though everyone—police and witches alike—was gaping at her in horror. She looked down at herself and realized why. Swirling black goop wrapped her naked form like a cloak. And it hurt like shit—she felt like she was being fried and frozen at the same time. She felt the black stuff forcing itself through her skin and deep into her marrow.

She yelled out. The policemen stood confused, unsure what to do.

Pagan saw Joker duck out of the grasp of the cop who'd been about cuffing her wrists. His eyes locked on Pagan's odd transformation, he made no attempt to stop her. Worming her way between two other policemen, and stepping over the prone Joe, Joker backed away from the altar, backing up all the way to the kicked-in basement door. There, she perched on the bottom step, watching Pagan.

Lt. Bradley was petting the rescued infant, who'd begun crying.

As the black swirl penetrated her flesh, Pagan realized she was in danger of losing her mind to it. She knew that much about demonic possession: whatever else happened, she must not let this creature, this thing she'd summoned from the pits of Hell, take over her mind. And the demon was doing its damn best to subdue her intelligence.

She shuddered with horror as she realized how desperate it was to own her. It *was* a monster; she felt intense evil pour through her as Avex entered the million doors her pores offered it. She wondered in shock how she'd ever been so naïve as to think she could control one of Hell's lords in the flesh.

But . . . it was supposed to enter that baby, not me! Not me!

And then it was over. The beast from Hell was completely inside her and she was no longer exactly herself. She didn't know what else she was, but she was definitely something other—both more and less—than she'd been merely seconds ago.

She frowned at the policemen. "Damn, that hurt."

Then, the next moment, she was seized by a force way beyond her control, a violent raging that demanded satiation. She was suddenly hungry, ravenous for blood and death. Something broke in her mind, her consciousness folded like a collapsing box, and the demon took her over.

Nooo!!! she screamed wordlessly as she blacked out, completely submerged under Avex's irresistible torrent of EVIL.

***

Watching from the bottommost step, Joker hardly believed what was transpiring.

'Something'—and it had to be the demon—had just taken Pagan over. Her eyes had turned completely black and her mouth had instantly filled up with big teeth. Her body was still normal but her previously beautiful face was now all distorted, horrid like an old crone's.

Moving like pink lightning, Pagan stepped around the black altar and up to the lieutenant holding the baby. She raked her hands across the infant's body. The child instantly fell apart in a horrendous shower of red. His arms and chunks of torso splattered the basement walls and pillars and the people. His head flew across into a corner. One of the boy's legs flopped down onto the altar.

Pagan snatched the bleeding leg up. Joker now saw that her hands were tipped by long black claws from which the child's blood dripped.

Sarah began screaming. Joker wondered why: *You happily gave up the kid to be sacrificed, didn't you? What's the difference, girl? He's still dead!*

Pagan stared at Sarah, her completely black eyes bulging with evil. Then, like one tearing Styrofoam, she ripped a corner off the stone altar and flung it at Sarah.

The chunk of stone hit Sarah in the forehead, and—Joker gasped—went right through her skull. The stone burst out of the rear of her head and hit the wall behind her, leaving a meat tunnel from which blood poured, and inside of which pulverized brains were visible.

Sarah swayed in place for a moment, then crashed to the floor and lay with her buttocks and legs flopping like a netted fish.

Joker perched there on her bottom step, torn between her desire to stay so she could report what was happening to her Abyss superiors, and the need to flee and save her own life. She really didn't want any part of this mess anymore.

The cops all seemed confused. Joker didn't know if it was the fact that Pagan now looked like a zombie's grandmother, or that she was simply moving faster than their brains could process, but even with two corpses the police officers still seemed stuck in slow motion.

Lt. Bradley was sputtering in disbelief and wiping baby guts out of his eyes.

Pagan flung the baby's severed leg into her mouth and bit down on it, crunching the soft flesh and bone like it was a cookie. She grinned like the infant flesh was delicious. She swallowed the whole leg.

Mouth smeared with blood, she regarded everyone in the room.

Joker stared back at her. She had no doubt that Pagan wasn't currently in control of the corporation of herself—Avex was. Pagan was buried somewhere deep under the layers of the monster's evil.

Fuck! At the moment, non compos mentis has a new definition.

The policemen now regained their wits. "Fire! Shoot her!"

But the demon-possessed woman was too fast for them. The cops fired, but she anticipated the swing of their weapons even before the bullets erupted from their flaming muzzles.

Steeling herself against mindless flight, Joker watched Pagan rip into the police officers. Her position in the doorway slightly

11

obstructed her view, but still she clearly saw several bullets hit Pagan's nude body and puff out her skin in red explosions. But Pagan was unfazed, and seemingly unhurt. Like a human tornado, she smashed into the cops and pulled them limb from limb. She stuck her claws deep into Lt. Bradley's chest and ripped his heart out, then ate it. She tore one man's head off, then pulled off both his arms, then dug her hands deep into his guts. Two other cops shot themselves to bits while trying to hit her; or maybe they did hit her, only the bullets passed harmlessly through her body and into theirs.

And suddenly, all the policemen were dead, and it was only the witches left. Joker now realized that there was no protection between Pagan and herself.

Oh shit! she thought. *The BPD are gonna take a really dim view of this slaughter.*

Pagan was covered in blood, running red with it. And she still looked hungry, even though her toothy mouth dripped with red liquid that fell to splatter her breasts and bare feet, feet now tipped with black claws like eagles' talons.

She stared down at her former coven. Sarah's husband Joe and the other two men were lying on their backs on the floor, their bodies covered with chunks of policeman.

"Help us, great Avex!" they cried.

"Yeah, free us before the cops bring reinforcements!" Joe added. "They'll be down the stairs any minute now!"

In response, Pagan/Avex laughed. Then she said—in a thunderous deep demonic voice that rumbled through the basement and made Joker want to crap herself, "Do not worry about the police. There aren't any more of them coming. Lt. Bradley played a lone wolf card on this one, and the card failed him. It is just us true believers here now."

"Yes! Praise Lucifer! Free us, great Avex—we your faithful coven!"

Oh, you fools, Joker thought. *Guys, at the moment, Pagan is far away from here. And as far as I can tell, Avex doesn't give a dog-turd about any of us.*

Lt. Bradley's lipless head grimaced from atop the altar. The rest of his body lay on the altar's far side, out of Joker's view.

"Help us, great Avex!" came the plea again from those bound on the floor.

Pagan looked instead across at Joker, and bared her bloody black teeth. Joker understood that look. *The bitch-beast is still hungry and it wants me as its next snack. To hell with that thought!*

Pagan dashed at her.

Joker, however, had anticipated the attack. She bent, grabbed up a pistol from a severed hand, and aimed it at Pagan. Pagan swiped at her; she pulled the trigger, firing point blank into Pagan's face.

Pagan howled in pain.

Joker was thinking on her feet now. While firing she was muttering a spell under her breath, imbuing the slugs with supernatural power. The gunshots flung Pagan halfway across the basement. She landed on her back on the altar. She lay there, limbs jerking, black ichor pouring from her face as she clawed the air.

But the damage was already healing, the shattered face repairing itself.

Realizing she hadn't a moment to lose, Joker pulled a cellphone out of one of the dead cops' pockets. Casting worried glances over at the monster on the altar, she hastily entered a number from memory.

"Hello! Hey, Nero, it's Joker! The poop has hit the propeller down here! Hey, Nero, can you fucking hear me!?"

Something hit Joker hard in the face. Momentarily stunned, she dropped the phone, then looked down to see what the missile was. Shit! It was Lt. Bradley's severed head, flung at her by Pagan. Blood dripping from a cut in her cheek, she glared at the demon-possessed woman.

Pagan looked completely healed.

"I'm going to kill you now," she said in that baritone rumble.

"The hell you are, bitch. I never liked you either." She bent down and plucked up an automatic rifle. She hastily checked that the safety was off. Then, she coolly regarded Pagan, who was absentmindedly stroking her sex.

The dropped phone had meanwhile fallen by Joe's ear. A drunken voice squeaked from it. "Hey, Joker, baby, what's happening? Say, this ain't your regular number, girl!"

"Pagan's gone nuts!" Joe screamed into the phone. "She's raised the demon Avex and—!"

That was as much as he got out before Pagan, leaping down from the black altar, stamped his head flat with a foot. Joe's brains squirted left and right from his ears. His body jerking in death below her, Pagan hungrily regarded Joker. The look on her wizened-zombie face was that of a starved wolf which has just sighted a juicy piglet.

Joker kept her place in the basement doorway with the weapon trained on Pagan.

Pagan licked her lips.

Joker muttered the spells to magically empower her bullets, then growled, "Stay back or I'll shoot!"

"You can't kill me."

The infernal vocal rumbling sounded like it was inside Joker's head. "No? Come one step closer and we'll see about that."

With a squelching sound, Pagan pulled her foot from the wreckage of Joe's head and stepped forward.

Joker pulled the trigger. The rifle fired one shot that chipped flesh off Pagan's left arm, then it jammed.

Joker gaped down at the gun in horror. *What the . . . ? I mean—now?*

Then, as Pagan realized what had just happened and began laughing at her, she flung the gun at the possessed woman and turned and legged it up the stairs.

***

Avex didn't pursue Joker. It was wary of the fleeing woman's weapons: those bullets had stung and it had no desire to feel that hurt again.

In its distorted body of human flesh, it instead looked down at the two surviving male acolytes handcuffed on the floor.

Still believing that it fought on their behalf, neither man had yet attempted to escape the basement.

Avex was frustrated. It already felt the rush of power of its incarnation waning—this woman whose body it currently occupied was strong in spirit, and would not long remain a prisoner. Even now, with her mind held in thrall by its own, her subconscious fought unceasingly for freedom, clawing its dogged way back from where it was stored.

No! It would not allow this! Not yet. It still wanted to feed its lust for ravening. It must control this witch—this Pagan! It must! At least for a while longer.

It regarded the bloody mess in the basement. The carnage of its creation. Like God when He'd made the universe, Avex was greatly pleased.

And still, there were these two men on the floor. These supplicants for its coming. They looked delicious to Avex. The twin oil-slicks of its eyes shone with pleasure. The lust to rend and tear flesh and drink sweet blood once again filled the demon.

In its borrowed female body, it grinned broadly at them, lips parted wide to reveal its massive teeth. "I thank you for summoning me from Hell, my good servants. Now I will eat you both."

"No! Please, Lord, no!" they both screamed.

Claws spread wide, Avex fell on the two men and began tearing their flesh to shivering shreds, digging its teeth in deep and biting out massive chunks of meat from their bodies.

Their dying screams echoed around and around the basement.

SATURDAY

CHAPTER 2

Britt

Britt Wilson pushed open the front door of her house and tramped into the living room. Due to an unplanned turn of events, she'd gotten back home early.

She lived with her mother on West Roxbury's Corey Street. The house was a spacious four-bedroom bungalow with an attached garage, a wide front yard, and a few trees for shade.

Unable at first to make up her mind what to do now that she had a free Saturday afternoon on her hands, Britt ditched her black jacket and shoes, then sat down in a green armchair and stared at the TV. The TV was on but muted, set to the Fashion Channel like her mother had been watching it before leaving to go do something.

Britt snickered her disdain. Her mom, Joanna Wilson, was obsessed with fashion, with new clothes and makeup tips; with Botox, with plastic surgery and eternal youth.

Since divorcing Britt's father, Joanna had also been on a sexual rampage. But then she'd been rampaging through beds even while married, which was why Boston pediatrician Jeff Wilson had cut the marital cord with her.

Britt was still pissed off by how that had played out. Her father had moved down to Attleboro and she, a third-year sociology student at Tufts University, had been forced to stay behind in Boston with her mother.

Britt neither consciously hated nor disliked her mother. The trouble was just that Joanna Wilson was so beautiful, so glamorous, so in tune with the moment—so desirable to all she came in contact with—that her 20-year-old daughter couldn't help but feel like an ugly duckling eternally cast in her sexy shadow. That overshadowing was a constant occurrence; it had happened so many times that Britt now utterly dreaded going anywhere in her mother's company.

Each time they were out together, Joanna seemed to suck the vitality from her.

The last time she'd been summarily deglamorized by Joanna had been at her Uncle Mortimer's funeral. (Uncle Mort had been a crusty old curmudgeon who never saw eye to eye with anyone. He'd died because he'd been so busy arguing with his wife Clarissa that he'd run a red light and parked his 1970 Dodge Challenger right into the side of a FedEx van. Clarissa survived the accident with just a broken leg and whiplash; at her husband's burial Mass she'd been a miserable shell of her former self, sitting up at the front of the Church of the Most Precious Blood on Dover's Center Street with her leg plastered up and her neck in a brace, and endlessly dabbing tears from her eyes.)

Britt, conscious of the solemnity of the occasion, had dressed sensibly in a black dress and hat which she felt conveyed her grief appropriately. Joanna, however, though also dressed in black, looked more like her older brother's young mistress than his grieving sister. Her dress was cut shockingly low up top and barely reached her knees below and was so tight she looked poured into it. Her makeup was Gothic red carpet, her lips as red as the communion wine. Sitting in the front pew beside her sister-in-law, with her large breasts pointing haughtily forward, it was no wonder that the young priest spent most of his time not looking their way, preferring to address his sermon to those seated at the rear of the church.

And afterward at the reception? Britt kept well away from Joanna. It took only the first few unspoken comparisons between mother and daughter that she'd read in men's eyes (*How the hell did THIS come out of THAT?*) to assure her that she'd rather be someplace else. She first stuck to two nerdy cousins like glue, then with deep relief, escaped to her father's side. She found it odd how she looked more like her dad's fiancée's daughter than her own mother's. Kelly dressed the way a middle-aged woman should, stylish but classy; not like—she gazed angrily over at where her mother stood surrounded by college professors all peering down her cleavage while complimenting her on her "exceptional choice of funeral attire" and shook her head. She'd been backseated again.

This crap had to stop. The eternally young Joanna Wilson had to give way to the younger generation. If she didn't . . . each time her mother stole her spotlight Britt felt so mad that she could have killed Joanna. (Afterwards, she was always shocked by the depths of her rage. And scared by how much resentment she was repressing.)

Britney Wilson definitely wasn't ugly. A straw-blonde like her mother, she just had the sort of face that was pretty with a little makeup, and 'almost plain' without it. The 'blank canvas' kind of face fashion designers crave in their supermodels; the sort that became whatever one painted on it.

Britt was tallish and slim and had large blue eyes. She was very insecure, however. Not where her personal competence was concerned, but with men. With the opposite gender, she tended to be awkward even at the best of times.

(Also, largely due to her mother's eternal overshadowing, she was rather uptight. She was very nervy and found it hard to relax.)

Still, even by her own exacting standards, she wasn't doing badly in the dating game. She was currently dating Chris Norton, a star MIT student (and football player too), and Chris was a prime catch.

Even her best friend Lori couldn't understand Chris's attraction to Britt. "I'm sure you look like his mom," she was always saying.

Britt put that down to jealousy. Though utterly gorgeous, Lori Kaminski had zero luck where guys were concerned. She couldn't even get pity fucks. The fact that she was on ATDs didn't help any either. And then there was that time, when, with a potential boyfriend in the house, her dad had busted her for adding their dog's Prozac prescription to her own. Her clean-cut young suitor had been out of the door like a flash.

Britt told Lori afterwards: "Most men don't mind having depressed, neurotic wives, they just don't like them ready-made. Guys want sane wives. You need to hide your neuroses until you're married. Then you let it out in carefully planned phases, preferably after you've had two or three kids. Then your husband thinks he's the one who's driven you nuts and the guilt makes him hang around."

"Britt, *your* dad left, and he's a doctor."

"My mom's madness isn't behind her eyes, it's between her thighs."

So Lori had no man of her own. And Britt, though unglamorous and no beauty queen and constantly being sexually eclipsed by her mother, had Chris.

She checked her watch. Saturday was a complete drag. Chris was busy helping his father out with a furniture restoration job. He and she were going to see the new *Avengers* movie later, but till then? What was she going to do with herself?

(Yeah, Saturday afternoon sucked monkey balls.)

She could go see Lori, but Lori had been on a really heavy low of recent. Best friend or not, she was currently a total drag to hang out with, what with her endless talk of suicide and being too scared to go through with it. (If she didn't really need a friend, Britt would have been begging Lori's parents to commit her.)

With the day promising to lead up to some great sex tonight, Britt definitely didn't want Lori's bad psychic vibes in her head. Oh no. She'd call Lori tomorrow and tell her how fantastic the cunnilingus had been, just to make her jealous.

She realized then that she was still seated staring at the muted TV. The channel had just auto-switched to something on 'E!' with lots of movie stars in long slit dresses sexily treading red carpets. Her mother must have programmed the change, but where was Joanna? On the toilet?

She checked her watch. *I've been back twenty minutes now. Mom where are you?*

Now she became worried. The bungalow suddenly seemed eerily quiet to her. She got up and paced the living room. Had someone gotten into the house? Was her mother being sexually assaulted?

"Mom," she called tentatively. "Mom, are you home?"

The only reply she got was the soft hum of the fridge from the kitchen.

Then, about to yell, she noticed a set of yellow panties tucked into the angle of the sofa. Those definitely hadn't been there when she'd left home at noon.

She walked over and carefully picked the panties up and sniffed them. Her nose wrinkled in disgust. Her mother was clearly at it again: in addition to their strong stink of female musk, the panties had a long pale discolored patch in their middle. The patch was still damp; Joanna must have left the living room barely moments before Britt arrived back home.

She replaced the stained panties on the sofa like they were infected.

Now that she was certain her mother wasn't being raped, Britt pondered what to do. She'd feel awkward meeting her mom's new male friend, knowing what they'd been up to in the mistress bedroom.

It would be awkward on both sides: Joanna making introductions while both she and the man attempted to be nice to each other.

But then, her mother might just be masturbating. No crime in that; Britt had even borrowed Joanna's rabbit vibrator (without her knowledge) on more than one occasion. (For easy access, Joanna always left the rabbit out on her nightstand.)

In fact, searching for Joanna's other sex toys in the nightstand drawer was how Britt had discovered her mother's gun, a small Taurus revolver. The pretty weapon had been loaded. Britt had checked the drawer since; the pistol was still in there. Still loaded; still daintily dangerous.

Remembering the concealed handgun completed Britt's chain of relief. Joanna could damn well look after herself.

That, however, still didn't resolve her problem of what to do with herself now. *It might be best to just go hang out in my room. Check out Instagram, or take a nap till they're done. But mom's like a sexual marathon runner; she screws like she's in long-distance training. She can go on for hours when the mood takes her.*

Then she changed her mind and got out her cellphone and dialed Chris. Like she'd half-expected, Chris's phone went straight to voicemail. She giggled "I love you, baby" into the phone then hung up.

She considered calling Lori and asking if she could come over, then decided a definite 'NO.' Lori depressed was bad news. Britt didn't want to walk in on her slitting her wrists. *Not like she has the guts to do it anyway, the little pussy; all depression and no action.*

Instead, she decided to just watch TV for a while. The sun was shining in through the windows and maybe, just frigging maybe, with the right programming the day wouldn't suck so much. MTV first, they'd promised an interview with that new Emo band Poison Temple. Then she'd (hopefully) escape to the safe haven of her bedroom before Joanna and her booty call got out of bed.

But first, I need a drink.

She walked through the dining room into the kitchen. The house was spotless, though she never cleaned it herself: her mother's other obsession was housekeeping.

Britt got herself a soda from the fridge, then feeling somewhat hungry, fished through the range of diet products in there for something fattening. Threatened bloat notwithstanding, she disliked compromising on the taste of her food. That was for Joanna, who was almost fifty, to fret about. Low fat yoghurts, salads, and diet recipes weren't for her.

She finally found a pre-packed sandwich with a lot of ham in it. She picked up a tray then made her back to the living room.

Halfway through the dining area, she remembered the jar of pickles on the top fridge shelf. Yeah, she'd like some of those too.

She put down her tray on the dining table and turned back towards the kitchen. That was when she noticed the white MIT baseball cap discarded by the hallway entrance.

The baseball cap had clearly been dropped by her mother's beau of the moment during their hasty retreat into the bedroom. She crossed the dining room and picked it up, intending to put it in the living room.

Then . . .

Hold on, this is Chris's cap. What's it doing here?

She knew the baseball cap was Chris's because of the red lip-shaped lipstick smear beside the MIT logo on its front. She'd put that smear there herself; an accident while they'd been making out a month ago. (She remembered the incident clearly. She'd just gotten through telling Chris that Joanna wanted him to help her fix some creaky deck chairs that she'd just pulled out of the garage; then she'd given him her mother's cellphone number so he could call her to discuss when he'd visit the house.) She'd lunged at him to kiss him just as he'd been pulling the cap off and it had gotten in between their mouths.

Afterwards, Chris had said the lipstick mark looked cool, like her badge of ownership on him, and he'd left it there.

So what was the cap doing here? It hadn't been here this morning. She was certain of that, and Chris was right now over at his dad's custom-built-furniture shop, sawing wood and hammering nails.

Or was he?

Britt suddenly didn't feel like eating or drinking or watching MTV anymore. A rage of nervous butterflies stirred her insides. She was so flustered, thinking was a chore. *Oh, hell no! It can't be what I'm thinking, can it? Chris might be out round back, fixing mom's chairs, but . . . he got them done a month ago. Or maybe mom called him over to . . . but then, why would he tell me he was working with his dad?*

The memory of the crotch-stained silk panties on the sofa simply aggravated her more. Barefoot and hoping she was wrong, she softly padded to the rear of the house, to her mother's bedroom.

Joanna's bedroom door was open. She clearly felt no need to shut it; there was no one else in the house.

Even before peeking in, Britt could hear Joanna's soft ecstatic moans.

Britt was shivering with dread now. *Oh, God, please, let it not be my Chris in there. Not with my mom. God, please.*

But it was. She looked in in cold disbelief at her darling boyfriend with his head bobbing between her mother's legs, giving her cunnilingus, while Joanna, beautiful as a movie star, gasped and moaned like she was in porn Heaven. Chris gave great head; Britt just knew how her mother felt at the moment, as her boyfriend's wet tongue laved her even wetter sex, teasing the swollen clitoris . . .

He's mine, you old bitch! Mine! She screamed internally, but the words didn't form in her throat and mouth. She had to keep quiet now, anyway, quieter than a mouse. Her heart was breaking, and she didn't want her mother to know.

No!—Joanna mustn't know that Britt had discovered this ultimate one-upping.

In the bedroom, Chris now flipped her mother over onto her belly and sank his penis into her from behind. Like he knew Britt was watching he'd positioned Joanna perfectly so she could see the glistening penis slide in and out. Joanna began moaning even louder. Each smack of Chris's crotch against her buttocks was loud as a gunshot in Britt's ears. She stood there powerless to do a thing, the victim of a kangaroo court's emotional firing squad.

She tried to cry, but the tears wouldn't come. She had no release in that direction. Instead, the cover of her well of rage—that store of resentment towards her mother that she'd stuffed away over years of being endlessly one-upped and pushed into the background—finally blew off.

Watching her mother enjoy her boyfriend, his penis entering her sex over and over again, anger flooded Britt like snake venom. It pulsed through her in violent waves. *Oh, mom, you've gone too far now! I'll teach you! And you, Chris, how could you? I frigging love you!*

Motivated by masochistic impulse, Britt waited till they were done. Chris's come seeped from Joanna's vagina. Love for him seeped out of Britt's heart to be replaced by raw hatred.

The moment Joanna rolled back over and kissed Chris's lips was the moment Britt irreversibly snapped. At that instant, her previously strong concepts of right and wrong imploded, and black and white blended into a gray zone, one in which she, like her mother before her, could do whatever she pleased to whoever got in her way.

Joanna was doing that right now, wasn't she? Taking the only thing Britt had had, the one fort she'd considered unassailable to Joanna's disgusting oversexiness?

Her first impulse was to charge into the bedroom, pull the gun from the nightstand drawer, and blow them both away. But no, this had to be done right. And death would much too simple an escape for her mother. Chris? She didn't give a rat's pee about him now. Whatever he got, he deserved. But her horrible mother? Oh, was Joanna gonna get it. *Really* gonna get it.

So she stood there in her shock, arms pressed tightly to her sides like they'd been glued in place, her hands balled into fists.

Joanna got through with kissing Chris. They sat back on pillows gasping for breath. Sweat dripped off Joanna's large breasts as they rose and fell.

Chris, all handsomeness and muscles and brown hair, regarded Joanna Wilson with awe.

"Wow! I don't get how you can be tighter down there than your daughter, Mrs. Wilson."

"Joanna. I've told you to call me Joanna."

"Okay, Joanna, how can you be tighter than Britt? Your grip down there is just incredible! It was all I could do to keep from coming once I got inside you. How do you do it?"

"You mean after pushing Britt out of the place?" She giggled, then stroked his face fondly, her voice a satiated purr. "It runs in the family, baby—Wilson women get better with age. No, I'm just joking—I do lots of kegels. I tried to teach them to Britt, but she's still too young to appreciate the need for a tight manhole." She reached a hand down and stroked his soft penis, then grabbed it and squeezed hard. "You ready to go again? I need a whole lot more stuffing and filling."

He was hardening under her touch. "I dunno, Mrs. . . . Joanna, I really should be leaving. Britt might come back early. She thinks I'm helping my dad out." His voice faltered. "I love your daughter, Joanna. I really do. I don't want to hurt her."

"Don't worry. You *won't* hurt her—she'll never know. I'm neither indiscreet nor jealous. I'll even pay for your wedding. Look at it this way: I'm simply teaching you what she likes. Like I said, it runs in the family. Admit it, doesn't my pussy look a bit like hers?"

Britt just stood there listening. The conversation was surreal. *He loves me and yet he's screwing her?*

"It looks a bit different," Chris said.

Joanna sounded piqued now. "How? In what way?"

"You've less hair down there."

Her respondent laughter reverberated through Britt's brain like thunder. "Like I said, women get better with age. By trial or error we work out what men crave." He was hard now; she wet her fingers with spit and fondled him expertly.

"Are you *sure* Britt can't come home early?"

"Positive. She's over at my sister-in-law's, helping her pack for a trip to Europe. Clarissa lives out in Dover, so Britt took my car. I'd be surprised if she makes it back home before seven." She raised her gaze to the wall clock. "And it's two-thirty now, so we've got all afternoon to make love." She straddled him facing the door. "Now I'm gonna teach you how to reverse cowgirl a woman. Trust me, once you give Britt a taste of this she'll never leave you; my prissy kid'll be begging to have *your* kids." She reached back and adjusted her buttocks on his crotch, spreading her labia wide around the head of his engorged penis.

Joanna began lifting and lowering herself on Chris's erection and grinding her buttocks on it. One hand braced her against the bed, the other squeezed her breasts in turn. She closed her eyes and resumed moaning in ecstasy. Below her, Chris pumped and grunted, his pleasured face occasionally visible behind Joanna's rising thighs.

Britt watched the sexual juice drip down her mother's thighs for a while, then decided she'd seen enough. She'd been standing by the door now for twenty minutes. Besides, with Joanna now facing the hallway, there was the chance she'd be exposed as a Peeping Tom. That insult added to her injury she could do without.

She turned and padded away from Joanna's bedroom. She was amazed at how calm she felt. Indeed she felt so calm, she wondered if she'd ever really loved Chris, if maybe she hadn't just been using him like her mother was now, as a sex toy.

She decided it didn't matter: personified by her mother, the world had shit on her one time too many, and she'd had enough.

It was time she shit back on the world, and she'd poop so hard and fast, the damn human toilet was gonna overflow.

Her mother's carnal moans pursuing her, she put on her shoes and jacket and left the house. First, however, she carefully replaced her food and drink in the fridge and put the tray back where she'd taken it from. She also both replaced Chris's white baseball cap where it had fallen (she'd been holding on to it all this while) and stuffed Joanna's panties back in the corner of the sofa she'd removed them from. (She was again surprised by how calmly she was behaving. Her movements were measured and precise, not frantic with the simmering rage she felt.) Joanna mustn't even suspect that she'd been in the house.

Also as part of her plan to not alert her mother of her early return from Dover, she left the silver BMW parked out front. (The noise of her starting it up might be a giveaway. She'd parked by the side of the house, in front of the garage. Joanna wouldn't see the car except she came to the front door, which was unlikely.)

Walking hurriedly down Corey Street to Highland train station, Britt rehearsed a plan in her head. It was crazy and outrageous, but she'd go through with it. She didn't care about anything anymore, all she wanted now was to get even. She meant to get even with her mother . . . with every-frigging-one.

And she thought she knew someone who felt the same way.

Her best friend Lori Kaminski. Assuming of course, that Lori hadn't either OD'd or slit her wrists yet.

A train was just pulling into the station. Suddenly overcome by a sense of desperate purpose, Britt broke into a run to catch it, pulling her phone from her pocket as she did so.

Lori you'd better be home!

CHAPTER 3

Lori

For the third time that Saturday, Lori Kaminski removed the gun from her mouth and laid it on the coffee table. She was sick and tired of her inability to kill herself. Disgusted with how she continually wimped out at the last moment.

She stared at the gun, her father's Ruger Centerfire. Its barrel dripped her saliva onto the table.

Britt's right: I am a damn pussy. Kurt Cobain I'm not. It takes real guts to kill yourself—guts I don't have.

Lori craved the peaceful blackness on the other side of death. It was the painful transition she dreaded.

She been trying unsuccessfully to kill herself for two years now.

Frustrated by this last failure to end her miserable life, Lori walked over to the living room window and stared out at the dark, cold, horrible world she wanted to be gone from already.

She considered flinging herself out from the fourth floor window and shattering her head against the sidewalk. That would be a nice way to die, lying there broken in pieces while people gathered around her. Maybe, even, she'd not be completely dead yet. She'd hear them asking, "Why'd she do it? She was such a nice girl, with a bright future ahead of her." Then they'd shake their heads in horror at the blood oozing from her, while she faded to delicious black to an orchestra of ambulance sirens.

But . . .

She shook her head. That would hurt too. Falling like that, one needed to hit the ground just right, so the skull fractured and the brain exploded. But what if she *didn't* hit the ground just right, and wound up in hospital instead, disfigured with all the skin scraped off her face and a quadriplegic to boot because she'd broken her neck? She'd never

29

be able to kill herself then. That would mean a lifetime of additional horror: her life being lived to the whims of others.

Sleeping pills then? No! She'd already tried that way out. Instead of killing herself, she'd had nightmares of demons torturing her, and woken up strapped down in bed, from where she'd been transferred to a padded cell in the Arbour-Fuller psychiatric hospital in South Attleboro. She'd been in there for three months. She wasn't ever going back to the madhouse again.

She looked longingly back at the gun on the coffee table. All she needed was one moment of crystal clarity, when her suicidal purpose was so lucid that it anaesthetized her against her dread of the pain.

And then . . .

What is wrong with me? Okay, sure, I'm not a guy, but lots of chicks have the balls to kill themselves. So—

Her cellphone rang. She picked it up. It was Britt.

"Hi, Britt," she said dully. "Yeah, I'm home, I'm off today. Nah, I feel like bullshit, you know those really shapeless cowpats after other cows have trampled on them? . . . Shit, you're coming over? I'm really not in the mood to see anyone. . . . You're coming over *anyway*? . . . Yeah, I guess you can if you insist on it. . . . Look, do whatever you like—the door'll be open when you get here. Just walk in. . . . What? I sound like I've been unsuccessfully trying to kill myself again? Britt, I'm not in the mood for jokes . . . Yeah, the door'll be open."

She hung up and went to unlock the apartment door. She left it open, then lay down on her blue sofa, staring out into the hallway with its horrible coat of orange paint, moodily wondering where she could find the courage to do herself in. It rankled when Britt mocked her over her endless chickening out of her suicide attempts.

And, she pondered as full-fledged depression set in again, *what the hell does Britt want anyway? Isn't she supposed to be over at her aunt's?*

***

Lori Kaminski lived in Roslindale, in an old apartment building on Bexley Road, about five minutes walk from Roslindale Village Station.

She'd moved out from her parent's house because she found it too depressing hanging around happy people.

Her parents had gladly supported and subsidized her move; they found it depressing being around her. (Her father had also bought her a car, a gray Mazda 3 sedan that he was perpetually terrified she was going to crash into a tree and total herself along with it. But he needn't have worried: Lori had seen enough car crashes to know dying that way was utter agony. And what if you didn't die quickly?)

She'd been their beautiful happy-go-lucky daughter till age seventeen, when suddenly she'd gotten upset about something (she didn't recall *what* now), and had fallen into the dark emotional pit from which she was yet to emerge.

She'd been on ATDs since age eighteen. They helped a bit but she seemed to have developed immunity to the pills.

She worked at Staples, an office supplies store almost next door to her house. Most days she coped okay and got along well with her boss and fellow employees. But there were days (like this black Saturday) when the hungry darkness really sunk its claws into her. On those days Lori hardly said a word to anyone either before, during, or after work; and once work was done for the day, she rushed home and locked herself in and lay in bed staring at the ceiling while playing metal music loud through her headphones.

She was a curvy brunette, with dark eyes that matched her umber hair. She had nice breasts and was extremely pretty. When she bothered with her appearance, she could look ravishingly beautiful, could have most young men eating out of her hands.

But, Lori felt, what was the damn point of getting made up? Or even of getting up each morning? What was the point of anything at all? Down here in her pit no one could see her. (Lori liked the 'Pit' metaphor—herself trapped in a deep and black cylindrical hole in the earth with just a circle of light overhead and her hands desperately reaching up for its rim, which was always just tantalizing out of reach. Whenever she leapt up to grasp the edges of the Pit, it became magically deeper, the outside world retreating from her. Meanwhile, people who didn't give a damn about her walked by the hole left and right. Occasionally, someone looked down into her pit, shook their head, then smirked and left her to drown in the darkness.

She dressed drab, acted drab, was constitutionally drab.

There was no frigging point to her life and that was why she wanted to die, die, die—to end the cosmic deception that was herself. Oh, she was so damn depressed. So negative that she needed to erase herself already to equalize out into nothing!

She stared at the gun again, her eyes pleading with its seductive black glint. *Oh, if only I had the courage to do it.*

***

It was mid-August. Summer—with all the fun and heat and craziness it brought—was just starting to wane. All the kids were out looking for beaches to laze on, to drain the dregs of the jar of warmth before the leaves started falling from the trees.

Britt and Chris both attended Uni, but were both currently slacking. Well at least Britt was slacking; Chris had to help his dad build furniture.

Lori just had the day off. (Lori had opted out of going to college—additional non-compulsory study seemed pointless to her.)

Britt had been Lori's best friend since high school, the only one who'd hung around when the cracks in her personality began showing. It was a good thing that they were both the same age—twenty—else Lori knew that Britt would be completely insufferable, eternally pulling rank on her and making snide comments on how 'young' she was. Britt was petty like that. Like age had anything to do with anything.

Britt constantly said she had no idea what they saw in each other, they were so much opposite. Lori knew better: they really weren't that much different. It was clear to Lori that Britt had her own Pit too—her mother Joanna. Britt's mother was a black hole that sucked all the light from her daughter. (Not that [as Lori saw it] there was much illumination to suck out of Britt in the first place.)

When Lori could muster up the psychic energy to mount vocal resistance, she and Britt bickered a lot. Their fights normally began with Britt calling Lori 'crazy.' (Like most female conflicts that weren't about men, their spats were catty and generally forgotten for good once over.)

"Your dad should have been a psychiatrist, not a plumber."

"He's not just *a* plumber, he owns the damn company. And *your* dad should have been a psychiatrist, not a pediatrician."

"Whatever. You're so touchy about your papa. And wow, Lori, your mom's so damn BIG. If genetics is anything to go by, say 'Hi' to your overweight future!"

And so on.

Lori simmered. Who the hell was Britt to point fingers anyway? *Okay, so my mom's obese, but at least she doesn't screw everything in pants.*

And she calls me crazy? Crazy? I'm NOT crazy!!!

Everything was *so* obvious to Lori. Britt had a deep thread of anger running through her. She blew up regularly, and though others might think she was just letting off steam at the latest jerk (or jerkette) to screw her over, Lori knew better.

Much better.

Lori *knew.* Finely balanced on the mental knife-edge herself, she instantly recognized fellow crazy when she saw it. Despite her appearance of normalcy, Britt was mere steps away from falling off the lunatic fringe. All she needed was the right trigger to set her off.

And Lori already knew the most likely trigger: Britt's mom.

The Joanna Wilson situation was a particularly jagged one; Britt's personal minefield. Lori saw the repressed rage in Britt's eyes whenever she spoke about her mother. Whenever she told of Joanna's latest offense of dumping her in the social shadows, Lori always felt that Britt was just waiting for Joanna to cross some unspecified line, then she'd loose hell on her.

The hatred Lori sensed Britt had for her mother was scary. How could anyone hate a parent that much . . . when they'd not abused you?

Britt, however, always protested otherwise. "I love my mom; it's just that . . ."

More than once, Lori had tried to mollify Britt. "Look, let it go. You're like me—inhabiting the dead-space. People like us don't attract attention, no matter what we do. It's not that Joanna shines too brightly and eclipses you, it's that you don't shine at all—you've not putting out any radiation to compete with her."

"Don't kid yourself that we're the same, alright? You're officially crazy, I'm not."

"Stop that. I'm *not* crazy. I'm just clinically depressed. I'm an emotional flatliner. Life drags me under."

"And misery likes company, is that it? You want to drag me down to your level and make me suicidal too. Hey, dopey, I'm not jumping off any cliffs with you!"

Lori had burst out crying at the taunt. Britt had stormed out of the room, then returned to apologize and hug and comfort her.

And Britt keeps calling me unbalanced? To Lori's mind, even Pagan Harris (who lived down Britt's street), with her Goth garb and black makeup, and upside-side-down-crosses and pentagram jewelry, posed less of a threat to society than Britney Wilson did. *At least the worst I'll do is harm myself, and Pagan'll brew a few love potions.* (She'd never seen Pagan with a boyfriend, or a girlfriend for that matter, so maybe she was hard up.) *But you, Britney Wilson, what will you do when you lose it big time . . . ?*

Lori was more than a little scared of her bestie. But for the fact that she was female, Britt struck her as the sort of 'normal, well-adjusted person' who suddenly snapped and took a loaded machine gun into a high school or movie theatre and mowed down twenty or thirty teenagers. Then everyone would find theories to explain how such a nice girl became a monster.

***

The moment Britt stepped through her front door that Saturday afternoon, Lori *knew* she'd just toppled headlong off the lunatic ledge. Like she'd always say, crazy knew crazy; it was like gaydar without the same-sex humping. Something about Britt's face, that expression on her lips that was half-smile, half-smirk, half . . . (how many halves could one have anyhow?), assured Lori that her best friend was now one beer short of a six-pack. She was clearly upset as hell, but she wasn't frowning, or more revealingly, ranting in Lori's face the moment the door opened.

Which meant her head was fucked. Likely for good.

She was clearly 'crazy' now, obvious once you knew the signs.

The fuse on her personal time bomb had been lit. Britney Wilson would never be 'normal' again.

To her surprise, Lori was pleased with the transformation. And no, it wasn't just 'misery likes company.' For the first time in memory, she was excited. This was the big scene; whatever Britt was about to do was going to be BIG.

Fireworks!

Lori decided there and then that whatever it was, she was going along for the ride.

CHAPTER 4

Britt

Britt glanced once at the gun on the coffee table, then sat across from Lori. Lori was draped over the sofa looking zonked, completely spaced out. Gorgeous as fuck but plain out of her ever-loving mind.

I was right. She was trying to kill herself again. Well, you pretty suicide candidate, have I got something much better for you.

It really made zero sense to her how she and Lori Kaminski were besties. And yet they were, had been so seemingly for as long as she remembered. No doubt about it. The zonked-out 20-year-old brunette lying opposite her was the only person she could tell everything on her heart. It didn't matter if she was planning to assassinate the President of the USA, she'd tell Lori, and . . . Lori, crazy though she might be, would understand exactly how she felt. Yeah, they were best friends alright. If that wasn't friendship, what was?

(To Britt's intense relief, Lori seemed immune to the weight-gain side effects of antidepressants. Lori looked *really* good, which Britt considered very important. Already unfashionable herself, it would have been completely mortifying to her to be additionally lumbered with a frumpish bestie.)

Too bad neither of us is a dyke, she mused, *or we'd have been lovers.*

Which would have prevented this current nightmare with Chris and Joanna.

Or would it? Britt suddenly understood clearly that even if she'd been a lesbian, her mother would have stolen her girlfriend simply to prove that she could. Motherfucker bitch!

Lori was staring at her like she could read her mind. She waved dully at Britt. "Hey, girl, so you got here."

"My mom's giving my boyfriend the MILF treatment."

"Huh? Speak English or at least YA."

"My mom's screwing Chris."

"What?" Lori suddenly wasn't so lethargic anymore. "Did you just—?"

"Lori, Joanna is fucking Chris. My aunt had to go to emergency confession and cancelled, so I got home early. I caught them in bed together, naked as sin. He was licking her like she was a popsicle. They're still at it as I speak; they plan on going all afternoon."

Lori swung her feet down off the sofa, then sat leaned forward, her elbows on her knees. "Shit, Britt, that's really crappy; it makes me sad just hearing it. What do you plan on doing about it?"

Britt noted the expectancy in her voice. Good, maybe this wouldn't be as hard as she'd thought. Lori had nothing she was living for anyway.

She hissed like a snake. "I wanna get even."

Lori brushed brown hair from her eyes. "Even? How? You wanna expose them, do a webcam thing like Sheila did?" Britt again noted how she sounded disappointed that that was all.

"No, nothing like that. I want to hurt them both. Really *hurt* them. And I want you to help me do it."

Lori frowned. "I just knew today was a bad day. You want to do something illegal?"

Britt leaned forward too. She placed her palms flat on Lori's coffee table and explained exactly what she had in mind. Lori listened, her excitement obviously growing, then she flung up her hands and slumped back in her seat, like life had just defeated again.

"What's wrong?"

"I like it, but . . ."

"But what?"

"We'll get caught and sent to jail," Lori pointed out. "We won't get out for ages. Maybe not ever."

Britt shook her head. "Not if we don't give a shit about the consequences of our actions. Jail is for wimps."

"Britt, the average penitentiary is chock-full of mass murderers, gangsters, pedophiles, crack dealers, rapists, terrorists, and psychos. Okay, except for the pedos, who technically qualify as bullies since they're adults targeting kids, how exactly do you classify any of those other categories as 'wimps'?"

"'Cos they didn't go the whole nine yards, girl. They didn't finish the race. They wimped out at the last hurdle."

"Which was . . . is?"

"They were scared to give up their lives for their cause. At the last minute, when they were staring 'life in jail' in the face compared to being blown away by government bullets, they chose *life* over *death*." She pointed a finger at Lori. "Which would *you* choose?"

Lori's answer was immediate and unhesitant. "Death. There's no way I ever want to be locked away again. You've no idea what being in a strait jacket in that padded cell was like."

"See what I mean? Only those guys didn't, they quit instead. What I'm proposing for us is that we go total kamikaze on this. We jump naked into the acid bath . We give the world hell and go out with guns blazing."

"I like the 'going out' part. I really wish I could die. But why make people suffer? Innocent people."

"Why not?" Britt checked her watch. "And Chris and my mom aren't innocent by any reckoning."

"Britt, you don't even sound heartbroken."

She rolled her eyes. "I heal fast. Mom claimed she was teaching him how to make love to me. Can you beat that for sheer gall?"

"Britt, calm down. She might have been telling the truth. I really think your mom loves you. She just loves sex more."

Britt ignored the inanity; such statements were typical Lori when she was doped up. (Lori stoned was an even worse animal.) "I don't need *her* to teach *him* anything. Chris knows what I like—I've told him over and over again. They both just wanted to hump each other" Now the hot humiliating tears threatened to come, but she blinked them away. She choked back on her heartache, buried it deep below her breasts, in her gall bladder, where it slowly congealed back into green malice.

"You love Chris. You want to spend the rest of your life with him."

"That was two hours ago. Now, I hate him with all my heart and I don't want him to have a life."

"You're absolutely sure of that?"

"Screw both of 'em—I'm getting even. Look, it's three-thirty now, we've got till about six to get this done. Lori, are you in with me on this or not?"

Lori shook her head as if to clear it. To Britt, the way she hung her head on the right for a moment looked like she actually expected stuff to trickle out of her ear onto the sofa. Maybe stuff did trickle out;

maybe, when no else was present, invisible chunks of madness leaked out of her.

Lori raised her head again and the illusion was broken.

Britt was confused. Lori looked like she was about backing out. *Oh, no, you're not frigging wimping out on me. I'm not doing this alone!*

Britt could tell that Lori was interested, she just needed convincing.

She said. "Look, my reasoning's simple. We both wanna die, but we're too chicken to kill ourselves, or each other, so we'll just drive around the country fucking lots of guys and killing people till our number's up, okay?

"Britt, you're not suicidal—I am."

"At the moment, I really don't feel life is worth anything anymore; not mine and definitely not anyone else's. I've lost too many times. As long as Joanna's there I'll never amount to anything. Don't look at me like that, like I'm nuts. It's true—as long as my mother is alive I'll never get out of her shadow, never be my own woman. But if I kill her, I'm a criminal, and the law will be after me. My damn life is a lose-lose situation."

She looked at Lori imploringly, and this time *there were* tears in her eyes. She blinked them back, then, when that didn't halt their flow, ran her hand across her face. She didn't understand anymore how everything had come down to this, how she'd fallen so completely to bits in just two hours.

She looked across at Lori. Lori was smiling and nodding at her. Her eyes were bright and caring.

She understands how I feel, Britt realized. But somehow Lori's empathy and honest sympathy made her feel worse.

Unable to keep meeting Lori's gaze, she instead glanced out of the living room window, its blue drapes parting in a breeze so she could see far and wide toward the train station. She watched the people walking the streets, their minds and bodies wrapped in their own concerns. (It was weird in a way: who'd ever imagine that a massacre was being planned in an apartment they were walking below?) Outside, the world was just the same as when she'd stepped out of it—full of assholes one couldn't trust. Screw 'em all.

She looked back in.

"I'm teaching my mother a lesson she'll never forget," she continued coldly. "And we hit the damn road after that and have the time of our lives. Maybe the cops will get us; maybe someone will have a gun in their house and shoot us both. Hell, maybe even, some serial killer will finally catch us, rape us both, then murder us, okay? We die when we die, together . . . however it works out. The only rule is: we don't wimp out for any reason—we don't let the law take us alive. But until then? We frigging live our asses off. Have ourselves a party of carnage. We drink, we fuck whoever and whenever we want, and most important of all—we don't take shit from anyone. And I mean anyone. Starting with Joanna and my asshole jerk of a boyfriend."

Lori mused a moment, then she grinned broadly. "Sounds like a plan. How many people do we plan on killing?"

"As many as we can without getting caught."

"I thought we wanna get caught . . . and killed."

"STFU, before I boot your ass out of your damn window and help you break your suicidal neck. Just pack the stuff you need, wilya? Don't forget tampons, or your meds."

"Yeah, sure. But, Britt, I really wish you'd stop bitching at me. I'm your best friend. I'm not the one currently screwing Chris."

"Okay, sorry . . . I apologize for that. But, Lori, I'm really worked up . . . and it's four o'clock, we're running out of time. Hurry up. Do you still have that big cordless nail gun you said your dad forgot here when he helped you put up your shelves?"

The scent of blood in the air, Lori instantly perked up. "Yeah, it's in the kitchen, in a cupboard."

"Get it, girl."

Lori got up and left the living room. Her voice floated back to Britt from the kitchen. "I've found it." There followed the sound of something thunking hard into wood. Next, Lori poked her head around the door. She was grinning. "And it's still charged up. This is gonna be messy, right?"

Britt had gotten up and was walking in tight circles around the coffee table. "Girl, you have no idea how messy." She began ticking off a shopping list on her fingers. We'll also need duct tape and some rope. And one or two knives. No, don't bother with the knives—I'll get those at home. Hey, Lori, you got enough duct tape to secure two people? We're out at home, and I don't wanna stop by the store."

Lori leaned out of the kitchen with a brand new reel of gray tape. "What else?"

Britt bent and picked up Lori's father's Ruger. Grinning wickedly at her best friend, she stroked the gun's barrel. "And we'll need this."

Britt was surprised at the deep excitement she felt running through her now that she and Lori were going into action. She felt surprisingly alive like never before. And from the unaccustomed excitement on Lori's face, Lori clearly felt the same way too.

CHAPTER 5

Pagan

Pagan awoke naked in a large bloodstained bed. For the first five minutes afterwards, while her heart beat rapidly and her brain strained to piece together the recent past, she had no idea where she was.

What the . . . ?

The bedroom was cream-colored and large, with two wardrobes and a TV opposite the foot of the bed. Looking hard right revealed a bathroom in which reddish water spilled over the edge of a china-blue bath. Looking the opposite way showed windows through which warm afternoon sunlight beamed in.

Where the . . . ?

While waiting for memories to occupy the blankness between her ears, she examined herself. Other than for her body being completely crusted over with dried blood, she seemed okay. She had zero cuts or injuries. She felt fine too.

In fact she felt absurdly healthy. Better than she had in ages.

She didn't feel calm though. She'd just noticed the severed female arm lying on the bedroom dresser.

She leapt out of bed and hurried over to the dresser. Tentatively, scared, she touched the bloodied hand's wedding ring.

Like the dead woman's finger pulled the trigger of a psychic gun placed to her head, the memories came then. A barrage of horrible visions that hit Pagan like bullets fired into her brain.

She saw herself (or rather her grotesquely clawed hands) ripping open a blonde woman in a bathtub, digging her hands into the blonde's belly and scooping out her intestines and raising them to her lips and biting into them . . .

She tasted again on her tongue sweet blood and dripping red meat.

Disbelieving the evidence in her head, she walked quickly over to the bathroom and peered in. The dead blonde lay beneath the overflowing bathwater, her eyes open, her guts scooped out. Her emptied belly looked like a feeding trough.

Oh, hell no. No!!! NOOOO!!!

Pagan's screams were all in her head though: some self-preservation instinct warned her against vocalizing them.

She felt like she was losing her mind. She staggered forward into the bathroom, her feet splashing the red water that covered the floor. She puked long and hard on the submerged corpse, her actions causing the water to overflow more violently.

Watching her vomit bob on the water surface both upset and calmed her. Slowly, she got a hold of herself. She peered down through the chunks of mess, at the dead woman's face. The frozen agonized expression was unnerving.

This is bad. Really bad. If I did this, what else did I do?

She left the bathroom and bedroom, and walked quickly along the corridor outside towards the next room. Her feet dripped water, but ahead of her were dried red footprints that headed towards her. She deduced that the approaching footprints meant she'd 'done' the blonde last. *Oh, God, who did I kill before her?*

The next room was a child's bedroom. Pagan took one look at the headless little body in the bed and bent over puking again. She heaved and heaved until there was nothing left in her stomach. She straightened up, wiping bile from her lips. She had no idea where the child's head was and she wasn't about touching its corpse to find out. She didn't want to discover that she'd eaten it.

Additional red chunks of gory memory arrived in her head like hearses delivering corpses for burial. She'd killed other people too.

Pagan wasn't so much scared as terrified by this new knowledge. She ran to the end of the stairway and stared down into the living room.

She gasped, beholding the site of a massacre.

The living room walls were splattered with blood and there were shredded body parts everywhere. Pagan trembled. There were more parts than would make up one person, and she remembered now (the memories tantalizingly cut in and out) that there'd been *two* men—two brothers—chatting when she'd looked in through the window. She saw one of their heads under the coffee table.

She sat down on the stairway landing and began weeping her eyes out.

God! Noooo!!!!

***

21-year-old Susan 'Pagan' Harris had initially become a witch simply for the thrill-ride of it. At that time it had seemed the cool thing to do.

When Pagan was eighteen, she and her two best friends had watched the movie *The Mad Witch of Fisher's Bay*. That film had started a Goth/black magic fad amongst the three of them that had lasted a year.

Then Terri, one of Pagan's best friends, had fallen in love with a trucker and moved down to Texas, where she now had two kids. Two months after Terri left Boston, Eliska, the other best friend, had been brutally raped and murdered in her home one night. The killer had never been caught.

Pagan had been particularly close to Eliska and she'd grieved deeply. Before Eliska died, she and Pagan had vowed to ditch both black magic and their black makeup, turn emo and dye their hair pink, then look for a couple of clean-cut young men to marry.

After Eliska's death, however, Pagan instead intensified her magic studies. She began holding séances, trying to summon her dead friend's spirit.

She'd not succeeded. She'd tried and tried again—even broken two Ouija boards in the process—but Eliska's spirit had eluded her.

But then . . . one night, after another exhausting failure to raise Eliska's ghost from the dead and ask who'd killed her, a mysterious young man who'd attended the séance in company of a friend had called Pagan aside.

The young man was called Nero.

"You're a crap medium," he'd said once he'd gotten her alone. "I doubt you could raise the 100 percent proof moonshine from my Uncle Matt's still."

Pagan had glared at him. She was seriously not in the mood to be patronized by some jerk with a superiority complex. "Who the hell are you to tell me—?"

Nero cut her retort short with a sharp gesture. "I haven't finished. Take it from me—you're crap as a medium. I mean, real bad. You lack the empathy to connect with the spirits of the dead. I believe they're scared of you—your dark aura repels them. But in some circles, that same dark aura which scares the human dead can prove priceless."

By now Pagan was more intrigued than pissed off. He seemed to be both praising and criticizing her. And besides, she was horny and Nero was quite hot.

"What I mean is—demons will *love* you. How would you like to join the Abyss Club?"

"What's the Abyss Club?"

He'd begun: "The Abyss Club is a sprawling multinational organization that seeks to bring Hell to Earth. We're not talking about playacting witchcraft here—orgies in graveyards and drinking blood and desecrating churches. Abyss is the real deal. I'm in Abyss, and with the latent dark talent I sense in you, I think you should be too."

She forgot about screwing him, at least that night. "Tell me more."

He did.

***

The Abyss Club was extensive and nebulous, a Satanic hydra with innumerable heads. Pagan usually described it to people as the 'Witchcraft version of the Illuminati.' The club embraced all forms of magic—black and white, high and low, ceremonial, Wiccan, folk, juju and voodoo, left and right hand—so long as they obeyed its rules and were willing to fulfil its stated intent of establishing the kingdom of Hell on Earth. It had branches all over the green planet, hidden hordes of faithful waiting for the day when the Dark Master, the Eternally Accursed One, the fallen Morning Star, would once again walk in Earth's desecrated garden of Eden. And those faithful who hastened his coming would have their dark reward, every one of them would sit on thrones of wet human flesh around their infernal king and assist him in judging the nations for believing in the usurper God and his Son.

The Abyss Club's world headquarters was in Nashville, Tennessee, a location chosen primarily because the city was a flourishing music hub. Where/how better, its leaders questioned, to spread our message of decadence than via the entertainment industry? A second, smaller, but equally influential sub-HQ existed in Los Angeles, where the organization had recently launched its own movie company, Abysmal Films. (The company's first project was a series of children's cartoons laced with subliminal messages.)

Even now, Pagan found it astounding how many of the US's rich and famous and powerful, how many of the influential and well-connected in society—from corporation heads to rock stars, from movie actors and TV anchorwomen to congressmen, and even in some cases evangelical preachers, were sleeper members of the Abyss Club.

The club had 666 covens in the USA, twelve of which were in Massachusetts.

Pagan heading one of those covens after just two years in the fold (and one of the four in Boston, even if it was 'the little unimportant one' down in West Roxbury) was viewed as a major achievement by her peers, subordinates, and superiors.

By everyone in fact, except herself.

She wanted advancement and she wanted it fast. And the time-tested way to get promoted was to show oneself as being better than everyone else at one's level.

Here, patience could hardly prove a virtue; the Abyssal pyramid was too high to scale slowly: In the US alone, there were 665 other coven leaders, and sixteen coven supervisors above those. (Nero, who'd recruited her, was one of these coven supervisors. Nero oversaw all the New England covens. Ironically for one in such a position of responsibility in the Abyss Club, he had negligible magic ability of his own; his main value to the organization was as a 'sensitive': like he'd done with Pagan, he could search out the magic—latent or otherwise—in others. The club valued that.). Overseeing the sixteen supervisors were the six high priests and priestesses, and finally, above those, the six members of the Overseer Council.

Pagan had never seen any point in remaining a mere coven leader, a satanic army corporal or sergeant taking orders from above and delivering them to the rank and file below. If she was dining with the Devil—and she was—it occurred to her that having already ditched the proverbial 'long spoon' by pledging her soul to the Kingdom of Sin, she might as well sit at the same table as her lord Satan, and not halfway across the dining hall where she'd only catch the occasional fleeting glimpse of the Dark Savior.

But how to impress? How to prove her worthiness to sit at that exalted table, on the Devil's left hand? How to stand out from the seemingly endless mob of other witches, from all those others who similarly existed only to propagate EVIL?

Pagan quickly realized that she needed to do something exceptional.

And that had been the root of her plan to raise Avex the Ravager from the pits of Hell. All the grimoires had it that Avex was barred by Satan from visiting Earth before the Apocalypse, and for damn good reason—the demon was a bloodthirsty son-of-a-bitch who didn't give a shit about humanity, but simply wanted blood and gore. Not exactly the best ambassador for the Kingdom of Darkness then.

But, Pagan felt, there had to be a way to neutralize the monstrous spirit.

And she'd finally figured it out: all she had to do was imprison the demon in a baby. How much harm could even the ravenous Avex do when stuck in the frail form of a newborn?

And her plan would have worked too . . . except for the police bust and everything that happened afterwards.

Most of which she couldn't remember.

***

Pagan sat in the middle of the staircase, trying to come to terms with what she'd somehow done to herself. Her memory was sketchy, a mental jigsaw with most of the pieces missing.

She clearly recalled, for instance, her initial success—the black wraith floating over Sarah's baby on the black altar—and after that the police interrupting.

Then a blank—like someone had randomly erased large swathes of an equation from a whiteboard—was drawn over her brain.

Then she remembered trying to sacrifice the child and cutting her hand instead, then . . . the Ravager entering her, filling and hurting her at the same time, making her someone who wasn't herself.

A bloody curtain of skin ripped before her eyes and she saw—and now understood—that she'd murdered almost everyone in the Hole Faith's basement.

With that horrible memory, she tasted their blood on her lips again. Six policemen, four of her coven members, and one child. She recoiled in horror. For a moment it seemed like she once again stood in the midst of their butchered bodies.

Then she sighed deeply. Heartless as it seemed, the dead baby was the most irrelevant of the casualties, the one no one would miss. Its parents had never cared about it from the offset; the child's conception had simply been the means to a bloody end.

The others though . . .

The Boston Police Department was certain to raise hell over this. 'Something' ripping six BPD officers into little wet bits of red meat in a nightclub basement (in the aftermath of what was clearly a Satanic ritual) wasn't about being overlooked. It didn't matter that the police chief's wife was herself a member of Abyss. The best 'Stormy' (one always used code names for those members in sensitive positions) could do would be to dampen the investigation, not stem it all together.

(There *was* the slight chance that someone had thought quickly, and had taken measures to minimize police involvement—had ditched the body parts in the incinerator and scrubbed the basement down with muriatic acid and Lysol, then deodorized it—but she doubted that that was the case. *She* ran the club and she'd been the one who'd run amok. Most likely, everyone upstairs had instantly taken to their heels, and then from a safe distance dialed 911 to come handle the mess.)

Pagan, however, was even more worried about her own people.

The Abyss Club's leadership would be incensed. With the club's blessing, lots of human sacrifice went on daily around the country. Stray people—runaways, homeless folk, hitchhikers, drug addicts, run-down prostitutes and felons on the run—just about anyone who wouldn't be missed was considered fodder for the dark lord's blood 'drainings.' (The 'drainings' were systematic, carried out at specific locations to build up a charge of atrocity that webbed the USA, till finally, the country would be ripe for Satan to walk the Earth again. And this time he wasn't coming as a serpent to tempt anyone's wife.)

But there were rules, the first being that nothing led back to the club. Nothing. The covens murdered in secret, taking the utmost precautions. The bodies of the sacrificed were disposed of in incinerators. Purged of incriminating DNA, the ash of the deceased was then used by the group's witches and warlocks in potions and philters to increase their powers of seduction and destruction.

Pagan winced. She had no doubt that she'd be reprimanded severely for breaking rule number one. Six months of making degrading porn would be considered a light let-off, the merest slap on the wrist.

Secondly, she'd conjured up one of 'The Forbidden,' those denizens of the pit considered too hot to handle; and she'd done it without either permission or supervision.

For a moment her mind flashed the image of Joker's face—the razor sharp nose, wide lips and haughty green eyes, and that trademark crimson hair. No, Joker didn't qualify as 'supervision': for all her skill in magic, she was Pagan's subordinate. And Joker had escaped—in a shard of memory she'd seen the redhead flinging down an automatic rifle and hightailing it up the stairs—and had likely tattled everything to the Abyss hierarchy by now, possibly seeking to take over Pagan's role as head of the coven.

But she doubted she even had a coven any more. Her third problem was that she'd endangered (and worse, killed) her own acolytes.

It got even worse than that. One of the dead men was a popular TV producer. There was going to be *a lot* of stink over his death. His wife, also an Abyss member, would be calling for Pagan's head.

So from what should have been a straightforward enough (if ill-advised) summoning, Pagan now suddenly found herself in a whole universe of trouble.

(She was intentionally relegating her final concern to the rear of her mind. She didn't want to think about it yet. She needed to pull as much sanity as she could around herself first before considering her current biggest problem . . . the demon within.)

Downstairs in the living room, a clock alarm buzzed. Pagan got to her feet and, step after weary step, staggered down the stairs towards the sound. The digital clock by the television read 03:00.

Stepping carefully over the strewn human body parts that dotted the blue rug, she sat her bloody self opposite the silent TV (which was showing an NFL game) and considered that detail.

It was 3 p.m. of the next day. It couldn't be longer than that; the corpses hadn't really begun stinking yet.

But . . . she couldn't recall a thing about how she'd left the Hole Faith club last night. On that account, no matter how hard she tried to remember, her mind drew a complete blank.

Which also meant that she had no idea where she was now.

Her gaze fell to the head that had rolled under the coffee table. It lay on its side facing towards her with its eyes closed, its neck skin ripped in shreds. It had short blonde hair and a mustache. Its bloody lips were parted in a grimace of pain, with two or three teeth missing (which she imagined she'd knocked out).

Her head hurt. She had no idea who the man was. Her guts heaved at the sight of his head, but her stomach was empty, she'd spewed all her vomit upstairs.

I killed fifteen people last night. And that's those I can account for. How many more along the way? And where the hell am I? There has to be a manhunt out for me at the moment.

She picked up the TV remote and surfed the channels for information about herself. She was terrified of what she might discover. There was no news, however; the rest of the world appeared normal enough: Down in Denver, Colorado, the Feds had just busted a sex slave ring specializing in girls imported from Ukraine. The president was explaining how increased trade with the EU would actually be bad for the economy. In Reutlingen, Germany, a woman claimed aliens had made her kill her lover and pickle his remains in their basement. Closer to home, the Massachusetts police were looking for six-year-old Nicklaus Johnson, last seen entering a blue van in company of a mysterious stranger. The BPD had also just pulled the rotted remains of two-year-old Cathleen Horner from a dumpster. The girl's savagely mutilated corpse had a red pentagram cut into its back. The cops thought the kid had been murdered as part of a black magic ritual.

There was more bad news, but nothing on TV about a massacre in the Hole Faith basement.

She felt momentary relief. *Maybe damage control was effective. Maybe Stormy managed to put a lid on things. Maybe I'll still make it out of this okay after all.*

That knowledge, however, only made her feel slightly better. She was still responsible for the deaths of fifteen people, two of those scattered in parts around her right now. And worse still—and now she had to face her deepest, most terrifying fear—the demon that had murdered those people was still inside her. And at any moment it might take her over again and wreak more havoc on the innocent and unwary.

She sat still, concentrated on herself, peered deep within her soul. She found the demon in her spirit, a black blot like spilled ink on her already desolate conscience.

It was a very angry tenant; its deep frustration throbbed like Satan's own heartbeat. Avex was *trapped* inside her—her unwanted prisoner—that was clear. Her knowledge of magic and spells (and sundry subconscious psychic defenses) made her too strong for it to take her over completely. It could only get out when she wasn't on her guard. And even then, after each brief period of self-expression it would fall miserably back into the prison of her flesh again.

She realized too now, with intense relief (and regret), that it had only been able to rage and murder with such abandon immediately after possessing her because she'd not been on her guard against it.

There was something more, something horrible that Avex was hiding from her . . . but she couldn't read that; and the demon wasn't letting on.

And she had no time to get insistent with it.

Shit. The longer I remain in this house, the more likely it is that someone'll come calling and discover the bodies. I've got to get out of this place!

Alarmed, she leapt to her feet, in her rush stepping on a severed leg that skidded like a skateboard over the blue carpet, bearing her toward a crash with the TV.

She leapt off the leg just in time, falling onto a sofa.

The leg hit a stack of DVDs piled under the TV, knocking them everywhere. It was the man's right leg; as it hit the DVDs a leather wallet spilled from the pocket of the pants blood-plastered to it.

Pagan picked up the wallet and flipped through the cards it contained.

She was thinking more clearly now, alert to the need to extricate herself from her current mess.

First of all, she needed to work out where 'this place' was.

A business card in the wallet that matched the credit cards belonged to Mark C. Larsen of 39 Brookline Street, Townsend, MA.

That stumped her. *I'm in Townsend? But that's up in northern Massachusetts, at least forty miles from Boston. How the hell did I get up here?*

Her current location shocked her so much that she began ransacking the house for confirmation. After stepping over various pieces of bloody torso, shaking off her foot a coil of intestine that she stepped into, and almost losing her balance again on a chunk of liver, she finally found the dead man's cellphone. There on the screen, the GPS confirmed it. She *was* in Townsend.

So I blacked out, and in that state, I travelled forty frigging miles. Whatever happens now, it's imperative that I don't black out again. If I do, who knows where I'll wake up next time. And worse, what I'll have done in the interim.

Time was running out. She had to leave this house quickly. *First thing, I need to have a bath and put some clothes on, then search for more money. There's four hundred dollars in Larsen's wallet, but I'll need more. And I'll need his phone, and maybe his car . . .*

She backtracked her train of thought a bit. His phone. There was something she needed to do right now, which was find out how she currently stood with the Abyss Club.

She dialed Nero's number.

The phone rang twice and he picked it up. "Hello. Who's this on the line?"

"Nero, it's Pagan."

"Pagan? Pagan, what the hell were you playing at last night?"

She could practically picture the grimace on his face on the other end of the line. "Nero, it was the cops' fault. I can explain everything. I—"

"No need to explain—Joker already told us everything."

On that statement, a white-hot flush of rage surged through Pagan. How dare Joker . . . ? Then she calmed. But . . . what else could Joker have done? The situation was completely out of hand.

After a pause, Nero continued: "Well the damage is already done. I've convinced the supervisors that it was an accident, that you just got your spells mixed up. Joker's agreed to go along with that, in exchange for control of your coven. The bosses are dubious—Amber was insisting on holding a séance so she can ask Jerry how he died, but I've overridden her. At least for the moment."

"Thanks, Nero." (Amber was the dead TV producer's wife.)

"Don't mention it, we go way back you know." (They did go way back; Pagan could still remember all the time they'd spent screwing.)

"Nero, what do I do now? The fucking demon is still inside me, and . . ."

"And what?"

She heard the sharpness in his voice, and hesitated before replying. "Well . . ." She explained how she'd blacked out and just now woken up to a scene of carnage. She left out her location.

Nero was silent for a while. She could hear him tapping on a keyboard.

Finally he said, "You'll have to come in to headquarters and let the warlocks exorcise you and send Avex back down to its pit. That's the only thing for it. We can't have another mess. Shit, Pagan, I honestly can't believe you'd pull a stunt like this: all the damn books warn people to stay away from that son-of-a-bitch Avex and you go and bring it to Earth."

"I . . . I thought . . ."

"That everyone else was wrong and you in your 21-year-old wisdom was right? The rules are in place for a good reason, Pagan: a demon of Avex's class—a Lord of Hell—won't ever take orders from us minions. Besides, once Satan discovers how we've set free a demon that he'd personally chained, heads will roll, and the more the merrier. Our Dark Master is nothing if not both capricious and unforgiving. You know how he often views punishment and reward as the same thing."

"I wasn't thinking that far ahead. I was going to imprison Avex, then . . . Look, I've got it under control until I black out again."

"And that's something we definitely can't have happening. One more massacre and the cops will be on us like white on rice. Okay, down to business: where are you now? Are you still in Boston? If so I'll send Joker over with a car to pick you up. I'll send a cleanup crew too; last night is history now. We put the bodies in the incinerator and cleaned out the basement. Actually, thanks to you, the club no longer has a basement."

"How?"

"How'd you expect? Magic. We filled the whole underground level with sand, then cemented the floor over. Anyone digging down there now is gonna hit a diverted city water main. The incriminating altar is now down in Texas."

"Smart."

"The point is, as long as you don't screw up again, you're in the clear. But where are you? We need to get a team over to that house ASAP, before the neighbors start wondering why the dead man isn't keeping up his Saturday afternoon ritual of mowing the lawn."

"I'm in . . . Nero, I-I-I d-don't know where I am," Pagan stuttered.

The lie had come to her on the spur of the moment. But she sensed danger: something was off about this; everything was being taken care of too smoothly. Other than saying that Joker would be getting the headship of Pagan's coven, there had been no mention of punishments. And Pagan knew how strict the Abyss Club was about violations of the rules. She'd personally overseen several punishments herself. The screams of those being disciplined had rung in her ears for days afterwards, haunting her nightmares and filling her waking hours with dread. Having demons stab you with pitchforks while others chewed on your flesh while yet others raped you with penises that looked like lobsters wasn't something she wanted to experience.

And those punishments had been for littler offenses than what *she'd* done. Mere trifles. And yet, Nero seemed almost nonchalant about her crimes.

"You don't know where you are? What do you mean, you don't know?" There was a sharp edge to his voice now, something Pagan recognized from when they'd been dating. Whenever she was late in getting ready for an outing, Nero's voice always took on this strident note. He was irritated and she again sensed danger to herself.

"I already told you, man—I blacked out. I don't know if I'm down in Connecticut or up in Maine, or out east. I've never seen that road outside before in my life. For all I know I could be right next door to you at the moment and not know it."

"Check the phone's GPS; the weather or . . ."

"It doesn't have one—it's some ancient almost-analog piece of crap. Total B.S., as in 'before smartphones.' Look, give me a few minutes and I'll call you back."

"Don't bother." He paused and she heard him tapping the keys again. "Don't worry, I'll just have someone trace this call. We'll have people at the house ASAP. Just stay put and . . ." he laughed, "don't eat anyone else in the interim."

"That's not funny."

"No, I guess not. Okay, stay on the line while I transfer you over to the—"

Pagan hung up. Her intuition of danger was too strong. Nero clearly wasn't being straight with her. *I know I'm in deep shit, so why's he acting like I've done the organization a favor? They're not going to punish me for invoking a dem—*

It hit her then: *They're coming to kill me! The Abyss Club has seen firsthand the destruction Avex can cause and they want nothing to do with it. They aren't going to try to control it because it likely can't be controlled. But if they kill me,*

Avex goes straight back down to its prison. And then I'm gonna be tortured for all eternity. Hell no to that!

Then another even more damning realization hit her: *Shit! They're not going to clean up this place! They don't need to. All they need do is kill me and leave my body here, and the cops have got an open-and-shut case—psycho bitch runs amok on a suburban family. My DNA has to be all over these corpses!!!*

The phone in her hand buzzed and she realized that it was ringing. Once she saw that the caller was Nero, she switched it off and dropped it on a chair.

Dashing back up the stairs, Pagan reviewed her current straits. With hindsight, she realized she'd been a big fool; all she'd done was ruin her life. She wished she'd thought this deeply earlier, during her year of planning her magic coup. *But, oh shit, it was going to succeed!*

She ran into the master bedroom, then into the adjoining bathroom with the dead woman in the bathtub. She toppled the gutted wife out onto the soaked floor, then pulled the plug in the bath, and without waiting for it to empty, got in amidst the woman's displaced viscera and turned on the shower faucet. The corpse bobbed up and down beside the bathtub as water flooded out into the bedroom, Pagan paid neither any notice. She was desperate now. She had to get cleaned up and out of the house before the Abyss Club's goons arrived.

She had one slim advantage: Townsend, where she was now, had no coven of its own. Those coming for her would have to drive up from Boston, a trip of about an hour; and this being Saturday, the murder crew might all be playing loving husbands to their wives and need to be roused from the everyday world to handle Satan's dirty work for him. *And if my hanging up on Nero prevents him from tracing my phone (Larsen's phone!) then all the better for me.*

(She'd of course have to ditch Mark Larsen's cellphone now that the Abyss Club had its number. But the device had already served its purpose.)

She gave herself thirty minutes max to be gone from here. That would be enough.

She stood under the shower for five minutes, scrubbing the red crust off her skin. She had the water as hot as she could bear and she scrubbed herself so thoroughly that she looked cooked afterward, her skin red like a lobster's.

She had to pee so she peed standing up, sighing with relief as the warm flow dribbled down her legs and washed away in the shower water. She was glad she didn't need to defecate yet—in her current crisis that would have meant a delay she could ill afford.

The warm water was so soothing, she almost lost herself in it. She felt it washing the slime of murder off her tainted soul. Standing there with the hot water drenching her was a deliciously lulling sensation, almost like sexual arousal.

Then, just as her feeling of relaxed wellbeing peaked, she sensed the demon in her readying itself to emerge into her flesh again once she'd let down her guard enough.

Shit! I need to be super careful about this!

Shuddering, she turned off the water and leapt out of the bath, again almost skidding on the corpse's arm. She grabbed a towel off the towel rack, then dashed out of the bathroom, shutting the door behind her so she no longer had to view the corpse. While pacing back and forth by the bedroom window and flinging glances down into the street, she hastily toweled herself dry.

Once dry, she flung the towel away and searched the wardrobes for clothes.

The dead woman was larger than Pagan, but she found some old jeans that fit, and also a blouse and a leather jacket. She found a pack of unused panties, and, after some deliberation on personal hygiene, she also borrowed one of her dead victim's bras. Finally she found some white sneakers that were her size.

She hurriedly pulled on the clothes and shoes, then sat in front of the dresser mirror and clipped her black hair back. Other than smearing on purple lipstick, she didn't bother with makeup. (*I'm not about attending a movie premiere, am I?*) She did however take the pair of expensive-looking sunglasses that she found and all the money in the dead woman's handbag (her bank cards revealed her name as Sandra Larsen)—sixty-five dollars and a pile of small change. And her wristwatch, her car keys, and (after first checking that it wasn't screen-locked) her cellphone. Then, realizing she needed a way to carry everything, Pagan decided to just take the handbag. It was a good size and not too flashy, a light brown in color, and seemed made from gator skin.

She regarded herself once in the mirror. Yes, she'd blend in okay. Divested of her usual Goth-girl makeup, she seemed a normal part of society again. That should help conceal her.

She checked the time on the clock. Twenty-four minutes spent getting dressed. The goon squad should be here any minute now.

Now to get the hell out of here. After a final look around the bedroom, she ran out of it and down the stairs. Stopping once to empty Mark Larsen's wallet of its money (she imagined she felt his head's anger at her while she stole from him), she crossed the carnage-covered living room and stepped outside into the early evening.

The street outside seemed devoid of life. Thankfully too, the driveway opposite was staggered with the Larsen's, all that faced her was the other house's hedge; meaning no one would witness her leaving.

The car keys she'd taken were for a white Honda Accord. She got in, permitted herself a moment's vanity to regard her reflection in the sun visor mirror, then, after taking an additional moment to catch her breath, started up the engine and backed out of the driveway.

Okay, so she knew this was Brookline Street. Her first priority now was to get well away from the house before the Abyss Club came calling. Any direction would do for a start. Once out of the Larsen's driveway, she intuitively went left. After making another hasty left turn off Brookline, she tapped on the GPS to find out where she was. Main Street. She was headed in the right direction: South.

She drove on past cars and people, making several turns till she was almost out of town. Then she parked by some trees, and did some thinking.

She couldn't just drive blind. She needed a specific destination, somewhere to hide while she came up with a plan for personal salvation.

She got out Sandra Larsen's phone from her handbag and dialed. The number she called was for Dover. It was burned in her brain from all the years she'd spent growing up there. Home.

"Hello, who's on the line?"

She smiled on hearing her mother's voice. "Mom, it's Pagan."

"Susan? What . . . ? How are you, darling? It's been ages since you last called. How's Millie?"

"Mom, I can't talk for long right now. Is it okay if I come over?"

"Yes, of course, darling. This *is* still your home, you know."

"Mom, dad kicked me out. You agreed with his decision."

"Susan, you're a witch and he's a deacon in the church. What did you expect? And besides you changed your name to 'Pagan' just to rile him up, didn't you? And then there was that *thing* you did with the crucifix; surely you didn't expect him to tolerate that?"

Pagan winced at the last memory. "Okay, I'll see you in about an hour."

"Susan?"

"Yes, mom?"

"You sound worried. You're not in any trouble, are you?"

Pagan couldn't help it. She began weeping on the phone. "I'm in big trouble, mom. I . . . I . . ."

"Darling, you're not pregnant, are you?"

She wiped her eyes, and almost laughed through her tears. She knew that to her mother's uncomplicated mind, her falling pregnant (and the young man not being interested in getting married, or worse still, being already married to someone else) was the primary kind of mess 21-year-old girls got into. "No, it's not that kind of trouble."

"Well, it doesn't matter if it is. You just come over and we'll talk about whatever it is that's bothering you. Your father's home too. We'll see what we can do to help."

Pagan hung up and stared at the wheel. She doubted anyone could help her in her current crisis. But at least she'd be welcome at home, and it was somewhere to plan.

She started the car up again and headed down the road towards Dover.

CHAPTER 6

Britt & Lori & Joanna & Chris

By the time Lori rolled her car to a halt at the foot of the driveway to Britt's house, Britt was buzzing with anticipation. It was a pleasurable excitement, the knowledge that things were looking up for her.

That shortly . . .

Lori parked and killed the engine. They were out in the street, there was no way Britt's mother could have heard the car arrive. So as long as she was still balling Chris, that was.

Lori turned in the driver's seat and winked at Britt. Her brown eyes were glistening like she was horny. "Let's do it," she said, then began fumbling around in the rear of the car for the carton containing the duct tape and the other items they'd brought over from her place.

Britt pushed her out of the space between the seats. "No, let me handle that. You check your gun. Remember: once we're inside the house, it's on—we're not taking any prisoners."

Lori nodded and checked the Ruger Centerfire. She slid the magazine out, winked at the bullets, then slotted the magazine back in place and cocked the gun. She was a good shot if not a crack one—she'd gone through the rehearsal of blowing her brains out so many times that she understood the weapon. She'd spent hours aiming at herself in the mirror, wondering what taking that final plunge into blackness would feel like.

"You good?" Britt asked.

Lori yawned. "Yeah, I'm damn good." She meant that literally. If she had to shoot, she'd not miss the target; not from close range. She knew she wouldn't hesitate either. The only person she couldn't bear to shoot was herself.)

They got out of the car and silently closed the doors. Then, two huntresses stalking prey, they advanced on the waiting house.

***

Like Britt had hoped, Joanna and Chris were still hard at it when she and Lori got to the mistress bedroom.

(Britt had the nail gun primed with six-inchers, Lori had her father's Ruger and the duct tape. The carton lay on the floor behind them, now containing two sharp knives from the kitchen and a circular saw of her father's [which, considering the use she intended putting it to, she found particularly fitting]. Also in there was a ball of twine.)

"Wow!" Lori whispered, peeking in through the slit in the doorway. "This is totally hot. We should be doing the webcam thing, not this."

"Don't get distracted," Britt retorted. Then she peeked in too, and instantly felt her heart crunch with hatred. Her mother was standing by the foot of the bed, bent over and gripping her ankles, while Chris thrust into her from behind. He was holding her waist, and they were positioned sideways to the door, so Britt and Lori could see his penis slurping in and out of Joanna's sex. Both their bodies glistened with sweat.

Peeking further into the room, a tray of fruit (everything organic, thank you!) and a half-emptied champagne bottle and two glasses rested on the nightstand, indicating that the lovers had refreshed themselves between bouts of screwing.

"Oh, yeah! Fuck me good, lover boy!" Joanna moaned, her blonde hair sweeping left and right over the carpet. "Deeper!"

Chris obliged, digging his fingers into Joanna's soft flesh and slamming his hips against her buttocks. The smacks of their bodies coming together filled Britt's head like gunshots blowing her brains out. Joanna's hair swished faster back-and-forth over the floor. When it swept away from her face, they saw that her eyes were shut and her mouth was open in a grimace, her lips pulled tight away from her teeth.

"Now?" Lori whispered, seeing the rage on her bestie's face. (*Yeah, Britt really has departed the shores of reason; the only question now is: how far will she actually go once this deed is done? Is she gonna just be all talk, or are we really gonna raise hell like she claims?*)

Britt shook her head. "No. We wait till they're done; they'll be weaker then. Remember, sex drains you."

"You really like torturing yourself, don't you?" Lori's gaze was glued to the scene in the bedroom. Chris's hips were moving back and forth faster and faster, his penis now a slick piston-like blur between them, his crotch smacking Joanna's buttocks harder with each thrust, while her moans and gasps had blended into a single agonized howl of pleasure. Her big breasts jerked back and forth with each impact, dangling as they did off her underside like ripe peaches. Her thighs were wet with her translucent juices.

"Just wait. We'll hit them in the afterglow." She hefted the nailer, taking comfort in its weight. "Remember how we planned it: I'll neutralize Chris; you keep my mom covered. Don't forget the gun she's got in the nightstand."

"Yeah, yeah. Wow, girlfriend, your mom sure can fuck, you know."

"Lori!"

"I'm just admiring talent. I wish I could go like that. But all the guys I ever got—"

Britt was relieved when a loud "Oh my gosh!!" from her mother that must surely have been heard out in the street cut Lori off. While Chris thrust even harder now, grunting like an overlabored engine about to explode, Joanna moaned out her orgasm like a cat being killed, and then, with Chris still humping her hard, she fell forward onto the bed and lay like she was dead.

They waited a few more seconds, till Chris's buttocks stiffened and he froze on top of her. Then they waited a bit longer, till he collapsed on Joanna, then slid sideways off her onto the bed.

Britt's rage hit fever pitch when her mother and her boyfriend turned and began kissing each other.

Damn! He's never kissed me after sex like that before.

But then, she admitted, she'd never screwed him like that, ever. Not bent over and holding her ankles like she was Brigitte B. being used for anal target practice. She'd be too embarrassed.

"Oh, fuck, Joanna," Chris said, "you're so so incredible!"

"It's the position, darling. You ever do it like that with Britney?"

"No, she prefers—"

"Many times younger women don't really know what they'll enjoy in bed. They just see a position and say, 'Oh, that looks just like porn—if I do that he'll think I'm a slut.' But once you persuade her to try it and you do it just right? She'll love you for it. So try screwing her standing up; we're exactly the same height. You enter her from behind at that same angle and she'll freak out."

"Oh, Joanna, I think I'm falling in love with you."

Joanna giggled. "Now, now, darling, remember the rules: we mustn't get emotional with each other. Let's not ruin your relationship with Britt."

"It's just that you're so . . . words fail me."

"Baby, I think the word you want is 'experienced.' It comes with age. Britt'll get there in her own good time. Usually after having three kids and realizing she won't get a refund on unused pussy in the afterlife."

"But Britt's so uptight; she's—"

"Uptight? Most women are at first; it comes with the hymen." She laughed loudly and tapped her forehead. "And we're not just tight 'up' here, we're tight down between the legs too. We all need to be loosened up, lovingly and gradually, by a good man who loves us with all his heart." She stroked his cheek. "You need to take your time, baby, she'll slowly slacken into your point of view . . . but, do you love my little girl enough to wait for her to open up to you?"

"Oh yeah, Joanna, I do—I really do. It's just . . ."

Britt had heard enough. What was annoying her even more was Lori's barely suppressed laughter like she found this disgustingly after-sex conversation funny. And it was so, so, so patronizing, hearing them both discussing her like this. *And I'm Joanna's little girl? Even now she still thinks of me that way, like I'm just out of diapers?* She could die of rage if she wasn't going to get even.

She was so going to nail . . .

And speaking of nails . . . She looked down at the tool in her hand, then tapped Lori on the shoulder.

Lori looked up at her, her beautiful face flushed with excitement. "We good? Now?"

"Yeah, let's get 'em."

Howling like Valkyries, they charged into the room.

***

Joanna and Chris's affair had started completely by accident.

That Saturday night, Chris had been drinking alone. Britt was down for the weekend in Attleboro visiting her father. Chris had wound up watching porn—big-titted Leigh Darby doing a MILF scene—and masturbating. He'd drunk too much beer to come though, so he'd quit on pleasuring himself and instead—with his stiff penis poking out of his pants and pointing at the TV—picked up his phone and decided to sex-text Britt.

Miss u babe. Luv 2 4k u, he'd typed. *If u were here rt nw, I'd rip ur pantz off & stick my tongue all d way down ur swit pussy :-p XXX*

Instead of sending Britt the text message, however, he'd sent it to her mother, Joanna.

This was an innocent mistake. Since he'd been helping her restore her old deck chairs, Chris had Joanna's cellphone number. Instead of saving her name in his phone as 'Mrs. Wilson' or even 'Joanna' though, he'd saved it as 'Britt's Mom.'

So now, when he'd drunkenly selected the addressee for his sex-text, he'd scrolled past 'Britt' to 'Britt's Mom.'

A minute later, the reply came in: *I'd luv 2 suck ur cock rt now. I'm so f'n wet n tchng myself; fingrs in my cunt.*

The reply had excited Chris so much that he'd resumed masturbating. While stroking himself, he'd replied: *I miss ur tight pussy, n ur tits, n I wanna lick d crak of ur ass.*

Oh, fk, I'm so wet now, gonna cum!!!!! :-O :-O :-O.

Chris was reaching orgasm too. This time, despite the beer in his system, he'd ejaculated all over the coffee table. Then he'd fallen asleep.

The next morning he realized his mistake. "Oh shit, I'm so finished."

After a nail-biting hour of indecision over what his best course of action would be, he'd called Britt's mother to apologize.

"Oh, don't worry, darling," she'd replied coolly. "I came too. You're a great text lover." Her voice turned serious. "Now, I need you to come over and look at something for me."

Relieved that she wasn't angry with him, and ready to do just about anything to stay in her good books (and he also wanted to plead with her to not say anything to Britt, and to please, please, please delete his texts from her phone) Chris dashed out his front door and hurried over to Britt's house.

Joanna met him at *her* front door, dressed in just a see-through lace bra and thong. She pulled him in through the doorway, locked it, then flung the key out of sight somewhere behind the sofa.

"Er . . . I'm s-so s-s-sorry," he stuttered, confused as much by her actions as by her physical perfection . . . the breasts, the body . . . svelte as hell.

Britt's mother had always looked great in dresses (annoyingly to Chris, way better than Britt did; but that was mainly because Britt was generally in a hurry when putting on her clothes), but now Joanna Wilson was smoking hot, literally smoking. Chris imagined he could see gusts of lust evaporating off her skin. (He was still too young and experienced with women to realize that Joanna had spent the interim since he'd called expertly putting on makeup, fixing her hair, douching and perfuming herself, which Britt never did when Chris said he was coming over.)

She stepped up close to him. "Sorry about what?" she asked. "Oh, you mean the text messages? Don't worry about those, they were fun."

Chris nodded, then gulped, then said, "I really think I should be on my—"

"C'mon, boy, don't play coy with me."

"Uh . . . uh . . ."

"You're a student, right? So think of me as your Sex Ed teacher. I'm gonna teach you how to really please a woman."

"B-b-but you-you-you're Britt's mom!"

"Okay, I'll teach you how to please *my* daughter then."

To remove any doubt from his mind as to what she meant, she kissed him, inhaling his male musk deep into her mind, and going limp against him for a moment as if the mere smell of him intoxicated her. Then she pulled him after her towards the sofa.

Once there, she pushed him down to his knees on the rug, sat facing him, and spread her legs.

"Now, Chris, darling, lesson number one in pleasing my little girl: cunnilingus. Get that right and you'll soon be in where it's deep, wet, and tight." With green-lacquered fingertips she pulled the flimsy front of her thong aside. "Show me what you've got." She giggled. "I hope you like strawberries."

Chris, now both confused and not believing his luck, got down to licking the proffered wet vagina. Oh yes, he did like strawberries.

That was three weeks ago.

***

Britt found the startled look on her mother's face as they burst into the bedroom priceless. It was a mingled stare of horror, fear, and yes, rage (rage at being upstaged?). It was great to see.

Swinging her gun left to right, Lori said, "Freeze, you two fornicators! Don't you dare fucking move a tit or dick!"

Chris looked completely baffled by their appearance in the room. His eyes roved from Britt to Lori, then sideways to Joanna. "Y-y-you said she was at—"

"She was," Joanna replied quietly. She wasn't looking at Chris. She was staring worriedly instead at the gun in Lori's hand, her own hands feeling around her for the edges of the bed sheet to cover her breasts.

Britt saw that she had her mother flustered. Time to do this before she got her cool back. She nodded to Lori, then climbed on the bed by her boyfriend.

His eyes were panicked. "Baby, I can explain everything! Your mom and I were just—"

She swung the nail gun up to his head and pulled the trigger. There was the sickening sound of metal puncturing bone and flesh and then Chris toppled slowly over on the bed, with the end of a six-inch nail sticking out of his forehead. With blood spilling from his head, he rolled over onto his back and began twitching.

Britt grinned wickedly down at his spastic face. "I'm sure you can explain everything, baby. I just don't wanna hear it." Then her eyes turned cold and she bent over and shot another nail into the right side of his chest.

"What the hell did you do that for!?" Joanna yelped.

Britt turned to look at her like she'd just remembered she was in the room. Her mother, the woman in whose shadow she'd quailed all these years, was staring horrified at her. Britt felt like laughing. Fear was leaching the beauty from Joanna's face, all those expensive facelift nips and tucks reversing so she looked like other skinny unenhanced bitches her age.

Enjoying the thrill of power, Britt leapt over Chris's twitching body and pressed the nail gun to the side of Joanna's head. "Now listen, mom, we can do this the easy way or the hard way. Lori is gonna tie you up now, and if you make any attempt to get away, or dare scream, I'll put four nails into your brain. Understand, you old slut?"

Joanna nodded, her eyes wide. She glanced at Chris, and her lips trembled.

"Good. Now roll over onto your belly."

Joanna rolled over. Lori sat on her back and duct-taped her arms behind her, then duct-taped her ankles together. Then she and Britt rolled Joanna back over onto her back and put a final strip of the silver tape over Joanna's mouth.

They both grinned at Joanna. Joanna stared imploringly at Lori.

Lori shook her head. "Sorry, Mrs. Wilson, but this is Britt's call. She says you're screwing up her sex life, and,"—she pointed her gun at Chris—"I have to agree. You were screwing . . ." She turned to Britt. "You ready to do him now, like you said?"

Britt nodded. Chris was about paying big time for his crime against her. And yet, in a way, she felt she was being somewhat unfair to him, treating him this badly: in reality he was merely collateral damage, burning flotsam in Joanna Wilson's wake.

But . . . this wasn't the time or place for mercy. She'd chosen her road and she intended walking it, come hell or high water. After locking gazes with her mother (Oh, how sweet the terror in Joanna's eyes!), she knelt on the bed beside Chris's body and felt between his legs for his scrotum.

She found the ball sack and pulled it up from under his penis, folding the penis back onto his pubic hair. Chris was still twitching, his arms were flapping by his sides like beached dolphins and it seemed like a river of blood was gushing from his head.

"Now, mother, see what happens to young men who screw renovated MILFs like you." Placing Chris's scrotum so his right testicle lay against his right thigh, she kissed the muzzle of the nail gun, then triggered it, shooting a nail through the testicle into Chris's leg. Her aim was true—there was a loud crack of bone as Chris's thighbone shattered. The nail stuck out of the mangled testicle and more blood squirted everywhere.

On his testicle being impaled, Chris's back arched high off the bed. Britt grinned at his tormented face and stroked his limp penis. "Oh, so you can still feel pain, baby? That's so nice to know." Stretching his scrotum taut, she pulled his left testicle across to his left thigh and repeated the process, once again successfully shattering the thighbone while impaling his testicle with the nail. There was lots more blood; this time some splashed on Britt's jeans.

Again Chris lifted off the bed. This time too, a loud agonized 'OOOOO!' spurted from his throat. Blood had now begun dribbling from his nose.

"You want me to duct tape *his* mouth too?" Lori asked.

"No, I like hearing him scream. Besides, the fucker's voice is low-pitched. Not like mom's." She looked at her mother. "See, mommy? See why it doesn't pay to mess with your daughter?"

Joanna wasn't listening to her daughter, she was staring horrified at what Britt had done to Chris.

But Britt wasn't through fucking Chris up yet. Not by a long shot.

While Lori giggled and Joanna goggled in disbelief, Britt now pulled Chris's penis up towards his navel, and then proceeded to shoot a series of nails into it from root to glans, nailing it to his belly. (Energized by adrenalin, she handled the bulky tool with ease.) The blood really got on her this time, into her eyes and all over her top. Meanwhile, Chris, his eyes almost bugging out of his head, was emitting a long agonized growl like a lion being strangled.

Britt found the sound very satisfying. She turned away from the squirming man to look at Lori. "I wonder what'll happen if I put another nail in his mind."

"Try it. Maybe he'll shut up. He's getting quite loud now."

Britt nodded. She placed the nail gun to Chris's head, just above his left ear and pulled the trigger. Again there was the same sick crunch of metal punching through bone into flesh, followed by a jet of blood squirting around the inch-long metal projection that now protruded from Chris's skull.

"Yeah, you're right, that did shut him up. I may have killed him though."

"You haven't, check out his chest; he's still breathing."

Britt looked and saw it was true. Though weakly and jerkily, Chris's chest was rising and falling. She studied his face. She saw no one there that she recognized any more, nothing of the laughing handsome man in whose company she'd spent so many happy days and nights.

Now, all that faced her was a pathetic wreck of flesh. And she'd done it.

An epiphany hit then: *I fucking did this! I successfully reduced another human being to nothing!*

At that thought/realization, a massive rush of power surged through her. It was a non-sexual power, just the knowledge and feeling that she'd finally escaped a mental cage that had confined her for so long.

How many other barriers existed, she wondered, that could be similarly broken through? Was this how serial killers felt? Was this why they endlessly went back for more after committing the first atrocity?

But still, one last thing. She leaned over Chris's bleeding head and kissed his lips, digging her tongue deep into their wet enclosure. Then she sat up again and spat in his face. His eyes stared at her miserably. She wondered what he'd say to her if the nails hadn't paralyzed him. Would he love her, or hate her? Then she looked down at his crotch, at the ruined penis nailed to his belly and the equally mangled testicles nailed to his thighs, and sighed. *Oh, he definitely hates me now. But you know what? I don't give a flying fuck.*

She gave Lori a thumbs up. Okay, now, lets do my mom here."

Hearing that, Joanna began thrashing up and down on the bed.

"Relax, mom, I'm not going to kill you . . . I've something way better planned for you. Lori, get the extension cord. I'll cut the twine."

Lori shook her head. "No, you get the cord—*I'll* do the tourniquets. I've done this once before when my dad broke his arm and was bleeding everywhere. They have to be *very* tight. Else she'll die on us and you don't want that, do you?"

Britt nodded. "Okay, I'll fetch our stuff."

Moving in a haste, she stepped outside the bedroom and retrieved their carton of things from the hallway floor. Once inside again, she dropped the cardboard box on the bed and nodded to Lori.

Lori put down her gun and picked the ball of twine out of the carton. She began measuring out a length of it, her eyes glazing over as she did mental arithmetic.

Joanna stared at Lori in confusion, her eyes asking questions. She'd been silent in the interim, tracking her daughter's departure and return with the brown box.

Britt looked down at her mother, then she picked the circular saw out of the carton, and brandished it at her. "Don't worry, mom. We're just going to tie off the blood supply to your feet before we cut them both off."

CHAPTER 7

Pagan

The drive down from Townsend had taken Pagan forty-five minutes. She currently sat in her 'borrowed' Honda, two houses away from her parents' place, on the opposite side of the road.

A large car was just pulling out of her parents' drive, a black Lincoln with tinted windows. That was likely someone from the church, maybe the pastor even, come to see her father.

She waited till the black car was well out of sight, then waited a bit longer to ensure that it wasn't coming back. Only then did she get out of the Honda and walk towards home.

None of those out on the street noticed her, just like they'd not noticed the car all the while she'd been sitting in it. (A man approaching with a dog on a leash gasped in surprise as if the white Honda had suddenly appeared from thin air, then navigated around Pagan like she was a tree planted on the sidewalk. But he kept his eyes on the car the whole time.)

Before leaving Townsend, she'd cast a cloaking spell over herself, one that ensured people wouldn't notice her. Like now, they'd look past her like she wasn't there. The spell worked on the police too; on her drive down here, she'd not been pulled over, even though she'd been pushing the speed limit the entire way. Even State Police patrol radar would ignore her.

The only people who would notice her were her fellow witches. Those she suspected were out to find her.

On that thought, her eyes widened in horror. *That black car! Oh no, it couldn't be them—they went up to Townsend!*

Spurred on by sudden desperate fear, Pagan burst into a run towards the house. Her handbag flapped against her waist as she ran.

In her haste she almost trampled on a cat's tail. The angered black feline hissed after her, which she took as a very bad omen indeed.

She turned the corner onto the driveway and stopped, panting hard. All of a sudden, staring at the white two-story building she'd grown up in, she was scared to approach it. The house almost seemed to be reprimanding her for abandoning The Faith.

She didn't doubt that her father would have a whole lot to say about that. They'd not spoken at all since he'd exiled her to go live with her aunt. (All her contacts during that time had been with her mother, and all over the phone; she'd never once returned here.) But maybe, like her mother had suggested over the phone, he'd relented. He'd always professed his undying love for her anyway, even when they were madly at each other's throats.

Then, despite the mixture of fear and worry almost driving her mad, Pagan had to laugh. *And I really did do bad then, didn't I? I'd have kicked me out too.*

***

Pagan's relationship with her father had disintegrated irreparably on the Sunday afternoon that he caught her masturbating with a crucifix.

A devout Christian and a deacon in The Dover Church, David Harris had not tolerated his only daughter Susan's 'slow descent into sin.' Pagan's sudden taking up black magic upset him no end.

She was his only child, and in his strict conservative way he loved her deeply. Up to this point also, even if she'd quit going to church at age sixteen, she'd remained obedient at home, been well-behaved, and had shown no signs of becoming a slut. (Once Susan had officially become pretty at age thirteen, David Harris had dreaded having to field off an endless stream of boyfriends.)

But then, for his cherished Susan to all of a sudden not only shun her parent's faith, but to actively take up promoting the Devil's works? And she'd insisted on being called 'Pagan' to boot?

But it would be unchristian to kick her out. And he loved the kid anyway. And her mother Linda did too.

Millie, his wife's younger sister who lived in Boston, kept asking that Pagan be allowed to come stay with her. But Millie was currently on her third divorce in ten years (which in David's eyes branded her a remorseless slut)—and not any kind of moral example for a girl already on the bad side of the tracks to have, so he kept refusing.

And so David lived with his teenage witch at home, endlessly fasting and praying that she repent and return to the Savior's fold before it was too late to save her soul.

But that Sunday . . .

David Harris had arrived home from church early. Looking for his daughter around the house and not finding her, he climbed up to her bedroom. He'd knocked, but gotten no reply, only some groaning. Thinking she was ill, he'd opened the door. Then he'd frozen in shock.

There, splayed out in bed, lay his beautiful daughter, her eyes closed, and stabbing herself in the crotch with a crucifix. He couldn't believe his eyes. *She's masturbating with a replica of the Savior on the cross?* The Savior's legs vanished up to His waist in the teen vagina with each thrust and reappeared smeared with blood. (Pagan was having her period at the time. Her father, however, believed she was wounding herself in some witchcraft ritual.)

David stood there transfixed. He wanted to leave the bedroom but couldn't, his legs refused to move. This was clearly the Abomination of Desolation of which the scriptures spoke. The enshrining of the Man of Lawlessness in the Holy Temple as written in 2nd Thessalonians. Or in this case, the *Woman* of Lawlessness.

But here, under his own roof? His own daughter was the Antichrist?

And then Pagan stabbed herself in the sex all the way up to the crosspiece of the crucifix, screamed, "I love you, Jesus!" and came. Her body stiffened and her legs trembled. Slowly she slipped the crucifix almost all the way out again, then slid it all the way back inside her body. Hard.

David ripped his eyes from the disgusting sight. He wanted to flee the bedroom, but his body felt like stone. (He was relieved that he had not even the ghost of an erection as he watched his daughter's nubile form pleasure itself. If this scene of sin had aroused him, he knew he'd have been lost forever.)

He managed to endure Pagan's ecstatic torrent of "Oh my Gods!" and "Thank you, Lords!" by looking away from his climaxing daughter to the wall, on which hung a poster of Aleister Crowley over a desk on which lay a broken Ouija board. Yes, evil had fully entrenched itself in his house. How had he been blind to it all this while? Had she hexed him with a spell?

"Dad? Dad, what are you doing in my bedroom?"

He turned back to stare at her. Her face was flushed, her breasts rose and fell, and she was sweating. Still she made no attempt to cover her impressive beauty, and her expression was mocking, almost teasing him: he could have some of her too if he liked; and . . . best of all . . . her mother would never know that he'd sampled her forbidden fruit—it would be their secret.

The crucifix was still stuck up her sex, and now blood dribbled red down its wooden length.

"Dad, what are you doing in here?" Pagan repeated. Her voice was still seductive, but she was less sure of herself now.

His cold reply was: "You trainee Whore of Babylon, you're outa here or I'll kill you. God help me if I don't."

He spun on his heel then and hurried downstairs to call Millie to come take Pagan to Boston to live with her. (Once he'd explained, a furiously giggling Millie agreed to drive over immediately.)

Then he went outside and sat in his car to cool off. Thinking of what he'd just witnessed threatened to scupper his Christian principles for good. It was all David Harris could do not to rush off and buy a gun to come shoot Pagan with.

I don't get it, he thought miserably. *Did she have to abuse the Savior? Couldn't she just buy a vibrator online like other young girls do nowadays?*

***

Pagan finally got over her attack of nerves. Caught between fear of her father's wrath and fear of what might have happened to him and her mother, she hurried up the driveway to the front door.

The closer she got to the house, the more worried she grew. She could sense a definite evil charge on the Christian abode now, the sort that resulted from blasphemous ritual.

She pushed the door open and it hit her: a blast of evil of the kind she'd never in her worst nightmares have associated with this house. It wasn't a stench, but a torrent of wind like demons were rushing out of the building. Her fears were further confirmed when she felt Avex—her resident evil that she was trying to ignore—stir somewhere

71

deep in her body. She shuddered; the creature seemed happy. She prayed that it wouldn't attempt to take her over again just now.

She stood there in the doorway as the putrid air surged past her, almost seeing demon faces in its passing winds. Then, steeling herself—she hadn't become head of her own coven by being scared of minor spirits such as these—she walked forward into the maelstrom.

Like she'd punctured their potency, the raging winds ebbed immediately she was indoors.

The building still smelt corrupted, however; a foul desecrated thing. And now . . . she saw blood smears on the wall by the foot of the stairs. She hurried over to examine them. Four thin lines, like blood from bleeding fingers.

Her heart beating furiously, Pagan rushed up the stairs.

She found her parents by the upper landing. Both had been crucified—nailed to the corridor wall—naked and upside-down, with their throats slit ear-to-ear. There was little blood in evidence though; it had likely all been drained into jars and carried off for use in some ritual. Bloody pentagrams were carved deep into the flesh of both her parents' naked bellies, and there was a puddle of melted black wax on the wooden floor between their bodies.

Pagan gaped at both corpses in horror, then sunk to her knees by their dangling heads.

"Mom, dad, I'm sorry!" she moaned. "I'm sorry!! I'm sorry!!!" Her father's gray beard was matted with coagulated blood, as was her mother's black hair.

Gazing into their sightless eyes, she wept and wept. The Abyss Club had *really* punished her; really *hurt* her. True, she'd on occasion wished both her parents dead. But she'd just been pissed off, angry at their refusal to accept her how she was. *Shit, I had no idea it would hurt me so much to see them like this!* One reason she'd stayed away from home was to keep her mother and father off the Abyss Club's radar, just in case of something like this.

More tears filled her eyes; she let them flow unchecked. She felt like a small crumpled toy thrown away by a petulant child.

But then, through her tears, she became aware of something. She sensed that the demon inside her was afraid. But afraid of what? *You're fucking Avex, for Satan's sake—the badass Ravager of Hell, so bloodthirsty that our Lord himself locked you away. What could you possibly be scared of?*

Except perhaps. . . being sent back to Hell and locked away again?

Forcing her gaze off her parents' dead faces, she reconsidered the situation.

Suddenly it no longer seemed like her parents had been killed just to discipline her. There *was* that part of it, but . . .

The pentagrams cut into their bellies and the black wax spoke of a summoning ritual. But to summon what?

It was at that moment that Pagan became aware of a tapping noise on the roof of the house. Soft and tentative at first, then louder.

Then it was really loud.

In a desperate intuitive flash Pagan's mind connected ritual to overhead sound. "Oh, shit no!"

A moment later, something thick and hairy burst down through the ceiling towards her. She rolled out of its way, smacking her head on the railing at the top of the stairs. The massive furred column— eyes goggling with terror she saw it ended in a dirty cloven hoof— punched a hole through the upper floor, scraping her father's body off the corridor wall as it did so. Accompanying the foot was a horrible stink of musk and a horde of flies.

It's a goat! They sent a goat after me!

Another equally massive leg crashed down through the ceiling, this one landing five meters ahead of the first. Amidst the ensuing rain of plaster, the first leg lifted again. It rose much faster than anyone would believe possible considering its size (each leg was at least four feet wide). In its wake, clouds of flies blew everywhere.

Pagan didn't wait to see where the foot would stomp next. She ran down the stairs.

I've gotta get outside!

Halfway down the stairs, she tripped, and had to grab the banister to keep from toppling headlong. That halt saved her life: the bottom half of the staircase suddenly vanished under the goat's descending hoof.

She hung there, half-sitting, half-falling, breathing hard and fighting not to scream with the demonic animal's leg less than a foot from her nose. (Any loud sound she made would give her position away.)

The massive hairy appendage teemed with swarming flies. Its hoof was buried deep in the ground. Slowly it lifted again, chunks of wood and shattered concrete pouring from it as it rose up past her face. She looked up to the ceiling. Through the clouds of green flies and the wreckage of the two previous holes she made out a dark and hairy underbelly.

Terrified by the infernal sight, she looked hastily down again and around. *How do I get out of here?* The gap in the stairs was too wide to leap across, the hole in the floor too deep to climb down into then out again. But the staircase descended along the wall, straight from the landing to the floor. She could leap over the banister to the carpet. A five-foot drop at most.

Deep inside her, she felt (or imagined she felt) Avex's fear of being cast from her flesh back into Hell's abyss.

She climbed over the banister, which, having lost its lower anchor, shook unsteadily.

Then the banister ceased to matter. The goat stomped again, this time demolishing half of the wall separating the living and dining rooms. The collapsing wall knocked the stair banister loose.

Banister and Pagan both crashed to the floor.

Again she sat stunned; again she was faced with the massive pillar of animal leg, the hoof so far buried in the ground as to be invisible.

She heard a loud noise behind her, and simultaneously felt the shock wave of a collision so strong that it lifted her off the floor. That was the goat's other leg coming down, somewhere out of sight in the rear of the house. The damned creature had to be stomping the house with its two front legs while balancing on its rear ones.

Feeling surreal, Pagan hung in midair for a moment, then crashed back down to the floor, smacking her head on a slab of concrete. She lay stunned again, watching the leg near her rising again. *Fuck! How the hell will the cops make any sense of this?*

Then, her mind clearing, she forgot about the police. The only important thing here was her life. She was currently buried under half of a sofa that had crashed against the remains of the staircase. A fallen wooden crucifix had ripped her jacket and was stabbing into her left breast. Her mind was filled with goat stink. The living room was filled with dust and the ubiquitous flies. She was choking and doing her best not to inhale the dust and flies.

She shoved away the crucifix poking her breast. She crawled out from under the sofa and prepared to dash across the living room and out the front door, the distance a mere ten yards.

Then she saw something—

A pair of black high-heeled shoes and an ornate steel dagger designed so that its hilt was four pentagrams stacked one above the other. The dagger's blade was bloody. Both it and the shoes lay on an undisturbed stretch of carpet over against the far wall.

Despite her dire straits, she froze in confusion. *Those are my shoes and my knife.* (She'd had the dagger custom-made from a drawing she'd seen in a comic book.) *I left them back in Boston. What in the world are they doing here?*

She had just enough time to note that her shoes also had blood on them, and that beyond the dagger and shoes lay one of her favorite magical surplices (a sleeveless red velvet robe dotted with glittering stones), before all of them were blocked off from her view by the goat leg's return. She felt the impact of its landing all through her body, like it would shatter her bones. (This was another concern: absorbing these kinds of forces at close range could actually rupture her internal organs and cause her severe internal bleeding if it kept up. And the damn goat wasn't about tiring.)

She stared adamantly at the monstrous flesh pillar with its thick bristling hairs. *You haven't gotten me yet, you stinky horned bastard.*

Suddenly mad at the goat, she considered running around the leg and at least retrieving her dagger, but then the tremors from another invisible further-off-in-the-house stomping flung her against the living room wall and she decided to just cut her losses and run for it.

She ran, flinging herself over the coffee table like a hurdler, then crashing out through the front door and rolling down the front steps. She lay stunned for a moment on the asphalt driveway (how many times now?) then pulled herself to her feet and limped down the drive into the street, where she joined the gathering crowd who were watching what seemed like the house's self-destruction.

Pagan stood among the crowd, bruised and battered, her heart filled with anger and agony. Alone spiritually sensitive among them, she watched her parents' front door crumble into the ground. She alone could see the huge supernatural animal stomping on the house; no one else there had even the slightest suspicion of its existence.

The goat was a massive shaggy beast, with apocalyptic curved horns on a head the size of a truck.

"What's going on?" an old lady on her left asked. "Why's Deacon Harris's house falling to bits?"

"I dunno," Pagan replied her, before realizing that with the cloaking spell still in place, the woman couldn't have seen her.

She was right. The woman was talking to a young man on Pagan's right, like just air separated them.

The young man grinned and stroked his goatee. "I dunno," he replied the old woman. "Maybe it's God's judgment on the old guy; the holier-than-thou religious hypocrite."

Her eyes brimming with tears, Pagan felt like slapping him. Instead, she turned and pushed her way through the now sizable crowd, as, to a chorus of 'oohs' and 'aahs,' two simultaneous crashes announced the total demolition of her parents' front porch.

Tears streaming down her cheeks, Pagan ran across the road and sat in her car. Ahead of her, the monster invisible goat was putting the finishing touches to the demolition. Now it was really getting into the swing of things, rearing up on both rear legs and coming down hard on what remained of the house with both front hooves at once.

The roof of the two-story, which already looked like the frame of a shack under construction, buckled with the impact. A chunk of pillar flew off through the air and out into the crowd. The crowd scattered in terror. Not everyone made it—two bodies were left flattened beneath the crashed masonry. One was the body of the old woman who'd been asking why the house was collapsing. The other body was a kid's; just two legs poking out from under the long slab of stone.

Pagan heard a loud howl coming from someone. That was most likely the child's mother.

The stampede reversed its direction; everyone rushed back over to help the fallen two. Meanwhile the house was still breaking apart (in everyone's eyes except Pagan's) of its own accord.

Shit! Pagan thought. *Now they're gonna say there were explosives in there!*

In her rearview she watched two squad cars turn into the street. Behind the police vehicles the sunset flared bright orange like the world was burning over there.

Yeah, this was going to be one hell of an evening in Dover. She could just see/hear it on CNN: "Police in Dover are still trying to solve the mystery of how a house on Haven Terrace fell apart. The mutilated bodies of the owners, Mr. David Harris, 63, and his wife, Linda Harris, 51, were discovered amongst the wreckage. Also discovered in the ruins were . . ."

Fuck—I've been set up! Pagan suddenly realized. *I've been framed. My dagger is in the rubble! Shit, that must be what they used to kill mom and dad! The goat was supposed to get me, but they'd already planted the evidence that I killed mom and dad in the house so it'd be an open and shut case!*

Shit, shit, shit! And if that was the case, then clearly the team that Nero had dispatched to Townsend, ostensibly to bring her back, would have planted even more damning evidence there. *As if all the fingerprints I left in the Larsen house aren't already more than enough to fetch me twenty life sentences without parole! Fuck!*

Feeling like the walls of reality were closing in on her, Pagan sat shock-still in the car, squeezing the steering wheel so hard that it felt like she'd break it.

She couldn't even feel additional horror when the goat kicked another massive chunk of house pillar out into the road. This one smashed through the windshield of the arriving squad car nearest the house, causing it to veer off its parking course and crash a crazy path through the desperately scattering onlookers. The pillar stuck through its windscreen like a concrete unicorn horn, the squad car finally swerved up off the road and through the Harris's hedge, hit one of Pagan's father's beeches and stopped, its rear tires lifting off the grass as its hood compacted. At least six more prone bodies lay in the crashed car's wake. Several weren't moving. A flood of blood poured from the car.

Its work complete, the invisible goat now vanished: a black 'poof!' of air, and it suddenly wasn't there anymore. All that was left were screaming, yelling people and carnage everywhere.

The cops from the second squad car began radioing for ambulances.

Slowly, Pagan got a grip on herself and put the white Honda in motion. She made a cautious U-turn. Even as she drove away from the wreckage of her onetime home, she realized she'd made a huge mistake by taking dead Sandra Larsen's car. *Like I'm not already in enough shit back in Townsend, the Honda links both murders, makes it seem like I drove down here just to kill my parents. Someone's bound to have noticed it while I was in the house.*

Somehow she managed not to weep again.

And deep inside her, she could tell that her pet demon was extremely relieved at her survival. So much so that it planned on behaving itself for a while.

Which at least was something to be thankful for.

CHAPTER 8

Britt / Lori

"Yeah, let's cut her feet off."

On hearing that, Joanna began thrashing wildly. With her hands secured behind her and her ankles taped together, however, she could do little more than roll herself towards the edge of the bed.

The panic and utter terror in her eyes was sweet music to her daughter's soul.

Returning to the bed after plugging the circular saw into the extension line, Britt paused a moment to regard Joanna. Was this really her mother, the woman who'd eclipsed her all this years, squirming in such terror? Now, even with her surgically perfect breasts, Joanna didn't look like much anymore, just another old hag who'd refused to grow old and let up-and-coming pussy have its say in the sexual race.

She retracted the saw's lower blade guard and checked that enough of the blade was free beneath the base plate. Then she flicked it on and tried to catch her reflection in the whirling metal.

She waved it at Joanna. "Hey, mom, now we just need to get your legs parted. But you're an expert at that, aren't you?"

She flung a glance at Chris. The bloodstained body's only sign of life was the rise and fall of its muscular chest. The end of the nail she'd fired into his right lung was a shiny metal nipple. Fuck him.

She looked back at Joanna. If her mother's eyes bulged out any further, they'd pop out of her face.

Lori had untaped Joanna's ankles. Joanna took that opportunity to kick her in the belly.

"Ouch! Hold still, Mrs. Wilson!"

Switching the saw off again, Britt walked to the head of the bed and whacked her mother over the forehead with Lori's pistol. She quieted down after that, staring up in a daze.

Lori tied two tourniquets above each of Joanna's ankles, two inches apart. Then she nodded up at Britt. "We're ready. No way is she gonna bleed to death now. So, you wanna do this, or should I?"

"I'll do it. I wouldn't miss doing this for the world."

Lori sat on Joanna's belly to hold her down. Britt sat on Joanna's knees. She played eenie-meenie-minee-mo to decide which foot to detach first. 'Mo' fell on Joanna's left foot. She shrugged.

After a moment's reflection on how sad it was to detach such a perfectly manicured appendage from its owner (unlike Britt, Joanna was religious with her footcare), she chose a point between Joanna's ankle and the lower of the two tourniquets on the left shin, switched on the saw again, and dipped its whirling blade into her mother's leg.

Blood instantly flew everywhere, zipping from the rear of the saw across to splatter the dresser. In a flash, Joanna came out of her daze and began bucking furiously as her foot was sawn off. From behind her gag came a horrible gurgling noise, all the more terrible for being denied proper expression.

"Hold still please, Mrs. Wilson," Lori said, pressing herself down even more firmly on Joanna's belly. "You wouldn't want it to slip, would you?"

Britt felt momentary nausea as the saw cut deeper into the leg. Her gorge rose; it seemed she'd puke. Then bits of bone sprayed out of the bloody trench in her mother's shin, and, feeling eerily empowered, she forced the saw deeper into the leg. The bed sheet was wetting with blood, but not overly so; Lori had done a stellar job with obstructing the limb's blood supply. What was falling on the bed was blood trapped in Joanna's foot flowing back and out. Britt bent over her work to see better. A splatter of ground meat hit her in the face followed by the wet crack of both sections of bone separating from each other. A little more pressure and the entire left foot was free of its leg.

She switched off the saw and lifted the severed foot, surveying its bloodstained perfection. The skin and meat exterior, the two bones inside. *Oh, there's two bones in there?* She smirked. *Yeah, one day I'm gonna have feet as cute and perfect as these. Heels and soles pumiced to baby-butt smoothness, and with the toenails all—*

She suddenly realized her mother had stopped bucking. "What's with her?" she asked Lori over her shoulder.

"Nothing serious. She's just fainted from the pain."

"Wimp. Still, it'll make it easier to get her other foot off."

"Hurry up."

Shrugging, Britt switched the saw back on and dipped its whirling blade into Joanna's right leg.

Getting this foot off was much easier. In fact, Joanna didn't wake up bucking and muffled-screaming until Britt was almost all the way through the bones.

Finally though, she was done. She switched off the saw, leapt off the bed, then picked up Joanna's two feet. Hefting them like barbells, she regarded Joanna's legs for a moment. They looked all funny now; something was definitely missing. Ha ha ha!

And, damn, did she feel good now or what?

She tapped Lori on the shoulder. "Get off her."

Lori got off Joanna's belly.

Britt waved her mother's feet at her. Joanna was already weeping, her cheeks drenched with tears. Now, seeing her feet so callously held in her daughter's hands, she began bawling furiously, her body shaking from agony and terror.

"And now, mommy dearest, my sweet revenge is almost complete," Britt intoned. She dropped Joanna's feet into the carton they'd used to carry in her tools of vengeance. "You can forget about having the surgeons reattach them. I'm taking your feet with me."

Joanna began shaking her head furiously. "Mhhhm, mhhhm!"

Britt figured she was saying 'NO! NO!"

"Fuck you, mom! Yes, *I am* taking them with me." She stared at Joanna's body. All that physical perfection: that face, those breasts, that surgically tightened or IntimaLased vagina (she didn't for one moment buy that story her mother had told Chris about doing her kegels regularly), that perfect ass, those long coltish legs . . . and down below, as the icing on the cake . . . no feet. No feet? A woman this perfect—sex on two legs—has no fucking feet?

She burst out laughing from the delicious irony of it. Once again she felt that thrilling power, just like she had with Chris. (She looked once at him, trying to catch his eye, but he was too far gone, or maybe the nails in his head were fucking with his mind?) Once again, she, ordinary Britney Nobody Wilson, had reduced another human to nothing. She'd been God to them, rendered them completely useless and impotent. It was the greatest feeling ever. She doubted anything could top this. *Oh fuck, and I'm just getting started.*

She stared again at the severed feet in the carton. *Yeah, mom isn't shit now.*

Behind her gag, her mother was still making pleading noises.

Lori sniggered at Joanna. "Of course, Mrs. Wilson, you can always see if they have spare feet on sale at Walmart. I don't recall so, but they do stock wheelchairs."

Britt found that impossibly funny. She laughed even louder.

***

"Careful with that!" Lori admonished as Britt picked up the nail gun to pack it away again. "You're looking to puncture yourself. The last thing either of us needs is a trip to the ER."

Britt nodded. She carefully laid the nailer in the carton, then did the same with the circular saw. Then she waved at her mother, who lay squirming in pain, and to her ex, who'd begun twitching again. Chris looked really funny with his manhood nailed to his belly. By now the blood in most of his wounds had clotted. In contrast, Joanna's stumps seeped red liquid. Slowly though, most definitely not life-threatening.

Britt looked at Lori. "I need to pack my stuff."

They went to her bedroom.

Britt considered her room with its surfeit of accumulated girliness: lots of stuffed animals (including a monster teddy bear and a unicorn), pop posters, an overflowing CD rack with an emphasis on easy listening and jazz standards, and a wardrobe stuffed with clothes she never wore. (Joanna insisted, Britt resisted.) Three racks of shoes. (Same logic: Joanna bought, Britt fought.) Then there were all those perfumes to consider, two makeup cases, her underwear, and the bookshelf crammed with bestsellers. Now that she was about deserting the one space in this house she'd really considered hers, she was confused. Everything in sight seemed important and essential to her wellbeing. (Well, almost everything. At least she was certain she wouldn't be needing her sociology textbooks.)

She stared at Lori. "How much should I take?"

"As little as possible. Follow my lead—just pack an overnight case and your laptop; we might have to walk at some point. And change the clothes you're wearing; you're all covered in blood."

The next ten minutes were taken up with Britt cramming things she considered indispensable into a duffel bag and Lori dumping them back out again.

Finally, Lori dragged Britt from the bedroom. Aside from her change of clothes, all that had survived the packing was underwear, a tube of pink lipstick, a pair of jeans and two tops, and a green dress. She'd forgone her HP Pavilion laptop for her Samsung tablet.

"We need cash," she told Lori. "My mom's sure to have some."

They returned to the bedroom. When they walked in, Joanna was barely conscious; she seemed to be in shock. Britt quickly ransacked her handbag.

"Thirty bucks," she grimaced in disgust, holding the money up for Lori's inspection. "Won't even buy us enough gas to . . . hold on a minute." She searched through the pockets of the handbag again, reappearing with her mother's bank cards.

"Yes!" she grinned triumphantly. "I know the PINs for these."

Lori nodded, then picked up the carton with the bloody tools. She gestured back at Joanna and Chris. "Are we just gonna leave them here like this? What if no one finds them for days?" (Lori thought Britt was being just a little too blasé now. To her mind, even if they were going kamikaze, they still had to use their smarts. That way they'd last longer and have more fun with it.)

Britt hadn't thought of that. "I'll untie her. Help me find Chris's phone. It should be in his jeans' pocket."

Lori dropped the carton and began searching. Britt rolled Joanna over onto her belly, and, using a knife, cut through the tape binding her wrists. Then she rolled her back over again, leaned forward, and whispered in her ear. "Okay, darling mother, we're leaving; and like I said, I'm taking your feet with me. So, bye, and have fun without them."

She paused for effect, then added, "We'll leave both your phones out in the living room. By the time you crawl that far and call 911, I'll be far out of your life. And one last warning, mom: wait at least ten minutes before making any noise. If you dare yell for help before we drive off, I'll come back in and cut your hands off too."

Joanna didn't reply. Though deep in shock, her gaze was riveted to the cardboard box containing her feet.

Britt understood the look. "No, and that's final. Fuck you, mom." An angry tear formed in her right eye. She wiped it away; this was no time for emotion.

She turned to Lori.

Lori waved Chris's cellphone at her. "We're good to go."

Britt nodded. She picked up Joanna's pink iPhone off the nightstand, then cut the cord for the bedroom phone.

Her gaze roved to Chris. He was twitching again, so much now that she considered trying to pull the nails from his head.

Then Lori caught her eye. Lori was tapping her wrist. A glance at her own wrist informed Britt that it was half-past-six. She was startled. *How'd it get so late so fast?* Then she smirked. *How time flies when you're getting even!*

"We'd better get a move on," Lori said.

"Yeah," Britt agreed. She shouldered her bag. Lori again picked up the carton with the tools and feet.

They left the bedroom. Behind them, Joanna Wilson began weeping inconsolably.

CHAPTER 9

Pagan

Pagan drove on. Out of Dover and past Medfield, heading southeast now towards Walpole and the I-95 Interstate. Vegetation, houses, people on streets and in vehicles, all passed her in a blur. Her heart was heavy, her mind packed with turbulent thoughts.

I still can't believe that they set up a goat to stomp me! A goat!?

Her horror made her pause. She pulled onto a shoulder and parked, got out of the car and sat on the hood. (Her body, particularly her ribs, ached from all the falling down she'd done in Dover.)

Front and back of her, cultivated fields stretched out into the distance. On her left, the sun was western blood now, the dusk sky heavy with pregnant-looking clouds. Right, her road to freedom continued.

She'd driven south on instinct more than anything else. Logic dictated that a big city was easier to get lost in; but there was also the counterargument that a big city was the first place they'd look. It might prove better for her to hide out in some unassuming out-of-the-way town. But how long could she dodge the Abyss Club anyway? Now that a tidy elimination had failed, they were certain to send assassins after her.

She got out her borrowed phone and tried to access the club's website, abyssclub.org. No luck; her account as a coven leader had been deactivated. Neither her username—Pagan666—or her password—Daddy'sLittleGirl—were recognized. Clearly, the club was trying to erase her from their database.

She dialed Nero's number. It went straight to voicemail. Shit, that hurt! Also from memory, she called his secretary, Sabrina. Her number too was unresponsive.

Finally, she called the one other Abyss number she remembered. A friend, Stormy, wife of the Boston Chief of Police.

This one connected.

"Hello?"

"Stormy, it's Pagan."

"Pagan? Where the hell are you? No, I don't want to know that— someone might be listening."

"Stormy, I'm in major trouble."

"Kid, you don't know the half of it. Nero's just sent an extermination squad after you."

"I know; they just missed me. A goat stomped my parents house— the bastards sacrificed my parents to summon it. How could they do that?"

"Oh shit! I'm so sorry to hear that!"

"They've also locked me out of my Abyss account. And Nero— the damned son-of-a-bitch—isn't picking up my calls. I deserve better—he used to be my boyfriend!"

As she sat there on the hood, her feet crooked up on the driver's-side tire, a State Police squad car zipped past. Neither cop looked her way. At least her cloaking spell still worked fine.

"Pagan, calm down," the voice on the line said. "Just listen to me, okay? You're finished with Abyss. This isn't Nero's call anymore. Even if he wants to help you, he can't; there's big politics involved. Orders from the top are to eliminate you. So just run and keep running. Don't trust anyone. Not even me if you call me again: I could be trying to set you up." There was a pregnant pause. "Better still, don't call me again; they might trace the call. It's unlikely, since Tom's Chief of Police but—"

"But what the hell am I supposed to do? You know escaping Abyss is like fleeing the mafia."

"Two words, but I'll deny telling you: 'Red Octopus.' Again don't quote me, girl, but I heard a rumor somewhere that they just might want the merchandise you're carrying."

"Thanks, Stormy, you're a real friend."

"Okay, I must go now. Tom and the kids just got back home from their grandparents. So look out for yourself. My regards to your aunt."

She hung up. Pagan sat there on the hood for a moment, a slight breeze rustling her hair. *Hell, I forgot Aunt Millie! What if the club's butchered her too!?*

It didn't seem likely, but then their killing her father and mother hadn't seemed likely either.

Since taking over running West Roxbury's Hole Faith and moving into an apartment in the club building, Pagan hardly ever saw her aunt anymore. On her own part, she was too busy running the club, while Aunt Millie—who had an addiction to husbands—was too busy trying to get remarried. Most of their communication had been over the phone.

She didn't, however, remember her aunt's number. Finally, she resorted to Facebook. She logged in on the phone, then checked out Aunt Millie's timeline. She heaved a sigh of relief: Aunt Millie was on holiday in Brazil. A new picture uploaded just an hour ago showed her laughing aunt, almost nude in a backless monokini, lying on a beach while a bald muscular man oiled her back. The photo background was a bright blue sky fringed with tall palms.

The picture was captioned: "Getting coconut-oiled by my darling Ronaldo! Planning on eating some Latin banana later ☺ Wedding bells in the air!"

Pagan had to smile. No need to worry about Aunt Millie then. She logged out of Facebook. While night fell around her, she considered Stormy's advice.

There was no helping it. She had to contact the Red Octopus Corporation. They really were her only hope now.

***

The Red Octopus Corporation (or ROC) was Abyss's primary rival where supernatural world dominance was concerned.

Red Octopus, though as steeped in evil as Abyss, however had a completely different (and even more sinister) motive:

Rather than enthroning mankind's Devil, the ROC sought to bring an 'Elder Race' called the Sinis to Earth.

The Sinis were a totally alien concept to the human mind, gods who had evolved to their current state, only to die and be reborn so they could evolve again.

What made the Sinis so attractive to humans was the fact that humans too, provided they were prepared to shed all their inhibitions and ethics—in short, shed their humanity—could also evolve into Sinis.

Man could become part of the eternal ultimate Elder Race.

The Sinis wallowed in filth—dirty bodies and dirtier minds; whatever worked to displace the humanity from mankind—and so Red Octopus was corrupt and filthy beyond belief, endlessly working to create new atrocities to worship, emulate, and please their nonhuman masters with.

***

Seated back inside the car, Pagan browsed to the Red Octopus website: www.sinisroc.org. She was faced with a purple page on which was a drawing of a creature that seemed a mixture of octopus (though with four times as many tentacles), bird (feathers and beaks abounded all over it), and lots of toothy mouths.

She shuddered. The drawing was supposed to represent one of the elder Sinis race. *Is this what they want to evolve into? Really? This thing that looks like it'd be comfortable living on Saturn?*

Other than this representation of the Sinis, there was little else on the web page. Above the creature was just a small 'Log In' link, and below it, what Pagan sought: a square 'Contact Us' window.

She mused for a moment on what to write, then typed: *Abyss coven head Pagan666 wants to defect to you. I'm possessed and time running out; hounds of hell hot on my tail. Get back to me ASAP.*

She read it over and decided it would work. *They either want me or they don't. And if they don't, I'm screwed good.*

She hoped both that they'd want her and that they wouldn't take too long in replying. By all rights, they should already be aware of her situation. Red Octopus had spies in Abyss; Abyss had spies in the ROC. Defections between the rivals were also commonplace. Rather than face the painful music, lots of offenders leapt over to the other side. Most came in with some arcane skill or the other, and every new entrant increased each side's knowledge of the other's activities.

She entered her email, hotdemonchic_666@gmail.com, then clicked 'Send.'

The text-filled window altered to a flashing, 'Got your Message. We'll be in touch.'

She put the phone away. *Now all I can do is wait.* A black car approached in the opposite lane. As it drew level, she checked to ensure that it didn't have pentagram hubcaps, then relaxed.

Damn! It's like the Cold War never ended. Particularly since Red Octopus had been started by a Russian, Peter Rostov. *Too much vodka and caviar and this is what happens: you have visions of angels, only instead of legs, the angels have tentacles.*

She stopped musing. Origins were for historians or superhero movies. What mattered to her now was that both sides—Abyss and ROC—left each other's' members alone. Even defectors were granted safe passage; no one attempted murdering or sacrificing them. *So once . . . if . . . I get accepted into the Red Octopus fold, I'm free. They'd likely ship me off to Poland or Ukraine, while changing my name to Susana Harizova or some such, but I'll be alive.*

Of course, that would be after they'd gotten Avex out of her . . .

With her trained witch sensitivity, she 'felt' inside of herself to see how the demon was doing. Once again, she was struck by how quiet it was: Hell's mighty ravager was uncharacteristically calm and well-behaved. Also, it didn't appear bothered in the least by her plan to switch allegiances. *Or is that that even the Sinis work for Hell? No, it's general knowledge that the Sinis are a completely different order of divine life. So . . . so why is this demon in me unconcerned?*

That unanswered query, however, was less of a concern to Pagan than something else she'd just sensed. Just like before, she could tell that Avex was hiding something from her. Something big. Something important.

The wiley rascal knows something it's not telling me. And that something has to be bad, for me at least. I never heard of a demon that did anyone favors.

She sat for a while staring at the road, then decided she needed to get a move on. Hell could wait. *I need to find a motel room and get some sleep.*

She started the car up and drove off the shoulder. Five minutes later she hit the I-95, and turned south towards Attleboro.

CHAPTER 10

Joanna

Once Britt and Lori had left her bedroom, Joanna Wilson instantly sat up. Because of Britt's warning, she didn't scream—it would be a complete disaster if she lost her hands too. But she'd couldn't just do nothing. She had to recover her stolen feet, no matter what.

Her only intent was to crawl to the living room and call the police.

In her haste, however, she'd forgotten the severity of her amputation. Sitting upright of necessity pulled her stumps in towards her buttocks. The twin knives of agony that shot through her legs as their severed ends dragged over the bloody bed sheets were so intense that she instantly fainted again.

Joanna regained consciousness forty minutes later. Even then she was too scared to move for fear of the pain returning. She lay in the bed wondering what to do. She suspected it was already too late, that her feet were lost for good, courtesy of her stupid daughter—*How could the little bitch do this to me . . . to us!?*

Us. She looked sideways at Chris. He was still alive, his body spasming like he was ejaculating through a wet dream. His head and torso were expanses of dark congealed blood.

She reached out a hand and touched his face.

At her touch, he began weeping.

Tears flooded from her eyes too. "Oh, baby, I'm so damn sorry! I never expected anything like this to happen to us!"

Joanna found it utterly inconceivable, what had happened here in her bedroom this evening. *Britney did this? She and Lori? But why go this far?*

Chris here would likely be a vegetable for the rest of his life. Her gaze drifted down to his penis, the six nails buried through its stretched length, to his scrotum—a nail driven through each testicle and deep into his thighs. Surgery could likely fix his cock but his balls were shot. The latter half of the thought didn't even strike her as ironic punning; she was in too much pain.

I raised a monster and didn't know it.

She considered trying to pull the nails out of Chris's head at least, then realized she'd only restart the bleeding. And that might kill him.

She twisted away from him. Pain again flared up her legs, accelerating up her spine to rabbit-punch her brain. She looked down at her twine-tied wet stumps—each white end of her lower flesh rimmed with bright red—and was horrified. *While I lie here, my feet are running away from me.* It was now at least an hour since Britt and Lori had left. Joanna was certain that even if the police caught them now, it was already too late to reattach her feet. She saw no point anymore in making the long agonizing crawl to the living room and their cellphones.

All I ever wanted was some harmless fun. Some no-strings-attached sex with a hot young stud. Was that too much to ask? And he'd have been a much better lover to my daughter afterwards too.

Slowly, biting her lower lip to cope with the pain, she rolled over and pulled open the top drawer of her nightstand. She got out her silver revolver and held it up to the light.

What she wanted now was death.

I need to end it quickly. I'm leaving this stupid life before any paramedics get here. A life without feet? My perfect face and tight pussy, and fantastic boobs, but no feet? Who'd ever desire me then? Who could possibly love and want me this way?

Weeping profusely, she looked gently at Chris one final time. *I'm so, so sorry this had to happen, kid.*

Then Joanna Wilson shoved the muzzle of the gun against her left nostril (*Why must it always be in the mouth?*) and pulled the trigger.

Red and pink brains squirted from the back of Joanna's head. She toppled over sideways.

She was dead before her body hit Chris's, which just made him twitch harder.

CHAPTER 11

Britt / Lori

"D'you think the cops'll be after us yet?"

"Nah. I mean, I dunno. I guess it all depends on your mom's tolerance for pain. It'll be utterly agonizing for her to crawl to your living room; and she might faint once or twice on her way there. I'd say we've an hour more at least before a manhunt's on."

"Womanhunt."

"Wha . . . ?"

"Before a womanhunt's on."

"Whatever." Lori steered the gray Mazda down Spring Street. They were just passing the Cypress Street intersection on their left, approaching the VA Medical Center on their right.

It was early evening and there was a disturbance up ahead; the police by the looks of it. Cars with flashing lights and blue-uniformed men running back and forth. The road just past the Morrell Street junction was jammed with them.

"Shit! Cops!"

"Relax, they're not after *us.*"

Britt tried to relax. She couldn't, but it wasn't from fear. Now that she was wanted by the law (though the BPD clearly didn't yet know that they wanted her) just seeing the officers was exciting. She peered at Lori, who did look relaxed, though she was repeatedly licking her upper lip.

Britt grinned. Yeah, Lori, with all her antidepressant medication, had years of practice in being calm.

Closer to the jam of police cars they saw that there'd been a fire. It must have been this morning or last night though: the blaze had long since been put out and there was neither a trail of smoke nor a fire engine in sight. Just the gutted husk of a two-story brownstone on their left with cops streaming in and out of it like uniformed lab mice navigating a maze.

Other policemen waved them through.

Though half-charred, the burnt building's wooden sign, hung on the second floor balcony, was still readable:

"Hole Faith Club. Enter the Abyss here, you who dare; the pit welcomes all."

Britt finished reading it off, then exclaimed, "Hey, Lori, this is Pagan's place!"

Pagan had lived down at the end of Britt's street. Though they'd never really hung out together, Britt knew Pagan quite well, mainly because after divorcing her mother and before moving to Attleboro, her father had been screwing Pagan's Aunt Millie. Britt figured that maybe her dad just had a weakness for sluts—Millie Vanilla (as all the female neighbors called her behind her back) was as bad as Joanna Wilson when it came to keeping erect penises out of her underwear. She apparently seemed to think that a vagina was meant to be filled— with dick—24/7.

Lori turned from grinning at the cute young officer directing her to the left. "Shit, Pagan's place burnt down? You don't think she died, do you?"

"I dunno. She might have." Britt regarded the place as they rode past. Two paramedics were just carrying out a stretcher piled high with body parts and covered with a sheet. Under one end of the sheet, a forearm swung free.

They drove on.

"Be real sad if Pagan's dead," Lori said after a while. "Though she kept to herself, I always liked her black makeup and stuff. Those satin dresses and big boots of hers were just totally *me*; only I was too depressed to wear them."

Britt rolled her eyes. "She was just a poser. The getup was just to get her attention. I mean, check out the name of her club: Hole Faith? Seriously? Only name suckier than that would be Church of Vagina."

Lori laughed.

Britt continued: "Back when my dad was dating her aunt, she once told me she worships the Devil. That was the end of my attempting to befriend her. I had enough problems with teenage angst and zits to add to them a crazy witch. Just imagine us arguing over a guy and her trying to hex me."

Lori laughed louder and stepped on the gas.

"We need to get money before leaving town," Lori said after a while. "Preferably around here." She turned onto the VFW Parkway, pulled up to a Bank of America ATM and parked the car.

Britt looked at her. "Can't we do this tomorrow?"

"Bad idea. Once your mom tells the cops we took her bank cards they're gonna try to track our movement through them. Here, we're still in West Roxbury; we could be headed just about anywhere."

Britt nodded and pushed open the door on her side.

"Hey, wait!"

"Yeah, what?"

"Withdraw as much cash as you can. We're gonna throw away the cards."

Britt nodded and dashed off.

Lori watched her for a minute then pulled out her phone and made a call. "Hi, Lonnie, it's Lori. Are you home? . . . I'm in bad trouble and I need your help . . ."

She listened, said some more, noted down an address on paper, then hung up.

Two minutes later Britt was back and fuming.

"Did you get it?"

"Got just five hundred bucks."

"That's all your mom has? I thought she's well-to-do."

"That's all her Citizen's Bank card would let me have. Her bank balance is $247,000. She's changed her Bank Of America PIN, so it's useless. We could hang around, take some more out tomorrow?" She looked pleadingly at Lori. "Or just take the Citizen's card with us?"

"No, it'll be too dangerous then. And no—we're not taking either card with us. Do you have any cash of your own?"

"I also withdrew my last three hundred and there was a hundred and thirty in my purse. You?"

"Hold on a minute while I withdraw too. Where'd I put my damn ATM card? Shit—I left it on the table at home! I thought I packed it." She grimaced at Britt. "I've three hundred bucks on me. Which brings our collective wealth to how much?"

Britt did the math. "Just over twelve hundred dollars."

Lori shrugged. "It'll last us a week or so. At least till we rob and kill someone."

Britt was taken aback. "We're gonna rob people too?"

"It's easy money. Except you want to work as a prostitute or stripper?"

Britt shook her head. "Count me out of that. Sure, I wanna screw a lot of guys, but not 'cos I have to, and definitely not 'cos they're paying me to. I want to fuck them on my own terms, pick and choose the ones I like, you know?"

"Yeah, that's the life, baby!"

Britt glanced over at the ATM, where a fat man in white overalls was now operating the machine, punching in instructions with one hand while the other scratched the crack of his ass. Yeah, Lori was right: they'd not lack for cash on the highway. Guys like this fat slob here would be easy to rob. Just look at him; she could practically smell the sweat on his body from this far away.

She put her purse away. "Alright, girlfriend, let's roll out of town!"

Lori, however, didn't put the car in motion.

"What's the matter? Engine trouble?"

"Take the card out of your cellphone. Get out the one in your tablet too."

Britt gaped at Lori. Lori already had her own cellphone out and was peeling off the rear cover. Then she plucked out her SIM card.

Then she noticed Britt staring at her.

"We don't want to get caught, right? We want to fuck and murder to our heart's content till we both die, but we don't want to be found. So we ditch our SIM cards. That way, the police can't track our movement."

"How'd you know all this stuff?"

"In between my unsuccessful attempts to kill myself, I watch CNN, which depresses me sufficiently that I want to kill myself even more."

"What's that got to do with my question?"

"Our armed forces regularly send drones to blow up terrorists by tracking their cellphone signals."

Without another word, Britt got out her pink iPhone. Being blown to bits while blithely chatting with a friend sounded horrifying. But then, instead of attempting to eject the iPhone's SIM tray, she pulled out a Sharpie and a notepad.

"What do you think you're doing?"

The question surprised Britt. "What else? I'm noting down the numbers I need: my dad, my aunt Clarissa, Terri Denton and Professor Trenchard at Tufts—"

"Gimme that!" Lori snatched Britt's phone from her grasp and flung both it and her own Vodacom mobile out into the road. A moment later, a passing truck crushed both devices.

Lori turned back inside, a beatific expression now on her face. "That's done with."

"What the hell did you just do that for?" Britt spoke slowly, but under the surface she was boiling like molten lead. She felt like strangling Lori with a length of the twine in the carton in the trunk, then she'd tie her down and saw off her . . .

She got a hold of her temper. "You Prozac-head, do you have any frigging idea how much that iPhone 6 cost?"

Lori's beatific smile never wavered. Angry as she was, Britt found her creepily beautiful and utterly intriguing. An insane Mona Lisa.

"Listen," Lori said, "it's over."

"What is bloody frigging fucking over!?"

"Both of our past lives, the records of our connections stored in our phones. Remember this is your idea—I was happily 'just suicidal' till you came along. What remains for us now is the future we're about making for ourselves. A notorious horrible future, so we'll be remembered with infamy. We're both young, free, and single, and we're going to fuck the world's ass to shreds. Sow our wild oats, or maybe that should be, receive our full share of lots of guys' wild oats. Ha ha ha! We're—"

Britt let her talk. Lori had been on ATDs for so long, Britt had forgotten how verbose she could be once given the opportunity. Before cracking up, she'd been head of the debating society at Hyde Park High (before the city shut the school down for lack of funds).

But . . . as Lori spoke on, Britt realized she was right: *This is a new beginning for both of us.* Losing her phone though made her feel naked. She stared out of their car into the road, where yet another truck was shredding her iPhone into its valueless individual components.

I've suddenly become disconnected. Rootless. I've no past, and my future is so uncertain that I'll better off not waking up tomorrow.

She felt a twinge of pain behind her breasts, deep in her heart. Then suddenly too, a deep joy surging through her, like she was a butterfly emerging from its chrysalis.

Then she became aware that Lori was staring hard at her. She was also extending a hand toward her, palm up.

"What?"

"Gimme the SIM in your tablet. It goes out too."

"I never call from it."

"Doesn't matter—it can still be traced. Don't worry, we'll access the web from Wi-Fi hotspots."

Wearily, Britt got out her Samsung tablet and extracted its SIM card. She handed it over.

Lori winked. "Oh no, I *haven't* forgotten. The bank cards too."

Britt handed those over also.

Lori cheerily tossed all the cards out of the Mazda's window to be deconstructed by the evening traffic. Then she looked back in at her bestie. "Okay. Now, girl, you ready to raise some hell?"

Britt nodded.

They set off. Britt fiddled with the dashboard radio. Almost prophetically, the radio blared out Lou Reed's classic *Walk on the Wild Side*.

***

They drove eastward out of town, heading for Dover. Lori, conscious of the severed feet in her trunk, took care to stay well below the speed limit.

"Who's this guy we're off to see?" Britt asked after a while of counting late evening clouds. The sky was a cool slate gray, the sun long since wandered off to have its evening drink in the Pacific bar. Wind slipped into the car and flirted with her blonde hair.

"Lonnie. He's a friend. I was on the phone to him while you were using the ATM. I explained our situation and he said sure, to come over to his place."

"You told him what we did!? How could you do that!?"

Lori tapped fingers on the steering wheel then checked the rearview. "Don't worry—Lonnie's cool. He's suicidal too. As far as I can tell, Lonnie holds the world record for Russian roulette."

"Isn't that the game where you spin a bullet in a revolver, then place it to your forehead and pull the trigger? How can anyone hold the record for that?"

"Lonnie's been playing it every night since he was fifteen. He's got the most incredible good luck. Somehow he hasn't succeeded in killing himself yet."

"How old is he now?"

"Eighteen."

"That's about a thousand failures. Wow. Yeah, that's some luck alright. Talk about a winning streak, or losing. I mean, in Russian roulette, do you win or lose when you succeed in killing yourself? Or both at once?"

"You know, that's a good question: I've never thought—"

"Hey, he's eighteen?"

"Yes, he's eighteen."

"He's just a kid."

"Britt, we're both just twenty."

"Exactly my point. *We* were eighteen two friggin' years ago. We're both grown up now. Next thing you know, he'll want a date."

"He won't. Not with us at any rate. He's scared stiff that he's gay."

"He doesn't know?"

"He's a virgin."

"A virgin?"

"He's scared to have sex 'cos, you know: what if he doesn't like girls?"

"Why?"

"It's complicated."

Britt grinned broadly. "Oh, am I so going to fuck him. I've never had boy-cherry in my life. Since losing my virginity to my bicycle at age eleven, all the guys I've been with have been so experienced, its given me an inferiority complex. It'll be great to be the teacher for once. Hell, I'm in love before even meeting the guy. We might even get married!"

Lori shrugged and left her to her daydreams.

After a few more minutes of driving, she remembered the address in her pocket and handed it over to Britt, who was tapping her feet along with a dance tune on the radio. "This is Lonnie's address. You know Dover, I don't. You know the way?"

Britt looked the address over. "Haven Terrace? Lori, this guy lives right opposite my aunt Clarissa."

Lori took her eyes off the road. "For real? You're serious?"

"For real. His parents drive a blue Ford SUV."

"Relax, your aunt doesn't know my car. And it'll be dark when we get there . . ."

She swerved around a patch of roadkill, a flattened porcupine.

They were close to Dover now and the road seemed strangely deserted. Then, up ahead by a turnoff they saw a hitchhiker with his thumb stuck out. He looked to about thirty-five, was dressed in denim jacket and pants with a brown knapsack on his back.

"Hit him!" Britt said suddenly.

"Huh? Why?"

"Because he's here? Just hit the asshole. Ram into him! Break his fucking legs!"

Lori considered it. Front and back of them the road was still deserted on both sides. She decided to kill the man; what business did he have being out here anyway? He might be a sexual predator, waiting to murder some innocent female driver.

She floored the pedal to ram her car into him, then eased her foot off the gas again. A truck was coming towards them in the other lane.

They sped past the hitcher.

"Oh, you little wimp!" Britt groaned when they'd gone two hundred yards farther. "I can't believe you didn't ram him. That's it, pull over, let me frigging drive!"

"Don't worry, I'll get the next one."

They didn't pass any more solitary hitchhikers, and they'd arrived in Dover anyway, so for the moment they had no further chance of committing an unsupervised crime.

Lori wasn't sure if she was peeved by this or relieved. She'd felt a definite thrill when she'd agreed to kill the hitcher: for those few moments she'd held the unsuspecting man's life in her hands. *Oh, yes, I want to feel that power again.*

Under Britt's guidance, Lori made a few more turns and then suddenly they'd turned onto Haven Terrace, a pleasant suburban close that was mostly grassy lawns and rose hedges with houses like concrete ships and tall trees like natural lighthouses. The road was a placid stone serpent sneaking inward through the grass.

All wasn't peace and quiet however. Fifty yards in from the turnoff, they saw a mass of police cars and ambulances. As they drove closer to the confusion, they saw barricades and yellow 'crime scene' tape that extended out into the road, along with hordes of harried and perplexed-looking police officers, and a crowd of equally curious onlookers that the police were vainly trying to disperse.

Then the oddest thing of all: The house outside of which all the vehicles were parked seemed to have been hit by a terrorist attack, rockets or maybe drones. Little of it remained standing—a pillar here, a solitary drywall there, an adamant strip of the second floor flooring with the ceiling collapsed in on it—and what there was was riddled with holes. The single surviving upstairs stretch of wall had two vertical stains on it that looked like blood.

Lori said, "Wow! It looks like someone blew it up, then blew the pieces up too."

Britt said, "I hope the bombs didn't affect my aunt's house!" Then she ducked low in the passenger seat.

"What's wrong with you?" Lori whispered. "These cops aren't after us!"

"I just saw my Aunt Clarissa in the crowd, talking to someone. "Thank God the bombs didn't get her."

Lori said, "I sure hope they didn't affect Lonnie's house either."

Britt peeked out, then sat up again. Her expression very sad, her aunt was hugging and comforting a thin weeping woman.

They were waved hard right. Lori had to drive up onto the sidewalk to get around a four foot slab of pillar in the road with bloodstains on it.

Then they were past. They both made sounds of relief. The devastation extended no further than the nearest trees, one of which had been cracked in two by a chunk of wall. The tree leaned over, an 'A' without the crosspiece. Both of the next houses were in perfect condition, concrete islands in the sea of grass.

"Park on the right," Britt directed, "the left one's my aunt's place."

Lori parked. Both residences were almost identical—white two-story colonial-style houses with extensive front porches and equally wide yards. Neither had either a fence or a hedge.

Britt and Lori sat in the car for a while, letting the evening air soothe them. Their unspoken thoughts were similar: it had been an exciting day; would it be an equally exciting night?

Finally, Britt turned to Lori. "Okay, here were are. Now remember our motto: 'We fuck until death.'"

"I guess so. That's our motto?"

"Except you got a better one."

"How about 'Suicide Girls Forever?'"

"The Suicide Girls already have a club. Besides, neither of us have tattoos or want to pose nude."

"Yeah, there is that to consider. We could call ourselves something cool though; like the Suicide Mechanics . . ."

"That sounds like a punk band. Suicide Freak Chicks sounds better. Or Hardcore Suicide Machine. Hey, what's with all this suicide theme anyway? I'm not suicidal."

"Kamikaze Girls!"

"Still suicide-themed. Also, it's too Asian, and there's a movie with that title. Think patriotic, girl—we're American!"

"There you go again. What's patriotic about murdering innocent people?"

"Lori, my depressed bestie, the innocent people we're gonna kill are Americans. What could be more patriotic than that?"

"You know, girlfriend, I'm not sure you should do any drugs on this trip. You're fucked up enough in the head as it is?"

"Hey, let's call ourselves the Murder Patriots or Patriot Killers!"

"Over my dead body."

"It soon will be."

"Look, fuck branding ourselves. We're not a murder corporation —"

"Murder Corp's a good name."

"Stuff it. Let's just get out of this frigging car and go buzz Lonnie."

***

Lonnie's front door was opened by two men. One was blonde, tall, and very muscular with a drooping mustache; the other, dark-haired and short and round and clean shaved. Both were middle-aged. The muscular man was very good-looking, the shorter one not too much.

"Hi," Lori said. "We're here to see Lonnie. We're friends of his from Boston."

The short plump man grinned. "Oh, please do come in. We're his parents." He extended a hand with a limp wrist. "I'm Tony, and my husband here is Rick."

"Oh, delighted to meet you both," Lori gushed in an excited voice.

Following them into the house, Britt grinned broadly. *Oh, he's got two dads. No wonder he's confused as to if he's gay or not.*

101

They were seated in a comfortable living room. Music—sounded like 90's REM—played softly in the background. A clearly recent wedding photo—Rick and Tony kissing before a minister—hung over the electric fireplace. Below it sat another, older picture: the couple, both much younger, with a small boy (about seven years old) who looked miserable. Britt figured that if the kid was Lonnie, he'd been depressed for most of his life.

"Lonnie had to hurry down to the library," Tony said. "He asked us to make you both comfortable."

"I was just about making some java," Rick said. "Would you two ladies care for some?"

Lori and Britt both nodded. Rick left to make the coffee.

Lori smiled at Tony. Rick had a low macho voice, just like his appearance. Tony was more of the stereotypical homosexual: the high-pitched voice, the limp wrist, the mincing gait, the barely restrained femininity. She decided she liked both men. Now the problem was: would Britt suddenly decide they should kill them?

(She rehearsed her counterargument in her head: "Look, we can't kill them: They're *gay!*" "So what? We're killing straight people, aren't we?" "If it gets out that we killed a *gay* couple, we're gonna be looked on as politically-incorrect killers!" She imagined Britt musing on this for all of two seconds, then rolling her eyes in disgust: "Does this no-killing ban of yours also apply to lesbians and Blacks and Jews and Mexicans and Arabs? Or is just gay *men?* The reason I'm asking is, if we tick everyone off our hit list, there'll be no one left!" "We don't kill them and that's all." "Oh, alright!"

Yes, that should work, but with the new and insane Britt, one didn't know for sure. *I mean she wanted us to kill the hitchhiker, right?*)

Mentally, she rejoined the conversation. Britt was saying, "What happened to that house back there? It looked like . . . was it terrorists?"

"It wasn't terrorists," Rick replied, returning with a laden coffee tray. "But what it was I've no idea. Damnest thing I ever saw in my life."

"Yes, darling," Tony continued while Rick set the tray down and began handing around their mugs. "We were having a siesta when these really horrible noises started . . . like someone was using a wrecking ball on old Deacon Harris's house—"

(On hearing the name, a memory triggered in Britt's mind: *Isn't Pagan's dad a church elder, and doesn't he live out here in Dover?* She let it go. *No, that would be way too much of a coincidence.*)

"It's so sad," Rick said, handing Lori her coffee, and staring directly at her as he did so, so that she saw his eyes were a lovely sky-blue. "Personally, we never did get along with David Harris. He was an unpleasant and crotchety old man, terribly set in his ways and utterly detesting the thought of gay marriage. He once said the mere sight of us holding hands threatened him with a coronary. So, so horrible."

"We were constantly scared he was going to have his church down here to picket us."

"Or even try to lynch us. His wife Linda, though, was a much nicer person. All sweetness and cream. She came over a few times for coffee and scones—"

"She brought us some of her homemade jam too, and we were surprised at how relaxed and outgoing she was. Once, when her husband was away at a church retreat, she met Clarissa Noble here—that's the lady who lives right opposite us; oh, an utterly delightful and wonderful neighbor to have—and we laughed the evening away."

"So . . . I mean, but what happened this afternoon?" Britt knew gay men liked a good conversation, but she was too curious about the destruction outside to oblige. And, oh yes, the coffee was delicious. She wondered if there was a stereotype attached to that too. Maybe gay people made better coffee than straight folk? She didn't know, but it seemed that since there were stereotypes attached to everything else, maybe in this case also?

After sipping from his mug, Tony resumed the telling: "I got out of bed and walked to the window, then I called my darling Richard. It was horrible. We couldn't really see from here, so we got dressed and headed outside for a better look. We got there and . . ."

"And *what?*" Britt pressed.

"The house was falling all in on itself."

"Collapsing?"

Rick gestured outside through a window, towards where they could still hear police noises and voices. "No, not like that. I'm a structural engineer. I design buildings and I know where all the loads and stresses on the different parts of a house are and what can happen to one. And I'm assuring you that no matter what happens, even in a tornado, a building can't fall apart like the Harris's did."

"And they were both still inside it too, darling," Tony said with a deep shudder, reaching to hold Rick's hand for comfort.

Britt was bemused. Tony's behavior was so feminine, it was easy to forget he had sausage between his legs, not a fun tunnel. Breasts and a little makeup and he'd make a fine woman.

She stared at Rick. "Okay, so what was so strange about the collapse then?"

Rick sighed. "Tony saw it too, but he says we hallucinated it."

"This is real life, not the X-files, darling. We did hallucinate it."

"What was 'it'?"

"It looked like something was stamping the roof in." Rick took a long sip of his coffee, then frowned at his two visitors. That sounds incredibly stupid, right? But trust me, I know what I saw . . . the way the holes appeared in the roof, there's no other explanation. Then, when chunks of the masonry detached from the front wall and flew out into the road, they looked like they'd been *kicked* out of place. I remember hearing an impact before each chunk broke loose. And in each case, it was only at that part of the wall. So something *kicked* them out." He leaned over and kissed Tony's cheek. "And nothing you can say, baby, will convince me otherwise."

"You're right," Britt began, "That sounds unbelievable as hell. Still—"

"And . . ." Rick continued, raising a finger for emphasis, "there was this horrible animal smell that hung in the air. Clarissa Noble smelt it too."

"Clarissa was just returning from confession. She most likely still had the scent of church incense in her nostrils."

"Baby, Clarissa said it smelt like *goat-smell*." He nodded seriously at the girls. "To me it smelt like unwashed dog, or—"

"Hey, Lonnie's back!" Tony announced in his feminine giggle. "That's his bicycle outside."

***

Lonnie Young was tall and plump (which Britt thought had to be the work of ATDs), with dark hair and gray eyes. He was quite handsome, and looked to be Rick's son (from before he'd discovered he was gay), rather than Tony's. Of course Lonnie might be adopted, but Britt wasn't sure how far back Massachusetts gay adoption permits went.

He waved to his parents, "Hi, dads," then grinned at his visitors.

Lori instantly recognized a kindred spirit in him, someone living in a similar 'Pit' to hers. It didn't matter that his parents seemed genuinely nice people; that had nothing to do with anything—her own parents were genuinely nice people too, they'd never once abused her or denied her love or hugs or ice cream or summer camp, and look how sick she'd gotten. So she understood and liked Lonnie on sight.

Britt also liked Lonnie. She felt strangely protective towards him. Behind his welcoming smile ran a clear vein of misery, like he was wearing a mask. And he couldn't be all there in the head, could he? Not with him welcoming them to his parents' house after Lori had told him what they'd done.

So another one in the rat pack. We're all crazy friends here.

After politely turning down an invitation from Rick and Tony to join them for dinner, Britt and Lori followed Lonnie down a short corridor towards the back of the house.

"I've got my own shack out back," he explained as he led the way. "My parents say I'm too depressing to keep indoors. Damn, that makes me sound like a bothersome pet."

His voice was bland, expressing neither anger nor regret, nor even a sense of injustice. He was just stating the obvious as he saw it.

"Tell me about it," Lori said. "My parents shipped me halfway across town to get out of my way."

"Your dads are both really cool," Britt said, as they exited the back door onto a short grass-enclosed walk that led to a large cabin.

"Yeah, I guess they are." As before, his voice was noncommittal. Overhead the sky was dark, and a breeze was blowing. The air smelt wet like it was raining somewhere.

Britt pointed to the cabin, a neat and glossy wooden box that seemed almost an organic part of the trees and flowers surrounding it. "Wow! This is your place?"

"Yeah, my parents are rich. Rick's an engineer and Tony writes novels. Have you ever read *The Sex Change Police* by A.W. Author?"

Both young women shook their heads.

"'Arthur Wright Author is Tony's nom de plume. It's a great book too," Lonnie said emphatically. "It was on the New York Times bestsellers list for three months last year."

"*Sex Change Police* is a weird title."

"It's a weird story . . . sci-fi about a world where everyone is male till age twenty-five, then they pass through a thing called 'The Pussy' and become female. So all the older members of society—including the entire government—are women who've once been men and who are all married to these young guys. Anyhow . . ." They'd reached Lonnie's front door now. It was a bright yellow. "Okay, the book's hero, Simms, doesn't want to become a woman, so he runs off, and the Sex Change Police are sent off after him to bring him back. They're all transsexuals, with big enhanced tits with laser technology built into them so they can shoot light beams from their nipples . . ."

"Frigging weird story," Lori agreed.

Lonnie pushed opened the yellow door. "And here we are, ladies. Mi casa es su casa."

Lonnie's cabin consisted of a living room, a bedroom, a bathroom, and a kitchen. It was comfortably furnished but painted a depressing gray (including the rear of the yellow front door). Stepping into Lonnie's living room, one felt displeasure with the world radiate at one from the enclosing walls. (This grim effect was only increased by the evening-gray now filtering in through the windows.)

"It's corpse-skin-tone," Lonnie explained. "I went to a lot of trouble to get it right. My dads hate it, they hardly ever come down here." He gestured around. "Please sit."

They both sat facing him, on a sofa to the left of a wall-mounted 52-inch LED television. Britt, closer to the TV, noted a pile of porn DVDs on the rug beneath it. Curious, she studied the titles: *Busty Texan Beauties, Hot Eighteen!, Barely Legal Sluts, Euro Ass Hardball.* Nah, this kid didn't seem gay.

Lonnie had vanished into his kitchen. He returned with beers. "My dads don't mind me raiding their stash of booze, so long as I agree not to pester them for a car of my own. They view that as a suicide machine." He grinned weakly. "I've got some of their wine too, for later. Dinner is sandwiches, if that's okay."

Britt nodded. "Thanks." She was studying Lonnie, trying to imagine how it would be to fuck a virgin for the first time. What did guys think about at times like this? Tearing pussy flesh, tears, and blood? And afterwards, there was the task of having to make insincere protestations of eternal love. And all for helping the girl get rid of a piece of tissue most modern women placed little value on.

She licked her lips. Of course, there was the possibility that he was gay after all and wouldn't even be able to get it up.

"So," Lonnie asked Lori while handing beers around, "how was your trip over? Did you have any trouble finding this place?"

Lori shook her head. "Nah, it was easy. Britt's aunt lives right opposite you."

Surprised, he swung his face towards Britt. "Clarissa Noble's your aunt?"

She nodded. "My dad's oldest sister. He's the baby of the family."

"Ah, she's a lovely old lady. It was so sad when her husband died last year. We all attended the funeral. Everyone on the street did. He's buried in the Highland Cemetery."

"Yeah, the whole family flocked here for that. It was like they were celebrating being rid of him."

Lonnie's brow crinkled. "Now that you mention it, I think I remember seeing you at the funeral. Yes, I do . . . and afterwards, you left with that lady who looked like a movie star."

Britt bristled; was Joanna going to upstage and smother her even now? "Yeah, that *was* me. The movie actress was my mom."

"Whose feet are currently outside in the trunk of our car," Lori added.

Lonnie's eyes widened; he sputtered his beer. "Outside? Y-y-you actually d-did it? . . . I mean . . . I know you said . . . but . . ." Then he calmed and said sadly, "Wow, you girls are the real deal. I've been trying to die for like three years straight now. No luck."

"Yeah, Lori said you're the world champion at Russian roulette."

He got up and lumbered off into the bedroom. When he returned he was carrying a Colt revolver. The gun was silvery, with a short barrel and a black grip.

He set it down on the coffee table.

"My dads don't know I've got this," he said, his voice suddenly feverish. "But I play every night. And I always lose. I spin the wheel, put the muzzle to my head and wait for the Big Bang, then the Rewind—"

"The Rewind?"

"You know, my entire life replaying in a second, but . . . damn, it never happens; all I ever hear is the hammer click on an empty chamber. It's fucking depressing."

"You don't seem *that* depressed," Britt said, eying the revolver on the table, that streamlined engine of death. (Viewed like that, the weapon held a strange beauty and fascination for her.) "At least, not like Lori here when she's in her bad zone. When she's out of it she's like roadkill, splattered everywhere and helpless to help herself. You, you're much more controlled. I can only *feel* that you're not doing so good; I can't see it on you."

He nodded. "I do some speed along with my ATDs. It helps sometimes. Sometimes I use a little pot and coke too."

"Does the mix work?" Lori asked in an expectant voice. Since entering Lonnie's pad she'd been on edge. Something great was supposed to be happening, wasn't it? She craved an additional level of excitement. If something new didn't happen soon, she feared she'd drop back to ground-zero energy level again, and from there back into the Pit. And Lonnie's corpse-toned walls would only facilitate that descent. "Everything I've read online warns not to mix antidepressants with recreational drugs; though some people argue that pot is okay."

Lonnie nodded sagely. "It works fine for me. I think it depends on your makeup and temperament. I know a guy on Xanax who did too much speed and wound up so wired he shot his parents and younger sister."

Lori grimaced.

Lonnie continued: "Yeah, he did. Then he put the gun to his head to kill himself too, but he'd run out of bullets. That's when the cops burst in. He's doing three simultaneous counts of life now." Lonnie shook his head in disgust. "Screw him—Joey was always an asshole anyway."

"Fuck, this is getting really depressing," Lori said. "Even for occupational suicides, we should be having some fun tonight." She shook her empty Bud Light can at Lonnie. Another beer?"

"Me too," Britt said.

He got up to get the beers. As he left the room, Lori whispered to Britt. "So?"

"So what?"

"You gonna jump into bed with him or not?"

"I'm still making up my mind."

"Well, hurry up or I'll be tempted. He's quite cute. And needy, clueless guys are always such a turn-on."

"Hell no—he's mine. You can have my sloppy seconds."

"Oh no, I'm not having any dick in my pussy after it's just been in yours. There's no telling what you've got."

Lonnie returned with their beers. "So how'd it feel . . . doing your mom?"

Britt shrugged. "It has to do with the moment, you know? Then, I was just so damn mad, and it felt great. Now, though, it's almost like nothing exceptional happened. And that's really surreal 'cos I'm sure the cops are after us by now. But still—"

"Stop it!" Lori said. "That's it—no more frigging death stories. Let's party!" She leapt up and began dancing without music. She struck the John Travolta pose from the *Saturday Night Fever* poster, then shot a gaze at Lonnie. "You got any dope or pills at home?"

"Yeah, sure." He vanished into the bedroom. He returned with several envelopes of pills. He handed each of them a blue and a white.

"Okay, wash those down. They work great with beers—you get a good buzz but feel mellow at the same time."

"Do your parents know you do all these pills?"

"Hell no! If they knew about these or about the gun they'd have me committed. They're cool with my drinking 'cos I never get into fights, but . . ."

They drank awhile, then Britt, feeling more aroused the more she stared at Lonnie's innocent 18-year-old face, with those baby-pure eyes, finally decided to take the bull by the balls.

She said, "Okay, Lonnie, out with it: Lori already filled me in you. Why do you think you're gay?"

He stiffened at the question, then slumped back in his chair. "I think it's 'cos my parents are, you know?"

"But how can you be sure if you've never had . . . been with a woman?"

He shrugged. "I'm scared of finding out *that I am* gay. There's this girl, Lisa, who works with me at the library. She's really hot, and she's been giving me all kinds of green lights. We've been on three dates and I've even kissed her, but . . ." he squeezed up his face like he was in intense pain, "what if we come back here and . . . it doesn't work out?"

Britt gestured to his collection of adult DVDs. "But what about all these?"

"They work okay. I get hard and all, but . . ."

"But what?"

"I'm not sure if I'm reacting to the pussy on display or the dicks."

Britt was stumped. She'd automatically assumed that any man watching straight porn would be naturally turned on by the women, but here Lonnie was, throwing a curveball into the works. Yes, what if *he was* getting turned on by the guys? *But, for the love of Hilary Clinton, how wouldn't you know if it's the tits or sausage turning you on?*

And now, she was really determined to capture Lonnie's virginity for herself.

"Okay," she began slowly, "so . . . ." Out of words, she looked over at Lori, who'd just helped herself to a yellow pill from the ranged envelopes on the table.

Britt watched her wash it down with beer. *Girl, do you even know what that is?*

"You know," Lonnie said. "I think having gay parents is even the reason I'm so depressed."

"Are they your actual parents? I mean one of them?"

"Yeah, Rick's my biological father. He was straight till my mom died when I was five, then he met Tony and they fell in love." He smacked his forehead with his palm. "Shit, it's so damn confusing. How 'bout if the same thing happens to me? I mean, I get married to Lisa only to find out later that I'm actually gay?"

His eyes dropped longingly to the Colt revolver on the coffee table. It had 'Python .357' etched into its steel barrel.

"I can see why you're depressed," Britt said with sincerity. She felt a deep impulse to mother him. He seemed to her like a large baby.

"Uh uh," Lori said. "Don't blame your dads. Your depression isn't their fault. So what if they're gay? My parents are straight as arrows; so what's my excuse for being depressed and suicidal?" She shook her head emphatically and wagged a finger at him with drug-induced sternness. "No. It's a copout blaming your parents: you're your own person, with your own genes and your own makeup—with your own unique brand of insanity."

"Look," Britt agreed, "I think Lori's right—you aren't depressed because your parents are gay. And them being gay doesn't have any direct bearing on your own sexuality. At most, you'll be very accepting of gay people, but not automatically homosexual yourself. Or else, straight parents would only have straight kids."

He looked at her, his eyes saying he wanted to believe her. "You really think so?"

She nodded. "Take me for instance: My mom's the living definition of the word 'slut,' but I'm sexually well-adjusted." She got up, then winked coquettishly at him. "Come on into the bedroom," she said, "let me get *you* sexually well-adjusted too."

Lonnie hedged for a while. "I . . . I . . . I . . ."

Britt walked around the coffee table to him. She bent and kissed him. Then, breathing hard with arousal, she pulled him to his feet. "C'mon, let's fuck. Confused as you are, it's best that your first sexual experience be with someone who cares about you. And besides, even if it doesn't work out, even if you are playing ball for the other team, you know for certain that me and Lori won't ever tell anyone."

Smiling weakly, Lonnie got up and followed Britt into the bedroom. The door clicked shut behind them.

"Shit!" Lori said then, rolling her eyes at the gray ceiling. "She sure took her time with getting him in the fucking sack, didn't she?"

After selecting three pills at random from the envelopes on Lonnie's table, she popped them in her mouth, washed them down with the rest of her beer, then walked into the kitchen to get herself a fresh can of Bud Light.

And she was starting to feel hungry; she wanted a sandwich too.

***

Once through the bedroom door, they got down to it. They fell onto the bed kissing. In no time at all, they were both undressed and she had his penis in her mouth. Like it was unsure what it wanted, the organ took a short while to stiffen fully, but once it did, it stayed up. She was pleased with that. She slurped her mouth down over it, pulling on his scrotum with her hands.

Lonnie quit gasping for breath and instead gasped, "Please turn around so I can lick you too! I want to taste you!"

"Oh yes. I thought you'd never ask!"

A few moments later, she was lying atop him with her vagina in his face and his tongue in her vagina, and gasping herself around the obstruction of his erection in her mouth. Damn! She'd had no idea whatsoever that she was so stressed out. Or horny, either. Her sex felt inflamed; each touch of Lonnie's tongue on it felt like a match touching the fuse of a stick of dynamite.

She tried to concentrate on fellating the hard penis between her lips (and damn, was it hard!), but she couldn't. Suddenly for Britt, this sexual experience wasn't anymore about establishing Lonnie's sexuality as much as getting off herself.

She rolled off him onto her back, pushed strands of her blonde hair out of her eyes, then spread her thighs wide and stroked herself. She reached an arm out to him and pulled him onto her. "Come inside me."

She gasped as his manhood filled her.

"Now," she instructed, "fuck me as hard as you can. As hard as you like. Just go 'Bang, Bang, Bang!'"

He stared worriedly at her, his soft pale face twisted with concern. "I don't wanna hurt you, Britt."

She had to laugh at his naiveté. "What the hell do you know about hurting a woman?" Then she softened. She stroked his face, looked deep into his eyes. "Don't worry, you won't hurt me. Just do what I say. Fuck me really hard."

"Okay, Britt."

He fucked her HARD, and he was fattish, so it felt like not just her body, but the whole bed was going to implode with each fresh thrust he made into her wet depths.

After the first ten or so strokes of his penis, she came, her entire self exploding inwards like that previously lit fuse of cunnilingus had just reached her sensual dynamite. She tensed, moaned out, then relaxed.

Above her, Lonnie was thrusting hard, his face red and warped with concentration like this was an exam he dare not fail.

Yeah, Britt realized, *in a way it is: The test to prove he's straight. He fails this and he's screwed, right? Literally condemned to rectal examinations by other men for the rest of his life? Shit, what's the fuss about being gay anyway? It's all just sex, isn't it? And his fathers both seem happy and . . .*

Her thoughts broke off as her body commandeered her mind again. She locked her legs around his buttocks and groaned. With her legs up like this, he was digging into a particularly soft and sensitive part of her.

"Oh, oh! Fuck!" She shuddered through another orgasm.

Lonnie was still slamming HARD into her.

"Okay, that's enough! Slow down!" she gasped, as the pleasure subsided. "And never, ever, fuck a girl this hard again unless she begs you to."

"Yeah, sure."

"And you're doing great. Just keep going slow like this. In and out." The penis inside her felt incredibly filling. It felt like a rod of delicious chocolate traveling a hungry mouth. "Kiss me, baby."

He bent down and kissed her.

He began panting hard.

"Okay, now come for me! Give yourself to me!"

He emptied himself inside her, and a particularly deep thrust of his sent her traveling the route of yet another orgasm. (She herself found her response tonight strange: coming thrice in less than four minutes? *Am I so excited that he's a virgin and I'm his first? Or is this just the culmination of this strange day; this day of killing my former self?*)

She held him tight and shuddered and moaned.

He finished ejaculating and crumpled on top of her. He lay heavy on her, but she enjoyed his solidity.

Finally he rolled off her. They lay side-by-side in silence for a while, two white bodies on sweat-drenched white sheets, in a gray room where the colors of the walls reflected the death-wish inside a young man's head.

"Oh no, you're not frigging gay," Britt finally announced breathlessly when her body had normalized enough for speech. "I'll be glad to write you a recommendation to Lisa the librarian if you like."

Lonnie laughed. "Thanks, I really needed that."

For once, the cliché seemed apt. She looked at him. He wasn't saying anything else, but the wide smile of relief on his face spoke bucketloads. Lonnie's previous weight of doubt over his sexuality seemed to have lifted off his shoulders like seawater becoming clouds.

"I discussed my problem with your aunt," he admitted shyly, cuddling up close to her, which she really enjoyed.

"Aunt Clarissa? You told *her*, of all people? What'd she say?"

"She said she thought the right girl just hadn't come along. She confessed that when she was younger, she'd imagined she was gay herself until your uncle asked her out." He laughed, then added, "I guess she was right—the right girl for me finally did come along."

Britt turned to him and hugged him hard. She buried her head deep in his chest so he wouldn't see she was crying.

It was much too late in the day for love.

CHAPTER 12

Clarissa

Still toweling dewy drops of water off her skin, Clarissa Noble emerged from her bathroom.

She sighed. Oh, it had an atrocious day, driving back from church to find the Harris's house falling to bits by itself, and with them still inside it. And the police said they'd been murdered. Sacrificed. Who on earth would want to sacrifice the Harrises? (True, the old deacon was a politically incorrect religious firebrand, but even the gay couple opposite found him more funny than scary—comic relief on their street—so . . .)

Watching the Harris's place fall apart had really upset her. Linda Harris had been a good reliable friend, not someone who should end her life nailed upside-down on a wall with her throat slit.

Clarissa sat in front of her dresser mirror. Like it generally did, her reflection annoyed her. She was a small mousy woman, and tonight, to her immense disgust, her face showed all sixty years of her age, the crow's feet and wrinkles (one or two for each year of her life), and the sagging pinched skin. But over that, her face gave the impression of having been well lived in, like she was an old house long overdue for renovation. Her once chestnut hair was now almost fully gray.

And her body felt as old as she looked. She regarded her figure. Thank God she'd not suffered from too much middle-age spread; her dresses still looked good on her. But what good was that? What good indeed? Since Mortimer had died, her life had just been so empty. Their shared life as spouses hadn't been just quarrels; there'd also been the delicious resolving of those quarrels, both in and out of bed.

The sex had been regular and very good. The result of years of practice, she knew exactly how to satisfy Mort, and he her.

And then suddenly, nothing. No husband, no arguments, no sex. Even her regular weekly flirtings with Onan held little thrill other than the release of tension.

Until recently that was, when she'd gotten masturbatory help from an unexpected source.

She squeezed her breasts. Though sagging, and with more blue veins than she cared for, they felt heavy, full of need, full of love. A real man would find them satisfying; they were large and had nice nipples.

But where was the man? She desperately wanted one, but all the ones her age were taken. As a national statistic there were more widows than widowers in the USA, and the few single sixtyish men that weren't attached and weren't recovering from coronaries hardly filled her with confidence that they'd give her much of a tumble in the sack.

She and Mort hadn't been able to make children either, so apart from occasional visits from her nieces and nephews, she lived alone.

Which reminds me: I need to see if Britney can come over tomorrow instead to help me pack. Ah, maybe I'll find some romance in Spain.

A wind parted her drapes, revealing the Young's house. The couple's bedroom window directly faced hers. The smell of the night filled the room. A romantic, but lonely smell. The half-moon was out, she stared desolately at it.

Clarissa disliked that she still felt so much at her age. At sixty (and a new widow) everyone expected that she'd come to accept that her really pleasant years of life now lay behind her, and that she'd also accepted her gradual decline towards a tombstone besides Mortimer's. It seemed like she had too, and her family respected her for it.

"Thank God you're not a walking scandal like my mom," her niece Britney had once whispered to her. "You know how to grow old gracefully."

Clarissa had smiled sagely, while inside she'd seethed at the comment. She deeply envied her sister-in-law.

Joanna Wilson had guts. She had style and class too. Above all, she was beautiful, and while still married to Clarissa's brother Jeff, had put his money to great use making herself even more so. Oh no, Joanna would never grow old gracefully; she'd be breaking hearts well into her seventies or eighties—she'd likely try to out-river Joan Rivers if that was possible, then die of a heart attack at age eighty-five while being sodomized by an eighteen-year-old football player. A highly probable scenario considering her voraciousness where men were concerned.

But Clarissa herself? It hurt to be a widow and not pretty.

Half the time she felt like a once-useful device now made obsolete by new female technology—the full bouncy breasts and pneumatic bodies of the next generation of women. The other half of the time, however, an erotic fire burned inside her: the desire for a man's arms squeezing her tight, for a body humped over hers in a sweat-drenched bed, for an excruciatingly stiff manhood filling her deep and tender female core, stoking her furnace so she roasted in Heaven's glorious lights.

She wanted to be screwed and screwed good, to have a man's bolt deep in her nut, fastening her to a bed so hard that it felt like she was becoming part of it.

But that so wasn't happening at the moment, so she'd found an acceptable substitute.

Almost on cue, the light flicked on opposite, in the neighbors' front bedroom. *Could it be?*

Acting on a reflex, Clarissa leapt to her feet and dashed across to flick off her own bedroom light. Then, padding breathlessly back to the dresser, she picked up the binoculars that lay beside her cosmetics.

Then she made her naked way across to the window, parted her fluttering drapes slightly, and raised the binoculars to her eyes.

Oh, yes! This is exactly what I need right now! A thrill filled her as she watched Rick and Tony Young shedding their clothes. Once they began kissing, Clarissa slipped a hand down between her legs and started caressing herself.

It's harmless fun, she told herself as tall muscular Rick (Oh, he's so darn handsome!) got down on his knees and began sucking on Tony's penis. *They don't know, and I'm not hurting anyone.*

Thanking God Almighty that she'd stumbled on the binoculars while cleaning out the attic, and sure that Reverend Father Nolan would likely move to have her excommunicated if she ever found out what she was doing, Clarissa masturbated to the two men having sex in the bedroom opposite hers.

Spreading wide the withered folds of her sex, she sluiced her fingers up and down the wet gap. She pleasured herself expertly; she knew what she liked—she'd had forty-five years of practice—at this age she could masturbate in her sleep. She slowly squirted the day's horror out of herself, burning away its depressing residue in the delicious fire between her thighs.

From across the road, homoerotism seeped into her brain, making her hotter and hotter by the moment.

What do you call a female voyeur? A Peeping Tina!

Rick was still fellating Tony, who stood with his eyes closed and his large belly quivering. The binoculars brought everything into wonderfully close focus for Clarissa—the lips sliding up and down the stiff manhood, the tongue swirling around the fat glans then licking the pearlescent bead of pre-come out of the slit.

And then Rick pulled Tony down, and bent him over the bed and began licking his anus. The binoculars captured that too for Clarissa. As Rick's tongue stabbed into the cleft of Tony's butt, she fingered herself faster, dipping her fingers deep into her sex now. She always loved seeing Rick dig his strong fingers into the meat of Tony's fat buttocks and spread those cheeks wide. *Oooh!* She was dripping between the legs now.

Tony climbed fully onto the bed, so he was on his hands and knees by its edge. Rick spat on his erection, got between Tony's legs, and slid it in. There was little resistance and his manhood sank in deep through the puckered brown ring of flesh.

While watching the swollen penis stretch Tony's anus and vanish inside it, Clarissa felt like she was right there with them. They seemed close enough for her to touch if she so desired.

Seeing Rick penetrate his husband like this felt to Clarissa like she was being penetrated herself.

Moaning loudly, she came. She groaned and shuddered and sagged against the window frame. She let her binoculars drop and hang on their strap, dangling on her breasts while she fingered herself desperately and her juices flooded from her.

Then, gasping out ragged breaths, she lifted herself upright, raised the spyglasses back up to her face, and began pleasuring herself again.

Across the street, Rick was thrusting hard now, while grimacing like he was coming into Tony's big ass. He had a hand under Tony and was masturbating him fast.

Clarissa licked her lips, and rubbed her clitoris harder. Her body shuddered as the dregs of her first orgasm began building up into another one. She was multiorgasmic, could come for a good hour if she chose to. *Oh, so today was bad. Tonight, though, is definitely going to be good.*

CHAPTER 13

Mostly Britt

By the time Britt and Lonnie returned to the living room, Lori was quite stoned. She was lounging on the sofa with the TV on and tuned to MTV at low volume. The program was something about the *Jackass* films. Yeah, there was Johnny Knoxville in all his demented glory.

"You guys took forever," she challenged in a manner that was half-happy and half-annoyed, then gestured at the six additional beer cans on the table and the two sandwich wrappings now covering Lonnie's gun. "I hope you don't mind that I helped myself."

Lonnie shook his head. "No problem. You're welcome to more of everything; as much as you like."

Lori winked at Britt. "Wow, you must *really* have convinced him he's straight." She swigged more beer.

Britt blushed. "I was cross-checking, to make sure I hadn't missed anything." What else could she say? Her body felt like a car just returned from the mechanic's—serviced, aligned, balanced, whatever . . . She must have come about ten times in the last hour, over and over again. And inexperienced Lonnie had proved quite the stud, pounding her tired vagina till now she felt sore down there, tender and lovingly bruised.

"You know what I've been thinking?" Lori asked.

"What?"

"While you were busy screwing, I worked out why Lonnie was so confused." She waved a hand at them. "Lonnie's problem is that he has male parents. If they were both women, and he liked girls, he'd never have even imagined he was gay. Push come to shove, he'd think he was a male lesbian, which is fine as both men and lesbians like pussy. So, in his current situation, he'd have been better off being a girl. Hold on a bit." She burped loudly, then scrabbled amongst Lonnie's pills for a black one.

"Hey, be careful with those!" Lonnie yelped. "They'll agitate you!"

Lori swallowed the black pill regardless. She burped again and continued: "So if *he* was a *she* and she had two daddies, then if he, sorry, if *she* discovered she liked sucking on a penis till it discharged semen, it would be natural, right? Girls and gay men do that, right?"

Unable to think of any logical response to Lori's outburst, Britt said, "Some girls dislike fellatio."

Lori giggled. "I don't, and you don't either. And you know that's a lie: all women—even some lesbians—like sucking dick. It's a great feeling of power having that manhood in your mouth, and knowing that if you suddenly bite down hard, the man won't ever forget you for the rest of his life. And also . . ." Then she seemed to completely forget what she'd been saying and pointed to the TV. "I've been through the news; there's nothing on about us. How's that for social irrelevance?"

Britt nodded and took a seat, Lonnie had gone to the kitchen to get them a bottle of wine and more sandwiches. He reappeared now and set the tray down, then sat beside her and poured them each a full glass.

"Look," he said afterwards, draping an arm over Britt's shoulders, "I still don't understand why you're refusing to let me travel with you guys."

"What's he talking about?" Lori slurred across at them.

"He asked if he could come along with us and I said no."

"Yeah, but why?"

Britt shrugged, and looked for an answer other than the real one: she didn't want to see him sprawled in a ditch somewhere, all riddled with cop bullets. She liked him too much for that. "I don't think you've got the right frame of mind for what we plan on doing."

Lori nodded forcefully. "Yeah. We plan on raising hell. This is just a brief interlude, for Britt to sow her wild oats, or rather, for you to sow yours in her."

"I won't get in your way," Lonnie pleaded. "And I can use a gun too."

"No," Britt said, "and that's final. We're going on alone. Forget you met us—"

"Particularly when the police trace us to here."

"But . . ."

Britt kissed him. "Look, Lonnie, you've got your own thing. You're the world champion at Russian roulette, for God's sake. Why give that up for a road trip to nowhere?"

He frowned. "But . . ."

Britt frowned back. "No 'buts' except this one." She smacked her ass at him.

Lori's eyes widened. "Hey!—I've got a great idea. Let's all play Russian roulette! I'll go first."

Britt's eyes widened too. "Hell no!"

But Lori had already picked up the Colt from the table and placed its muzzle against her forehead.

Britt felt her heart in her mouth as Lori pulled the trigger.

'Click.' The hammer had hit on an empty chamber.

Her heart fell back into her chest; but her stoned bestie wasn't done yet. Giggling, Lori pulled the gun's trigger two more times, on each instance of which Britt felt like the Earth was slowing down so much that she could have gotten off the planet and walked off into outer space had she chosen to. Beside her, she felt Lonnie tense up too.

But nothing happened. Lori's brains remained firmly in her head. After the third hammer fall had faded into the sound of the TV, Lori lowered the gun and looked expectantly at her companions. "Okay, who's next?"

Britt looked worriedly at Lori, then back at Lonnie. "Are you *sure* it's loaded?" It was hard for her to imagine that Lori (now staring at her with her pupils all dilated) was still alive.

"Sure, it's loaded," Lonnie said. He reached across and took the revolver from Lori. He broke the gun open, so Britt could see the single bullet in the cylinder.

Lonnie put the cylinder back into the gun, then he grinned at Lori. "You're incredibly cool to take your chances like that," he said.

"What d'you mean?"

"It's a six-shooter. I played last night, but I didn't spin the cylinder again afterward. So your odds were actually shorter than normal—4 to 1 rather than the normal 5 to 1."

"Huh?" Lori said, her eyes too bright.

"You've got to spin the cylinder afresh each time. That way you reset the odds. Otherwise you already know the previous cylinder's empty, right? Which lowers the odds so you're in essence cheating yourself."

"Wow," Lori said, "That is so damn profound. Britney Wilson, I heartily congratulate you—your boyfriend's a Russian roulette genius."

Britt nodded. Suddenly—maybe it was all the sex—she felt as hungry as a starved fox. She grabbed a chicken sandwich off the coffee table and bit into it.

"I'll show you the proper way to do it," Lonnie said. (Britt stared sharply at him, but he shrugged it off.) "First, you spin the cylinder to reset"—he gave it a hearty spin—"then you place the muzzle to your head like so . . ." He put the Colt's muzzle to his temple. "Then you pull the trigger, like so . . ."

He pulled the trigger.

Britt and Lori were both surprised at the loudness of the bang that suddenly filled the small living room. They gaped in surprise at Lonnie. His eyes stared wide and his mouth hung open. He had a little hole in his right temple and a big one over his left ear. The wall behind his head was covered with blood and bits of skull. A wedge-shaped jet of blood squirted from the large hole.

Lonnie's gun fingers went slack and the revolver dropped into his lap. Then he collapsed left onto the sofa, falling away from Britt into the pool of blood that was still spilling from his head.

Britt's half-eaten sandwich fell from her fingers to the floor. *NOOOO!!!* Lonnie was the Russian Roulette world champ, right? Britt couldn't believe she'd been so dumb as to let him play tonight. But was it actually her fault? She'd blithely taken it for granted that if Lori—stoned-to-fuck Lori who even now was regarding Lonnie's corpse with an undertaker's dispassionate gaze—if Lori could survive three attempted shots to the head, then Lonnie, the unexcelled maven of this game of death, would definitely survive just one?

Shit!

"He's stone cold fucking dead," Lori said simply.

Britt nodded. "And it's your stoned fucking fault."

"Yah, maybe." She picked up two more black pills and washed them down with Lonnie's untouched glass of wine.

"Stop taking those! Lonnie said they'll agitate you!"

"We've got a problem."

Britt regarded Lonnie's corpse, his eyes staring like he was looking at something under the coffee table. A line of blood was still dribbling down his forehead from the bullet's entrance hole. She nodded at Lori. "Yeah, I fucking agree we do have a problem. What if his parents heard the gunshot? They'll have the cops down here in no time. And—shit!—the cops are just next door at that collapsed house."

Lori nodded. "That's our problem, girl. We can't take that chance. We need to kill Lonnie's parents."

**

Britt stared at Lori like she was crazy. Yes, *she was* crazy, but even for her this was a new level of crazy. "Kill Rick and Tony? Are you out of your frigging mind?"

"Yes, I am . . . we both are . . . but that's not the point."

"*What is* the point?"

Lori pointed to Lonnie's corpse. "They'll think *we* blew him away."

"No, they won't." Her voice was pleading. "Look, we'll just leave before they find out."

"We can't just leave. It's 10:30 now. So, picture this: Rick and Tony hear us start up our car. So they look out of their window and see us driving away, but they don't see their darling son walking back into the house. So they come downstairs to check on him? Are you getting the picture?"

"We could all just be going off somewhere; to a party maybe." Britt felt she was fighting a losing battle. *And why the hell is Lori making so much sense when she's stoned?*

"Stop arguing with me. We're the devil's handmaidens. I say we kill them."

"Lori, they're genuinely nice people!"

"They were nice when I was sober. Now I'm drunk—let's kill those two cocksuckers." Like she was making a point by doing so, she reached down to scoop up another handful of pills.

"Lori, I just fucked their son!"

"Yeah, that's true; and see what good it did him—his Russian roulette luck ran out on screwing you. Britney, I already told you— you're just like me, a denizen of the dark space without any positive emanations, but you disagreed." She burped loudly. "Besides, I didn't get laid tonight and I'm sexually strung out and I need to take out my vagina's frustrations on someone."

"This is a bad idea."

Lori rounded on her, her eyes wide and staring like something was ringing a doomsday bell inside her head. "Fuck bad ideas. We already agreed on this, and now you're chickening out on me."

"They're gay; it'll give us a bad rep."

Lori sneered. "So what? Fuck gay people, fuck straight people, fuck the lesbians too. Everyone's a frigging label or color or creed nowadays. Fuck the Blacks, fuck the Whites, fuck the Chinese and Japanese and Indians, fuck the Jews, the Germans as well, and the damn Native Americans, the Italians, the Mexicans, in fact particularly screw *all* the Latinos—"

"Your mom's Puerto Rican."

"So? Fuck us too. And my dad's parents were both Polish, so what? Fuck them as well. Fuck every fucking body on the planet. I say we kill them all—the majorities, the minorities, the oppressed, the depressed, EVERYONE!!!"

Britt rolled her eyes. Yeah, the government had a good point saying that drugs were bad for you. (They were clearly VERY bad for Lori Kaminski who, to Britt's knowledge, had never done anything harder than pot before.) "Okay, yes, fuck everyone like we agreed, but first, fucking lower your fucking voice."

"If I do, we go kill those fags together?"

"No," Britt said. "I'm not doing it." *Wow—did she just say 'fags'? Fags? Lori, who's marched in numerous pro-gay-rights demonstrations, with her 'Support Gay Marriage!' placards held high? Fags? Where the hell did that come from? Are those things she's swallowing Anti-Gay pills?*

Lori walked round the table and picked up Lonnie's revolver from his lap. "Well I am. You can wait for me."

"The gun's empty."

"Not for long. The bullets are on top of the fridge. Makes you wonder how his dads never noticed."

"He said they hardly come out here."

Britt watched Lori enter the kitchen, then a minute later exit with the box of ammo. She snapped the gun open, forced out the single shell casing, then loaded it up.

Britt watched her entranced. Lori really intended to do this. She really was going to kill two people she'd just met; nice decent folk

who'd never hurt her in any way whatsoever; people she actually liked
. . . okay, whom she'd liked before doing all these damn pills. *It's weird:
Lori seems to have converted her need to kill herself into a desire to kill Lonnie's
parents.*

She made no further attempts to stop her. Watching her, Britt was
reminded of how goddess-like she'd felt while shooting those nails
into Chris's head, and also while sawing off Joanna's feet.

Suddenly she wanted to experience that thrill, that rush of power,
again. Too bad it had to be Rick and Tony who would provide her
with her superlative feeling. She'd hate herself for killing them, but
she'd hate herself even more if she didn't.

Lori was already leaving the living room, opening the cabin's front
door.

"Hey, wait!" Britt called after her.

"What?" Lori had a pissed off look to her. Britt wondered if Lori
would shoot her too if she angered her enough.

"Okay, I'll go with you. But we don't use the gun—we use knives.
They make far less noise."

Lori thought about it. "O.K.," she agreed finally, an evil gleam
flickering in her eyes. "We do it with knives." She stuffed the revolver
into her waistband, then followed Britt into the kitchen, where they
armed themselves with two long, gleaming, and sharp knives.

Outside, the half-moon was half obscured by clouds, as though it
was scared to see what they had in mind.

The back door to the main house was still unlocked. They let
themselves in.

"Ssh," Britt cautioned Lori as the door swung to. "They might be
in the living room watching Jerry Springer."

"They're more likely to be upstairs fucking," Lori retorted.
"Licking each other's brown eyes."

They made their way in along the corridor, then finding the living
room empty, made their way up the stairs.

"This one," Lori said when they were upstairs, pointing to a door
on their left. Her face was all flushed, like her head would soon pop
open from internal pressure. "Yeah, this one. I can hear heavy
breathing behind it."

Britt nodded, though she wasn't hearing anything. She had one
admonition before they opened the door though. "Okay," she
whispered, "we need to plan this. Which of them do you want to kill?"

"Both of the . . ." Then Lori understood the question. "Er . . . Rick, that big handsome—"

"Okay, I'll take the short fat one." Now, Britt felt all jacked up again, ready for the kill. It was an unbelievable rush of emotional power, one that seeped from her soul into her muscles, making her fingers tingle. "Okay, on 'three' we kick the door in."

"No need to kick it, just un-click it. It'll be open."

Britt didn't question how she knew that either. Personally, Britt was in a strange place now, filled with an expectation that threatened to crush her mind if she didn't satisfy it soon. "One more thing—no screaming. We don't want to alert the neighbors. And your gun's only to be used as a last resort."

Lori yawned. "You're taking longer with this than Obama reading the State of the Union address to Congress. When did murder become so complicated? Fuck, can we just do this? We need to get it over with, okay? O-frigging-K?"

"Okay, here we go! One . . . two . . ."

Lori was right, the door wasn't locked. They burst into the room.

***

Rick and Tony were lying on their backs holding hands and giggling when the two girls charged into their bedroom. Exhausted from three rounds of sweaty copulation, and completely confused on seeing Britt and Lori, neither man offered any resistance to the attack. (The gunshot announcing their son's departure had occurred right at that delicious and delicate instant when Tony was ejaculating into his husband's mouth, moaning loudly and with his hands pressed tight over Rick's ears to keep his head firmly in place in the deep-throat position so the semen went directly into this stomach. As such, neither man heard the shot.)

Neither man stood the chance of a snowflake in hell of surviving the attack.

Once her eyes worked out which of the two men was Tony, Britt pounced on him like a cat on a mouse. Her entire focus was on *him*— she forgot there was anyone else in the room. Her first stab caught Tony in the throat. Then, while he was gurgling blood and plugging the wound with his fingers and gaping at her with startled and terrified eyes, she moved down to regard his pale and plump torso. He was unnaturally hairless, looked like he'd been waxed.

She stabbed him deep in the belly, right under his heart, then ripped the knife diagonally across his body down to his right hip. Her knife was deathly sharp; there was scant muscular resistance. Tony's belly skin parted like pork in a butcher shop, blood flowing like it was desperate to escape him. Tony let out a loud wet gurgle and blood splashed her bowed head. She looked up at him, his eyes were still confused. She slashed him deep again, this time tearing his belly open from upper right to lower left. Her hands were now stained a bright red.

Beside her, she was aware of soft sick noises: the wet sounds of meat meeting metal, Rick's grunts of horror—which sounded almost like he was coming—and Lori's giggles of delight.

She didn't look their way: Lori was clearly handling her own business: "Fuck gay assholes, and fuck straight assholes, yeah . . . and fuck all the ones porn hasn't yet fucked already. Yeah, fuck everybody! Fuck every fucking body! Fuck every living and dead fucking body!"

Excitement flowing through her like blood, Britt regarded her own handiwork. Tony's belly now had an 'X' sliced across it, only it was bloody red, not green like the X-Box one.

She roughly peeled back the flaps of stomach, revealing his bloody massed intestines. (She'd cut him so deeply, she'd severed his guts in several places.) Then she dug her hands deep into his guts, and, lifting her head to look him flush in the eyes, she began pulling them out of him.

Tony was fading fast now. He'd plugged the bleeding in his throat with his thumb, but there was blood all over his mouth and spilling from his belly and . . . his eyes were pleading with her.

"Rick, darling!" he gasped, looking right. Then his voice erupted in a shrill moan: "Oh no, Rick!!" Then he began crying.

Britt let him cry. Fuck him. He was her plaything and he was dying for her pleasure. She was still yanking out his intestines, but her fingers had now struck something hard inside him.

She looked down. Her bloody hands were touching a large smooth purplish expanse. *Oh, it's his liver! How do I get that out?*

After a moment's thought, she hooked her hands around the liver's edges, gripped it tightly, and tugged. Its arterial and venous connections meant it didn't leave Tony's belly easy, but, without letting go of it, she squatted, then leapt up on the bed so she was standing over him. That worked: the liver followed her up, Tony remained below, stone dead now. He might have been dead even before she'd plucked out his liver, but she wasn't sure.

Britt looked herself over. She was totally stained red. But—what was important here—she felt damn great, like Tony's happiness had transferred itself into her body on his death.

She finally paid attention to Lori. *Holy Mother of . . . Christ!*

Lori had cut Rick's head completely off. And . . . Britt was speechless—*What the . . .?*— she had her pants down and was defecating in the severed head's open mouth. Lori had the head wedged between Rick's thighs and was squatted bare-butt over it grunting while a thick unbroken rod of black poop dropped between the spread dead lips.

She noticed Britt watching her in shock, and waved. "I really needed to go, maybe that's why I was so worked up earlier downstairs. You know what I mean, don't you? I feel really constipated all of a fucking sudden, like a month's worth of poop has backed itself up all the way into my skull. I just need to get all this crap out of me—damn, it feels like there's so much of it still left inside. I feel all blocked up back to my frigging neck!"

Then she squeezed her eyes tightly shut and began grunting to force the still-unbroken tube of excrement completely out of her anus. Once done, she left the head there, shit all over its face. Some of her shit was coming out of the severed end of Rick's throat.

They both got down off the bed. Lori was as blood-soaked as Britt. She picked up Rick's silk robe off the floor and wiped her ass with it.

"How do you feel?" Britt asked Lori while she pulled her pants up.

"Oh, completely evacuated." Lori's pupils were huge now; her words were coming out in fast bursts. "I really needed to take that shit, you understand me, Britt? It was coating all over my insides like rotten ice cream with maggots crawling in it . . . I needed to be rid of that frigging poop. And now that it's out of me, I feel . . ." She gazed admiringly at Britt's murder work. Tony's entrails lay strewn over the bed and draped down over its edge to form a bloody mess on the floor. "Now *this* is the right way to end someone's life. You deserve a medal for such excellence in killing. Yeah, and my damn poop's gone too." She nodded at Britt, "You okay too, Britt?"

"Oh, holy fuck, do I feel great right now! I feel like two million bucks. I feel like . . ."

"Hey, what's the matter? Why's your face suddenly all gone like I dirtied up your mouth not Rick's? Tell me, tell me, tell me! I'm getting agitated now! What's the frigging matter!"

"Lori, look!" Britt pointed out through the window drapes and across the road, to where Lori too could clearly make out a single nude female figure outlined in the opposite bedroom window, with something pressed up against her face.

"Oh, that's your aunt," Lori said, her words coming out fast as bullets. "She's fucking seen us. Shit, what are we gonna do now? Do we have to run over there and kill her too?"

"Lori, forget it—we're not killing my aunt. I need her to attend my funeral. She looks breathtaking in black."

Across the way, Aunt Clarissa vanished from sight.

Lori glared fiercely at Britt like she'd insist on butchering Clarissa Noble, then she nodded equally fiercely. "We'd better leave in a hurry then. I mean, like get away from here before the pigs arrive. We're not gonna kill your aunt? Okay, that's O.K., but we gotta go then. She's likely dialing 911 right now. And . . ." with both hands she gestured down her bloodstained body, "we need to change our clothes, we both look like shit." Then she pointed to the corpse with her excrement in its mouth and began laughing. "Ha ha ha!!!!"

After cursing whoever had made the illegal chemicals Lori was tripping on, Britt said, "Alright, raid the wardrobes for shirts and let's go."

Britt's mind was in countdown mode. *So we've got like how long now before the law shows up?*

Her worries about being apprehended, though, made no difference to her emotional high. At the moment, she felt too alive for anyone to kill successfully. Even if came down to a shootout with the police tonight, she knew they'd both make it out alive.

CHAPTER 14

Clarissa

Clarissa had been about dropping off into blissful afterglow sleep when she'd heard the sharp groan "Oh no, Rick!!" from across the street.

True, her gay neighbors had gotten extra-loud before, but this, this sharp howl sounded like Rick had just ripped Tony's anus to shreds.

So she'd leaped out of bed, grabbed up her binoculars, and again trained them on the opposite bedroom, and then . . .

Hey . . . that's Britney! What's she doing here . . . over there!? Britt was standing with a bloody knife in her hand. She was so covered in blood, she could easily be mistaken for Elizabeth Bathory.

And her niece wasn't alone.

Another girl—a beautiful brunette, equally crimson-splattered— was wiping her ass with a bathrobe. The pale robe came away smeared black like she was on a course of blood tonic pills.

Clarissa swung the binoculars right. What she could see of the bed made her shudder—Rick and Tony's bodies. Rick's head wasn't on his neck anymore, but wedged down between his legs. And what was that mess on his face? Tony, all split open, looked like a pig carcass that a butcher had taken a hatred to. She looked back at Britt and the other girl. Both were laughing.

Clarissa was utterly horrified. *I have to call the police! Yes, she's my favorite niece, but no, this is really, really bad. How could she? . . . Oh, why did she kill them!? And I've been calling and calling her phone without response all evening and all the while she's been just next door? Yes, I'm calling the police!*

Then a gust of wind blew the window drapes off her bare body and she gasped in fright. She knew they'd seen her, with her binoculars pressed up against her face like a pervert.

Britt was pointing her way, then the other girl looked too, and then both young women began arguing.

Clarissa tried lip reading. She made out Britt saying, ". . . Killing my aunt."

Her horrified mind, however, put the wrong interpretation on her bloody niece's words, words that had just saved her life.

Oh, the ungrateful little bitch is coming to murder me too!

Her emotions overloaded. The world spun before her eyes. The binoculars dropped from her hands and she collapsed in a dead faint.

She was still out cold ten minutes later when both young women exited the Young house, both with their hair wet from a hasty showering and both wearing male shirts several sizes too large for them.

SUNDAY

CHAPTER 15

Pagan

She woke up shuddering, as abruptly as a clown shot from a sleep cannon, or semen shot from a virgin boy's testicles. She lay there, her chest rising and falling for a full minute, trying to figure out why she felt so wrong this morning.

When she sat up, she understood.

She was in her motel bed, but she was covered in blood. (Finally deciding to take her chances in a small out-of-the-way town, Pagan had changed her mind about hiding out in Attleboro. Instead, she'd turned off the I-95 onto the I-495 and stopped in Raynham last night; and was currently staying at the Sunflower Motel.)

She looked around her, horror filling her as she did.

Oh no, not again!

Next to her on the bed lay a headless body with blood splashed everywhere around its shoulders like a blooming rose. The corpse was male. The dead man's guts and viscera lay outside of him, piled aside like he was being readied for cooking. Most of his liver was missing.

Pagan leapt out of bed and ran into the bathroom to throw up. The puke poured and poured out of her. She was startled and scared at the amount of it. When she studied the mess in the toilet bowl afterwards, she was stunned: the toilet was half-full of brownish chunks that she figured had to be the dead man's liver. There was also a lot of skin and some hair mixed in with it.

After spitting out more meat onto the pile, she staggered back to the bathroom door and grimaced out at the dead man.

I ate him? Who is he? How could I forget?

Like it had done at the Larsen's house up in Townsend, her memory returned in short brilliant flashes like she was browsing a phone's picture gallery with half the JPEGs missing.

His name was Kyle Bennett. He had the room next door to hers. He'd been standing outside on the front walk when she'd pulled up, a stocky middle-aged man, but handsome. Not the kind of guy she'd normally take a shine to, but for some reason, the moment she'd set her eyes on him, she'd felt a rush of heat between her legs.

He'd said "Hi" and they'd gotten to talking. And talking had led to them sharing his six-pack of Coors Light in her room.

There was a blank space here that could have been three minutes or three hours.

Her next slice of memory showed them having sex.

They'd given each other head (she had a vibrant flash of his penis throbbing on her tongue, while electric thrills filled her vagina like soapy bathwater) and then she'd gotten on top of him and ridden him hard, digging her fingers into the thick carpet of his chest hair like it was a horse's reins. His penis in her sex felt like it was piercing deep, deep into her guts; and then she'd been coming hard, coming hard and loving it, because the sex was helping her forget her troubles. Her sexual juices creamed her thighs and soaked his crotch and yet she still wasn't done. Leaning back, she was howling like a wolf; he was reaching up and grabbing her breasts and squeezing them hard, thrusting his delicious male hardness into her wet depths while grinning and moaning, "Oh fuck, I'm gonna—!"

Another blank, and then he was staring up at her in horror and a pair of monsters' hands—*no, they're MY hands!* (she could feel herself controlling them)—were wrapping themselves around his neck.

Horrified, Pagan backed away from the door with its framing of the headless man, as if doing so would enable her escape the memory of how he'd gotten that way. No such luck—the memory remained and no blank spaces existed in it now when she earnestly desired them.

In flashback, she watched herself rip Kyle's head off his shoulders, then shred it and hurl the bloody pieces around the room. (His brains splattering the bed looked like chunks of peeled shrimp.) Worst of all, though definitely hers, the hands doing this evil work weren't human, they were big and scaly and dark green; calloused, and with huge horny black nails. The arms controlling them were also green and muscular and decorated with fat veins that looked like creepers on trees.

Her whole body was scaly . . . and covered with the red effusion of Kyle's passing.

Kyle's truncated neck spurted out blood, which she leaned forward into and lapped up like a thirsty dog. Oh, the crimson liquid tasted so good and refreshing . . .

But still, she needed more. She was *hungry*, and also, in this her altered state, there was a satisfaction in tearing flesh, in ripping a body to pieces; a primal, elemental blasphemy achieved in so carelessly destroying what The Creator had lovingly knit together over the course of three trimesters in a mother's womb.

She'd reared up again and stared at the dead man's belly, a flesh-mine taut and ready for her claws to excavate . . .

Thankfully, Pagan's recollection ended then. Her body once again as red as if she'd been dipped in paint, she stood in the bathroom, arms wrapped around her breasts, shivering.

I-I-I . . . I-I-I'm . . .

Then, staring at her reflection in the mirror, she froze.

Oh, shit! What is this?

Her eyes were darker, like someone had injected chestnut-tinted ink into their irises. From a pale blue, her eyes were now hazel-colored.

She blinked. It wasn't a deceit of the light. She did indeed have light brown eyes now.

And it wasn't just her eyes. Beneath her bloodstained skin, she could feel that her body was somehow different, unsettled, in a state of flux.

Oh, shit! I'm altering, transforming! Shit! I'm becoming—

Becoming what? She covered the toilet bowl (there was no way it was going to flush with all the meat in it) then sat on it to think. Out in the bedroom, with Kyle's remains everywhere, would be too distracting.

What am I becoming? Oh . . . Avex! Yes, Avex will know!

She said aloud, "What are you doing to me, you infernal son-of-a-bitch?"

She fell silent, and tried to listen inside herself.

All she heard from the world of darkness beyond her heart was silence. But Pagan had the clear impression that the demon Avex was extremely pleased with what was happening to her body. With its evil work in her flesh.

And somehow, horrifyingly, she knew the demon wasn't done with her yet.

Not by a long shot.

***

After a while of worrying, Pagan got off the toilet and walked back out into the bedroom. First point of call was her stolen cellphone. She opened up the browser and checked her email.

There was no reply yet from the Red Octopus Corporation.

Didn't they get it? She considered going back to the ROC webpage and resending her message, but then she remembered that the page had yesterday given her a 'success' confirmation.

So all I can do now is wait. I just hope they understand how desperate my situation is. She looked around her blood-spattered motel room, from Kyle's headless corpse to the myriad bits of him scattered everywhere, and winced. *Yeah, it's desperate alright. I'd better get some cleaning done.*

She grabbed Kyle by his feet and pulled him off the bed, then dragged the corpse into the bathroom. She deposited the body in the bathtub, then returned to strip the bloody sheets off the bed.

Those, along with as much of the dead man as she could scrape off the carpet, also went into the bath. (One pillow was totally crimsoned, it too went into the bath.)

Next, she filled the washbasin with water, made suds in it with the bath soap, and used a ripped-off corner of the sheets to mop up. She was certain that if she racked her mind enough, she'd remember a spell to magically clean up, but she needed the work—it was something to do. *And, besides, so long as I have this demon inside me, I need to be very careful with casting magic spells. I've no way of knowing what sets the damn thing off.*

She painstakingly wiped down the walls and furniture. The blood on the carpet wasn't going to come out; the light brown flooring was now maroon in patches.

Finally, using all her remaining strength, Pagan flipped the mattress over so the blood was out of sight. There, that looked better.

It was now noon. She was bushed; the cleaning had taken her two whole hours. She drained the washbasin of water for the nth time, and to its liquid gurgle stood in the doorway, regarding her work.

The effort had definitely been worth it: close the bathroom door, and except for a faint seeping odor of decay like a rat had died under the bed, there was no way of telling she had a corpse in the bathtub.

After a hot shower to get the blood off of herself (she had to stand in the bathtub with the corpse; there was no other way), she stretched out in bed and stared at the ceiling while wrestling with her thoughts. *Maybe I should watch TV, see if there's an APB out on me? Maybe I should go for a walk? Maybe I should . . . .*

She lay there for ages unable to make up her mind. *Hey, Red Octopus, frigging get back to me already!*

CHAPTER 16

Lori, mostly

Lori woke to a bright blue sky. She was outside. The sun was directly overhead. She felt like total shit. Oh, hell! This drug comedown from last night felt like someone was kicking her in the head. Damn, this was way worse than any hangover.

After working out that she was lying on her back on the hood of her gray Mazda, deep in the middle of a lush green cornfield (the car was surrounded by five-foot-high corn plants), she rolled over a little and puked down by the front passenger side wheel.

It wasn't a lot of vomit, but the act cleared her head a bit. Her brain still felt like it was being squeezed though, so she rolled back over on her back and resumed staring at the sky. She'd never come down off a drug binge before and navigating the treacherous descent from this one wasn't an experience she ever wanted to repeat. *How the hell can I feel so bad now after feeling so good last night?* It felt like there were needles stuck into her, not just into her body, but into her soul also, and through them, her essence was being drained off elsewhere.

Then, remembering she wasn't supposed to be alone, she looked around for Britt. Doing that meant she had to twist herself up like a contortionist.

Britt was snoring, open-mouthed in the driver's seat. Her blonde hair was all over her face, some of the short ends on her tongue. She looked like Courtney Love from *Hole* on a bad day, without the smeared lipstick.

Lori uncontorted herself and let her head fall back down on the hood. Eyes closed against the midday sun, she tapped fingers on the warm metal and put last night in perspective.

No doubt about it, the police are after us now. Do I frigging care? Not a flyspeck. Let the womanhunt begin! There's no going back now.

She recalled last night's kills with a deep thrill. Unlike Britt—who the hell knew what Britt had felt, likely she'd been on some hardcore ego-trip then, imagining that she was Queen of the World, or even Mistress of the Universe—Lori had just felt a deep satisfaction on stabbing Rick to death, and then . . . *Oh, did I actually do that? Ugh, gross!* . . . pooping in his dead mouth.

Drugs are great for helping one shed one's inhibitions, she concluded. *Too bad I was too stoned to grab the rest of Lonnie's stash before we ran. But then, Britt's aunt had seen us.*

Despite which they'd escaped. She recalled their flight in vivid hallucinogenic color. Actually it had been a disappointing anticlimax. The cops at the demolished Harris house up the road had just looked into the car, seen two harmless pretty girls, and waved them past. That was the great escape? *I mean no one even heard the gunshot?*

Britt, however, had been jacked up on herself, spouting some rant about being the Spinster Goddess of Dover. *And I thought I was the stoned one.*

Anyhow, they'd driven and driven till they were out of town. At some point, Lori was sure they'd turned onto the I-95, but she wasn't sure. Not her fault—Britt had insisted on driving. "Don't even suggest it," she'd retorted when Lori had suggested that she take the wheel. "You'll just kill us both. You can't even *walk* straight at the moment; you're staggering like you just survived a gangbang."

And then, somewhere along some road, south of Dover and out in the middle of nowhere in the middle of the night, Britt had suddenly yawned at the wheel. "I'm tired. I'll just pull over here into the fields and we'll doze till morning."

"I've told you to let me drive," Lori had protested. "I know how to drive, don't I? It's my car after all. I—"

"And I've told you, no, I'm not letting you kill us both. We turn off here and go to sleep." And then, driving over the speed limit herself at 11:17 p.m., Britt had suddenly twisted the steering wheel hard left and sent them rumbling away across the cornfield. A short bumpy ride with several abrupt drunken turns, which, now that Lori considered it, was certain to have put paid to her car's transmission.

Her head stopped expanding and contracting at random; the drained feeling receded from her flesh. She got down off the hood of the car and looked around.

She made out the expressway/Interstate about two hundred yards off by the bright metal flashes of passing cars, which flickered through the corn plants like sunlight reflecting off shards of broken mirror. Behind her own Mazda, a long deep double furrow paved with crushed corn—flattened stalks, stripped husks, and crushed yellow cobs—marked the path the vehicle had cut through the cornfield. Here, all four wheels looked stalled in mud.

So it was likely her car wouldn't be leaving here any time soon. But still, on a positive note, for the most part the walls of green stalks hid them from view. *Well, at least we're out of sight for the moment.*

Kicking over two nearby cornstalks that had survived the field's re-plowing, and taking care not to sink in the wet earth, she walked back around to the driver's side window to wake Britt.

Then she grimaced.

Britt was already awake, but she also had her fingers stuck down the front of her jeans and was masturbating. Her eyes were shut tight. Oblivious to Lori's presence, she was making loud noises and licking her lips as she fingered herself. Her left hand was inside her shirt, squeezing her right breast.

Lori poked her in the head. "Hey, what are you doing?"

Britt's eyes popped open. "Isn't it obvious? Let me finish, please? I'll just be a minute."

Lori shook her head. "No. Here's Kaminski's law—you don't *ever* masturbate in front of me. Stop wanking right now, and get out of my damn car." Then, when her best friend still kept rubbing her crotch, Lori grabbed the offending hand and yanked it out of Britt's pants.

"Hey, frigging stop that!" Britt howled. She angrily zipped up her pants and got out of the car. "What was that about? What the hell is wrong with you?"

"I've a headache. Hearing you wank was aggravating it."

Britt digested that, her breathing hard. She at first looked like she'd attack Lori, but all she finally said was, "Alright, I'm sorry; you really didn't need to see that. But, Lori, for some reason I just feel all horny this morning. I even dreamt that Justin Bieber was giving me head."

"Maybe it's the leftover from last night's virgin?"

Britt grimaced and wiped her hand dry on her too-large shirt (which had to have been Rick's.) Then a dreamy smile spread like pink oil over her face. "Oh yeah, last night was so frigging awesome."

(Lori *had* remembered to pack her Prozac pills. She considered taking them, then changed her mind. She felt too good for the tablets. She also had the weird idea that if she took her meds now, this magic feeling of wellbeing she was currently experiencing would evaporate and she'd be back down in the Pit again, down in that horrible black space where all was gloom and doom and there was no way out. And this would be one of those really horrible times when, no longer content with just ignoring her, the faceless mob above her deep hole would gang together and torment her with her helplessness.

She honestly didn't feel suicidal anymore. So, for whatever it was worth, this road trip was already paying dividends.)

"So, okay," Britt prompted, when it looked like Lori wasn't about saying anything, "why'd you pull me out of the car?"

"Yeah," Lori replied slowly, running hands through her brown hair. "Last night was just incredible. "I still can't get over the feeling of cutting Rick's head off and . . ."

She controlled herself. One mustn't dwell too deeply on the past; not when there were more people to kill awaiting her in her future.

She pointed up at the sun, then out towards the road, where over the tops of the corn plants a blue 18-wheeler was rolling past like a rectangular ship riding distant green waves. "It's noon. We should get a move on. But, Britt, where exactly are we now? I was too wired last night to keep proper track of the turns we made."

"State Route 138, just past South Easton."

"Where are we headed?"

"Anywhere we like. Everywhere is exactly the same now. The world is our roulette wheel. I say we spin it, just be random; wind up wherever the ball falls."

The answer satisfied Lori. *In this case, one place is as good as another, so long as it's away from the police. I want to live a little longer before dying.*

"We'd better hitchhike from here on," she suggested. "Just leave the car here."

Britt thought a bit then nodded. "Okay, lets get our stuff out of the trunk."

Lori yawned and stretched.

Britt opened the Mazda's trunk then gagged. "Shit! I forgot they were in here."

The thick stench of decaying meat quickly jogged Lori's memory. "Oh, you mean your mom's feet?" She walked over for a look. "What are we going to do with them anyway? Leave them in here?"

Britt considered. "Nah, we'll throw them away." Then she began laughing. "Oh, no . . . I've got a much better idea."

Lori wondered what she meant. Britt wouldn't explain. Instead, she took both white, well manicured feet out of their carton (now in death, Joanna's feet seemed like twin marble sculptures), then got out the roll of duct tape.

"Help me open the driver's door," she instructed Lori.

Lori did so, then watched in amusement as Britt duct-taped her mother's right severed foot to the car's gas pedal and her left one to its brake pedal. She did so with a single band over the arch of each foot, so it looked like they were in gray slip-on sandals. The beautiful maroon toenails reflected the sunlight.

Britt straightened up laughing. "You know how dumb cops are in movies? Maybe they'll think her feet drove the car here themselves."

Lori found that hilarious. Together they got their bags out of the trunk.

Lori made a point of leaving all her ATDs behind.

***

Twenty minutes later, changed into their own clothes again, the two of them stood by the roadside thumbing a lift south.

They'd made one bad discovery: "Lori, I left the wallet with our money in it in Lonnie's house."

Lori shrugged. "Don't sweat it; I've still got that $300 on me. We'll just need to rob someone sooner than later." To her, losing their money like that wasn't even an inconvenience; it just made them pro-active. Now they wouldn't be able to laze in comfort. And they had *two* guns now: both her dad's Ruger and Lonnie's Colt Python revolver (for which Britt had thankfully remembered to bring along the box of ammo).

A dark green Ford stopped for them. They ran to it.

The driver was a young man in his mid-twenties, dark and good-looking, and wearing a suit the same color as the car.

Best of all, to Lori's mind, he seemed quite clean-cut, not the psycho kind who stashed female travelers in his trunk and took them home to rape for months in his basement. (Her observation gave her major cause for thought: *How in the world, when we're both armed and dangerous, am I still thinking of myself as prey instead of predator?*)

"Hi, ladies, where you headed?" He had clear gray eyes. Lori instantly liked him.

"Just south," Britt replied. "Anywhere's good, so long as it gets us out of the state."

He grinned even white teeth. "Well, hop in then, I'm headed for Westville."

They hopped in. Britt sat in front, Lori in back.

"I'm Billy," he said as the car sped down towards the West Bridgewater State Forest. "But my friends call me Billy Two Shoes, 'cos I'm a shoe salesman. In fact, I'm on my way right now to a shoe sales convention in Westville."

"I'm Lori, and she's Britt."

"Delighted to meet you both." Billy grinned over at Britt. "So," he laughed, "what's your story? How'd two good-looking girls come to be stranded by the roadside on a Sunday afternoon? You both seem rather old to be running away from home. What'd you do, rob some bank?"

Lori laughed from the backseat. "Nah, we're sociopaths fresh out of college."

"Serial killers?" Billy laughed loudly, then honked angrily at a red pickup truck that had just carelessly overtaken him. On both sides of the car the forest was a dark green wall. "Aw, now, c'mon . . . Serial killers? Ha ha ha! You really expect a guy to believe that?"

"Believe it, Billy," Britt said, sticking the Colt's muzzle in his right ear. "You know what, man? Pull over between these trees right here and find us a nice quiet spot. I've got something I need you to take care of for me."

Gulping, Billy Two Shoes nodded and veered off the road into the bordering woods. At Britt's urging he guided the car between the trees till it was invisible from the road, then parked.

Lori was filled with a mixture of dread and anticipation. *What? Is she nuts? We're going to kill him out here?* They couldn't start arguing in this situation though.

But instead of shooting Billy in the head, Britt looked back at her and winked. "Okay, get out, and keep watch in case anyone's coming."

"What?"

She licked her lips. "I'm about to be a serial *fucker* for a bit. Yes, Lori, I'm about to get laid . . . *again*, and I don't want to be disturbed at it." Then she turned back to Billy. "Okay, man, you get out too, but only into the back seat, and lose your clothes somewhere between here and there."

Billy nervously complied.

Lori got out too, and went and sat cross-legged on the car's hood. The hood was hot, so she wadded up Billy's trousers (which he'd draped over the driver's door) and slid them between her ass and the metal.

A cool breeze blew in from the surrounding trees. Insect and bird noises fluttered around her like butterflies. She didn't understand Britt's sudden burst of arousal. *Last night, and now this afternoon too? I just hope she's not turned into a fucking nympho overnight, and this won't become a three-times-a-day thing. Shit—I should just have let her finish wanking back there!*

She herself wasn't aroused. She was more into the thrill of the chase which wasn't actually happening yet.

And then the car began bobbing up and down and she decided, *What the heck, I might as well watch—it'll pass the time.*

She rotated herself on the hood so she was peering in through the windshield.

In the rear seat, Britt had herself positioned breasts-up on Billy and was slamming her buttocks down on him. With the front passenger seat in the way, Lori couldn't make out either of their faces, but she could see the glistening penis appear and vanish between their bodies, and occasionally a bit of Britt's breasts. Then Britt twisted herself off Billy and repositioned herself so she was facing him. She knelt, then began rising and falling again. Now, her head occasionally appeared between the seats, pink ears and a wash of straight blonde hair sweeping over her shoulders.

Lori was impressed with Britt's sexual energy. *Wow! She's really riding this guy!* She felt the start of a tingling in her own lady parts.

Around the car the trees rustled pleasantly.

***

A broadly grinning Billy Two Shoes dropped them off in Raynham, at the Center Street junction.

"You sure you don't wanna go any further?" he asked hopefully. "My sales convention is actually tomorrow. I can easily drop you both off down in Rhode Island—say in Providence or Warwick if you like—and drive back up to Westville."

"No, we're fine here," Britt said. She leaned in through the car window and kissed him on the cheek. "Thanks, baby, you're a total darling."

"O.K., if you say so, but it really wouldn't be any bother."

"No, we're really okay here, Billy. Lori's got a cousin in town we wanna drop in on."

"O.K. You've got my number, give me a call sometime. Let's get together."

She nodded. "I'll definitely do that."

He drove off.

"There goes one happy, not to mention lucky, guy," Lori said as the green Ford diminished in the distance. "You think he really believes we're serial killers?"

"Not on your life. The way he was looking at me after sex, he was thinking of taking me home to mother."

Lori pointed to the business card Billy had given Britt. "He's cute. You gonna call him?"

Britt studied the card. It was a light brown with the surface artificially roughened to feel like leather. 'Billy Branham: Sales Promotion Executive.'

With a wistful sigh, she ripped the card up. "No I won't. I don't plan on living long enough to be a wife."

"You know, that's twice now that you've gotten laid since we left your house yesterday. If our motto's 'fuck until death,' how come I'm not getting laid too?" (Okay, so she'd not been interested earlier, but now the tingle between her legs was fast becoming a buzz.)

Britt frowned. "You need to be like me—more proactive with guys. Shove that fat ass of yours right in their face and yell 'I want a goddam fuck, goddammit!' Even the mentally challenged will get the message then . . . and a hard-on."

"No way do I want to screw a guy with Down's syndrome."

"That's your trouble; you're too boxed-in, too uptight. A hard penis is a hard penis—it's the fuck that counts. You need to remember that we've now left the so-called 'real world' behind. We're off the grid, so to hell with conformity. Now we do what we want, say what we want, and . . . finish it for me."

"What? Oh, yeah—we screw who we want, when we want." *(And, did I just hear Britney Wilson—tight-ass supreme—call me 'uptight'?)*

"Yes. Even if it's the same damn cop who wants to arrest us, we fuck the hell out of him. We tie that son-of-a-bitch down and ride him like we're Paul Revere off to warn everyone about the British invasion. Do the Old Colony proud."

They studied their surroundings. Billy had dropped them off close to what appeared to be the town center. This being Sunday, most shops were shut and there were few people about. Every now and then someone rumbled by in a truck, but that was about it. It was a little town anyway, a good place to take a breather, which was why Lori had suggested they stop here.

They ambled around awhile, getting a feel of the lay of the land, then stopped an old wino and asked where they could find a good motel. Lori had specifically waited till they found someone who clearly didn't have a TV at home.

"A motel? Ah, you'll be wanting the Sunflower then. Right back the way you came, on Carver Street. About a quarter-mile's walk. "

"Thanks." Lori gave him ten dollars to buy some booze.

The wino grinned. "Well, thanks, ladies. That's mighty nice of you both." He shambled off towards a liquor store.

Lori nodded at Britt and they set off.

A short distance up the road, they saw a woman collecting money at a Cardtronics ATM.

Britt nudged Lori. "Her? Now? She's just recharged her purse and there's no one in sight."

Lori shook her head. "No, tonight. Then we can hide the body if we need to."

The woman, unaware that her violent death had just been averted, finished collecting her money and walked past them, flashing them a smile.

They smiled innocently back and kept going. Further up the road, they stopped at D'Angelo's Grilled Sandwiches at the Carver Street intersection for some food and drink.

***

The Sunflower Motel was just off the road enough, and just secluded enough to make them both feel safe. Three blocks of rooms and a reception building with an all-gravel parking lot.

They walked into the motel lobby. The receptionist was a bearded old man wearing a red plaid shirt and faded overalls.

Wow, what a wonderful cliché this old guy is, Lori thought.

They told the old man that they were sisters traveling up from Kentucky, that their car had broken down just south of town and had had to be towed, and that they were stuck here in Raynham till the auto garage got it fixed. They paid cash for two nights and were given the keys to Room 5.

"Front block," the old man instructed. "An' call me if you need anything else."

***

The room was comfortable and neat, with light green wallpaper, brown carpeting, and a single wide bed. It also had a wall TV, a telephone, and a small fridge. The bathroom had an actual bathtub in it.

To Britt's relief, the air conditioning unit worked.

According to the old receptionist, the motel didn't have a restaurant but there were lots of eateries within strolling distance.

After dropping their bags and flopping down on the bed, Britt said, "So we're safe for the moment. What now?"

Lori was turning on the television. She found it gratifying how Britt kept turning to her for answers. "For the moment we relax and watch TV to see what the latest news on us is."

Britt picked up the motel room phone. It had no dial tone. She frowned at Lori. "It's dead."

"Perfect; exactly what we need."

"I really wish you hadn't made us throw away our phones. Now that we need info I'd just have called Debbie—"

"Who you told me can't keep a secret, and then everyone would know where we are. At the moment, the only person on earth with an inkling of our whereabouts is Billy Two Shoes, and he's away at his shoe convention. By the time we're real news and he realizes we told him the truth about being killers, we'll be far away from here."

Britt nodded, making herself comfortable and twirling her blonde hair round her fingers. "D'ya think? Which way are we finally heading anyway? East, South, North . . . ? Hey, Lori! Stop! Don't change the channel!"

"Wha . . . ? Why?"

"Turn the sound up! That's Pagan on the news!"

Surprised, Lori paid more attention to the female face on the screen. Yes it was Pagan, in black makeup like a vampire queen. Her picture was captioned: 'Boston Witch Sought in Satanist Slayings.'

What the . . . ? She quickly upped the volume. "The Massachusetts Police are looking for this young woman, Susan Courtney Harris aka Pagan, to question in regards to three sets of ritual murders, one in West Roxbury's Hole Faith nightclub, and two others in private residences in Townsend and Dover. The Dover murder involved Ms. Harris's own parents, David and Linda Harris. Police are yet to release any details of the three murders other than to say that altogether seventeen people were killed, and that the killings appear to be linked to the witchcraft coven that Ms. Harris, a known and prominent Boston Satanist, was heading. They also admit that Ms. Harris appears to be directly involved in the massacres. If seen, please call . . ."

Lori muted the TV. She peered hard at Britt. "I don't believe this. Are you sure Al-Qaeda didn't spike our high school water with something? Or even our elementary school milk? Maybe the terrorists plan on taking over the USA that way—you know, turning us all into raving homicidal maniacs?"

"Wow," Britt said. "Seventeen corpses. And I always thought Pagan was just a poser."

"Ah, you were just sore that her aunt was screwing your dada."

"No, I wasn't."

"You know," Lori continued seriously, "there's some positivity in this for us."

"How . . . how d'you mean?"

"Well, with that sort of body count, no one's going to be seriously looking for us for a while. We'll practically be flying under the state radar."

"Don't count on it, girlfriend. Massachusetts has loads of cops, and they all need targets to shoot at. Drug dealers are becoming passé."

Lori plumped herself down on the bed too. She began removing her pants. "I need to take a bath."

"Me first," Britt said, jumping up and running off into the bathroom ahead of her, then shutting and locking the door.

"Hey!" Lori ran after her and began pounding on the bathroom door. "Come out of there, you—I'm first!"

The door opened a crack. A miraculously already naked and mischievously grinning Britt peeked out. "Uh uh, I need it more than you do. Remember all the time I spent sweating in the car with Billy? I need to clean my pussy."

She shut the door in Lori's face.

Lori heard the key click to keep her out. Defeated, she walked back over to the bed. After taking off her bra, she leaned back against the headboard and watched the latest episode of *The Bachelor*.

CHAPTER 17

Joker

Joker was having sex with two dogs when the call came. With the cameras rolling and capturing everything in crystal-clear HD, she was down on her hands and knees on a pentagram-inscribed rug, masturbating an oversized St. Bernard that was busy ejaculating in her mouth. Behind her a Great Dane was preparing to flood her vagina with yet more semen.

As punishment for her failure to stop Pagan's madness—*But what in the world could I have done?*—Joker had been sentenced to two months of making animal porn. (She was currently at a multipurpose Abyss facility in Medfield). She was very aware that she'd gotten off lightly; the Abyss Club had an array of alternative punishments, each more horrifying than the last.

The St. Bernard was just pulling its penis out of Joker's mouth, leaving a stream of semen pouring from her tongue while she did her utmost not to vomit before the scene was over. She let go of the hand with which she'd been masturbating it. (The dog had come so fast and furiously in her mouth that she'd had no other recourse than to swallow about half of its horrible effusion.) Here, her iron self-control was essential. She was getting through this by compartmentalizing her feelings, and the sensations from her flesh too—the Great Dane's penis felt like it was shredding her vagina, it had knotted up inside her and the knot felt like she was being fisted—even if one was worshipping the devil, there were limits to degradation. This kind of crap made you want to become a Christian. But—the disgusting thought brought bile to her throat—hell no, screw those God-fearing pussies, Satan still rocked fulltime!

And I've got two damn months of this shit to get through? And meanwhile, this is all Nero's damn fault, not mine?

But Nero was too high up to fuck with—rumor had it too that he was fucking someone even higher up the Abyss chain of command (and that old bird wasn't having the same mouth eating her withered pussy eating cow pussy beforehand)—so low-down Joker was the scapegoat.

"Okay, good girl," Boy Toy the movie director said. (Boy Toy was fat and black and was smoking a large joint.) "Now suck on that doggie bone! And yeah, swallow all that nutritious come. It's just vitamins, girl."

She sucked and swallowed, feeling like she'd murder Nero if she could just get her hands on him. Then the camera filming her mouth shifted its focus further back and she dropped her head and puked out the dog semen onto the rug.

Meanwhile the Great Dane behind her stiffened, beat its forepaws on her shoulders, and spurted into her body.

For its ejaculation, the stupid dog had rammed itself DEEP into her sex, hard against her uterus. *Oh hell, that knot fucking hurts!!!*

At the sudden jolt of pain, Joker jerked her head up and found herself looking directly at Nero's secretary Sabrina, who'd apparently just walked onto the set.

Sabrina was small and fleshy and had cropped black hair. She wore a short red dress and long red boots. An aloof smile on her face, she stood and watched the shoot.

And now that the dog was done coming, Joker suffered the further indignity of having to wait—with the cameras still rolling of course (the 'slack' would be edited out)—till the Great Dane's penis unknotted inside her and it could disengage itself from her.

She remained on her hands and knees on the rug, while an assistant kept the dog calm and held it in place on her back so it didn't turn around. While they remained joined at the crotch like that, she pondered her miserable life. How in the world had she ever fallen this frigging low?

From time to time Joker's green eyes flashed angrily at Sabrina, wondering what the hell she wanted. (Sabrina had so far said nothing; now she sat cross-legged in a director's chair and stared wet-eyed at the canine penis stuck in Joker's sex like she wanted some of it herself.)

Finally, fifteen minutes later, the Great Dane was done with Joker. She sighed with relief when she felt the knot in its organ start to shrink inside her.

She raised her head and nodded at the director, who instantly leapt back to life.

"Alright, action, everyone—here comes the money shot!" he called. "Hey, Jones, get your punk ass down there! Cameras, zoom in on Jones's head."

The dog pulled its pink penis out of Joker's sex. There was no spillage of semen. Jones, a bony teen similarly on punishment duty, quickly took the Great Dane's place between Joker's legs, sucking out the doggie ejaculate and swallowing it all down.

And Joker could feel it really gushing out of her—there was a lot of that dog semen for Jones to drink. She doubted he'd be thirsty for the rest of today.

Once the shoot was declared over, Joker rolled over on her back, and again considered that she still had about sixty more days of this nonsense to get through. *I might just take the frigging easy way out and slit my wrists and throat. Either way I'm going to Hell when I die, so why bother to wait?*

For that matter, she wasn't even done with today's work: Boy Toy had informed her that they still had a goat flick to film (Witches/Satanists loved goats!). The two dogs had meanwhile ambled off to different corners of the studio. The St. Bernard was already asleep.

Something wet splashed her thighs so she looked down. Between her legs, Jones was puking up dog semen.

She looked away from Jones to Boy Toy. Sabrina was telling the black director something. He didn't look too pleased. He glanced over at Joker, then back at Sabrina, then nodded.

Oh, shit, Joker thought, *What now?*

Boy Toy grinned over at Joker. "Okay, girl, courtesy of the Overseer Council, you've just been promoted to horse-fuck duty. Hey, everyone, lets have a round of applause celebrating our star's upcoming vaginal expansion!"

Everyone including Sabrina clapped. Joker's heart instantly fell. *Shit, not the horses!* Horse flicks—particularly those involving full penetration—were generally reserved for 'more experienced' witches, meaning those who'd given birth to at least one child (preferably two), and as such had 'more stretched' birth canals. (The younger witches had all vetoed involvement, explaining that while 'hung like a horse' sounded nice in principle, human vaginas were meant for *human* organs.) Women who did those kind of films for too long always had major problems getting together with men. It was like spending one's entire life being fisted and then trying to get satisfaction from a normal penis.

"Aw, c'mon, man!" Joker whined, flinging Sabrina a look of pure hatred. "Someone throw me a frigging break here! What the hell am I supposed to have done now?"

Sabrina laughed. "Relax, hon. Boy's just having some fun at your expense. Actually, Nero's pulling you off animal flicks altogether; your punishment's been cancelled for good."

Joker looked at her in confusion. She couldn't even hope that Sabrina was telling the truth. "Cancelled? For real?"

"As real as that dog turd you've got in your hair."

"Why?"

Sabrina gestured over at the two now-dozing canines. "Do you honestly care?"

She was right; Joker honestly didn't.

"Bye, baby, we'll miss you," the director said. "You got real talent for this game."

Relieved, Joker got to her feet. "Screw you, man."

He puffed on his joint. "I ain't kiddin', mama. It's damn hard to find a chick who can really suck dog-dick, know what I mean? You're a natural."

"Ignore him," Sabrina said, "he's stoned."

"And you, hot stuff, have just been boned! You know dogs have a bone in their dicks, don't ya?"

Joker wiped mingled dog semen and puke from her mouth. "Why can't we simply do animatronics for this shit? Sooner or later, someone's gonna wind up with a dog-baby, and don't you dare tell me that it can't happen. We're working for the Devil."

Boy Toy said, "You mean *whoring*, baby, not *working*."

Joker gave him the finger, then stretched her six foot frame, flinging her head back so her red hair spilled behind her like a cascade of blood. She remembered the dog-turd that Sabrina mentioned and felt around in her hair for it.

Sabrina winked at Joker. "You know how it is, girl: pervs like it real. They've got wanker instinct—we use CGI animals, they'll detect it in an instant. C'mon, don't feel too bad about it—according to an online zoophile survey, forty percent of female dog owners have screwed their pets at some point. Of course, they'll never admit to it."

"Tell that to my hurting puss."

The black man laughed. "Oh you witches are such bitches." He turned away from them to an assistant. "Mo, get those black goats in here; make one of them female so Jones can fuck it—the kid deserves some fun. And bring Candy Kane in, let's film some shemale shit for the freaks—"

"Candy's strung out, man. She close to O.D.'d again last night."

"Great, then she won't frigging bitch so much like she always does." He did a histrionic imitation of Candy's voice that had everyone laughing—"I like man, man, man. I not like fuck women-animal's pussy. Or have dog fuck me in poor ass." He finished up in his own voice. "But like I always say: 'Candy, I don't friggin' get it: if you don't like getting punished, why d'you always screw up so damn much?'"

The assistant left to fetch Candy and the animals.

Sabrina looked at Joker. "You coming to see the boss or are you growing to like this place?"

Joker flung one last look around this den of her recent degradation. The Great Dane was snoring now. Her costar Jones still lay on the rug. The kid was holding his belly like it hurt and looked sick. And according to Boy Toy, he was going to have to screw a nanny-goat in a few minutes. Well there was always Viagra.

She saw Boy Toy looking over at her.

"What?"

"You still here, darling? 'Cos we can use you for the goat scene if Candy starts bitching. You can use a strap-on instead." He made a wide two-armed gesture like he was unveiling a marquee sign. "We'll bill you as 'Joker Jackova—Satan's Soviet Strap-on Slut.' How's that sound?"

"What? Are you serious?" She tugged on Sabrina's arm. "C'mon, let's get outa here. I need to have a bath, wash the filth off my soul."

Sabrina grimaced. "Baby, you know how that never works. I've been down in this filth before and I know from painful experience."

***

"I hate you," Joker told Nero.

It was thirty minutes since she'd left the animal shoot. She'd washed for ages; at least she'd gotten all the dog-stink off. She'd brushed and douched, but she could still taste dog semen in her mouth; and she couldn't forget that even now she was still digesting some of it, using it as nourishment. She was also still scared that one of those mutts might get her pregnant with some human-canine monster.

No point denying it: Satan works in mysterious evil ways.

Sabrina was right; clean up all you liked, except you naturally enjoyed bestiality, the psychic degradation stayed with you for days afterwards. That was the point of the thing though: the degradation served the Master's lower purpose—it kept you compliant. In addition, it soiled your spirit, blackened your heart, so you felt more like you belonged to him. And wasn't that a good thing?

Not as far as Joker was concerned. *I've had two days of that animal crap. That's more than enough for two lifetimes. No way do I intend ever going through it again.*

"I really fucking hate you," she repeated for Nero's benefit.

Smiling, he walked out from behind his desk. He wore a long black vestment, with collar and sleeves trimmed with crimson. In addition he had on pointy black shoes. A wizard's clothes, when he wasn't really gifted.

In contrast, Joker was dressed like a secretary, in a calm gray pantsuit and sensible black shoes. She carried a small black purse. Her red hair was done up in a tight bun, the best she could do with it after two days spent cleaning the farm floor with her ass. She also wore zero makeup, just lip gloss.

Her sex still smarted; the Great Dane had left its mark somewhere inside her.

(Sabrina was currently outside, in her adjoining office, painting her nails red and listening to black metal music while her black cat paced the top of her desk.)

Nero sat on the front of his desk facing her. Though darkly handsome, he'd developed a heavy paunch over the past two years, the result of an easy life of constant hedonism. "Don't hate me. Until I got Azalea to intervene, they were going to put you into SADE."

Joker gasped. (Azalea was Nero's reputed elderly Council mistress. In her everyday life, Azalea was one of the nation's most popular female Republican senators; there was even speculation that she might make it to US President one day. Azalea was also a very wealthy widow. Not bad for a sixty-five-year-old in Joker's opinion.)

Nero laughed at her shock. "Yes, SADE, baby. So what do you think of me now?"

She smiled grimly. "I still frigging hate you." But this was just show. Now she understood how she'd gotten off so lightly.

(SADE—an acronym for Sex, Agony, Detention, and Enlightenment—was one of those massive pocket spaces that existed parallel with Earth; neutral realms that were equally adaptable to good and evil. God and his angels, however, generally couldn't be bothered to use the places. [Whenever the Almighty needed a new realm, he just up and created one. Satan, lacking that sort of ability, had to be more resourceful.] The demons had 'colonized' SADE and now used it for different purposes, one of which was the torment of those not yet ripe enough for Hell. There was also great pleasure available there, but to Joker's knowledge, few people ever got to taste that side of it.)

Nero said. "They were going to drop you in the Cube." He was clearly amused as her eyes widened in additional horror. "So, baby, be damn *grateful* to me, by now you might have been skinless and impaled upside-down and yet not dead."

Joker shuddered. "Thanks, Nero." Then she was angry. "But . . . this . . ."

"Was my idea?"

"Yes, that's why I'm so angry with you. Do you have any idea what dog semen tastes like?"

He grimaced. "No, and I hope never to have to sample the delicacy. Look, I apologize for that. Hold on a minute."

Nero made a hand gesture and suddenly his office vanished and they were in a black space in the middle of nowhere. Walled in by darkness so intense it seemed solid. Hell was over there somewhere, as was Heaven—they could feel the spiritual pressure of Evil and Good that came from each realm. Earth was somewhere far away.

Joker frowned. "This is a neat trick from someone without any magic ability."

(They were both still seated on chair and desk, and Nero's laptop still seemed to be working. A pinging had just announced an email being delivered. But where in the universe was it being delivered from?)

He shrugged. "It's one of the things I *can* do. We can speak here without being overhead by man or devil."

"Where is this place?"

"If I told you that, I'd have to kill you. Seriously."

She rolled her eyes. "Okay, man, what's this all about? Why'd you pull me off farm girl duty?"

"We need you to go after Pagan."

"What?" Okay, this was serious. "Nero, what exactly is going on?"

He frowned deeply. "Simply put, we're trying to abort the biggest crisis to the Abyss Club since its founding, and we need to do it without either our own hierarchy or our inglorious master the Devil himself finding out about it."

Pagan was stumped. "Why me?"

She had a good idea though. Six months ago, Nero had come to her with a proposal. "I want you to keep an eye on your coven leader Pagan. She's a loose cannon, and I sense that she's going to attempt something crazy." Joker had agreed. (The deal was simple: if Pagan *did* screw up, Joker got to head the coven in her place.) A month later, Pagan had also come to her with a proposal. "I want you to help me raise the demon Avex from the pit; and I need you to keep quiet about it."

Joker had also agreed to Pagan's request. She'd not paid too much attention to the job. She'd reported regularly to Nero on Pagan's plans to sacrifice Sarah Downe's baby a week after it was born, and prepared to take part in the ritual herself. She had, however, taken one thing VERY seriously: Nero's constant warning that the ritual could prove very dangerous, and that she needed to be on her guard against the unforeseen.

Yes, the unforeseen like the police breaking down the damn door and arresting everyone while a just-summoned bloodthirsty demon floated over the sacrificial altar.

Nero sighed. In the vast emptiness surrounding them both, it was a miserable and desolate sound. "How about if I start by filling you in on the problem?"

Before she could reply, he continued, "This—I mean raising Avex—has been attempted before; always with disastrous results. A few notable examples: In 1396, at the Cluny Abbey in France, an overly inquisitive monk named Jacques de Marolles, custodian of his monastery's store of ancient occult texts, accidentally became possessed with Avex. The result? All the monks in the abbey were massacred by the possessed Jacques, along with all the inhabitants of the three nearest villages. It took a special dispatch of holy Jesuits from Rome to snare the beast the monk had become, and then return Avex back to Hell, by which time the death toll was well over two thousand. In official Church records the affected villages were devastated by packs of hungry wolves."

Joker gasped. Nero nodded solemnly and went on. "Jump forward two hundred years, to Imperial China. In 1602, the Ming Dynasty astrologer Wu Xian made the same mistake as Jacques de Marolles. As a result, approximately ten thousand northern Chinese were killed and eaten by the mysterious 'Yaomo Beast,' before, with the help of several sorcerers, Emperor Zhi Yijun's frontier guards successfully cornered and killed it. In this case, the Chinese officially recorded the deaths as being caused by 'hordes of cannibalistic Mongol barbarians.'"

He paused and scratched his chin, then nodded to Joker, "Are you getting the gist of this?"

She nodded back. "So if it's that dangerous to raise Avex, why didn't you stop Pagan right from the offset? Why'd you ask me to spy on her instead?"

Nero sighed again, and the darkness surrounding them both seemed to press in deeper. "I'm coming to that bit. But first, I need you to understand that these two examples I've mentioned are merely the tip of a colossal iceberg. There've been quite a few others across the centuries; all ending just as disastrously.

"The last and most recent occurred in 1943 in German-occupied Poland, when Menahem Ben Goldberg, a Jewish rabbi imprisoned at the Auschwitz concentration camp, was used by Nazi occultists in an experiment; their aim being to use The Ravager as a weapon against the Allies. Unfortunately for them however, the possessed Menahem proved uncontrollable, and instead of heading towards Allied positions as instructed, turned and attacked the German battalion stationed at Auschwitz. The change of destination may have been deliberate; some occult scholars believe that the rabbi—an extremely pious man from all accounts—altered the demon's destination by the force of his good spirit. There were seven hundred German casualties, all blamed on saboteurs exploding artillery shells stored in the armory.

The soldier's bodies were so shredded, no one ever questioned the cover-up story. But then, this was Hitler's regime, who would?"

Joker was flabbergasted. "And you want *me* to go after this bloody thing? Just *me*? Are you nuts?"

He smiled. "There's more."

"I'm listening."

"First, I'll answer your question as to why we didn't stop Pagan once we found out what she was up to. The answer's simple: she was going to store the demon in a *baby*. The idea was total genius. Apparently no one had tried that solution before. True, in an adult, Avex *is* completely unmanageable, but in a newborn baby that can't even coordinate its limbs yet? The mighty Ravager of Flesh would be helpless."

Joker nodded. "Pagan said as much. She was right then?"

"We assume so. We don't *know*, because, like you said, the police showed up and the demon possessed her instead."

"Yeah . . . they did. Alright, let me get this straight: You still want *just me* to hunt down an unmanageable demon. Why? Why not send one of your hit squads after it?"

Nero got to his feet and walked back behind his desk again, the black floor tiles duplicating him perfectly in reflection. He placed both palms on his desk and regarded Joker. He appeared calm, but she sensed disquiet in him.

"Ah," he said finally, in a long explosion of breath that the darkness swallowed up like a thirsty throat, "now we come to the complicated part of the story."

Joker crossed her long legs. "We're *just arriving* at the complicated part? Alright, man, I'm all ears."

Nero looked very pained. "Well, you see . . . Satan currently doesn't know that Avex is missing."

"He doesn't?" She recalled that he'd said/implied as much earlier, but then she'd thought he'd been using the expression as a mere figure of speech.

"No, Satan doesn't know it's gone yet. Our dark master is too busy running the other parts of his empire to bother with such trifles. And thankfully, along with omnipotence and omnipresence, only the Almighty—He whom we blaspheme daily—has omniscience." He sighed. "You know, sometimes I think I joined the wrong side; I keep feeling that we're going to lose."

She smirked. "Talk like that will get you dropped into Detention, or worse yet, Agony; and from either of those places it's a one-way trip down to Hell. I could rat on you. And get promoted for it."

"You won't. Who'd watch your back then? You're a smartass; everyone else here hates you."

She agreed, disliking him for stating that fact. He was right: Nero was the only one who recognized her true potential for the order. The rest—like Pagan—knew she was too good and considered her a threat.

"Okay, so I won't rat on you, provided you keep me sweet. Go on."

"O.K., but stop interrupting. This is hard enough to explain as it is."

"Sorry."

"Pagan was smart. In freeing Avex, she somehow bypassed the guardians of its prison completely. Yes," he replied her incredulous stare, "the demons guarding Avex's cell had no idea it had gone missing either. But once they did, they came to me. Last night. Thirteen of them. They were hopping mad."

Joker tried to imagine the spectacle of thirteen angry demons gathered around Nero's bed last night. It was funny, but she couldn't laugh. "What did they say? Did you poop yourself?"

"Be serious. They were angry, but they were also scared shitless. They *begged* me to help them get Avex back into the pit before the Devil finds out."

"That bad?"

"Worse. Except for a few of my superiors, our people know nothing about this either. Everyone thinks Pagan's simply run off to start her own occult society. And we *need* to keep everyone in the dark. So, we capture Pagan before the six-day incubation period is up and—"

"What are you talking about? What six days? What incubation?"

He gave her pained look for interrupting him again, then relaxed. "Shit. I forgot that I hadn't finished explaining. After Avex possesses a person, it slowly transforms their body into that of a monster. A horrible invulnerable monster that's more demon than human. The process takes six days. During that time, the person still appears normal, but their eyes might change color, becoming darker. Also, during that time, Avex makes them black out now and again so it can feed. The host wakes up to a scene of total carnage, dead bodies and gore, with no memory of what happened in between, except for a series of incomplete flashbacks of their actions."

Joker nodded, throwing her mind back to the basement when Avex had first possessed Pagan, and to the horrifying massacre that had followed. The memory made her shiver. "Okay, so it incubates for six days. I get that."

"And during that six-day period is when it's at its most vulnerable. If the host is killed then, the demon automatically falls back into the pit. If we wait until afterwards, there's going to be a whole lot of dead Americans for the cops to clean up, and then Satan *will* find out— likely from watching CNN—and our guys will too, and lots of heads are gonna roll." He stared pointedly at her. "Including both mine and yours."

Joker nodded. "Okay, I'll do it. Where is Pagan now?"

"We don't know."

She gaped at him; this got worse by the minute. "Man, how can you not frigging know?"

Nero looked embarrassed. "It's that damn demon inside her. Understandably, Avex doesn't want to be found. It's blocking us off from locating her."

"So how am I supposed to find her if the almighty Abyss Club can't?"

Nero walked back around the desk to sit on its front again. "Just look around and ask questions. She's likely still in Massachusetts."

"How can you be sure of that?"

"Mainly because, being a coven head herself, she knows how far-reaching the organization is; that there's no point in running from us." He turned on the desk and stared at the wall of solid black on Joker's right. "Don't think I'm leaving you to go this alone. I've already got two warlocks tracking Pagan's spirit trails fulltime. That's something Avex can't block."

A cold wind from the void whipped Joker's red hair around her face. She tucked it neatly back in place, then asked, "So, are they having any luck with finding her?" Spirit trails were reliable tracking aids. The latent 'scent' left behind by a person's aura was almost impossible to mask. Spirit trails were one reason why it was useless fleeing the organization.

He nodded, then shook his head. "She was last picked up at her parents' house in Dover. The trail went cold there, but once we find it again, we'll know her general location."

"It went cold? How did you lose it?"

"There was a commotion at the house." He looked pained again. "We set up a goat to stomp her, but it missed. The crowd of onlookers dirtied the trail. The warlocks say it's as bad as trying to determine who gave a hooker herpes after a fifty-man gang bang."

Joker winced. "Couldn't you use a nicer simile?" Her ears pricked up on hearing they'd used a goat. This was clearly desperate business. Goats were reserved for only the highest level emergencies. To date, she knew of only two other incidents where goats had been used: both down in Texas and blamed on tornadoes. "Okay, so when . . ." Then she realized that she was overlooking something. "Hey! So let's say I successfully take care of your demon trouble. What do *I* get out of it?"

Nero grinned broadly. "I thought you'd never ask. How'd you like to head the organization's Alaska branch?"

She considered that. "Alaska's just a block of ice. Give me somewhere warm: Mexico or Brazil."

He thought a bit. "Both Mexico and Brazil have *live* overseers. Alaska's vacant at the moment: Francois Martin had a heart attack."

Joker shrugged. "I don't frigging care. Transfer either the head of the Mexican or Brazilian branch to Alaska and give me their job. They both need a rest from the heat anyway."

"This is all hypothetical, of course. You might not catch Pagan."

"The hell I won't. Just assure me that I've got the promotion—I'd prefer Brazil by the way: all those handsome Samba boys—and I'll bring you Pagan's head on a silver platter."

Nero winced. "No need to do a Herodias versus John the Baptist here. Her Abyss tattoo will be more that sufficient proof of the kill."

"Are you certain you want that? It's on her left breast."

"Bring it along with the nipple if you like. And now, let's talk about *how* to neutralize Avex."

"I thought I could just shoot Pagan."

"You already tried that down in the basement, didn't you? Any success?"

Joker shook her head. "I pumped an entire clip of bullets into her ugly face, and she still healed herself and came after me. But . . . she was transformed then, Avex was in control. I'm supposed to hit her when it's not, right?"

"She'll still be hard to kill."

"Okay, how do I do this?"

Grinning like a wolf, Nero explained.

Joker was appalled. The blackness over them suddenly felt like it was falling on her; that which walled in the space felt like it was squeezing her body; it was a horrible feeling of claustrophobia. "*What? I need to get *that* close to her?"

"View it like this: When you're head of the club's Brazilian branch, no one'll be able to say you didn't earn the promotion."

Nero raised a hand to dispel the darkness.

"Hold on a moment before you do that."

He paused mid-gesture. "Yes?"

Now it was Joker's turn to grin like a wolf. "Seeing as we're conspirators in this, share a confidence with me."

He looked at her confused. What do you want to know?"

"Is Azalea as freaky as people claim? The rumor is that all she likes is cunnilingus and getting splooged on."

"*That's* what you want to know?"

"Yes. *Tell me.*"

He tapped his fingers on the desktop, then shrugged. "Azalea? Oh, she's weird alright. You women all are. Azalea likes me to eat her pussy while she reviews pending legislation. She claims that sex helps her view legal issues with penetrating clarity. She sits on a sofa reading, with her fat legs spread; I kneel between them and start licking. And boy, she can read for ages. Then afterwards, I wank over her while calling her 'mommy' and come on her breasts and she rubs the semen into her skin like she's a porno star."

He shrugged. "I guess in my own little way I'm affecting national policy. Other than that, she's an utterly evil fat old witch and I can't get enough of her. Hey—stop giggling. I swear, if a word of this gets out, I'll recommend that you're dropped in Detention with that crazy Schoolmaster and Peaches."

CHAPTER 18

Pagan

Once it was properly dark, Pagan drove off from the Sunflower Motel with Kyle's body in the trunk of his car, a red Dodge sedan. His luggage and possessions—a laptop and piled shoe boxes—were on the back seat. His wallet was in her handbag: she didn't want him being identified too quickly; that would lead directly back to the motel.

After driving around Raynham for a while, searching for a suitable place to ditch the car, she finally found a truck stop on the north road out of town.

'Rudy's Truck Stop,' as the red neon sign announced, was actually close to the Sunflower, about a quarter mile farther up Broadway, at its crossing with the Blue Star Memorial Highway (aka Interstate 495). She'd missed it yesterday when motoring in from Dover because it was hidden by the flyover.

The lot had a large number of parked trucks and cars, several stationary 18-wheelers, and some motorbikes. Bikers rolled in and out on Harleys. Back off from the parking lot stood a rowdy roadhouse where people were noisily eating and drinking. Strains of country rock music rode like agitated witches on the night breeze.

The lot was quite large. She parked the Dodge in a corner at the rear, on the right of the roadhouse building, and locked it up. With any luck (if the smell of rot from the trunk didn't get too bad), no one would think of looking inside it till midweek.

As she was walking out of the lot, a yellow Jeep pulled in off the main road; a 4-door Wrangler. The streetlight at the turnoff let her see into it. Two men sat in the car. Both looked like drug dealers, the stereotype kind one saw on TV: long dirty black hair, greasy mustaches, and hard cold smiles. Their clothes were a combination of old leather and denim.

The ruthlessness in both men's eyes made Pagan shiver. The driver was fortyish and fat, the other man young and slim; handsome but with tons of zits.

The car stopped; the younger man looked her way. "Hey, hon, you want some?"

She was about telling him, "No thank you, I don't," when she realized that with her cloaking spell in place, he couldn't see her. She looked round. A bone-thin prostitute was hurrying her way over to the Jeep.

She brushed past Pagan like she wasn't there and leaned in the Jeep's front passenger window.

"C'mon, Snake, where's my fucking meth? I've been waiting for ya for hours."

The fat driver scowled at her. "I had to take Sin to the doctor's. She was having contractions, but Doc said they're just early."

"Hey, puta, you got our fucking money?" the younger man asked. "We ain't no goddam charity, you know. You try 'n run off like last time and I'll break both your damn legs."

"Yeah, yeah, Boner, I got some money. I've been turning tricks since six a.m."

Wincing, Pagan quickly walked off. What sort of a name was Boner? Or Snake either, for that matter?

She quickly forgot the drug dealers and their skinny client. She had problems of her own. Red Octopus hadn't yet gotten in touch with her, and her nerves were shot with the tension of waiting. *So what do I do now? Hang around here or run?*

It was a quandary. As far as she could tell, this town Raynham was the kind of place where nothing happened, so no one would expect she'd be here. But maybe she'd be better off further away from Boston?

The weather was warm, so much so that she felt overdressed. This Sunday night saw the road practically deserted. The half-moon overhead looked like the eye of God, angrily accusing her of all the murders she'd committed.

Pagan had been racked with guilt all day. She'd done her best to convince herself that the killings weren't her fault, but they weighed heavily on her soul nonetheless. That was another reason why she'd been so desperate to remove Kyle's corpse from her motel room.

Now, after crossing the connecting road in from the highway, she suddenly remembered that she still had Kyle's wallet on her. That was so dumb. *I need to get rid of it.*

She quickly opened up the leather folder and extracted all of Kyle's money, about $285. She then wiped the wallet over twice with a tissue to erase her fingerprints.

Satisfied, she turned off into the roadside trees to ditch the wallet. No point leaving it by the sidewalk where some good Samaritan would find it and try to return it to its owner.

Steeling herself against the shadows between the trees, she made her way in a short distance from the road. She dumped the wallet under a shrub, then began the walk back.

Suddenly she froze. She'd heard a noise. Had someone seen her walk in from the road? She reminded herself that with her masking spell in place, no one could see her except she let them.

Except for fellow witches.

The sound came again. This time it was accompanied by a voice: "Cut it off!"

Cut what off? The sound was coming from ahead of her, towards the motel.

The noises continued. Curious as to what was going on, Pagan quickly made her way towards the sound, pushing aside the denser foliage in her way. Her cloaking spell meant that she had no need to be careful: whoever was there in front of her wouldn't hear her approach, no matter how many fallen branches she trampled and snapped or leaves she rustled.

She paused just outside a small grove about ten yards in from the road. Some light penetrated the space, and through the bordering trees on her right she made out the All American Assisted Living building.

But right in front of her?

Two women were cutting a dead man's penis off. He was clearly dead, that was for certain: he had a long bloody slash across his throat, and his white T-shirt looked like someone had splashed it with a bowl of tomato ketchup.

"Okay, roll him over," one of the women said. Both were facing away from her, so she couldn't see their faces, but the voice she'd just heard sounded strangely familiar. But here? *No, it can't be her. It's some sound-alike lady psychopath. But maybe I shouldn't judge too quickly—maybe the guy once raped her?*

She watched the two women rolling the dead man over.

"Alright, spread his legs, let's shove his dick up his ass."

"We need to take his pants off first; otherwise there won't be enough space in his butt crack."

Then: "Ugh, Gross. He shit himself while dying."

Then: "His ass is really tight. I don't think his dick will fit up it at all; maybe we should cut his balls off first?"

Then: "No. I'll just open him up a bit with the knife. See?"

There was animated laughter as the two women shoved the dead man's manhood up his sliced-open anus. "Hey, asshole! Here's what you get for screwing with us."

Disgusted with both the world at large and herself in particular, Pagan made her silent way away from the place.

CHAPTER 19

Britt & Lori

After they'd pulled the man's stripped and mutilated corpse back close to the sidewalk (for easy discovery in the morning), Britt and Lori headed up the road towards Rudy's Truck Stop.

Robbing the man had been super easy. He'd collected money from the ATM at the VERC Gulf gas station near the motel, then crossed the road and proceeded up past Calvary Chapel towards Rudy's. That was when Britt had quickly walked up to him from behind and stuck her revolver into his ribs. Then she'd ushered him into the trees bordering the road, where Lori waited. There they'd both set on him with their knives, slit his throat and stabbed him to death. He'd been slightly drunk, had hardly put up a fight. They'd just slashed and stabbed while he first looked confused—grabbing his neck and staring at the red leakage spurting over his hands—then keeled over, then lay still in the spreading pool of his departing life. Then when the blood had all soaked away into the grass, they'd pulled down his pants and gotten down to work severing his genitals.

Best of all, Britt had again gotten that incredible feeling (that came from reducing someone to nothing) from killing him. She really couldn't get enough of that. Neither (by her own admission) could Lori.

Lori had also thought to bring a bottle of water along, so they could wash their hands clean afterwards. In a morbid sense, they'd been lucky: their victim's drunkenness had had the additional advantage of allowing them to kill him without messing up their clothes. Other than for some blood on their arms and shoes that easily wiped off (and a splash from his throat that had streaked across Lori's cheek), they'd gotten through the murder (and subsequent mutilation) remarkably spotless.

(There was something else too, that Lori was considering: So far all their victims had been easy kills, all unsuspecting their deaths, but what if they met someone who offered resistance, or worse, was armed and dangerous? What then? To Lori, it was an exciting uncertainty.)

"That was a great idea of yours," Britt congratulated her BFF. "Now everyone will think Pagan killed him."

"Yeah," Lori agreed. On her suggestion, after shoving the dead man's penis up his anus, they'd also carved several pentagrams into the corpse's flesh to make it look like a ritual killing. So, yes, everyone would blame Pagan for his death. But then, she was apparently already responsible for about seventeen other deaths anyway. One more would hardly make any difference when she was being sentenced.

"Gimme his phone," she told Britt suddenly. "I saw you sneak it out of his pocket."

Grumbling, Britt handed the cellphone over. "Oh, I feel so disoriented without a phone, like I'm disconnected from modern life. You aren't going to throw it away, are you?"

"Not until I've called home."

"What? But you said . . ."

"Don't worry, my parents won't rat on me, no matter what. Besides, we'll just remove the battery and ditch the phone afterwards." She looked pointedly at Britt. "Look, we've been gone since yesterday. We need to find out what's been happening in our absence."

"It's not my fault that we keep missing the news. You insisted on watching MTV all day."

"Whatever, just let me dial. Shit, now see what you've done: you made me enter a wrong number. No, no, cut the call, you damn phone! Phew! Okay, now don't say anything . . . anything . . . let me finish this.

"Hello? . . . Dad, it's me Lori . . . The police were over there? . . . They said *what!?* . . . When? . . . No, we didn't do it. . . . we didn't . . . Sorry, dad, I can't turn myself in, and I can't tell you where I am; this is too far gone now. . . . No, don't worry, I'm fine. . . . I love you too, dad. Say hi to mom for me."

Tears in her eyes, Lori hung up.

Britt placed her hands on Lori's shoulders. "What's the matter? Say something!"

"Your mom killed herself. Blew her brains out."

Britt's eyes went wide. "Shit. Once we tied her up I completely forgot that her gun was in the nightstand. Aw shucks, I should have known she'd do something vain like that—try to one-up me even into the grave. Hey, but is that why you're crying?"

"No, it's not that! I miss my parents! My dad sounded so scared on the phone! And he said my mom had had to take tranquilizers and go to bed early!"

Lori dashed the phone down on the sidewalk. It blew apart, the battery flying out into the middle of the road. She picked up the shell and flung into away into the trees. When she looked at Britt again, her eyes were once more dry and calm.

"Also," she said in a soft voice, "Chris died of a brain hemorrhage. And your Aunt Clarissa only this morning reported last night's murders."

Britt nodded. "My aunt's cool like that."

"And yes, we *are* a news item now. My parents watched two appeals for info on our whereabouts."

"And so . . . our body count's rising. That's five corpses to our credit now."

Lori laughed and jerked a finger behind her. "No, four. That last one's on Pagan's account."

Britt burst out laughing. "Yeah, I forgot that." She stepped out along the dark road, tugging Lori along behind her. "At least we got the asshole's money if not the credit for offing him. C'mon, let's go get some drinks at the truck stop."

***

"They're gonna ask us for our ID," Lori pointed out as they stepped onto the parking lot at Rudy's Truck Stop. "Neither of us is twenty-one yet."

Britt rested a hand against the grill of an 18-wheeler, then tried to catch her reflection in the chrome. "Don't worry, we both look old enough. Besides, it's night and everyone's likely to be too drunk to notice anyway. And"—she leered at Lori—"undo your top."

"What? Oh shit!"

"Uh huh. Cleavage works wonders in bars. The horny male bartender will be mesmerized by our irresistible female breasts and serve us."

Lori unzipped.

"More," Britt instructed, "a little more." She undid her own blouse so her breasts were showing. Almost like she'd known this would happen, she wasn't wearing a bra.

"We look like sluts," Lori said. "Absolute hookers."

"Give it a rest. Part of our plan is to get laid, isn't it?"

Lori nodded, then grinned. "Okay, let's go get 'em. And the first one's mi—"

"Hello, ladies," a voice said on their left. "Are you two looking for a good time?"

They pulled up short. A tall thirtyish man had just stepped out from between two parked 18-wheelers. Looking into the space, they saw a bright yellow Jeep 4-door slotted in there. A fat man sat behind the wheel smoking a joint.

They looked the thin man over. He was handsome but pimply. Had long greasy hair and a handlebar mustache.

"Hey—we ain't hookers!" Lori retorted. "We're just going to the bar. We wanna get a few drinks and some food."

The thin man gave them a greasy smile. "Sorry, but no offence meant. My name's Boner." He gestured back at the yellow Jeep. "Me and my buddy Snake over there, we're salesmen handling the chemical entertainments for this town. We were wondering if you're buying. We got way better stuff than booze. Pot, coke, meth, horse, pills, you name it. Whatever you want, we got."

Then he frowned. "Say, haven't I seen you two girls around somewhere before? Your faces look damn familiar."

They both shook their heads. "We're new in town," Britt said.

Boner lifted his eyes from studying Lori's breasts. "So what's it gonna be? You two girls wanna buy some shit or not?"

Britt looked at the yellow Jeep. The fat man was now following their conversation with interest. "How much is this gonna cost us?" she asked.

"Britt, we haven't got money for this," Lori insisted. "Let's just get some beers and head back to the motel."

"Motel? Oh, are you girls rooming at the Sunflower?" Boner smiled winningly at Britt. "Well, see, as touching prices, it all depends on what'cha want to purchase, and, seeing as you're both new in town, we'll give you our special discount for new customers. Weed, for instance only costs . . ."

Then he paused and took a quick look around the truck stop lot. Two couples were just stepping out of the roadhouse and heading their way. "You know," he said nervously, "how 'bout we discuss this in the safety of my ride?"

Lori tugged on Britt's sleeve. "I don't like this," she whispered in her ear.

Britt ignored her and grinned at Boner. "Lead the damn way. It's been such a boring day. We could both do with chemical pick-me-ups."

CHAPTER 20

Lori

A minute later they were both sitting in the rear of the yellow Jeep and the fat man was pointing a gun in their faces. Lori winced; this was just the kind of thing she'd been expecting. Now, they were going to be robbed.

"Snake, what the hell are you doing?" Boner asked. "They just wanna buy some dope."

"Boner, you bonehead, you never were much for faces. These are the two girls we saw on TV this afternoon, that killed the gay couple up in Dover, and cut that city socialite's legs off."

Boner, sitting beside the captives, gaped. "Shee-it. I knew I'd seen the both of 'em somewhere before."

Lori gave Britt a hard look that said, *See what you've just got us into?*

"There's blood on your hand," Snake told Britt. "Now where'd that come from?"

Lori at first wondered if he was speaking figuratively, but when she looked down, there was indeed blood on Britt's hand, from the outside of her left thumb back to the wrist.

"Answer me, you little bitch! Have you gone and killed someone from this town?

Britt said nothing. Lori asked, "What do you want with us?" The fat man was undressing them with his eyes. She remembered that they'd just put their breasts on storefront display; that didn't seem such a great idea anymore. The fat man was pulling on his joint, but his dark eyes never left their bodies, neither did the gun in his right move off covering them both.

Lori felt both excited and disgusted. *Are they gonna rape us? Damn you, Britt. Maybe next time you'll listen to me.*

She looked at Britt. Britt's eyes were wide open with fright. Then Lori felt Britt's right hand slowly moving between their bodies. She was trying to pull her gun.

Britt was seated on the driver's side of the back seat, Lori was in the middle, and Boner (What the hell kind of a name was 'Boner'?) was behind the front passenger seat. The gun was tucked between Britt and Lori. She waited expectantly for Britt to shoot the fat guy in the face. But then he said:

"Hey, Boner, frisk 'em both." He swung the gun towards Britt. "Start with Blondie here."

A few seconds later, Boner had their Colt revolver in his hand, along with Britt's bloody knife. He regarded the gun musingly, turning it left and right to catch the light. "Dangerous, dangerous," he said.

Outside the car, a biker couple strode past towards the bar; the man was built like a mountain of rock; the woman was short and curvy and had long red hair down to her waist. Lori hated how, being on the run, they couldn't scream for help. That would mean the cops coming, and them going to prison for life. It seemed so damned unfair to be in trouble and not have any options, like competing on *Who Wants to Be a Millionaire* without lifelines.

Snake said, "Now tell me: what's a couple of little girls like you doing with a gun this big?"

"We could ask you the same question," Britt replied sharply.

Snake laughed his oily laugh and ditched the butt of his joint between Lori's legs. "Well, see, the way I view it, having a big gun is like having a big penis: you don't need it, but it sure fills you with confidence."

Boner laughed out loud. Britt rolled her eyes.

Snake nodded to Boner, then pointed his gun at Lori. "Alright, check out Miss Pretty here for weapons too, then we're all gonna have us a little talk."

Boner shortly found Lori's knife also. "There's blood on both knives, and it's still fresh," he said with some disbelief. "Snake, I think they did just kill someone else."

Snake shrugged with grave disinterest. "Maybe he or she pissed them off; young ladies have a right to defend themselves. How much money they got in their bags?"

Boner checked through both handbags, and held up his findings. "'Bout three hundred bucks and some small change."

Snake took the cash from him with a dirty hand. Lori winced as he tucked it away in a jacket pocket. It hurt her no end, seeing the money go like that. *Damn, that's all the cash we just stole from that sucker down the road!*

Snake patted his stuffed pocket and grinned in their faces. "Alright now, ladies, this is part payment for the favor we're gonna do you both."

"What favor?" Britt asked coldly. Her eyes were red like she was going to cry. "For fuck's sake, just let us go. You've already got all our money."

Boner laughed and relaxed back in his seat. "He means, we're not gonna turn your murdering butts over to the cops."

"Oh, thank you, thank you!" Lori immediately gushed. That at least was the worst that could happen.

"But see," Snake continued, "criminals though we may be, we're both good American citizens at heart nonetheless . . . and, we're sure to both have sleepless nightmares of bad conscience if we let you two go without punishing you in some significantly memorable and proper way." He looked over at Boner. "How'm I doin' with the explanation, buddy?"

Boner grinned broadly. He'd been cleaning his nails with Lori's knife. "You're doing great, Snake."

Snake nodded. He pointed his gun down at Lori's thighs. "So's, the way I reckon this is, we'll just take our payment out of your flesh. That should teach you not to kill people just 'cos you feel like."

Britt said, "You're gonna *what?*"

Boner explained: "What he means, is—we're gonna do America the favor of fucking you both silly. Fill all your holes with drug-dealer jism."

"Yeah, that's right," Snake agreed and burped.

"You're gonna r-r-rape us?" Lori asked. Once again that strange combination of lust and disgust filled her. She waited with eager anticipation for the reply to her question.

"You can call it that if you like; or you can just cooperate with our hard-ons, and take it like a woman." Snake leered at Britt over the barrel of his gun. "One way or the other, however, Blondie, my dick is gonna be stirring up your poop tonight."

"Hell no!" Britt yelped. "Let me out of this goddam car! Help, someone! Somebody help us! They're gonna rape us!"

Lori quickly turned to her. "Shush! You're just gonna make things worse for us!" There was no one in the parking lot anyway. And hidden where the Jeep was—between the two 18-wheelers—Lori doubted anyone could hear Britt either. As far as she could see, it looked like they'd both be donating their sexual organs to a nearby dope-dealer charity tonight.

Britt, however, was freaking out big time and trying to lower the window on her side. "Help! Somebody fucking HELP!"

"Shut the dumb bitch up," Snake calmly instructed Boner.

Boner pulled Britt away from the window and smacked her hard in the mouth. Her lower lip split and blood spilled. Dazed, she sat back in the seat.

"Now that's better," Snake said. He pointed to Lori. "Boner, you and Ella can have this one." He reached forward and stroked Britt's thighs. Dazed as she was, she didn't resist. "Blondie here's all mine, though Sin might wanna join in." He grinned broadly. "We both like screamers. Ha ha ha!"

"It's not just the two of you?" Lori queried worriedly. "You're sharing us with other people?"

"Just our old ladies—my wife Sin and Boner's girl Ella. They like runaway pussy too."

Lori stared at him. Things had really gotten way out of hand and still, she felt excited. She didn't understand it. *Aw, well, I haven't had a guy for two whole years, and Britt's been hogging all the ones we're met so far. At least Boner's almost good-loo—but . . . what kind of a nickname is 'Boner'?*

"Alright, get down low in the back, both of you," Boner instructed. "Make sure you're outa sight."

"What?" Lori asked.

Snake grimaced. "We don't want anyone seeing you in the car with us while we take you home."

"But why?" Lori asked, suddenly frightened.

"Because this is just a ruse; they're gonna kill us after they rape us," Britt said dully, her eyes still glazed over. "That's what scumbags always do."

Boner regarded Britt disgustedly. "Use your damn brains, girl. We're taking you home with us to fuck, but you two are both wanted for murder and other dastardly acts, like cutting that beautiful woman's feet off. If Snake and I are either seen or caught associating with you, we'll both get accessory raps for not turning you in to the cops."

Lori looked enquiringly at Snake. He nodded back. "Yeah, that's it. Now hide yourselves and let's get a move on." He winked at Britt. "As for me, I can't wait to try some of Blondie's hair pie."

"Fuck you," Britt said.

A deep belly laugh. "You're going to, baby."

Lori ducked down into the rear foot well. After a moment, she felt Britt's weight fall on her. It felt like Boner was forcing Britt into concealment.

She felt some resentment towards Britt. She twisted her head and whispered, "Try to be reasonable for once. Hopefully, like they say, they won't kill us afterwards."

"And if they do?"

"We intend to die anyway."

"Not like this we don't. Kidnapped and—"

"We discussed and accepted it as a distinct possibility."

Lori didn't hear Britt's whispered reply. The Jeep started up then and they began their bumpy ride to only God-knew-where.

Once again, Lori felt that intense thrill of the unknown; an elation totally opposite to the rage she sensed bubbling in Britt.

CHAPTER 21

Britt

All the time the Jeep was in motion towards their destination, Britt was furious. Pressed down on top of Lori by Boner's hand on her back, she fumed and fumed and fumed.

This wasn't supposed to happen. These two hairy bastards had stolen their weapons and all their money. Losing the money hurt after what they'd had to do to get it.

But getting it *had* been fun. With a thrill, she remembered how great she'd felt on stabbing the guy they'd robbed in the neck—she'd instinctively understood that if you stabbed someone deep in the neck, you destroyed their ability to yell for help, all that came out of their throat afterwards was a wet gurgle like the sound from a dying TB patient's lungs. And they began spitting out pretty red blood.

Then Britt's rage returned, but not for long. Fear overwhelmed her. She didn't want that fat disgusting guy Snake anywhere near her, speak less of inside her body. The very thought of him taking her against her will made her want to vomit. And it looked like she couldn't escape it. Blood still dripped from her swollen lip and her head felt like a door that the ATF had just kicked in. And did he say two women also wanted in on the rape action? *We're gonna get gang-banged? And stupid, complacent Lori* (who was crouched underneath Britt as quietly as if she was asleep on her hands and knees) *says we should grin and bear it? Bear what?*

And worst of all, bent over like this in the foot well, she had utterly no idea where they were.

Finally, the car slowed and made a sharp left turn. Then it bumped up and down over an unseen trail for a while and halted.

"Okay, ladies," Snake said from the driver's seat, "you can both get up now. We're home."

***

'Home' was an old dilapidated cottage. There were lights in the windows. A gravel footpath led to the front porch and the wide yard was surrounded by trees.

Looking back, Britt couldn't see a main road. Add that to the fact that the moon was playing hide-and-seek with a bank of clouds, and they could be just about anywhere in the town.

Her fear returned; she hoped they'd survive tonight. She looked from Lori, who had a feverish expectant look in her eyes, to their two captors. Snake and Boner both had guns pointed at them now. To Britt's dismay, both men also had visible erections in their pants. Being thinner that his partner, Boner's boner was particularly prominent.

Britt quailed before the stiff penises. *What the hell is it about forced entry that excites men so much?*

"Okay, pretty young ladies," Snake said, a lecherous grin on his fat face, "now here's the rules we're playing by: Just behave yourselves. If you kick up any fuss—start screaming or try to run away—we'll simply gun you both down. Then you'll vanish—ground up into pig food. Ed McKinney's farm ain't but half a mile away. He's always looking for free feed for his hogs, and human meat is considered particularly nutritious. Do you both get the picture?"

Britt gulped, then nodded. She looked at Lori. Lori had a weird dreamy smile on her face, like she was in a trance.

Maybe she's thinking how great it'd be to be ground up into pig mash.

"Alright, come on, both of you," Boner instructed, leading the way to the front door. "And don't you dare sass our ladies."

Inside the house wasn't much different from outside. It was dilapidated, unkempt and had cheap old furniture. A trail of rat droppings along one wall made Britt cringe.

In the living room, two women sat watching TV in their underwear. One was dark and plump and quite pretty. The other had a face like a hawk, was skinny as a bone, and was heavily pregnant.

"So, girls," Snake said with gusto, "meet the ladies." He gestured from the plump to the pregnant one. "Ella and Sin." He nodded at the question that formed in Britt's eyes. "Yeah, that's right—Sin . . . S . . . I . . . N."

Britt and Lori said nothing. Ella and Sin, however, stared at both of them.

Sin said, "Aren't they the ones . . . ?" In addition to looking like a hawk, she had a horrible caw-like voice like she used moonshine for mouthwash.

Boner laughed. "They sure as hell are! Oh yeah, America's most wanted pussy, both here to donate some good loving to our communal fund. Now are you girls in or is it just Snake and I gonna enjoy these two young adult honeypots?"

Ella instantly stuck up her hand. "I'm in. Makes a change from watching *CSI* reruns."

Sin regarded the two captives, then pointed at Britt. "I wanna fuck *her* . . . but later." She indicated her belly. "Snake, this damn brat of yours has been kicking like I'm a damn soccer ball all evening." She winced. "Oh, I'll be so glad when it's out of me."

"It's because you're having kids so late in life," Ella said. "It's usually best to start early, and then . . ."

"Well, what the hell are you still waiting for!?" Snake thundered at Britt and Lori. "You heard the ladies—get your damn clothes off!"

Feeling like she'd somehow fallen through a broken floor and down into Hell, Britt complied, reluctantly dropping her clothes in a pile on the floor. She'd have felt a lot better if only Lori looked as scared as she did, but no, Lori looked almost beatific. She was stripping with rapidity, like the clothes had been annoying her all day.

Both men were peeling their pants off, revealing their erections.

And then it began. Snake grabbed Britt roughly by the hair, pushed her down on her knees, and stuffed his penis into her mouth. "Now give it the old college try, city girl!" And she was gagging and doing her best not to faint and his hairy sweaty belly was all pressed up against her forehead and, oh God—the horrible stink of him!

***

Britt discovered that being raped was worse than she'd ever imagined it would be. It wasn't so much being invaded by another— the violent physical aspect—that upset her so much, as did the horrible feeling that all of her massive emotional gains since yesterday (when she'd freed herself from her mother's sexual domination of her psyche), were being leeched away by this one act.

Snake sweated away on top of her, using first her mouth, then her vagina, then—oh, God, no!!!—her virgin anus. Shit! She felt a hard penis slide up inside her ass for the first time . . . shit, it hurt! He was tearing her up! And all she could do was hate him; hate him for once again reducing her to *nothing*. Making her a big *NO ONE* again.

She was lying flat on her belly with her arms by her head, on the rug, with him heavy on her, thrusting into her rectum like he owned it. The pain was so intense she was almost fainting. Sin was laughing and clapping her hands on top of her immense belly.

But what upset Britt most of all were the moans of pleasure coming from her left. She looked that way: Lori was on her back on the dirty rug, with Boner between her thighs. Her feet were up on his shoulders as he thrust. Boner's plump girlfriend Ella was kneeling over Lori's face and gasping as she ground her sex on Lori's mouth. Lori clearly wasn't in *any* pain: she was playing first with her own breasts, then with Ella's bigger ones, then reaching a hand forward to grab Boner's buttocks and pull him deeper into her body.

Ella gasped and rolled off Lori's face. She lay on her back by Lori's side stroking herself between the legs with one hand and stroking Lori's face with the other. Lori was gasping herself, her eyes shut.

Then as Snake emptied what felt like a liter of semen up Britt's rectum, Lori visibly stiffened.

"Harder, I'm coming!" she growled.

Boner humped her harder, and Lori *really* came. To Britt, she looked like she was in Heaven.

Britt, though, was deep in Hell. The hell of her shame and her aching flesh. Snake got off her. She rolled over, the semen pouring from her anus, and, tears in her eyes, regarded the fat man (whose beer belly sat on his penis like the phallus was propping it up) with hatred.

Snake saw her look and laughed. He turned to Sin, who'd begun stroking herself between the legs. (Snake's gun lay on the sofa within easy reach of her fingers.) "Hey, babe, now *this* is some tight pussy here. Not like that slack bag you're carrying around."

The hawk face scowled, the dark eyes glimmered with anger. "Snake, lay off me, okay? It's just till this kid of yours is born. It's your damn fault I'm so slack now. And it ain't like you give me any bed rest even now anyway."

"Aw, Sin, you know that Dr. Sloane says fucking one's pregnant wife regularly helps with an easy delivery."

"He's a damn quack." She stopped stroking her sex and got up. She eyed Britt wickedly. "You know, I think I'll have a go with her myself now. I'll just go get ready."

Britt had no idea what Sin meant. She was lying there impaled on her rod of pain, and horribly having to listen to Lori having yet another orgasm. Did the stupid bitch have a rape fantasy?

She looked their way. Lori was on top of Ella—they were going sixty-nine at each other—while Boner was kneeling behind Lori and thrusting into her that way. And it looked like he was in her ass too. So why wasn't she screaming and weeping?

And what was up with all this lezzie shit that Lori was doing?

Then Lori collapsed on top of Ella. Boner got off her and walked over to Snake, who was sitting in the chair Sin had vacated, playing with his gun. Britt winced. He too was hard again.

Boner winked at Snake, then pointed over at Lori. "Let's change places. She's super hot—real sweet."

"Yeah, I do think I'll have me a go with your brunette." Carrying the gun, Snake walked over to Lori's side, pulled her up onto her knees again, and sank home his erection in her dripping flesh. The penetration was greeted by a loud moan—of delight—after which Lori began grunting again as he thrust into her. Shortly afterwards she was coming again. Under the pair, Ella was moving her mouth from sucking Snake's scrotum to licking Lori's clitoris.

Britt on her part, screamed as Boner sank his penis into her sex.

NOOOO!!!! Her degradation was doubled. He began fucking her hard. Unlike Snake, he was very fit and his thrusts seemed to peel the walls off her vagina. She was as dry as the Mojave Desert down there and it felt like he was rubbing sandpaper inside her. *Oh, God, please help me!*

Then just when it felt like she'd pass out from the pain, Boner ejaculated inside her.

He got up and regarded her anguished face, shaking his head. "You're real pretty too, Blondie. You just need to put in some effort, like your girlfriend there."

Britt's angry retort was tempered by the shadow that suddenly fell over her. She looked up and wailed. Sin had returned from the bedroom. She was wearing a harness from which protruded a massive black strap-on dildo. The sex toy looked almost the size of Britt's forearm.

"Oh, God, no!" Britt squealed. "NOOOOO!"

Sin laughed. "Oh yes, bitch! After I give you some of this, we'll see who's the slacker of the two of us."

"No!" Britt protested in horror. "You'll tear me to bits!"

Boner grabbed her arms and held her in place. With seemingly unnatural strength, Sin forced her legs apart. Then, after carefully balancing her pregnant belly on Britt's own flat one, she slipped the black strap-on into Britt's vagina and began sliding it in and out hard.

I'm being raped by a pregnant woman wearing a strap-on! The thought was so obscene, the image so ridiculous, that Britt finally gave up the fight. It couldn't get any worse than this. She watched Sin's hawk-like visage sweating bullets over her, her milk-swollen breasts and massive belly wobbling as she thrust harder and harder, and the sadistic smile on her face as Britt squealed and moaned in pain.

And then Boner was hard again and sticking his penis in Britt's mouth, and filling her throat with it. And it tasted of Lori's shit.

And, just making matters worse, beside her Lori—damn the fucking ATD'd hussy—was having yet another orgasm. What the hell was going on here? This time she was riding Snake, who lay with his arms folded behind his head, while Lori slid up and down on his manhood. Ella was standing facing Lori and rubbing her clitoris against Lori's mouth.

And then Britt screamed. Sin had just savagely yanked the dildo out of her sex, and it felt like she'd torn something down there. Sin got up. (In other circumstances Britt would have found her utterly hilarious: she was so skinny, and with that huge tummy on her, she looked to be fully one-half pregnancy.) Britt stared at Sin's crotch in horror, expecting to see her entire inner sexual lining extracted and messily draped over the black phallus. But there was nothing. The dildo didn't even look bloody. That had to be a miracle.

(Looking up, she saw a solitary spider making its way across the ceiling. Looking down, she noticed yet another line of rat droppings trailing the other side of the room . . . and the completely unperturbed rodent dropping them. On the TV, Obama and Putin were laughing at some summit meeting in Germany.)

Sin stroked the dildo and laughed. "Okay, now that your pussy's looser than mine, let's have your ass." She winked at Boner. "Turn the girl over."

Britt was summarily flipped over, and pulled up on her hands and knees. A moment later she howled as something was shoved up her anus. It was hard and didn't feel round like a penis and . . .

When the hard object was well inside Britt's body, both Sin and Boner collapsed into chairs laughing.

Britt, her backside in fierce agony, was completely confused. What had they done to her? Bent over as she was, she couldn't see. (But she *could* see that Sin was still wearing the dildo.)

She looked over at Snake. Snake was looking at her and laughing too.

Then, Ella, just coming down from her orgasm, gasped out, "Oh, my God! Is she really that slack back there? You stuck the TV remote up her ass!? Oh my God, Sin, you're so nasty! I didn't even know one could do that!"

"I'm just trying to turn the bitch on, girl! Ha ha ha ha ha!"

Britt lost it then. She began weeping, bawling her eyes out, not caring who was watching.

Once again, it wasn't the pain that was the problem, it was the fact that she'd just been publicly humiliated again, reduced to a big fat zero, and all for another woman's pleasure. Having a fellow woman do it to her just made it much worse. It felt like her mother's ghost was haunting her.

And worst of all, beside her, that stupid slut Lori was gasping and moaning her way through still yet another orgasm.

And then, to compound her shame, Snake came back over to her and, leaving the TV remote stuck up her ass, pushed her to the ground, rolled her over onto her back, and inserted himself into her front entrance again.

"Aw, Sin, what have you done to this sweet tight puss? She's so slack now that I can't come!"

And all around her everyone was laughing. Yes, they were all laughing at her. She was truly nothing now, much less than zero even.

***

Much later—after a while the pain and penetrations and moaning and humiliation all blended into a single swirling soup of degradation—they were let go.

Outside it was dark, dark night. The unsympathetic wind whistled through the surrounding foliage like a flock of ghosts.

Once again, they were both made to duck down in the rear of the Jeep while Snake and Boner drove them back.

"Alright, out you get, ladies."

Britt was surprised to see that they'd been dropped off at their motel. The drive in was deserted now. The lobby lights were all off; most of the room lights were too.

The night was chilly; an unmerciful breeze gave her abused flesh goose pimples. She was literally out on her feet; the only thing keeping her awake was the pain between her legs. There was blood on her pants and it wasn't her period.

Snake sat humming and tapping the wheel. He wore a contented smile on his fat face.

Boner got out of the car and handed Lori their revolver and their knives. "Alright, hon, here's your stuff."

Looking from him to Snake, Britt regarded both men with disgust. Now that their ordeal was over and they'd not been killed, her anger was slowly rekindling. She was going to get even with these bastards; maybe even right now.

Boner shook his head at her. "Don't'cha think it, Blondie. I unloaded the gun first."

He forgot about her and grinned at Lori, who smiled back, albeit weakly. "Now, sweetheart, I recommend that you both get rid of this firearm in a hurry. The knives too. They're what the police call *evidence*. Wash 'em, wipe 'em off, and bury 'em somewhere. Throw the gun in a river outside of town. That way anyone could have used it to kill whoever you killed with it."

"It's not ours and we haven't killed anyone with it yet."

"Alright then, just be sure you ditch it once *you have* killed someone with it."

"Hey, Boner, hurry up! We don't want anyone to see us talking to them."

Boner frowned, his pimply face half-shadow in the night. "Yeah, that's another thing: the cops catch you; we ain't seen you, you ain't seen us? Understand?"

"Sure," Lori agreed. "We've no idea who you are."

"Good girl. You're as smart as you're hot."

"Can we go now?" Britt said. "It's been great being violated by you both, but I really need to get to bed so I can have nightmares about it all."

Boner leered at her. "Aw, Blondie, ain't you even gonna invite us in for a nightcap?"

Lori apparently assumed he was serious. "C'mon, man, both of us can hardly walk as it is. I'm practically bowlegged now. You guys fucked the living daylights outa us."

"Boner!" Snake growled. "Get your bony ass in here and let's roll!"

"Yeah, I'm coming." He reached into a pocket and handed Lori several small packets. "Some joints and other medications for your hurts."

He patted her on the cheek and walked round to climb in beside Snake.

Snake leaned out of the driver's window. "Okay now, both of you, a little neighborly warning."

Britt grimaced through her pain. "A warning?"

"Yeah, or you could call it unfriendly advice. Now see, girls, Raynham here's a real peaceful town like. So don't'cha start stirring up shit by killing our pretty ladies and gay folk. And definitely don't start cutting people's hands and legs off, alright?"

"Fuck off, O.K.?" Britt spat. "We kill whoever we want, and when and how we want to."

Snake looked like he'd get mad, then he laughed in her face. "Too bad it ain't us, right? But still, I like your spunk. And I know you liked mine—ha ha ha! Alright, you two, get your sweet asses off to bed. We'll see you both around."

He blew them a kiss and drove off.

"Shit, what a pair of assholes," Britt said.

Lori supporting her, they made their way back to Room 5. Every step of the way hurt Britt like she had gravel in her lady parts.

MONDAY

CHAPTER 22

Pagan

This morning Pagan woke up with the shakes. After opening her eyes, she lay in bed for a full ten minutes feeling like she was dying, twitching and shivering, and with her eyes watering.

Finally, she composed herself enough to get up. She ran into the bathroom and puked into the now-empty toilet bowl, then she sat on the edge of the bath to collect herself. She felt nauseated and her head swam like she'd lose her perch on the bath edge and topple forward onto the floor.

What on earth is wrong with me?

She felt sick, sick, sick. She'd never been a junkie before, but now she wondered if this was how withdrawal felt: this horrible feeling like you were being sucked inside yourself, like your body was feeding on itself.

The vomit came again. She stuck her head deep into the toilet bowl and let it out. When she seemed empty, she sat up again, only to be instantly hit by another wave of nausea which ducked her back into the toilet.

She remained there like that, seated naked on the side of the bath with her head in the toilet, for another ten minutes. Enduring the stench of her vomit was less torment than the feeling she got once she straightened up.

At last, her body seemed to resolve its irritation with itself. She sat up again, then when she didn't instant fold over with nausea, stood up and washed her face.

My eyes are still brown.

If anything, they were a darker brown now, like Belgian chocolate. That was the only *obvious* difference. Under her exterior, however, she knew she wasn't normal. She didn't *feel* normal. It wasn't only this sick feeling—even now she could feel the nausea threatening to return—her body just didn't feel right.

"Oh, Avex, what in Hell's damned blaze are you doing to me?"

That uttered, she flushed the toilet, wiped the edge of the bowl, and put the seat down. She urinated, flushed again, then got up and brushed her teeth. She spent a good while brushing her tongue to get the thick vomit stink off. Then she returned to the front room and flopped back down in bed.

Outside her window, the day was bright, the sun strong and high in the sky. It was a lovely day, but she didn't feel at all lovely.

After a while, feeling stronger, she checked if she had any email. On seeing a reply from the Red Octopus Corporation in her Gmail inbox, her spirits instantly rose.

It was a cautious reply: *We're discussing your request. Where are you?* It was signed 'Squidkid.'

She typed: *Thanks, I'm in Raynham. Please hurry.*

After a thirty-second interval, another message came in from Squidkid: *Don't worry, we're definitely interested in what you're carrying. Also, don't leave town. Everything will be resolved by tomorrow. Will contact you then.*

Pagan turned off the phone, and lay there considering the future.

Thank God I'm almost out of this nightmare. Soon, I'll be free of this goddamn demon and—

A knock on the front door startled her from her thoughts. The knock came again.

"Hold on, I'm coming!"

She pulled on her top and pants, then walked over to answer the door.

It was the cleaning woman, a tall, frumpy, mid-twenties redhead who in some cartoonish way reminded Pagan of Joker back in Boston. Her cleaning cart, loaded as it was with soap bottles and polish cans, vacuum cleaner and mop, and brushes and dusters and cleaning rags, looked like a surreal weapon of mass destruction.

"Can you please come back later?" Pagan asked. "At the moment, I've got this horrible splitting headache."

She wasn't lying: standing up was bringing on her nausea again. Her head felt like it was spinning, and the floor wasn't exactly in focus. Once this frumpy chick split, she was dashing back into the bathroom again. "I feel like . . ."

Then she saw that the cleaning woman was doing her best to look around her, checking to see who was in the room, perplexed as to who'd opened the door.

Pagan uttered the two syllables required to neutralize the spell making her invisible.

To the cleaner it seemed like the room's occupant had suddenly materialized from thin air in front of her. She stepped back and crossed herself. "Oh my God!"

That was a mistake. Pagan was repeating herself, "Please, can you clean later? I'm feeling . . ." when she noticed that the woman had a long cut on the back of her right hand, revealed when she'd raised it to make the sign of the cross. The wound was fresh and bleeding.

"How'd you suddenly appear like that?" the cleaning woman asked. "You startled me!"

"You've hurt yourself," Pagan said. "Your hand is bleeding."

She looked at it. "Oh, it's nothing. A door in the—"

Pagan never heard the rest. From deep inside her body a raging torrent surged up and consumed her.

She saw the cleaning woman's eyes and mouth spread wide with fright. Then she blacked out.

***

When Pagan came to, her motel room was full of blood again.

"Oh, unholy shit!"

In a panic she leapt off the bed and ran to shut the door. She latched the chain and leaned back on the door panting.

How long has it been open? How long was I out for? I stupidly turned off the cloaking spell; did anyone look in and see?

But clearly, no one had come around and looked into the room. If they had, there was A LOT to see.

The cleaning woman's remains were strewn everywhere like a USAF drone had blown her up. One of her legs (complete with bloodstained white pantyhose) was sticking out from under the bed; the other leg was wedged between the headboard and the wall. Half of her ribcage was on the bed, a lake of blood pooled inside it. Her lungs and heart were missing.

Did I eat them? Pagan realized that she did indeed feel full. She looked down at herself; her belly bulged out prominently, stretching her skin taut like she was in mid pregnancy. *Also . . . I don't feel those shakes anymore.* Instead she felt full of wellbeing and strength, like she was ready to tackle any challenge the world threw at her.

A wide splash of blood was up on the ceiling. The motel room walls were red in patches. The wall opposite the foot of the bed was covered with crimson polka dots as if she'd been throwing organs and body parts at it after ripping them off her victim's body.

She walked into the bathroom. The rest of the cleaner was in there. The woman's head was stuck upside down in the toilet bowl. Most of her innards were piled in the bathtub, though a few coils of intestine (topped by an eyeball) lay inside the washbasin.

Pagan groaned with almost physical pain at the sight. "Fuck! This nonsense really has to stop soon!" She pulled the woman's eyeless head out of the toilet bowl, then bent over it and began puking up some of the meat she'd eaten.

Afterwards, with the cloaking spell firmly back in place, she opened the front door, wheeled in the cleaning woman's cart, and began cleaning the room again.

CHAPTER 23

Joker

Joker was finishing a late breakfast. Wrapped in a peach-colored bathrobe, she was seated in the kitchen of her West Roxbury apartment with the radio on, listening to the morning news and drinking orange juice. Outside, the day was proceeding as normal for everyone else.

This morning, Joker wasn't in a good mood at all. Earlier, she'd woken up from a horrible, horrible nightmare in which Jesus had been nailing *her* to a cross.

She'd been lying on her back on the wooden cross. Her feet were already nailed in place and her right arm too. The Savior, who looked like Rob Zombie—just a whole lot meaner—held a hammer larger than Thor's, and nails that looked like those things that held ships together.

In addition, He was pissed off at her. Big time irate.

"I died for your sins, you little fool!" Jesus growled. "And you're wasting your time making magic and having sex with dogs? You think that's why I went to the cross?"

"I'm sorry, Lord!" she moaned. She was scared turdless, and even though Jesus looked like Rob Zombie, she just knew He could seriously fuck her up if she angered him any more. Yeah, Jesus *was* Lord, and now, where the hell was that horn-headed bastard Satan when she needed him?

Then she'd screamed as Jesus pummeled the last nail through her left palm. Straining her head that way, she could see the horrible mess her hand had become. There was blood all over the end of the wooden crosspiece and the damn nail felt like it had fractured all the bones in her hand.

"Oh, *now* you're sorry," He said. "Well *now* you'll know just what it feels like; what I went through to save your damned soul."

Her hands and feet felt like they were being roasted. Next, Joker screamed even louder when Jesus produced a crown of coiled barbed wire and jammed it down on her head. Now it felt like she had all the migraines on the planet combined.

Jesus raised her up and stuck the bottom of her cross in the ground. She was looking out over a landscape dotted with similar crosses on which were crucified all the members of the Abyss Club that she knew.

Damn, she thought through her agony, *the Savior's really been busy.*

Then He'd gotten out a whirling chainsaw and jammed it in her left side.

"Just for realism," He said.

An endless torrent of blood and water poured from Joker's side. She'd woken up covered in sweat, unable to move for five full minutes.

Even now, seated at her breakfast two hours later, the horrible dream refused to budge from her mind. She was a witch, her soul eternally pledged to Satan. She didn't believe in any Jewish messiah— Jesus was for pussies (and she didn't mean the one between her legs!)—but she did believe in her subconscious. She suspected it was warning her that something was about going awry in her life.

Her cellphone rang. She put down her glass of orange juice, pushed away her emptied cereal bowl, and picked it up.

"Hi, Nero."

"Good morning, Joker. Hope you slept well." Behind the calm greeting she sensed excitement.

"No, man, I frigging didn't. I had the most horrible . . . Aw, man, you're not calling about Pagan, are you? I've no leads yet. I'm just about hitting the streets to start asking around."

"Don't bother. We've found her."

That shocked Joker. "Where?"

"She's down in Raynham."

"Are you sure? How'd you find her so quickly with the masking spell she's using?"

He laughed. "Through the papers. Our girl's been careless. Last night she killed a man down there, then carved pentagrams into his body."

"She killed someone else?"

"Real nasty. She cut his dick off then shoved it up his ass."

"Really? That doesn't sound like Pagan."

"I didn't think so at first either, but I had the warlocks working on the case check Raynham for her spirit trails. It's her alright; she's all over the town like glue." He paused, then added, "Only thing is, because of Avex's doubled masking influence, the warlocks can't locate her exactly, else we'd have just dispatched a goat to fix her once and for all."

"You already tried that."

"Last time was an ambush. This time it'll work. We'll send the goat at night when she's sure to be asleep. But of course, we do need to know her exact location first."

"So, what should I do now?"

"Get down to Raynham and ask around. See if anyone's noticed a strange Gothish chick."

"If she's using a masking spell, no one will have noticed her."

"Yeah, that's right. Still, she might have slipped up, switched it off while trying to book a hotel room or something."

"O.K., I'll do that. Anything else I need to know?"

"Yes. We've got an agent there in Raynham. Her name's Sin. Sin Corbin. Only thing is—she's heavily pregnant at the moment, about to put to bed. She likely won't be much use in your enquiries, but she's a local—if you need anything, she'll know where to get it. I've told her to expect you, and she's already arranged for the stuff you need to take Pagan out. She'll drive you out to pick it up."

"O.K. I'll get packed."

"Girl, I . . . we're all counting on you to finish this."

"Forget the goat then. I'll clean up your mess."

"You do that, and you can write your own ticket with the organization. Say, Joker, baby, instead of exiling yourself to Brazil, how'd you like to run our Hollywood operation?"

"Wh-wh-what? Abysmal Films? I-I-I'd love to! But Mo Jackson . . . ?"

"Is dead. Four a.m. this morning, his wife Karlie walked in on him balling some black porno chick and shot them both. Then she stuck the gun in her own mouth and pulled the trigger."

"Oh . . . I'll take the job."

"Alright, kick Pagan's missing butt for us and it's yours: signed, sealed, and delivered, you're in the movie business. I gotta run now.

Sabrina will transfer funds for expenses to your account. And, yeah, call me at any time—day or night—if you need anything else."

He hung up.

Joker sat back, unable to believe her luck. *They're offering me Hollywood to get rid of Pagan? Wow, they're really desperate! Guess my bestiality shoot really impressed them.* Then she smirked. *Poor Pagan, you're so dead now, it's like you were never born. I'm erasing you from the human list.*

***

Joker was pragmatic. She would rather profit from the mistakes of others than make those mistakes herself.

Still, though she didn't doubt Nero, something about the matter felt odd to her. Yes, it must have been Pagan who'd sacrificed that man in Raynham, but why in Hell's glorious blaze would she give herself away like that by carving pentagrams on him? Or maybe the demon was making her act erratically?

Better for me, she enthused, now on an 'up' after the downer of her waking nightmare. She did the dishes, then walked into her bedroom. (The bedroom, like most of her apartment, had pentagram-inscribed wallpaper.) Her bed and other furniture was all carved with inverted crosses.

Pulling open her wardrobe, she got out a small suitcase and began packing. Her sense of urgency notwithstanding, this took a while. Joker always had a problem with making up her mind what to pack for a journey. Clothes and shoes were stuffed into the suitcase and ditched again, only to be repacked five minutes later. Finally, she reached a compromise with herself and got enough stashed in the suitcase to keep her for five days.

As always, getting packed had completely stressed her out. She got out her favorite vibrator, and sinking to the bed, parted her labia and stroked herself with it.

In a short while she was moaning and groaning and writhing all over the bed, losing herself in the delights of her body. Thoughts of a vengeful Messiah and the cross and nails were far away; soon they were all gone. Her fingers splayed the lips of her sex open, the vibrator buzzed sensation through the swollen bud of her clitoris and deep into her aroused flesh; through her body, seemingly into her very soul.

"Oh, my God!" she moaned as she came, embarrassed as always because, at this most critical of moments, she always called on the Hated One's name.

(She had tried saying [as was recommended in the *Satanist's Handbook*] "Oh, Praise Lucifer!" instead during orgasm, but that never worked for her. Somehow, it sounded false. Orgasm was the highest human pleasure; you needed to link such sensations to the highest deity available to properly express what you felt; which was God, not the Devil. She hated to admit it, but it was true. From what she'd read, lots of atheist chicks had a similar issue. She'd once shared these thoughts with a close friend who'd had the same experience, and who'd replied, "When you masturbate or copulate or ejaculate, Satan is second-rate.")

She rubbed the dildo at the entry to her sex, then slowly eased it in and stroked herself gently. She was careful not to penetrate herself too deeply: yesterday's doggy bruises. Her left hand teased her breasts, tweaking her nipples.

In a short while, her body reached its boiling point again, and another orgasm rendered her both mindless and powerless.

"Oh, oh, Jesus!" (This too was very annoying.)

After one more orgasm (she was glad that she'd not this third time called on the Holy Spirit to celebrate her passion), she got off the bed and walked naked into the bathroom for a shower. On returning, she dressed in a short blue dress and black ankle boots.

Carrying her suitcase, she left the apartment. *Raynham, here I come.*

The last word of the thought reminded her that she forgotten to pack her vibrator. She had no way of knowing if she'd meet any guys she liked down south, so she reentered her apartment and fetched the sex toy.

Thus fortified, she exited again and rode the elevator to the ground floor.

CHAPTER 24

Lori & Britt (Mostly Lori)

"Boner lied to us," Lori said. "The revolver's still loaded."

She replaced the cylinder, gave it a spin, then placed the lethal piece of metal on the nightstand. She peered at Britt. "How'd you feel this morning?"

"Utterly lousy."

The pair of them had just woken up. It was eleven a.m. on a bright Monday morning, and they could hear distant cars arriving and leaving town.

Lori got up and went to pee. While sitting on the toilet, she examined her emotions for signs of breakage. Last night had been . . . strange. The robbery, then the rape.

(At the moment she found it hard to apply the usual terminology for such nonconsensual sexual situations to herself. Though yes, okay, technically she'd no say in the matter, was it still rape when you enjoyed it so much?)

To her surprise and delight, she felt both whole and wholesome. She did still feel like killing herself (the gun on the nightstand tempted her with its promise of blissful annihilation) but it was a feeling like a 90-year-old might have; anyone that old had reasonably had enough of life and viewed death as a welcome exit from their decayed flesh.

Murdering herself could wait, however. At the moment she was having too much fun.

Now that the killing was properly underway, Lori was truly happy for the first time in years. She felt like she'd found herself, like she'd discovered her true purpose in life. There was no point in being depressed when *you knew* you had no future, when all that awaited you at the end of the road was death—the big zero.

She finished peeing and flushed, collected her brown hair into a ponytail with a rubber band, then walked back out into the front room.

Britt, though, clearly wasn't having any fun at the moment. She'd sat up in bed now, had two pillows behind her against the headboard, had the quilt up over her breasts, and was switching TV channels with the remote.

Her face . . .

Britt's lips were squeezed into a tight frown. (The lip swelling from last night was largely gone now.) Her blue eyes as she stared at the television reflected her trademark anger, all the more scary now that they'd both cast off society's restraints and were spitting in the eye of its demand for good behavior. There was a fundamental hatred in her eyes, one that roved like a caged tiger behind the pretty mask of her face.

Britt looked like a bomb primed to explode . . . again. And yet, she looked so vulnerable too, so hurt. Or *was she* hurt? Lori's heart went out to her.

But what can I do? What can I say?

She said, "How do you feel this morning? Does everywhere still hurt?"

Britt replied, "My pride hurts worse than my pussy." She dropped the remote control, and, eyes blazing cold flame, spun to face Lori. "*We're* the ones on a rampage here, for goodness sake. *We're* the ones supposed to be doing the robbing and fucking. And what happens? We get robbed and fucked by two greasy drug dealers! Shit—I feel so foolish."

Lori reached out a hand and touched Britt's. "Try to get over it. That's simply life for you: sometimes you win, sometimes you don't. We were simply on the wrong end of the dick last night."

"They didn't use rubbers, you ditz. They could have given us AIDS."

"Britt, we plan on dying at the end of this. What the hell difference does getting AIDS make?—AIDS takes years to kill you. And besides, I don't you remember you using rubbers when you deflowered Lonnie."

"That's 'cos he was a virgin, he *couldn't have* a disease!"

"Okay, that's true, but you didn't use condoms with Billy Two Shoes either."

"Lori, stop being such a goddamned sexual abuse apologist. You make a crap devil's advocate. They *raped* us! And that bitch Sin stuck a TV remote up my ass. It HURT."

Lori decided that an angry Britt was better than a feeling-sorry one. *At least I won't need to baby her.*

She said, "And *we've* been murdering people. Stop being melodramatic; it comes with serial killer territory—you fuck people, they fuck you back; sometimes twice as hard." She grinned coyly. "Besides, last night we were looking to get fucked anyway."

"Not against our will."

"Speak for yourself. I came six or nine times."

"It sounded more like sixty-nine. Look, stop talking before I start hating you instead of them." Then she appeared to calm a bit, which didn't deceive Lori: Britt never cooled down that easy. "How can you be so calm about what happened to us? We've been friends since childhood. You never once told me you had rape fantasies"

"I just told you, girlfriend—I had a come-fest. I haven't had orgasms like that before in my life."

"You're just a masochist."

"No, I'm suicidal, remember?"

"What's your point?"

"I'm viewing it this way: We both went out last night, right? And both got caught. *You* got raped, *I* didn't."

Britt suddenly looked close to tears. "You're my best friend; we're in this together. How can you say that?"

Lori tapped herself on the head. "Because it's all in the mind. Rape only occurs when there's no consent."

"So?"

"So, once it was clear that we couldn't get away without being screwed, I simply decided to go along with it. I made up my mind to get what I wanted out of it. That is, to have fun."

"That's forced consent; dubious consent at best."

"So? You don't know what it's like, not having a guy up your . . . for two whole years." She left a pause for Britt to reply. Britt didn't, so she continued: "You, on the other hand, were so angry that you didn't see the same opportunity I did, and seize the moment to—"

"Lori, for crap's sake, just keep quiet! *I get it.* One thing's for certain: you're no feminist advert. And as for Sir Galafat and Prick Charming, they also stole all our damn money."

"Not entirely. They gave us some dope in return. I think Boner actually gave us more than our cash would have bought. We've got pot and pills too. Even some of those nice black ones that Lonnie had. At least I think they're the same kind."

Britt made to get up from the bed, then winced and sat back again. "Hell, I'm so damn bruised! And it's my back door, not my the front yard."

Then her eyes turned cold as ice. Lori felt chilled when she spoke next:

"If I ever see Snake and Boner again, I'll kill them both. I'll cut both their stinking dicks off! Okay, so you got your depraved rocks off. But you've no idea how *I* felt. I felt . . ."

With a loud howl of rage, Britt suddenly leapt off the bed and ran into the bathroom, slamming the door after her.

Lori walked over to the bathroom door. She tried the handle. It was locked from within.

"Britt . . . Britt . . . are you okay? Look, I didn't mean it like that. I'm not saying that you weren't hurt, or that it wasn't a horrible thing to happen, just that I . . ." (*Just that I fucking loved it?*)

Inside she could hear Britt sobbing loudly. "I'll fucking kill them both! I'll murder them both if it's the last damn thing I ever do!" More loud weeping followed, then loud pissing, then loud flushing; then farting, then the sound of the taps, then more crying.

Lori walked back over to sit on the bed. *Yes, but they didn't kill us, you ditz. And they could have. Just forget the both of them already. They're armed and clearly dangerous, and can clearly look after themselves, and we'd better stay out of their damn way, for chrissakes!*

Lori really felt for Britt. Which (she suddenly realized) meant that this 'murder therapy' (if it could be so called) was working wonders for her. She couldn't recall when last she'd felt compassion or pity for someone else; usually all she felt was immense self-pity.

So yes, if I feel Britt's pain—and I do, I do!—even though I find it childish and misplaced, I'm definitely getting better!

Britt stormed out of the bathroom again.

She glared at Lori. "So it's official—you're a slut, I'm not."

Lori rolled her eyes; were they about starting this all over again? "I'm not a slut."

"Yes you are. Thank God you're dying at twenty. If you lived to be forty you'd be a duplicate of my mother. Oh, that's my *late* mother, fuck her departed soul."

"Whatever." Lori rubbed her crotch through her panties. "My pussy hurts a little. I'm sore, but I want more men—a whole lot more."

Now Britt rolled her eyes. "See? You're—"

"Britney Wilson, I just want to pack forty years of sex that I'm never going to have into my last week or so of life." She grinned. "You should too—like your mom said, they don't give 'unused pussy' refunds in Hell."

Britt ignored the reference to Joanna. "Hell?"

"Where else do you think we're going when we die? Do you honestly think God's going to let us into Heaven?"

"Does God frigging give a shit about what we do down here? Does he? Does he?" She was pacing back and forth across the room now, scuffing her feet on the light brown carpet while glaring at the pieces of furniture like *they* had sexually molested her. Oddly enough, her nipples were stiff. "Sometimes I wonder why I even believe He exists." She glared at Lori. "You know, maybe God doesn't even exist. Maybe religion is just a cosmic con? Maybe—"

"Don't get into a swivet over it." Then she had an idea of how to cool Britt down. "Hey—let's smoke some of the joints Boner gave us. Let's just mellow out for awhile." She grinned expectantly at Britt, "How 'bout it?"

Britt stopped pacing and looked at Lori. "O.K. But this doesn't change anything: I'm still going to kill your pimply Prince Charming before this is over."

Lori felt like she needed to salvage some self respect from this situation before Britt locked it into her head. Then she'd never hear the last of it. "Hey, don't get it twisted, alright? That ugly punk is by no means my Prince Charming. He's way too thin, and has almost no ass at all."

"He's your sixty-orgasm man. You just said he was great in bed."

Lori sniffed. Britt was such a donkey at times. She wondered why they hell she was even feeling sorry for her. Maybe she needed to be gangbanged more often? And this time by burly biker types who'd shred her condescending ass, so she'd need to have it stitched together? "Look, he was just a means to a frigging end. Let it go, O.K.?"

Britt looked to retort, but Lori was glaring so angrily at her that she gave in.

She lay down on the bed, groaned, "Shit, my ass hurts! How am I ever going to poop now?" then smiled contritely at Lori, "Okay, girl, lets smoke those joints."

Lori got out the marijuana; nine fatties. She began rooting around for matches, then pointed to the TV. "Hey, see if they're showing *The Bachelor* anywhere. I haven't yet watched this week's episode."

***

After they'd been smoking pot for thirty minutes or so, Lori said. "Look, I've a solution to your anger issue."

"I don't have an anger issue, just an asshole issue—my aching asshole and the assholes who made it ache. But . . . okay, I'm listening."

"Let's just take out your . . . our frustrations on someone else. We'll go out and look for a guy that looks like Snake—fat, middle-aged, and with a mustache—and completely fuck him up. It's a displacement therapy I learnt from my shrink—mentally shifting my depression onto another person, then imagining they've got my horrible life."

Britt creased her forehead. "Did it work?"

"Once or twice, then it seemed as pointless as everything else. That was how I wound up eating the dog's Prozac. I tried to shift my depression to Fifi, but apparently she was more depressed than I was. The little bitch had hardcore separation anxiety like you wouldn't believe. So I wound up twice as depressed and needed more medication."

Britt did her best to keep a straight face. She couldn't and burst out laughing.

"But in this case I'm certain it'll help," Lori finished solemnly. She wondered what Britt found so funny. This wasn't any kind of a laughing matter.

Britt thought awhile. "Yeah, let's do it. We need more money anyway."

CHAPTER 25

Britt

Standing there beside the highway, Britt already felt much better. A sweet sense of anticipation filled her. Soon now, soon, she'd get payback for what had been done to her last night.

She and Lori had meticulously planned this. After bathing and eating breakfast, they'd left the Sunflower Motel and walked up Broadway, heading out of town towards Raynham Park, looking for a suitable spot to take their victim to.

Finally, about two miles from the motel, they'd come on a seemingly disused right-hand turnoff which led through the woods to another turnoff.

There were actually two turnoffs here. The right one led down a muddy road. The weather-bleached sign beside it read: "McKinney's Pig Farm."

They went left. That road led in turn to a dirt track which led to an old wooden gate that seemed unopened since the days of President Eisenhower. Beyond the gate the road vanished into a paradise of overgrown grass and bushes, like the farmer had died on the road and become weed food.

Deep in here, there was no way anyone would see or hear anything they did. They'd nodded and grinned at one another, then headed back to the road.

There, they'd walked another hundred meters up the road and waited like birds of prey. Britt carried her travel bag so it looked like they were hitchhiking. The bag didn't contain clothes and cosmetics though, but instead held their guns and knives; and duct tape and a length of sturdy rope (both of the latter hastily purchased at a store); and also, a large bottle of mineral water to clean up with afterwards.

They were ready to strike.

They posed by the roadside chatting, regarding the passing cars and the woods opposite. Neither stuck a thumb out until Lori said:

"Hey, this one coming looks like Snake!"

Both quickly stuck their thumbs in the air.

The SUV—a blue Toyota RAV4—passed them, stopped, then reversed.

The driver flashed a smile. "Why, hello, young ladies. Do you need a ride south this Monday morning?"

Britt was delighted. Oh yes, Lori had excellent eyes. This man did indeed look like Snake. He was fat and middle-aged and had a black mustache and beard. He looked respectable in his gray suit and striped tie, and his face bore no traces of either lechery or dissolution, and he definitely didn't stink like Snake did, but she could overlook those faults in him. He'd do nicely.

She smiled demurely. "We're looking for a ride to Taunton, sir. We're—"

"Oh, that's on my route. Hop in, hop in!"

He unlocked the doors for them. Lori got in the front, Britt in the back.

"I'm Matt Lewis," he explained, as he put the car in motion again. "I'm a shoe salesman. We've a convention starting today in Westville, and—"

"Shut up, fattie, we've heard it before," Britt said from behind him.

"You're gonna be really late for your meeting," Lori added with a broad grin.

"Huh?" Matt asked, looking confused.

"Yeah, you are," Britt agreed, sticking her gun in his ear. "Now pull over into this turning right here. It's either that or lose your brains all over the windshield."

***

Ten minutes later, they had Matt Lewis tied naked to a roadside tree. His arms and legs were drawn around the tree trunk and bound tightly to each other by a rope running behind it, and he was also gagged with duct tape. Two more coils of rope bound his torso and neck around the tree. He wasn't going anywhere without help.

His blue RAV4 was parked by the abandoned farm's gate.

Matt's eyes were bulging with fear and he was sweating copiously. Britt liked him reeking of sweat—it made him smell more like Snake. (Oh, how she hated that bastard. Even now, she could feel Snake's fat stinky weight pressing on her suffering body as he used her for his dirty enjoyment, compressing her freed psyche and the expanded horizons she'd only recently discovered back into nothingness.) His body was pale and soft and hairy. Divested of clothing, she found him disgusting, which was another huge plus in his favor.

She turned to Lori. "How'd we make out cash-wise?"

Lori looked up from studying Matt's wallet. "Not bad at all. Three hundred bucks and two bank cards."

Britt nodded, then prodded Matt in the belly with the tip of her knife. She stuck the knife in about an inch deep, till blood was streaming down his body to his legs.

"Hmmph! Hmmph!!!" the bound man groaned.

She looked up at his face, a cold, cold smile on her lips. "Great, I've got your attention. Now listen, Matt. I'm giving you a choice. Do you understand me?"

He nodded.

"Good." She pointed over at Lori, then looked back at him. "Now, you're going to give us the PIN numbers of both your ATM cards or . . ." She reached down and grabbed his penis and testicles and squeezed hard. "Or . . . we're gonna castrate you." Still holding his genitals, she frowned at him. "So, man, which is it gonna be? Which would you rather part with: your dough or your dick?"

He began nodding fiercely, which she took to mean that he considered his penis his more valuable possession.

"Okay, now listen. I'm gonna take the tape off your mouth. If you dare yell for help . . . do you understand?"

He nodded again.

She ripped the tape off his mouth. Some of his mustache came along with it, leaving his upper lip all bloody.

"Please, please!" he gasped now that he could talk again. "I'll tell you!"

"I'm listening. Lori, you got a pen?"

She was still holding his genitals in her hands. She squeezed them painfully while Lori took down the bank card PINs. Already, she felt powerful again. No, Snake and Boner hadn't really leeched her of her new-found strength, they'd only introduced a little self-doubt into her.

Her female power was still there, packed under her painfully cracked exterior. Yes, even cramming that remote control up her ass hadn't been able to switch it off.

And now, using Matt here, she'd complete this ritual of rebuilding herself.

She looked at Lori, wondering how she was feeling—was the greatness of what they were doing affecting her too? Did she even understand this source of power, that by reducing someone else, you simultaneously increased yourself by the amount of self-worth you took from them?

She couldn't tell: Lori looked like regular Lori, consummately pretty but bland as dogshit. An emotional zombie. Lori was thoughtfully tapping her notepad with a pen.

Britt asked, "You got both numbers?"

Lori replied, "Stab him in the belly again. Not too deep though."

"No, don't!" Matt protested. "Somebody he—!" Britt instantly replaced the duct tape over his mouth. "Hmmpp! Hmmmph!"

She slapped him. "I warned you not to make any noise!"

She looked at Lori, eyebrows raised. "Stab him?"

"Just do it."

Britt didn't know what she was getting at, but she was feeling too good to argue. She stabbed Matt in the belly.

"Not too deep, and twist it a bit. Yeah, like that."

As Britt twisted the knife, Matt squirmed and wobbled his large form as best he could. He was too well bound to the tree, however, to stand any chance of freeing himself. Trussed up like he was, all he could do was suffer.

Britt kept twisting the knife in his belly. She dipped it another inch into the hurt flesh. She grew intensely aroused on feeling Matt's abdominal muscles rend at her command—the knife was her cock and she was fucking him painfully with it. (Oh, why was Lori saying to keep this shallow? She wanted to be deep inside this fat fool's body, like Snake had been deep inside hers.) She viewed with pleasure the fat in the cut, egg-yolk yellow beneath the spilling blood which dripped to redden his black pubic hair.

"Okay, that's enough," Lori said finally.

Britt pulled the knife out, releasing a further dribble of blood. "What now?"

"Take off his gag and ask him the PIN numbers again. The pain was to clear his memory. If he was lying before he'd have forgotten them now."

Britt laughed. "Lori, you're a genius."

"No, I just watch too much TV."

Britt ripped the tape gag off again, plucking off even more of Matt's mustache. Now his upper lip looked like he'd applied lipstick to it. She grabbed his sexual organs again and squeezed painfully.

Matt howled.

Keeping a straight face, Britt said, "Okay, ladies and gents, I'm Britt Honeypot Wilson, presenter of *Who wants to be a Eunuch?*, the TV show on which one unlucky contestant has to answer a series of fourteen questions to keep his manhood intact! On the hot-tree today we have shoe salesman Matt Lewis. Now, Matt, this next question is for your left testicle and half of the right one. Tell us, Matt, what are your two bank PIN numbers? Remember, one wrong answer means you'll never fuck a woman again. Sorry, that's a politically incorrect assumption. Are you *gay*, Matthew? In that case you'll never fuck another man! You'll become a permanent pillow prince, always receiving and never giving! Alright now, you've thirty seconds to tell Lori those damn PIN numbers. Better get them right, Matt!"

Lori was meanwhile laughing her head off at Britt's skit.

Still looking comic-serious, Britt nodded to the bound and bleeding man tied to the tree. "Lori's listening, baby! Spit out those numbers!"

Matt told them again. He was looking dazed now, like either the blood loss or pain had him entering shock. His pale body hung from the tree like the carcass of a dead whale, blood dribbling from him like he'd been harpooned.

When he was done speaking, Britt looked a question at Lori.

She nodded back. "They're both correct. He told the truth the first time." Then she frowned. "Yeah, one more thing: Hey, man what's your damn ZIP Code?" She shrugged at Britt. "Just in case. You know how finicky banks are about handing people back their own money."

Britt dug the knife into Matt's belly again but refrained from twisting it.

Matt howled out a further stream of numbers.

"Okay, we're about done," Lori said after noting the numbers down. She gazed sternly at Matt. "Hey! Are you sure this is correct or should we cut off your nose to confirm it?"

He nodded quickly when Britt waved the bloody knife in front of his face. "It's correct! It's correct!"

"So what now?" Lori asked Britt.

"Please let me go!" Matt pleaded. "I've never hurt either of you! You've got all my money! I was only trying to help you girls. I won't report—!" That was as far as he got before Britt slapped a new roll of duct tape over his mouth. She doubled, then tripled the tape. She didn't want it coming off while they did what she had planned.

She stepped back. Lori put her notepad away. Together they regarded Matt.

"I almost feel sorry for him," Britt said. "Considering what we're about to do."

"What d'you have in mind to do to him?" Lori asked. "Do we stab the shit out of him and stuff his dick up his ass like the last one?"

Hearing that, Matt began squirming and groaning loudly against the tree.

Britt licked her lips. She felt really aroused now. The power—the ability to do, to be!—filled her, intoxicating her. (At this moment, she viewed Snake and Boner and Ella and that horrible bitch Sin who'd stuck a remote control up her ass . . . she viewed them as little inconsequential turds floating in the toilet bowl of her greatness.) She shook her head. "No, while doing that comedy skit, I had an idea." She gestured over at Matt. "Besides he won our game show—we're not gonna cut his penis off."

Matt made a loud moan of relief and slumped against the tree.

Britt laughed wickedly. "Oh no. What we're gonna do instead is, we're gonna make him have sex with himself—help him fuck his own ass."

"Girl, are you losing it? How in the world is that possible? His penis won't ever stretch that far."

Britt laughed, "Oh it's possible alright; I got this all figured out. Just you give me a hand."

Matt squirmed as they advanced towards him and Britt knelt between his legs.

"Now don't be scared," Lori said, clapping her hands excitedly, "Britney here claims she's about granting you the indescribable pleasure of making love to yourself—no hands required. Just imagine those delicious endless hours of future enjoyment of wanking without touching yourself."

"For fuck's sake, will you stop jerking about?" Britt angrily reprimanded Matt. "I'm not going to castrate you. Just hold still. I have to cut your anus out of your ass."

On hearing that, Matt's eyes bulged with disbelief and he began squirming even harder and squeezing his buttocks tightly together.

Britt dug her knife into his buttock crack and sunk it in deep. Matt let out a moan that filled her brain. She loved the sound. She dug the knife in even deeper. Blood wet her fingers as she sliced first forward, then across.

Above her there was a sudden loud 'thump.' To a strangled noise, Matt went abruptly limp. Britt looked back and up.

Lori shook her gun at Britt. "I knocked him out. The noise?"

Britt looked angrily at Lori. *Shit! She doesn't understand this at all! She has no concept of the glory involved.*

Even so, the thrill of the kill was still hers to take. And . . . Matt being unconscious made the work at hand much easier to do. For one thing, he'd stopped clenching his ass shut. Now his hairy anal ring was bared for her surgical attention.

With his blood covering her fingers, she stuck the knife deep into the flesh around his anus and sawed around it, deeper and deeper—cutting through obstructions of meat and navigating around bone—until finally, Matt's entire rear passage—both his anus and rectum—popped out of him. Blood was pouring out in torrents now.

What she'd sliced out of his body was slightly ripped (excrement squirted over her fingers from tears in his rectum), but still in one piece.

Matt now woke up. His thick thighs trembled against her shoulders. It was such a sensual feeling. He was groaning again, but it was a weak sound, and she knew she'd finished him by relieving him of these organs she gripped in her bloody, messy hands.

(Yes, she decided grimly, Lori was right—this displacement therapy stuff really worked. After cutting into this man's body, she felt practically reborn. Him bleeding felt like she was the one bleeding, releasing in his blood all the poisonous semen that Snake and Boner had ejaculated into her.)

Without severing the colon attached to it, Britt pulled Matt's rectum forward between his thighs. She faced quite some stiff resistance from the colon, but the stubborn tissue holding his lower gut in place in his abdomen gave way before her own dogged insistence on extracting it. Slowly, like a python emerging from its hole, Matt's bleeding gut emerged from his body. Like spilled lubricant, blood streamed down his legs onto the grass.

"Gimme a hand," she grunted at Lori. "I wanna get this done before he croaks."

Crouching beside her, Lori helped. Together they dragged out about three foot of intestine so it looped between his legs like a skipping rope. Next, Britt stuck both her index fingers into Matt's anus, then pulled his sphincter open, fitting in her middle fingers too once there was enough room for them. To a muffled pathetic plea from the bound man, she forcibly stretched the anus wide.

"Okay, Lori, now stick his manhood into it."

While Britt held Matt's anus as open as a fisted vagina, Lori stuffed his penis into it; then she forced his entire scrotum in after his penis also.

Smiling with satisfaction, Britt released her grip on the anus so it shut around Matt's genitals like a cock-ring made of meat. Like she'd thought, including Matt's testicles in the package prevented the penis from slipping out through the anus again. Now it looked like he was wearing a tube on his manhood, a wet loop that connected the front of his crotch to its rear.

The grass between his legs was covered with blood, as was the bark of the tree he was secured to. The stuffed rectum bulged and there was feces on Britt's fingers which she wiped off on his belly.

They stood up.

"Wow!" Lori said in admiration

Britt grinned, dabbing squirted blood off her face. "See? Now the fat pig is screwing himself—doing himself in the ass. We should ask him what getting buggered feels like."

Lori scratched her head. "I'm confused. If a straight man fucks his own ass like this, does that make him bisexual or what?"

Had they asked him either question, Matt couldn't have replied: he had died sometime during the ghastly operation. His head lolled sideways. His eyes were wide and staring. There were tears on his cheeks.

Britt shrugged. She'd felt it happen—felt him die that was, felt that intoxicating rush of power fill her as he went limp for good. He'd served his purpose, which was to reinstate her in the pantheon of New Adult gods.

"Britt, you know how they say there's a thin line between genius and insanity? Girl, I don't know if you're psychotic or just super creative."

"Please bring the water over and help me get cleaned up."

Lori fetched the water.

"What now?" Britt asked once she'd gotten the majority of the blood off her face and hands, if not her clothes. (Lori only had dirty hands.) "Do we mark him up for Satan and blame it on Pagan again?" Now that she'd gotten what she wanted, she was willing to let Lori resume doing their thinking. In a way, it was almost essential that a goddess like herself—even one temporarily so—permit an underling to handle the mundane affairs of existence.

Lori slipped smoothly into the role of postmortem organizer. "Yes and no. We'll slice him up in case he's found, but we won't drag him off to the road like the last one."

"Why not? That defeats the whole point of it."

Lori grinned, then pointed at the corpse with its penis stuck up its anus. "You don't realize we've hit the jackpot with him."

Britt descended from her goddessness. "What are you talking about? What jackpot?"

"Remember he said he was driving down to a shoe salesman's convention in Westville?"

Britt nodded, then her eyes widened. "Hey, wasn't Billy Two Shoes headed there too?" (Ah, she wished Billy was here now—she'd ride him silly, ride him till his manhood broke. Her sex felt so wet now. She was so aroused, she'd explode if she just touched herself. But Lori had already made it clear that she didn't want to watch her relieve herself. Damn Kaminski's law.)

"Yes, yes, that's my point," Lori agreed. "Billy said the convention starts today. That means no one is going to be expecting Matt here to be anywhere else at the moment. Even if he doesn't call home for a couple of days. Even his office aren't likely to be too worried if they don't hear from him."

"Any picture of a family in the wallet?"

"Two little girls and a wife."

"*They'll* wonder where he is."

Lori walked over to Matt's blue SUV and got his wallet off the hood. "No, she won't be looking for him. He's a salesman; she'll be used to him being away. If he doesn't call home quickly, she'll likely think he's shacked up in a hotel room somewhere, screwing some prostitute." She handed Britt a color photo.

"Ooh, she's really mousy. Great boobs though."

Lori licked her lips and scuffed her feet on the grass. "What I'm getting at is, we've free and uncontested access to Mr. Matthew Lewis's car and money for at least three days before he gets reported as missing."

"This place is so secluded, no one might find him for weeks."

"Exactly." Lori grinned now, her eyes like a hungry wolf's. "We should be able to get several thousand dollars from his bank accounts before there's any kind of alarm raised." She shrugged. "Assuming of course, that he's got that much in the bank."

Thousands of dollars? Britt looked at Matt's corpse and laughed herself silly. It was utterly hilarious, how this corpse she'd painstakingly made had just provided all their needs.

She waved her knife at Lori. "C'mon, let's slice our message into his flesh."

"What should we write?"

"We need something really unholy, really nasty. What would a Satanist write?"

"How about 'Fuck Jesus, Satan is Lord?'"

"Hey, I like that! Yes."

Giggling like kids frolicking on a kindergarten playground, they got down to mutilating Matt's corpse further.

"We need to change our look," Lori said reflectively, while cutting a deep 'J' into Matt's chest, in the depths of which his ribs were visible as pale struts amidst his flesh. "Once done here, I suggest we change clothes at the motel and go shopping. Hair dye's a necessity at the moment."

Afterwards, they ditched the contents of the RAV4's trunk—shoeboxes, shoes, and a black travel bag—amongst the trees and drove off.

CHAPTER 26

Kev

Raynham Police detective Kev Parr was calmly having his lunch—donuts and muffins and bagels and a large cappuccino—in his parked squad car when he saw the two girls walking down towards him.

This was the south part of town. Kev was parked facing east by the Dunkin' Donuts on the New State Highway (or Route 44, if one preferred). Subway was right across the road from him and McDonald's was about sixty yards further up the road. It was a great area to have his daily lunch.

Kevin Parr—twenty-six, sandy-haired, and grossly overweight (the result of too much fast food while on duty, and too much steak and beer when off work)—at first regarded the two young women with merely routine male interest.

It was a warm Monday afternoon and the Raynham Shopping Center area was quite busy. There were lots of cars driving in and out, lots of people coming and going with shopping bags, and since it was summertime, lots of kids on the streets too angrily demanding that their mothers buy them stuff.

There wasn't much else to do, so Kev was enjoying a relaxing well-earned lunch, while keeping an expert eye out for trouble at the same time. And yeah, these Dunkin' donuts sure did taste good.

The two young women, both carrying full shopping bags, were walking towards him. One slim blonde, one curvy brunette. Both wore T-shirts over tight trousers and brand new pink sneakers.

Damn, Kev thought, *they're both really good-looking.* Especially the super-hot brunette, who had this slightly spacy look about her eyes that made her look real innocent. The blonde had a hard look to her which marred her prettiness somewhat.

For a moment, Kev wistfully imagined that he wasn't engaged to Honey Maxwell, one of Raynham PD's dispatchers: *Oh, lordy me, what I wouldn't do to that brunette if I got her into bed.* But it was just harmless fantasy: Kev loved his darling Honey, and while she was really skinny, with zero breasts and minus-zero butt, she more than made up for that with her culinary ability.

Kev never joked with his food. (It was largely why he always had his lunch in this part of town.) Since he and Honey had gotten engaged, Kev, already a four-hundred-pounder back then, had gained another thirty pounds, mostly around the gut.

He grimaced. Maybe in retrospect, a large guy like him dating Honey Maxwell was a bad idea. Two or three years from now, he'd likely be as fat as Beth McKinney, the pig farmer's wife; and wow, would that be a really bad thing. Beth McKinney was HUGE, almost the size of one of her husband's prize sows. Kev was stumped: how on earth did the old guy manage in bed? Or maybe he didn't bother? Maybe his groove tube simply didn't work anymore, scared into soft submission from fear of the bulk it had to penetrate?

Laughing, Kev snapped out of his reverie. The blonde and brunette were just at the hood of his car. Carrying their stuffed bags, both were looking straight ahead, and chatting.

There was a moment when the blonde looked into the car at him, waved, said a bright "Hi, officer!" and then they were past.

He regarded their rears as they crossed the road. Yeah, the dark-haired one had quite a behind on her. *Wouldn't I just love to sink my tongue between that fat ass and lick up her honey. But . . . yeah, I already got my very own Honey.*

Okay, but something was odd here: these two young ladies looked mighty familiar to him, and he didn't think they were from Raynham. Or were they the Town Clerk's nieces, who'd come around last year during the big August barbeque?

Then it hit him: these two were the ones in that BOLO they'd got yesterday, about two runaway girls from Boston, who'd . . . what they'd done almost made him lose his lunch.

He picked up his car radio to call into the station for backup, then hung it up again. Were these really the fugitives? (One thing about Raynham was, lots of shoppers drove in from Taunton, Attleboro, and Middleborough also to do their buying here, so just seeing familiar/unfamiliar faces didn't mean anything.)

He looked across the road again. Both young women were outside Subway now, talking like they were trying to make up their minds whether to go in for sandwiches or not.

No, he decided, *it ain't them. These ones are too pretty to be serial killers.*

Then the blonde one looked across at Kev's squad car. He saw her nudge her friend, who looked back at him too. Like they were sharing a joke, they both began laughing.

That laugh decided Kev. For some reason, he got the idea that they were laughing over having outsmarted him. It was irrational, but he also felt they were laughing about how big he was: "Just look at the big super fat cop." Or, "Hey, girlfriend, so now you know why they call the police 'pigs,' right? See how much like a hog that one is?"

Angry now, Kev decided to investigate. He quickly chomped the rest of his donut, finished up his cappuccino, brushed the crumbs off his uniform shirt and pants, then stepped out of the vehicle. He loosened the strap on his holster and hitched up his pants.

He prepared to cross the road to interview the two young women, who were both looking away from him and towards Subway again.

"Hey, Cousin Parr, how's it going?"

Kev knew the voice. A tattooed hand was waving at him from the shotgun window of a passing yellow Jeep. That would be Boner Hewitt, along with Snake Corbin, his partner in crime. Boner was a distant, distant, distant cousin of Kev's (so distant that their family connection could be a flock of migrating gulls) and they'd attended high school together, but they'd never hung out, or wanted to.

The Jeep turned the next corner and vanished. Kev grimaced with disgust and relief. He couldn't stand his punk cousin. He had his suspicions—still unfortunately unproven—that Snake and Boner were dealing drugs.

And then there was that case a year ago when a hitchhiking junkie couple had gone missing and their ID had later been found in Snake's possession. Snake, however, had claimed that his wife Sin found the missing couple's wallet in the parking lot at Rudy's when she'd driven out there looking for him after they'd had a fight; and that he'd been about returning it to the police station but had forgotten. As was to be expected, Sin backed him up, as did Boner's girlfriend Ella, who said she'd been in the car with Sin that night when she'd noticed the wallet. How anyone could notice a black wallet in the dark, no one had explained. (And as to why Snake had walked down to Rudy's rather than drive his Jeep? Sin claimed that during their fight she'd hidden the car keys so Snake couldn't leave the house. The fight had supposedly been because he wanted a kid and she didn't.)

Try all they might, they couldn't pin either a murder or kidnapping rap on Snake and Boner. Besides, the junkies were never spotted again. So maybe everyone had just imagined them, right?

Kev Parr thought otherwise. He'd heard rumors that the pigs at McKinney's farm were occasionally fed 'enriched' mash as a treat, 'enriched' with meat generously provided free of charge by Snake and Boner. And since both sleazebags claimed their everyday occupation to be 'scrap metal dealer' not 'butcher,' where did all that free meat come from?

But, even in investigating that, there was a problem . . . a BIG female problem . . .

By now Kev was almost beside the two young women, who'd apparently forgotten about eating and were on the other side of the block of shops, gazing into the window of Trends, the jewelry store.

"Hey, ladies, hold on a moment. I wanna ask you a few questions."

He was shocked. Both girls turned startled faces towards him, then set off walking fast down the row of shops.

"Hey, you two, I said wait up! This is the police!"

They pretended not to hear him, almost knocking over Amy Truffet's baby carriage in their haste. (Amy was coming out of the Copy To Copy next door to Trends.) And poor Amy with another bun baking in her oven too.

Kev hurried after them. *Aw, shucks! Are they really the ones?* Still he didn't grab his radio and call the station.

There was a reason for that; the same reason he'd so far not dared investigate Snake and Boner's meat contributions to McKinney's pig farm.

The problem was, Raynham's Chief of Police Tina Kravitz was old Ed McKinney's daughter. Kev wasn't risking his job by going against her.

The Chief was a naturally bad-tempered woman who was always on Kev's case over his being, "Too fat for police work, kid; you need to either jog the slob off or emigrate to Japan and take up sumo wrestling."

The accusation always stung Kev. *Chief shouldn't nag me . . . no, not just me . . . everyone . . . so damn much.*

An irascible woman at the best of times, Chief of Police Kravitz was currently lighting firecrackers under everyone's asses because of Cody Jones's death. She'd known Cody since he was a kid; was a tight friend of his mother's. She'd sworn she was gonna get the Satanist bastards who'd cut off Cody's dick and stuffed it up his ass if it was the last thing she ever did.

Kev, a good honest cop, agreed in principle. Still, at the moment, he was keeping well out of Tina Kravitz' way. (The brief memory of how Cody died almost made him lose his lunch again. How the hell could anyone stuff a man's manhood up his ass?)

And this was all of course before the BPD showed up this morning saying Cody's death was likely connected with their runaway Boston witch, the one who'd already killed seventeen people.

Kev was appalled: *Good Lord! Is the crazy bitch training for the Murder Olympics or what?*

(There was additional weirdness involved here as well: According to the BPD, AT&T had twice picked up signals from the murdered Townsend woman's line bouncing off their Raynham cell towers. Data usage: the fugitive witch [who'd stolen her victim's phone along with her car] had apparently been sending/receiving email. Even then though, the phone company had found it impossible to narrow down her location in the area. AT&T's tracking software had apparently all gone mental once assigned the task, claiming the witch was both here in Raynham and not here at the same time. And meanwhile her cellphone signal had been leaping from tower to tower like it was a hare. Now how was that for strange?)

So, no, Kev wasn't calling into the station till he was damn well sure that these were the right fugitive girls he had here. Definitely not with everyone so on edge over yesternight's Satanist murder.

Kev knew that if he got everyone worked up over nothing, he might as well just retire from the cop business, his life wouldn't be worth living otherwise.

The girls walked on faster, past the Mass Audiology shop now, their tight asses bubbling in their pants, purchases clutched to their breasts, while Kev huffed and puffed after them like the big bad wolf. Thankfully this was a short block; the end was just fifteen yards off.

"Hey, you two! Stop in the name of the law!"

Then the girls suddenly ducked into the last shop on the block: Alice's Boutique.

Seeing that, Kev slowed his gasping run to a gasping walk. He'd seen this before: the perp ducks into a shop and next thing you knew, you got a gutful of lead if you weren't cautious.

Kev pulled out his gun and double-checked that the safety was off. He cocked it, then, after peering in between the storefront manikins to confirm that the girls were still in the boutique, dashed past the display window to the front entrance.

He ducked into the shop, then growled, "Hey, freeze, you two! Put your goddamn hands up where I can see 'em!"

Then he froze, puzzled. He looked quickly around the shop, then at Alice Spring, the elderly proprietor, who stared back at him equally perplexed.

"What's the matter, Detective Parr?" Alice was a kindly old widow with a dignified handsome face.

"Alice," Kev wheezed, holding his gun pointing into the shop and fighting to make himself heard through the layers of chest fat that felt like they were smothering him, "where's the two girls—the blonde and brunette—that just ran in here?"

"Oh, they're over there by—" Alice shut up and looked twice as perplexed as before.

Other than for Kev, herself, and her niece/assistant Tricia, her shop was empty.

Tricia gasped. "I coulda sworn I saw 'em come in a minute ago. Look, here's their bags, right here."

Kev looked down. Yes, four shopping bags stuffed with clothes and shoes and makeup sat by the counter.

Whilst peeking between the racks of clothes and rows of manikins, Kev Parr smacked his head in disbelief. *Oh no, there's no way I'm reporting this back at the station. The Chief will have my balls for lunch.*

CHAPTER 27

Britt, Lori, & Pagan

Detective Kev Parr had deduced correctly: the two fugitive girls *had* ducked into Alice's Boutique just so they could ambush him before continuing their flight.

Britt and Lori's stolen blue SUV was parked just across the road. They could simply have run to it, climbed in, and sped off, but then the cop would be certain to note down both the make of their car and its number.

So they'd decided it was more pragmatic to kill him instead.

The two shopkeepers would just be collateral damage. An excitement fluttered in Britt's body. *Oh, yes! Our body count is about rising again.*

Her finger tightened on the trigger of the revolver as the fat cop ran into the boutique. She glanced left: Lori also had her Ruger out and was aiming at the door. "Let's fill the pig full of holes. Make an example out of him."

"Don't shoot," a voice whispered just before they squeezed their triggers. "He can't see you."

Shocked, they both looked back.

Pagan—Susan Harris—was frowning at them. She nodded. "Yes, *it is* me, and yes, I said 'don't shoot.' They can't see or hear you now. Just listen to what they're saying."

Confused, Britt spun back to stare at the fat policeman, the old woman, and the young girl.

"I'd swear they were standing over there a moment ago," the old woman was saying.

"Me too," the assistant added.

Gut hanging over his belt, the fat cop—Wow, was this guy BIG or what?—was scratching his head while sweating profusely. He had large damp patches at his armpits and all. He looked as confused as a cobra dropped into the mongoose pen in a zoo.

"Hey, where'd they just vanish to?"

Now quite scared, Britt turned to stare at Pagan again. "How come they can't see us?"

"Yeah," Lori seconded. She looked worried too.

Pagan rolled her eyes. "Duh? I'm a witch, remember?"

"Oh . . . *that.*"

"It's a simple masking spell."

Gun held at the ready, the policeman was now walking between the clothes racks, peeking into empty spaces. They got out of his way, pressing themselves against a lingerie display. Britt found it creepy, the way he stepped past them without noticing. He even looked right at her, but didn't see her. He brushed against her, so close she smelt the sweat forming on him. His expression was so baffled that her fear departed her and she laughed.

The cop strode past them and began peering through a manikin display of summer dresses.

Britt returned her attention to Pagan. "Pagan, what are you doing here?"

Pagan shrugged. "In here? Girl stuff—I'm shopping." She hoisted up a bag full of clothes and frilly panties. I'm wearing everything else I've got, and it stinks to high heaven now, particularly my underwear."

"I mean *here* as in *Raynham?*"

Pagan pushed a wisp of black hair out of her eyes. "It's a long, long story. C'mon, let's go back to my place, I'll explain there."

Lori asked, "You're sure they can't see us?"

The witch grimaced. "You'll see. Pick up your bags and let's go. My car is outside in the lot."

The policeman had just completed his tour of the store. Back at the counter, he holstered his gun then said to the two women, "There's frigging no one in here."

"Kev, we can both see that," the girl replied.

"Okay, here's what we're gonna do," he said in a hushed voice like the walls had ears. "Look, if we tell this to anyone, they'll all say we're nuts, okay? I mean, vanishing women? So let's just keep it quiet—there never were any girls." He wiped his brow with the back of his hand. "I must've just imagined them in the heat."

"I'm fine with that, Detective Parr," the old lady agreed. "No girls came in here today." She looked sternly at the younger woman. "Tricia?"

"Okay, Aunt Allie, I didn't see no one, either. I hallucinated it too. B-b-but if that's the case, where'd these four bags come . . . hey, where'd those shopping bags go? I'd have sworn they were here a moment ago!"

"I won't." The cop wiped his brow again, catching the sweat before it dropped onto the front of his overstuffed blue shirt. "I don't know what's going on today, and I don't care anymore." He slammed a hand down on the counter. "Nothing happened, and damn . . . now I'm feeling hungry again."

Shopping bags firmly in hand, Britt, Lori, and Pagan pushed the front door open and stepped out of the boutique.

Behind them the conversation continued:

"It has to be that new Satanist cult that's in town," the old woman was saying, "the one that killed poor Cody Jones."

"Oh, but that's just horrible, Kev, ain't it? Have you guys any idea who—"

The closing door truncated the sentence and then the three of them were standing by the parking lot.

"This way," Pagan said, leading them over to the tree-shadowed lot extension and a white Honda Accord. "Here's my car."

Then she gestured back towards the shops. "Shit. I'd wanted to get some earrings from Trends too, but that'll have to wait."

Britt pointed across the road. "That's *our* car over there. Lead the way, we'll follow you.

Pagan nodded then opened the Honda's rear door and dropped her bag of clothes on the backseat. When she straightened up again, her face wore a puzzled look. Britt and Lori were still on the sidewalk, waiting for a black truck to roll past so they could cross the road.

"You know," Pagan called across to them, "you guys must have heard what that old lady back there said about the 'new Satanist cult in town?' I know she was referring to me, but I swear to God I never killed that guy. I didn't do it."

Britt nodded sagely. Lori made a point of studying a black cat sitting by one of the elms shading the lot.

Inwardly, both were wincing, remembering how they'd just left another corpse to be blamed on Pagan.

***

The drive over to Pagan's place was uneventful: no cops; not even a red traffic light to slow their passage.

The big surprise came when all three girls realized that they were staying at the same Sunflower Motel. And that Pagan's room was only four down from Britt and Lori's.

They parked in front of their respective rooms, dropped their shopping bags by their front doors, then walked back, meeting halfway between them.

"Okay," Pagan asked, "your place or mine?"

"Yours," Lori said. "I could do with a change of wallpaper."

"Okay, but don't complain about the smell when you get there." Then she frowned. Shit! Meeting you guys made me forget to buy food. Not like I'm hungry now, but for later?"

Britt said, "That's okay, we bought some. It's all cheese sandwiches though. We were going to get other stuff, but then"—they were standing beside a window, so she lowered her voice—"that cop sighted us and . . ."

"Wow," Lori whispered, "did you see *the size* of that guy?"

"Look, guys, *relax*. No one can see or hear you as long as you're with me."

Britt had forgotten. "It doesn't wear off?"

"Not until I tell it to." She grinned. "So don't either of you dare piss me off or I'll hand you both over to the law myself." She gestured down the walkway linking the motel rooms. "Come on then, I need to get off my feet."

"I'll join you two," Lori said. "Let me put our stuff away in our room and bring some sandwiches."

She jogged off right, Britt followed Pagan left.

"Wow, I see what you mean about the stink," Britt said once they were inside Pagan's room. "Did a rock band die in here?"

Pagan said. "Go look in the bathroom."

Britt opened the bathroom door. Then she stood stupefied amidst the reek of blood, excrement, and other miscellaneous spilled body fluids, staring at the completely destroyed body that filled the bathtub.

She could just about make out that the human remains in the tub were female: the splayed fingers had chipped brown nail polish on them, and the severed and eyeless head under the toilet bowl had smeared lipstick on it . . . but the rest was just a jumble of shredded cloth and gore. Two feet in blood-splattered white sneakers lay at opposite ends of the tub, separated by a mound of torn flesh that was studded with part of a bra, intestines, half of a liver (Where was the other half?), shattered bones, and diverse other stuff that she assumed must be from within the human body, but which she couldn't place.

Fuck, she thought, *this is just so frigging awesome.*

She turned in the doorway to face Pagan, who was sitting on the bed with an expectant look on her face.

"Judging from what I heard about you guys on the news, I thought you'd appreciate the sight," Pagan said drily.

"Wow!" Britt said. "I thought me and Lori were good, but this . . . this is just so—"

Loud knocking interrupted her.

"That must be Lori." Pagan got up to let her in.

Lori walked in and dropped a bag of food by the fridge. Then she wrinkled her nose like she'd gag. "What the hell is that smell?"

Britt began giggling like mad. "Come see, come see."

Lori walked into the bathroom, yelped once, and then next came the guttural sounds of her throwing up.

Britt walked over to the bed and lay down beside Pagan. She kept on giggling.

When Lori appeared in the bathroom door a minute later, she had a tight but manic look on her face. "What the fuck happened in there? Who the hell is that? What did you do to her? Why did you do it to her? Shit, I need some pot to calm me down!"

Before they could stop her, she'd opened the front door and left again. They heard her footsteps running down the walkway.

After a pause of a few moments Pagan looked from the open door to Britt. "Is she always like this?"

"Lori? Nah, she's super-cool most times. Just don't ever feed her uppers . . . or those black pills—I've no idea what they're called—or she'll go total loco on you." Then she pointed to the bathroom door. "So it's true, you really did kill all those people? Seventeen of 'em?"

Pagan sighed loudly. "It was actually fifteen. I got framed for my parents' deaths."

"*I* wasn't," Britt said musingly. "At least, technically I *didn't* kill my mom, but I'm wondering if I should have, you know?"

"No, I don't frigging know," Pagan retorted angrily. "Do you think I'm enjoying this crap?"

"You're not? We definitely are." She grinned. "Hey, look! Miss Pothead's back! How do you feel now, you wimp?"

Lighted joint in hand, Lori stamped in through the door and slammed it shut, then she dropped onto the bed beside them. "Much better, thank you very much." She pointed to the bathroom door. "It was just the shock of seeing *that*." her gaze flitted to the bag of food. "And now, puking up like that's got me all hungry. You two don't matter if I go ahead and eat something, do you?"

Without waiting for their reply, she got out a sandwich, ripped off the nylon wrap, and bit into it. "Ah, that's better." Then she looked at Pagan, who in the meantime had kicked off her shoes and lain back on the bed with her arms folded behind her head. "Hey, why're you looking so glum? If you're gonna fuck people up that good, you might as well take pleasure in it like we're doing, right?"

"Shut up, both of you, please!" Pagan shrieked. "This isn't some goddamn game."

"It is for us," Britt said. "We're heading on out and taking as many miserable souls as possible with us."

"You tell her, girl," Lori said, taking a deep drag from her joint.

"Listen," Pagan said, "you've no idea what I'm talking about." Tears pouring from her eyes, she pointed to the dismembered body in the bathtub. "That is part of a nightmare of the kind you never, ever, want to experience." Then seeing their confused expressions, she added, "Look, I don't even remember killing her."

"Wow, that's really messed up," Lori said.

"It sure is," Britt agreed. "Tell us more."

"Oh, I'll frigging tell you alright," Pagan growled. "Just don't interrupt me, or I'll zap you both into frogs."

Lori grinned. "We won't, we won't; tell, tell, tell, tell, tell!"

Britt winced at her. "You know drugs are really bad for you, right?" Then she looked at Pagan. "Please go on. Seriously, we won't interrupt."

Pagan nodded. "You won't believe what I'm gonna tell you, but what the hell—someone needs to know the truth."

She began recounting all that had happened to her over the past three days.

CHAPTER 28

Pagan

Pagan was surprised to find that Britt and Lori didn't doubt her tale.

"Oh, we definitely believe you," Lori said when she was done speaking. "What's happened to you is the sort of thing that happens, and keeps on happening, but no one ever believes it, see? Everyone thinks that that's just movies—like the X-Files sort of stuff—and if you go around telling people about it you wind up in the madhouse. But it does happen, you know? Witchcraft and demon possession and all that other weird stuff." The room was full of marijuana smoke now and Lori had just lit a third joint. She nodded sagely. "Oh yeah, this kinda shit does actually happen for real, in real life. It's just that people never believe that it actually does."

After Pagan had understood the basic gist of her stoned ejaculation, she looked at Britt.

"Hell yes, we do believe you," Britt agreed, her face all screwed up and serious where Lori's was lax. "Even Hollywood's best scriptwriters would have trouble making this stuff up. *That's* what happened to your parents' house? Wow! Ah, so *that's* what happened to your eyes—I thought you had dark contacts in . . ." Then she frowned. "Hey, Lori, stop being so damn selfish and pass the fucking joint."

"Sorry." Lori handed it over. Britt took a long drag and lay back, holding the smoke deep in her lungs. Then she focused her attention on her toes, wiggling them and checking between them for dirt.

Lori, meanwhile, was saying, "So, Pagan, this demon of yours, it needs blood and murder, right? I don't see too much of a problem there. Just hang out with us—we'll provide it plenty to eat. Yes we will, it can have our leftovers. We're gonna do a whole lot of killing. Sacrifices? Oh, well, we don't mind sharing the corpses."

Pagan winced. "Guys, I keep telling you—this isn't any fun for me. I'm just barely holding on here: my own people the Abyss Club are out to kill me. And worse, something is very messed up inside my body, and I'm hoping to God that the ROC get back to me before it's too late to save me." She almost burst into tears but managed to control the salt water threatening to spurt from her eyes.

Pagan was more-than-a-little confused by her two companions and their motivation for mass murder. She quizzed them both, but the results were largely non-conclusive:

"Why do you two want to die?"

"I'm suicidal," Lori patiently explained through exhalations of pot smoke. "Existence is a black hole constantly vacuuming out bleeding chunks of my sanity."

Pagan nodded blankly, then looked at Britt. "What's *your* reason?"

"I'm her best friend. She's contagious."

"And so . . . ?" she prompted.

"Yeah, I'm suicidal," Lori said. "You know, like in a good way? The more people I kill the less I feel like dying myself? I think I've discovered my true calling in life now. It's almost like I could start a religion, you know. Kick-life's-ass Temple."

"Hey, I like that, Kickass Temple. Let's do it."

"No point though—we won't live long enough."

"Yeah, I forgot that part."

"So, anyway, like I was saying, I feel *good* now. For like the past three years I've felt like my own excrement, you know, those hard round things you pass out and flush away 'cos they're no use to your interior anymore. I mean that's how I felt, and it was just horrible. Feeling like turds, I mean. Then half of the rest of the time, I'm down in this Pit, which is a black, black, black, sort of cozy hole place which makes me feel like I'm floating in outer space . . . it's nice and warm and I'm happy in there . . . I think the Pit loves me, but then I realize that it's just fattening me up for the kill . . . the Pit I mean, it views me as food, and suddenly it grabs me . . . then it sucks the life out of my brain, you see . . . ? But now, I'm free and I'm killing people and suddenly . . . well, view it like this: the people I'm killing are now the turds I'm pooping out, you know, and once I've flushed their worthless lives down life's toilet I feel great, much much much better than I do on Prozac . . . so okay, like I was just saying, yeah, I'm a really wonderful suicidal right now."

She grabbed the joint back from Britt and took a long pull of its contents.

"But don't you feel bad about it? The killing, I mean."

"Do you?"

"Yes I do."

"We don't. It's fun. Screw the dead."

"Yeah, fuck 'em. And . . . fuck gun control too. If they'd owned guns they'd still be alive now."

Pagan didn't get more than that from her companions. To her mind, both seemed to have batted reality way out into the stands: a sociopath's 'home run' logic that permitted the ditching of the rules of everyday life.

Yeah, these two were playing for keeps.

She wasn't actually judging them (though it was hard not to). Each time she looked through the bathroom door at what remained of the cleaning woman, she figured she was just as bad as Britt and Lori.

The afternoon continued in a similar vein. None of them had anywhere to go.

Lori went off to fetch their pills. They smoked, doped, and joked the hours away. Pagan also had some beer in her fridge, which they drank.

As they got progressively more stoned, their discussions grew even more surreal, inane, and (to Pagan's mind) insane. Some of it the seeming disjointedness of Britt and Lori's conversation clearly had to do with the drugs they were all using; the rest was likely just because it was spillover or fallout of other talks of theirs that Pagan hadn't been party to. Particularly about their (primarily Lori's) need to get laid:

"Lori, aren't you tired of dating your vibrator?"

"Britt, I can't get a guy."

"That's 'cos all the guys we know, sorry . . . once knew . . . all knew that you were crazy."

"Stop calling me crazy. I'm not—"

"You've been in a madhouse. Sorry, but you are crazy. Look, these guys we're gonna fuck, we'll pick 'em up in bars, like that one, Rudy's Truck Stop. One night stands. They don't know shit about your mental history, and even if you shouted it out with a megaphone, most would be too drunk to care anyway."

"That's so cold and unromantic."

"Lori, you can't have everything in life. You wanna get laid or not?"

"I do . . . I do . . . but, it's not as simple as that, you know what I mean? I'm not a particularly social girl at the moment, and down in the Pit where I've been living all this while, it's not helped my romantic networking capability any. I believe what I'm trying to say is, that I'd like to meet a guy who actually cares about me, someone who recognizes that I'm more than just big breasts and big buttocks and a beautiful face. A guy who understands that I'm more than the sum of my individual parts, great as those admittedly are. So, I think that particularly at this vulnerable stage of my life——you know how I mean that——with it being so short now, I mustn't settle for anything less than the best. So yes, I want romance, even if it only lasts five minutes, our eyes meeting over a chill glass of beer, but it'll mean something, Britt. I want a fucking soul mate not a hole-mate!"

"Lori, what's the big deal? You didn't give a shit about it last night with that idiot Boner."

"That was different, that was so very different."

"Why, because you weren't stoned and drunk up to the gills then?"

"It was just different. I was in an existentially sexually tormented place, being restrained and pumped delightfully hard by Boner's boner, and I came and I saw stars and I conquered my fears of the Pit, and then I came and saw yet more stars and conquered my fears again, and I came and came and came again, and saw and conquered the Brits. And I don't mean your Britt, Britt, I mean the European Brits way across the Atlantic. Julius Caesar said that, you know."

"Not unless he was in bed with some English hooker, he didn't. Fuck, Lori, drugs are oh so bad for you."

"No, they're not; they enable me see clearly, for miles and miles."

Lori popped another pill, said, "Aw, screw you, Blondie," to Britt, then turned a dopey grin to Pagan.

"Hey, witch girl, do us a magic trick!"

Pagan stiffened. Despite keeping pace with them as far as the drinking and pill-popping was concerned, she still maintained a barrier of caution. "I can't. With the demon lurking inside me; it's much too dangerous."

"Aw, come on, witch girl! Just a little one! Just a small one."

"Yeah," Britt seconded, "Lets see some MAGIC!!"

The pair began beating on the bed. "MAGIC! MAGIC! MAGIC! MAGIC!!! MAGIC!!!!!!!!!!"

The noise convinced Pagan to oblige them. "Okay, but only a little, tiny, teensy-weensy trick."

"So long as it's . . . MAGIC!!!!!" Lori screeched.

Pagan winced as the noise hit her ears. "Give me your hand," she told Britt. She didn't trust Lori in her state of inebriation.

Britt stuck out her hand. Pagan turned it palm upward then traced out a pentagram on Britt's palm with a finger. Then she muttered a spell.

"Wow! This is real magic!" Britt exclaimed as a tongue of flame burst into being over her hand. The fire, a mingling of bright orange and yellow, was about four inches high; it flickered and licked the air over Britt's palm, spilling light and heat into the motel room. It had a curved base and between it and her hand was a space of about an inch.

Britt stuck a finger into the space between the flame and her hand. "Wow, I can feel that it's hot, but it's not burning me."

"Not bad, huh?" Pagan asked with a touch of pride.

Then the next moment, she was deeply regretting her action. Like a rising tide, she felt Avex stir inside her. Her eyes widened in fear.

Her terror that the demon was about overpowering her mind though, was cut short. Instead, what happened was: she suddenly had the shakes again. Her body began trembling like she was doing uppers (she was!), but it was way more than that.

Suddenly, Pagan felt just a wee bit hungry, and it wasn't for cheese sandwiches. Alarmed, and realizing what she'd unwittingly done to herself with her innocent display of sorcery, she stared at her companions.

The fire still burnt over Britt's palm. Lori was lighting a fresh joint in its orange flames. Pagan waited till she was through, then she leaned forward and blew out the fire.

"Aw," Britt moaned in disappointment, "why'd you do that, Pagan? It was so pretty. I saw myself in it: a purging fire consuming those unworthy of life."

"Yeah," Lori said in a low voice that seemed made of smoke. "That was a great trick, one of the best ever." She grinned broadly. "Hey, do another."

"That's way too much magic already," Pagan retorted. She knew it was the drugs preventing them from sensing how bothered she was. She lay back, and let the alcohol and pills in her bloodstream attempt to divorce her from the madness she sensed about to consume her existence again. Avex's hunger tingled in her belly, its kindled appetite at the moment a subtle buzz that would in time become a deafening rumble.

And then . . .

Her thoughts fuzzed out for awhile. *Oh, God, let Red Octopus get back to me fast!*

She became aware of two female faces peering down at her on the bed.

"Are you okay?" the one with blonde hair asked worriedly. The other face had a joint in its mouth and was puffing smoke at her. She wished it would stop.

"No," she replied. "I'm *not* okay—not in the slightest. Now I fucking need to get laid too. My girly bits feel like they're aflame."

CHAPTER 29

Joker

Joker arrived in Raynham early that afternoon. Following phoned directions, she drove directly over to see Sin Corbin, her Abyss Club contact.

Sin's house was a ramshackle old cottage buried deep off the main drag as one arrived in town. Two miles before reaching the Blue Star Memorial Highway one turned off onto a nameless bumpy road that seemed hand-built and kept going.

Meeting Joker at the front door, Sin Corbin gasped, "Wow! You're so tall. And you've got the most wonderful red hair."

Sin herself looked unkempt in a blue maternity dress, old felt slippers, and her hair up in curlers.

Joker winced on entering the Corbin house. It was a stinking dump; one that showed unmistakable signs of rat and roach infestation. The disgusting 'wet newsprint' smell of rat urine was everywhere.

Once seated in the living room, Joker quickly disagreed with Nero's appraisal of the mistress of the house: Sin Corbin was way more than just 'heavily' pregnant. She was so pregnant that it hurt Joker's brain to look at her.

It was odd. Sin was, say, five-foot-four, and without her bulge likely didn't weigh more than a hundred pounds max. But that belly? All by itself, her pregnancy seemed to add another hundred pounds of weight to her. It stretched her maternity dress to bursting.

And she looked particularly weird because she was one of those women who didn't gain body weight during gestation. Both her feet and her nose were immensely swollen though, her fat nose giving her a hawkish look, not least because she had a thin face.

Joker was worried as Sin carefully levered herself into the easy chair opposite her—Sin's immense belly looked like it could fall off her body if left unsupported for too long.

"You're certain the doctors got the scans right? You're not actually expecting triplets?"

"Nah, it's just one," Sin wheezed. "I don't understand either how I'm so damn big. It's alright though, really. I get around just fine."

"You don't look like it."

Sin leered back. "Ah, I just had some fun last night. Some hot sex with my husband and a couple of just-arrived-in-town girls he'd picked up at the truck stop." She groaned. "Oh, it was ill-advised— I'll admit that now. I'm definitely paying the price at the moment."

"Satan be praised," Joker said, lost for words as to how a woman this gravid could be having sexual foursomes. Hell, her pregnancy looked like the result of a foursome: like three men had all impregnated her at once.

"Yeah, praise the evil old son-of-a-bitch."

They chatted for a while on life: the weather, healthcare ("Oh, doctors are nothing like what they used to be. Take my doctor, Dr. Sloane, for instance: Can you believe that he actually advised Snake to keep screwing me up till my delivery date?"), and gender politics ("We're getting there, but we keep stabbing ourselves in the ass. It beats me how all the women in America can't simply get behind Hilary Clinton for prez? How damn hard is that to figure out? We all vote for her and she's in the White House?" "We won't vote for her except she agrees to pass legislation making breast enhancement surgery a basic human right." "And lipo too! Of course the first thing she'll likely do is paint the White House pink as pussy! Ha ha ha! I guess that's what the guys are all scared of!").

Every now and than, Sin would wheeze and grip her belly like the fetus was kicking her extra-hard. "Doc says I'm due next week. He'd better be right: another fortnight of this and I'll be ready to kill Snake for doing this to me."

Joker laughed, then admired the photograph of Sin's husband that hung by the TV. A 'thick' man he was, hairy as an old-time bandido. Joker found him quite attractive: being tall and thin herself, she got off on chubby men. Okay, judging from the unkempt state of his house and wife, Snake Corbin would need to take a long bath—soak in a tub for an hour at least—before she'd ever dare bed him. (While chatting, she also mused on the strangeness of relationships: how they were often based on deceit, even if that deceit was benign. As far as she'd understood from Nero, Sin's husband Snake had no idea that his wife was a supernaturalist. He thought her inverted 'A' tattoo (situated under the curve of her huge belly) was something she'd taken a fancy to in Vogue magazine.)

They didn't discuss Pagan. Sin had no idea that Joker was tracking a traitor witch. She'd been told that Joker was in town to have a look around and see if Raynham qualified for an Abyss coven of its own.

Having heard that, Sin was of course delighted to be of every assistance required. "Just let me know if you need anything. If I can't get it, I'll ask Snake to find it for you."

At a point, her hostess asked her to pass the TV remote control. Joker did so, instantly noting that the unit felt greasy. On returning to her seat she instinctively sniffed her fingers to see what the oily substance was. She was shocked: her hand smelt of poop. She gaped at Sin: how in the world?

Sin giggled at her bafflement. "Oh, you know. Like I said—we had some dirty fun last night. I used the remote to turn one of the chicks on."

Joker nodded. Sin tuned the TV to a news broadcast. Two runaway Boston 20-year-olds who'd killed one of their boyfriends with a nail gun and then hacked up a gay couple in Dover and shot their teenage son in the head. The police believed the pair had fled west and were now in either Michigan or Illinois, from where they might try to hop the border into Canada.

Sin smirked, then muted the news.

After a while, another woman came in from the back of the house. She looked a bit like Sin, but was say, eight or nine years younger. She was plump, but pretty with it. Dark hair, dark eyes, and only the barest suggestion of Sin's hawk face. She wasn't wearing a bra; her large breasts swung in her white halter.

"My kid sister Ella," Sin introduced. "She and her boyfriend Boner live here with me and Snake."

(While speaking, Sin made the Abyss Club's 'Caution: she's not one of us!' hand gesture to Joker, tapping her right thumb and index finger thrice against each other.)

Joker nodded back while thinking, *Her boyfriend's name is 'Boner?' What kind of a name is that?*

"Sis, old Mr. McKinney just called," Ella said. "He's holding the line. One of his sows just dropped a litter. He wants to know if you need the piglet today or tomorrow?"

Sin mouthed a silent question at Joker, who nodded back, then replied, "Tell him tomorrow. We'll both be over at noon."

Ella walked off to deliver the message.

Once they were alone again, Joker said, "Thanks for your help, I really should go find a motel now and unpack."

"Are you sure you won't prefer to stay here with us? I can make the spare room ready. Snake won't mind a bit."

Joker grinned. "No, but thanks for offering. I really need to be alone to focus my magic energies." Inside, she quailed at the offer. *Oh no—no way above Hell am I sleeping in this dump.* She dreaded waking up surrounded by rats, and with roaches crawling all over her.

She similarly declined an invitation to stay for lunch. Though hungry, she was scared she'd find rat droppings in the food.

After she'd made her appointment with Sin for tomorrow, Ella saw her out. Joker was relieved at not having to get Sin Corbin out of her easy chair. It would have been a wicked thing to do, considering how front-burdened she was.

Ella gave her directions on how to find a good motel, the Sunflower.

***

Raynham was much how Joker had envisioned it: sparsely dotted buildings along two or three primary streets that fed a web of other smaller roads. She doubted the town's population would be more than fifteen thousand people. It was much too small for a coven. In a place like this, where lots of people knew each other (and often tended to be closely related), it was far too easy to attract police attention to Satanist activity. For the foreseeable future, Sin Corbin and her Abyss converts would remain under the Attleboro branch.

***

"Well, here's your key, miss," the old man at the Sunflower's reception desk told Joker. "Your room's just round the back there: third block, Room 36. You just call me if anything's out of order."

She thanked him, put the key in her pocket, and was about leaving when his desk phone rang.

"Hello? . . . No, Zak, I ain't seen her. I've no idea where the heck she's run off to. I'm about calling the cops in case she's been kidnapped. . . . We gotta wait twenty-four hours first 'cos she's an adult? . . . She-it! . . . Check the rooms again? I told you, son: I've already been over them twice asking the guests if they've seen her. No one has. It's like she just up and vanished into thin air! . . . What, son? . . . No, Zak, I ain't being funny. I don't get it, either; that's how that nice shoe salesman—Mr. Bennett his name was—went missing yesterday too."

The old man hung up. He saw that Joker was looking at him confused and ventured a hassled explanation. "It's my grandson's wife Cherry. She's gone missing. She works here, helps me out with the cleaning and stuff. This morning, she left about ten o'clock and ain't been back since. And her mobile phone ain't working either."

He sighed. "That was my grandson on the phone just now. He's freaking out already, he is. He's really jealous-like, thinks she's run off with some other kid. Shee-it! It's like aliens came and grabbed her." Then he forced a smile. "Maybe I'm just getting into a swivet over nothing tho'. Maybe Zak's right and she *has* eloped with that Perkins boy."

He shooed Joker out. "Nothing to worry your pretty red head over, miss. Cherry don't show up soon, I'll get the cops on the case. You now, you just get over to your room and kick your heels up." He flashed her a disarming grin. "Oh yeah, and welcome to the Sunflower."

Joker walked out from there. Then, about to leave the lot, she got out of her car again and headed back for the lobby.

She got the lobby door half-open, then paused. The old man was on the phone again, his back to her. She'd been about asking him if he could check his guest register for a Susan Harris, a friend of hers who was also supposed to be here in Raynham at the moment. Now though, it occurred to her that with a statewide manhunt on for Pagan, she was very unlikely to have registered here using her real name.

The old man's phone conversation filtered into her thoughts.

"No, Zak, Cherry ain't showed yet. . . . Hell no, I ain't going around and asking the guests again if they've seen her. Kid, are you damn sure you and she didn't have another fight again last night? Did you beat her up again? Kid, I've told you over and over: you keep whipping her with your belt just 'cos you're jealous and she's gonna leave you someday. . . . What? . . . You stopped beating her last year after she lost the baby? . . . Yeah, sure I know you love her, but . . . now c'mon, kid, don't you start crying now—we don't know for sure that Cherry's run away, do we?"

Wincing, Joker left them to it. Yes, there really was no point asking. If she'd stayed here, Pagan would likely have registered under another name, or . . . she might not even have bothered registering at all—simply take unpaid occupancy of one of the rooms here. Spell-obscured as she was, no one would remember the room existed till after she'd left.

And Nero said the demon has additionally masked her whereabouts. So how the heck am I supposed to find her then?

The two missing people might be a clue though. That was definitely abnormal—two people vanishing in quick succession without a trace. Clearly something to investigate.

Climbing back into her car, Joker's gaze caught on a blue Toyota RAV4 parked in front of the fourth or fifth room in the front block.

Nice set of wheels, she thought. Driving past the RAV4 on her way to loop round to the rear blocks, she was struck by a sudden wash of evil pouring at her from the car. It attracted her like catnip attracts cats.

She stopped her car for a moment and focused back on the evil efflux. No, this wasn't Pagan's car, nor was the room it was parked outside—Room 5—her room either. There were no supernatural hangovers here, just a routine stench of death: the RAV4's previous owner had died violently at the hands of its current owner.

Joker grimaced at that knowledge, then let it go. She drove round the corner to her own room.

At least she'd gotten here. Time to relax and have a hot bath, then drive out to have lunch and see the town. Do some old-fashioned sleuth work.

***

Even if Joker hadn't been preoccupied with her own thoughts she'd have missed the spell-obscured car that pulled away from Room 9—four doors down from the blue RAV4—just before she reached it, its three occupants occupied with the gory business of going to dispose of Cherry Duggan's dismembered corpse.

Equally preoccupied—in her case, Pagan was busy trying to wrest a half-smoked joint from Lori's grasp (currently the soberest of the trio, Britt was driving)—Pagan didn't see Joker either.

As Joker's Lexus turned round the end of the motel block, the white Honda pulled out of the motel's drive and turned up north, towards the hidden backwoods road where Britt and Lori had earlier left Matt Lewis's corpse bound to a tree. They'd decided it was best to keep all their stiffs in one place from now on.

And after that, all three of them planned on getting laid good and hard tonight. Nailed like with hammers.

"We need dick! We need dick! We need dick!" they howled as they rode along. Then, inspired now, they began loudly corrupting an 80's pop classic into, "Girls just wanna get fucked! Girls just wanna have sex!" though none of them sounded even remotely like Cyndi Lauper.

CHAPTER 30

Britt, Lori, & Pagan

They discarded the chunks of Cherry without incident.

Pagan's only comment on seeing the mutilated body bound to the tree with its 'Fuck Jesus! Satan is Lord!' inscription was: "Oh shit—that was you guys?"

On their way back into town, they decided to get some more food and wine from the Market Basket down on lower Broadway.

Britt was still at the wheel. Just past the Center Street turning, she spotted a pregnant woman in a yellow maternity dress pushing a pram towards them.

Next thing, she'd gunned up the accelerator and was speeding towards the approaching female.

"What's up?" Lori queried beside her. "Why're we suddenly going faster? There's no hurry, the day's not about to end right now, and even if it did the night follows immediately after. So what's your hurry, Pretty Britty?"

Britt didn't reply. She couldn't control herself: all she saw as the white Honda drew nearer the woman in the yellow dress was the image of similarly preggered Sin abusing her with that huge black strap-on dildo, then forcing the TV remote up her anus, and everyone there laughing at her. Except for Lori, who'd betrayed their friendship by having orgasms instead of screaming.

The woman's yellow dress made a further subconscious link to Snake and Boner's yellow Jeep.

The pregnant woman stopped pushing the pram and stared wildly ahead of her. She instinctively sensed danger in the air, but (as the onrushing vehicle was invisible to her) was confused as to its location. She stared down into the pram like she was unsure whether or not to

241

remove her child and run for it. But if she ran, in what direction was she to flee? Where exactly was the danger? What exactly as it?

Finally, all she did was bend over the pram to ensure that its little passenger was okay.

With her foot down hard on the gas pedal, Britt swerved the Honda up off the blacktop onto the sidewalk and rammed pram and mother hard.

The young mother vanished from sight under the white hood. The pram, which might have been knocked free into the road had she not been bending over it, was already being crushed beneath the car.

All three of them in the car felt the impact, then the meaty crunch of their vehicle rolling over the woman's body, coupled with her single surprised shriek of pain.

They bumped down over the woman.

"Ha! Gotcha!" Britt yelped in delight. In a flash, she shifted gears and reversed back over mother and child, then drove forward over them again, just to make sure that she'd *really* gotten them both.

Ten yards farther on, Britt parked and looked back between the seats out of the rear window. The pregnant woman lay on her back, with blood squirting from between her thighs. She wasn't dead . . . not yet. They'd apparently driven over the fetus though—the hill of her baby bulge was now leveled to a plateau. The woman's limbs were twitching, and her tongue stuck out of her mouth like a thirsty dog's.

The baby carriage was now just an upended ruin of cloth and steel with shredded skin and bones sticking out underneath it, and its wheels knocked off. Blood and some smeared pink stuff was running from beneath it to join the blood from the dying mother.

A long blood smear extended from the corpse in their direction. In the road beside them, traffic had begun stopping as people gaped.

Britt was silent, accepting into herself the sheer delight of having 'reduced' yet another person to zero. And this was a person who'd accomplished something great in life—she'd made a child. No, she'd made *two* children. In a sudden burst of inspired understanding, Britt realized that she'd actually reduced *three* people to nothing, not just one. In her human demolition derby, babies counted too, maybe more so because they had no idea what was going on.

Like pure honey, the glory filled her from buttocks to brain.

"Now that's what I call an abortion," Lori said admiringly. "Somehow I don't think she'll be giving birth any time soon." She grinned glassy-eyed. "Hey, you stupid bitch, haven't you ever heard how overpopulated the world is? Serves your fat ass right for being in our frigging way to get to the mall in the first place. Didn't you get that we were in a rush? And I don't even get what you need *two* kids for anyway, huh, you greedy bitch? One child should be enough, just like in . . . what's that mother-frigging commie place called? Yeah, Red China . . . Birth control—"

"What the hell did you do that for?" Pagan asked in a low and startled voice.

Britt promptly replied, "We're leaving our mark on the world. Dammit, Pagan, for a witch, you're such a pussy."

Pagan tried to get her drunk mind around Britt's explanation. 'Leaving our mark on the world' made sense in a way. Viewed now through the crowd arriving to aid her, the pregnant woman and her children (fetus inclusive) were quite smeared on the world's surface. Yeah a real mark: parent blood and kiddie brains. (It was pandemonium back there now, with everyone dialing 911 at once [likely jamming the lines] and all puzzled as to how the woman and her baby had sustained such horrific injuries with nothing causing them.)

Pagan almost got the logic of it, then something struck her as totally unacceptable. "Britt, you just killed her damn kid! No one should kill kids!"

Britt smirked. "Collateral damage; it's paying for the sins of its mother. Consider the little fucker a sacrifice to my ego."

"Yeah, a sacrifice sounds good," Pagan slurred. "You'd make a kickass witch. I was gonna sacrifice a kid too, but I missed and . . ."

"Look," Britt said with finality. "Fuck 'em, alright? Let's just get some food already and go sleep. As it is, we aren't in any state to meet guys."

"Yeah, that's so damn true," Lori agreed. "When you meet men you really need to look your best so they can take advantage of you." She burped. "Sorry, I mean 'look your breasts' so they can see what they're getting. Oh, is that what I actually mean? Does it matter what I mean? Does anything matter down in the pink pit of our sweet magnetic kittens that the dogs of our species find so irresistible? Hump, hump, hump! Look, Britt's right—what's important here is that we go lay in bed. It's practice, you know: later, when we're getting laid, we'll lay in bed too, and then they'll all lie on top of us and tell us lies about how pretty and tight we are and we'll like those lies and they'll make us have de-lie-ghtful orgasms, or . . . yeah, well, what-the-fuck-ever, you sluts know what I mean."

After a moment of silence, in which her companions both shrugged and exchanged 'Yeah, drugs *are* bad for her' looks, she spurted again: "And we should get some rubbers too—safe sex, you fucking know? Who knows where their goddamn penises have been?" She pointed back at the crowd around the (now dead) woman. "One of them might even have been in *her* pussy. That's how she got the baby. She might infect us with her pregnancy."

"Lori, we haven't even met the guys yet. How can they have—"

"Men cheat on you a lot. They fuck your mom, suck off your dad, eat your wife, impregnate your daughters. They watch porn and fuck onscreen women they can't even touch. And . . . and . . . and they plan to fuck . . ." She pointed back again. "Look, a man got her preggered, didn't he? You wanna tell me that a man didn't fuck *her*!? Huh? Huh!? I don't buy that Virgin Birth nonsense!"

Sighing, Britt started the car again, and drove off for the Market Basket.

CHAPTER 31

Joker

Joker was having a late lunch of a greasy burger and fries at Rudy's Truck Stop when the text message came in from Nero:

Our spies in ROC just confirmed that Pagan's contacted them. U need 2 get her b4 they do.

She texted back: *Yeah, I know. Seen Sin, working on it. Any fix on her location yet?*

A few seconds later: *None. Gotta run. Meeting Azalea for lunch. She says urgent as fuck.*

Which likely just meant that Azalea wanted her pussy eaten while reviewing the latest constitutional amendment proposal; the wizened old slut.

Grinning, Joker dropped her phone in her handbag and looked around. Rudy's was the quintessential small town joint: dark wood-paneling, a black/white checkerboard floor, lots of round tables with graffiti drawn/etched on them, a few side booths, a bar—large glass steins, chrome taps on wooden casks—and a vintage nickelodeon.

A biker chick had just put Slain Jane's *Antidote for God* on the jukebox. Joker appreciated the song. In addition to its nihilistic feel, *Antidote* was the sort of track you didn't need to think about. You just sat and let it smother you in multitracked layers of noise.

Attending everyone were two pretty waitresses who looked like they never slept. (As far as Joker could tell, Rudy's Truck Stop was an inn too—there were rentable rooms on the building's second floor.)

Up in a corner, a TV showed a muted UFC rerun: two men grappling on the floor, the one with a broken and bleeding nose choking out the one with two black eyes.

Rudy the proprietor/barkeep was a muscular man in his fifties dressed in faded blue jeans and a white shirt with the sleeves rolled up above his elbows. He looked mean as a grizzly bear (and was as hairy as one too), but he was a jovial chap, and the place had a jolly enough ambience to it. Joker wondered what it'd be like at night when everyone had been drinking. Particularly the bikers.

Except for two bikers and their women, the truck stop was currently deserted. She'd been flirting with one of the bikers, a burly bearded guy of the sort she liked, but then his old lady—who looked like a pro wrestler—had come back from the ladies' and that was off.

One of the tired-looking waitresses came in from the back of the bar and whispered something in Rudy's ear. Joker caught the word 'police.'

Rudy nodded, then leaving the woman at the bar, left via the front door.

Joker, who'd been facing away from the door towards the jukebox, trailed him with her eyes through the window till he vanished from view. She wondered what the matter was. *Police?*

Then she forgot about that for a moment and regarded her burger suspiciously. *Hey, this ain't roadkill, is it?* Then deciding she was too hungry to care, she went back to eating.

She finished her meal and coke and left. Walking over to her car, she caught sight ahead of her of two cops standing by a red Dodge with its trunk open. Rudy was with them and he looked sick, like he'd throw up any moment.

What instantly struck Joker as odd was how fat both cops were. The male cop was immense. His female partner was even larger than he, a squat blonde mountain of flesh that Rudy was referring to as Chief Kravitz.

The car with the jimmied trunk was separated from Joker's by a gap of just five yards. The cops' patrol car was parked on the other side of it, its doors open.

The fat policeman had begun rooting amidst boxes on the red car's rear seat. He looked up, an indecipherable expression on his face. "Hey, Chief!—these are shoe boxes back here. Loads and loads of 'em."

"Alright, so he was a shoe salesman then," the obese policewoman agreed. "A number of them have been through here in the last two days; they've a get-together down in Westville."

"This one definitely didn't make it tho'."

A shoe salesman? That rung a bell in Joker's mind. Hadn't the old guy at the Sunflower said a shoe salesman had somehow vanished into thin air?

Joker had reached her car now and both Rudy and the cops were looking at her.

"Hi," she said, slightly on her guard. She pointed at the red car. "Is anything the matter, officers?"

The police chief grimaced. Despite her huge size, she had a small head and so retained some attractiveness; she looked to be in her early forties. "Yeah. Someone we don't know turned this other someone we don't know into pig feed."

Joker stepped closer. The homicidal stench of murdered meat reached her before she reached the red car. Being a Satanist—participating in black magic rituals, many of which involved human sacrifice—it was a smell she was well familiar with.

The policeman quickly blocked her view of the carnage in the car; with his immense girth it was easy to do. "Sorry, miss, this ain't something for ladies to see." Then, like he'd realized the Chief might be pissed off by that remark, he added, "except they're police ladies, of course."

Chief Kravitz nodded slowly at Joker. "Yeah. Kev and I just pulled in to have some lunch and spotted that spot of blood under the car. Rudy says it's been parked here since yesterday." She squinted coldly at Joker. "Did you by any chance see anything?"

"No, I just drove in here an hour ago." Behind the Chief she could see the dried pool of blood, looking like spilled oil. The stink from the opened trunk was the sort one usually only smelt in nightmares.

Chief Kravitz was regarding Joker with sudden interest. "You live here in Raynham, miss?"

"Just visiting." She extended her hand and shook the Chief's. "My name's Jo Carroll. I'm here to clear my head from the Boston smog for a day or two." She smiled and added, "I'm also checking on an old friend of mine, Sin Corbin. She lives just up the road."

The Chief raised an eyebrow at that.

"I'm rooming at the Sunflower."

The police chief apparently decided that Joker was harmless enough. She said. "Alright, you head along then, Ms. Carroll. I know both Sin and her husband; they're good folk." (Joker noted that when

she said 'good folk' her subordinate's face creased in disagreement.)
"And say 'hi' to old Clint for me."

"Who?"

"Clint Duggan, the motel owner," Rudy explained. He'd moved
away from the trunk to stand with the cops, they three forming a
rough semicircle around Joker. He still looked pale. Joker couldn't
fault him: the unseen body in the car trunk smelt truly puke-worthy.
She did, however, find being hemmed in by three large people
intimidating. It felt like she was a meal they planned on eating.

"Yeah, sure, I'll pass on your greetings to him." She nodded coolly
to the three of them, then turned back to her car. She'd decided not
to mention that the Dodge likely belonged to old Clint's missing guest.
Or to mention for that matter that his granddaughter-in-law/cleaning
lady had also vanished.

"And, young lady . . ."

She turned back. *What now?*

Chief of Police Kravitz was frowning. "Be careful, alright? This is
usually a quiet town, but these past few days, lotsa strange things have
been happening. Bad people attacking townsfolk . . . or visitors. This
dead man, for instance, he wasn't from around here, if you understand
what I'm getting at. So you watch yourself."

The two men nodded solemn agreement with her advice.

"Thanks, I appreciate the warning." Joker got in her Lexus and
drove off. In the rearview she saw the Chief holding a radio to her ear.
Likely calling for forensics to get their asses out here.

Joker knew the shredded body in the trunk had to be Pagan's work;
she was convinced of it. She was glad that she'd not mentioned the
motel connection. With any luck, it would take the police a day at least
before they'd get round to checking with the Sunflower.

The game was getting faster and deadlier, its walls closing in on
everyone, even—like the cops back there—on the unsuspecting. Time
was running out fast for all of them.

Pagan was a trapped animal seeking the only bolt-hole available—
the Red Octopus Corporation. Were the ROC considering accepting
her into their fold? Joker couldn't tell. It was very important to her
though that either the ROC reject Pagan, or that she, Joker, found the
fugitive witch before they did.

If *they* didn't, or if *she* didn't, she could kiss that sweet Hollywood
job goodbye.

But that was a minor hassle. For her attempt to fix things, she'd at the very least get a coven headship of her own and accelerated promotion through the ranks of the order.

Except if . . . Except if things got out of hand.

The real problem—and the scariest part of this—was Pagan's pet demon Avex. Pagan herself was almost innocent in all this, a walking time bomb who had no idea of what she was about to become.

All the killing she's doing now is nothing compared to what she'll be capable off if I don't stop her.

Three days left, Joker calculated, driving down the road to the motel again. *Three days, then we'll be faced with a massacre the likes of which the modern age has rarely seen. And it'll start here in Raynham.*

And after that? *Well, there'll be literal hell to pay once our lord Lucifer watches the disaster report on CNN. Then I might want to defect to Red Octopus too.*

She frowned. *There's still time to fix this; I gotta think positive. Poor Pagan. Sorry, girl, but you're in the way of my running most of the West Coast. That's a seven-figure-salary job. And so, I'm getting rid of the obstruction you pose . . .*

Feeling better, she drove on into the evening.

CHAPTER 32

Britt, Lori, & Pagan

"Coffee is great for a woman's sex drive," Pagan explained while serving them steaming mugs of black instant brew. "It helps you concentrate on what's being done to you. The dick feels like it's in much deeper."

"You sure 'bout that?" Lori asked. She, Britt, and Pagan had just woken up after two hours of sleep. Thankfully, considering the night's plans, the world outside her head looked less than woolly.

Pagan, looking miraculously recovered from their drug and alcohol binge, grinned. "Trust me, it works. It helps hangovers too, particularly if you take an aspirin as well."

"For some reason, I'm not hungover."

"I'm in for the sex benefits," Britt said brightly. She didn't feel hungover either. *It's the aftereffects of my killing that bitch and her baby . . . sorry . . . babies . . . I mustn't forget I flattened her womb. Oh, fuck, but do I so need to get laid already. But no dick goes anywhere near my ass—damn, it hurt to poop just now!*

After two cups of coffee apiece and using the last of Lori's uppers, they took some time to alter their appearance.

(Pagan had moved into Britt and Lori's room: hers smelt too bad now to live in, and there were maggots in her bathtub.)

After the hit-and-run incident with mother and child, they'd raided several shops at the Raynham Shopping Center. Their coffee table now looked like a shelf in a beauty salon. Hair dyes, eye pencils, blusher, lipsticks, eye shadows, foundation and concealer—the bottles and jars stood in alarming array. There were also several wigs, a full manicure set, a veritable rainbow's worth of nail paints, a lady's electric razor, and a portable hair dryer.

For Lori, they'd also filched gray contact lenses. (Shoplifting was easy when no one could see you.)

Two hours of cutting, dyeing, and applying later, they were done. Pagan and Lori were now both blondes, Lori with her hair cut short and butch.

Britt had black hair and bangs, and bookish red spectacles. (She kept being startled by her reflection in the mirror.)

Finally, they all stripped nude to get dressed.

"Hey—that's a great tattoo," Lori said, pointing to the inverted "A" just on the outside of Pagan's left nipple.

She shrugged back. "It's our Abyss trademark. All the members have one."

"But on your breast?"

"Two guys I know have them on the heads of their dicks."

"But why is it upside down? It's an 'A,' isn't it?"

"Yes, but it's also a symbolic arrowhead pointing down into Hell. Also, set upside-down like this, the top half looks like a hole, representing Hell. See how the tips of the A's legs are angled? Also, in this inverted position, the A's crosspiece now forms a platform over the abyss, symbolizing how we, Satan's faithful, live in his domain of evil without being harmed . . . we're above the burning depths, so to speak, under his love and protection . . ."

Then she saw that, with a frown on her face, Britt was staring at each of their crotches in turn.

Lori had noticed too. "What's the matter?" she asked. "You're not suddenly thinking of carpet-munching instead, are you?"

"Girls, we forgot to dye our pubes," Britt announced.

The other two looked and confirmed that it was true.

"How the hell did we all forget something that important when we're going to pick up men?" Pagan asked.

"Anyway it's too late now, no time to remedy it," Lori said. "It's already ten."

Britt scowled. "We're gonna look super-freaky all having upper and lower hair that's different colors."

"We'll say we did it as a sorority dare."

"What sorority? Alpha Kappa Slut?"

"Shave it off. Use the electric razor."

The razor, previously used to clear armpit and leg hair, now came back into play. Britt denuded herself completely, as did Pagan.

Lori, though, shook her head. "Nah, I like the contrast. And it won't seem strange if I'm the only one."

They dressed: hot pants, T-shirts, hussy-high heels. Britt, conscious that her legs were thin, wore pants cutoff at the knees. They applied bucketloads of makeup. Britt and Lori went dark and sexy, Pagan kept her look deceptively simple.

Blue nail paint for Pagan, red for Lori; black for Britt.

"No bras permitted, Big Tits," Britt informed Lori on snatching a cute lace number from her bestie's grasp. "This is a hunting trip. Nipples rock."

"Britt, we look like total sluts—prostitutes."

"That's the *hole* point—to fill our *holes*."

"Remember what happened the last time you advised a sexy look?"

Britt pouted angrily. "Will you frigging stop bringing that up?" Shit, trust damn Lori to try to deflate her latest high.

"What *did* happen?" Pagan asked quietly. "You two never said."

Britt didn't reply.

"Don't ask," Lori said.

Britt changed the topic. "Okay, now remember: we need three guys who're together, but without any women."

Pagan cached her curiosity over what was so hard or sordid for Britt to confess to. Maybe it was even better not to know. Britney Wilson was clearly a young woman of many parts, all of them equally disturbed. The afternoon's mother/child hit-and-run incident had instilled massive respect for her special brand of crazy in Pagan. Only now, with the drugs largely out of her system, was it really hitting Pagan just what her newly-blonde companion had done.

She actually ran a car over a pregnant woman's belly? And I was in that car and did nothing to stop her?

(Pagan's eyes were coal-black now. With that optic change and her new 'Blondie' look and nice-girl makeup, she looked so little like her previous self, the police would need a fingerprint test to ID her.)

"Oh, and just in case I forget later . . ." Britt glared at Lori, "no lezzie nonsense. I mean it. I don't care if it's the heat of the moment or whatever, but if you dare stick your tongue in my muff, I'll kick all your teeth out."

She stared a challenge at Pagan. "That goes for you too, my darling witch."

Pagan was taken aback by her vehemence. There was that 'crazy' showing again. "Frigging lighten up, wilya?"

Lori just chuckled. She was amused at discovering how true it was that the apple never fell far from the tree. At the moment Britney Wilson looked the spitting image of her dead mother: bed-bait body and lust-filled eyes; ready to fuck His Holiness the Pope himself if he were temptable. Lori knew better than to point this out. She didn't dare tell Britt that, teetering on those criminally-high heels like she was, she currently looked like a clone of the late Joanna Wilson.

Instead, she said sweetly, "Britt, darling, you're the most uptight slut I've ever met. And, oh yes, Pagan's got much better tits than you."

Britt looked pained. "Whatever. You two lick each other till you dissolve if you like. Just leave my vag alone."

"I have absolutely no intention of giving Lori head," Pagan said soberly. "But if we don't head over to Rudy's damn quick, I just might eat both of you."

Britt instantly dropped her belligerence and gave her a worried look. "Is it that bad?"

She shook her head. "Not yet, but I can feel the stupid demon rising in me. Soon it'll be hungry again. I should never have done that magic trick for you guys."

"Sorry."

"It's not your fault; there's no way you could have known. Shit, right now I feel like a pipe being stuffed with evil from below."

Lori giggled. "I wanna get stuffed down below too with a pipe."

Britt nodded. "Me too. Alright, darlings, let's get our pussies over to the truck stop."

Guns and knives in their purses, they set out on the hunt.

**

Before hitting the truck stop, one last order of business remained to attend to.

On leaving the motel, they drove both cars out and ditched Pagan's Honda at their secret turnoff where they'd earlier left Cherry's body. That took a while, as they had to navigate off-road with their headlights off so no one saw them.

Then, while Britt and Lori waited, Pagan drove the white Honda Accord as far beneath the right-hand trees as she could to defy any air searches for it. Five minutes later, they made out her figure tramping back to the dirt road. There had been a light drizzle that afternoon while they'd all been asleep; Pagan had to clean a lot of mud off her shoes before getting into the RAV4.

Finally they arrived at Rudy's. Snake and Boner's yellow Jeep wasn't in the parking lot tonight. Britt was disappointed about that: she'd have liked to slit both their throats before getting laid.

***

11:28 p.m. The dead of night.

The half-moon was a voyeur's eye peeking in through the living room windows. Maybe the sky god was aroused too.

The three young men were all quite drunk. They were also very good-looking and very horny. Stiff penises poked at their zippers all round.

Perfect, Britt thought, looking at the boys they'd snared.

She, Lori, and Pagan weren't drunk at all. They were all, however, equally as horny as the guys.

The three young men were friends: Josh, whose parents' house this was (they were over in Europe on holiday); Omar (a black soldier on leave); and Roddy (who was at Boston's Northeastern University with Josh).

They'd been waiting for hours at Rudy's for Crystal, a local prostitute who was supposed to hook them up with two of her sexy friends. Crystal hadn't showed though, and her phone had kept bumping into voicemail.

Slightly depressed (Rudy's other regular working girls being already all taken by burly truckers), they'd drank even more and then . . .

And then, at about a quarter to eleven, just as they'd been about leaving, three angels of the night had walked in the front door of the truck stop and made straight for them.

"Nah, it's 'cos we're all drunk, that's all," Roddy had replied Omar's cross-eyed whisper that the three young ladies hadn't actually walked in the front door, but had actually materialized right before their eyes out of the thin air. "We just didn't notice them crossing the room 'cos of all the dancers."

Josh nodded his agreement to that explanation.

The truth was, Pagan had forgotten to switch off her masking spell until she'd realized that the three young men couldn't see or hear her, hence the 'sudden appearance' trick. But all three guys were sufficiently drunk that everything seemed logical, particularly because the 'everything' in question was three beautiful young women who were making no bones of the fact that they wanted *their* bones.

"Hi, boys," Lori, hand cocked on her right hip, said in her best hookerish drawl, "y'all lookin' for a good time?"

"Maybe. What's it gonna cost us?"

"Nothing you ain't got."

"Well, I guess we can afford that."

And that was that. Forty-five minutes later and here they all were in Josh's living room.

"So," Pagan whispered to her two friends, "let's do this."

"Alright, everyone!" Britt yelped, pulling her T-shirt over her head so her breasts bounced free. "Time for some fornication!" She felt incredibly potent, like she could gangbang a thousand men now if she so chose. Just none in her ass please.

It was a rush after that to see who could lose their clothes fastest. The girls won simply because they had less on—Lori wasn't even wearing panties. They'd already each picked the young man they wanted and so got right down to business.

Josh vaguely murmured about safe sex and waved a strip of condoms in the air, but a giggling Lori snatched the rubbers from his grasp and flung them out of sight behind a couch.

After staring angrily at Lori for a moment, Britt realized that she too honestly didn't give a shit about contraception or STDs or AIDS anymore, and besides, should a social disease like herself really worry about catching another social disease? She looked over to see what Pagan thought, then realized that Pagan clearly didn't give a flying fuck either—or maybe the witch just had magic genital protection—she was already pulling Roddy down to the rug.

Lori pushed Omar down on one of the two living room couches then knelt over him and took his chocolate-toned penis in her mouth. He groaned as her lips and tongue rose and fell on him. She grabbed his testicles in both hands and squeezed; gently, then firmly.

Britt didn't bother with such preliminaries. Already soaking wet between the legs, she pulled Josh after her, then bent over and grabbed her ankles, instructing him to enter her from behind. She came the moment he did so; the penetration felt so goddamn deep, like he was right inside her stomach, stirring up her digestive juices. *And oh, fucking yes*—she thought, a single moment of lucidity in her daze of pleasure—*mom really knew what she was talking about! Oh, fuck! Maybe I shouldn't have cut her feet off!* Then another orgasm sparked in her sexual tunnel—it felt like an explosion falling out of her womb into her vagina—and she forgot everything except the bliss filling her and the strong male body connected to hers by this rod of flesh, and the firm hands steadying her around her waist and keeping her from toppling off her high heels.

Pagan was riding Roddy cowgirl style, her freshly-blonde hair whirling about. She had him flat on his back on the rug, with herself kneeling on him and grinding back and forth. It was a great feeling. In under a minute she was coming too, a body explosion that had less to do with sexual desire than sheer animalism. She felt violent, brutal, degenerate; but above all she felt like a primal force of nature, something dark and forbiddingly evil and completely unstoppable. She reached down and kissed Roddy, looking into his eyes. She almost felt pity for him—this poor misguided instrument of her pleasure. But still, pity or not, she continued grinding her sex against his adamant penis, in their contest of which would outlast the other.

Omar had been doing Lori missionary-style on the brown leather couch. She'd had one orgasm and it felt great and she could feel another one coming. It was a real turn-on watching her friends getting fucked at the same time as she was. The conversation of penis and vagina was such a fascinating sight. Watching Britt wobbling on her black *sex*-inch heels, with her breasts also wobbling left and right, was particularly erotic, like live porn. *Go, Bridgette B., go!*

Omar twitched and ejaculated into her sex. As his eyes spun in his head and his body froze, she reached down and stroked her clit so she met him halfway. Afterwards he collapsed on her groaning. "Damn, mama, you're so tight down there, it hurts."

She sighed with passion. "I should be—it doesn't get much use."

They lay together on the couch and watched the others screw.

Britt's legs had finally given out on her. She was now kneeling on the rug, bent over the coffee table with her hands gripping its opposite edge. She was whimpering like a whipped bitch as Josh humped her hard. Clearly, the booze in his system was preventing him from coming. Britt looked like she was both enjoying herself and in pain.

She made one final loud yelp and flattened out over the coffee table. Mission half-accomplished there.

Roddy was giving Pagan head. While she squeezed her breasts, her feet high up in the air, he lapped between her shaven vaginal lips like a dog would, his tongue furrowing through the musky wet crevice. The canine similarity didn't end there: Roddy's limp penis swung left and right between his legs like a puppy's tail. His ass was a hairy purple cave above it.

Omar kissed Lori. She felt him between the legs. He was hard again.

"Hey!" she called out into the room. "Everyone stop what you're doing!"

When she had everyone's attention, she said, "Alright, now don't you dare laugh at me . . . but (she managed to look just a little bit embarrassed) . . . I want to fuck all three guys at once."

Pagan nodded at Roddy. "Go do her. I gotta see this."

Britt, completely fucked out for the moment, pushed Josh off her with relief (the guy was like a sex machine—didn't he ever go soft?). "Hey, go slam it to her."

Lori got down on her hands and knees on the rug. Omar stood by her head; she took him in her mouth (she was wary of both Britt's and Pagan's vaginas, but particularly Britt's: her anger might be catching). Josh lay on his back and slid underneath her. With a grin and a loud slurp, she slotted him into her sex. Roddy knelt behind her, between both she and Josh's legs. He grabbed her hips to steady himself.

"Yeeesss!!!" she moaned around a mouthful of penis as he entered her backside.

Lori found being filled in all her holes a transcending experience. It was definitely fun, but also had a strange element to it where she felt like she wasn't in control of herself anymore. Then she understood: that was the *hole* point: this was almost a BDSM thing—you let go and *let others do*.

She relaxed, didn't even bother too much about sucking Omar's penis anymore, just let her mouth go slack around the turgid rod of sexual meat throbbing on her tongue. Like he'd been wishing she'd do just that, Omar now grabbed her behind the head and began thrusting hard into her throat.

Lori let them have her. The gagging feeling in her neck (and the corresponding stink of male musk each time Omar's pubes struck her welcoming lips), Josh's relentless plumbing of her sex, and the completely unnatural distention of her excretory passage (each of Roddy's thrusts into her anus felt like feces was being stuffed backwards into her colon), were individually strange sensations, but combined, they worked wonders in her tender nubile flesh. Before she knew it, she was coming again. And, oh my, what an orgasm it was! It ravaged her. She felt like she was shitting, pissing, and vomiting all at once, and yet it all felt so incredibly and horribly good, like she was voiding herself of all the useless emotions she'd never needed in her life. She wanted to fall prostate on Josh's chest and hug him, but Omar didn't let go of her head, he kept thrusting his brown manhood between her lips, so she couldn't fall flat; she was helpless and it was a delicious helplessness, and before she knew it she was coming again, and this time, remembering what she and her friends had planned for these three boys afterwards, she almost spilled the beans and warned them to run for their lives, but she couldn't, no, she would never rat on her friends, and "Oh, God, yes!" another orgasm took her over and this one felt like her shit would come out of her mouth (Roddy was pumping her ass so hard and good!), but the excrement couldn't find its way up her throat because Omar had that blocked, and (her sex felt like it was exploding!) Josh was flopping up and down under her, in and out, in and out, in and out of her, and her whole body was a candle melting from both ends at once and on all sides too. Oh, and now suddenly the feeling reversed like a swing: it felt like she was going to vomit out of her anus, but the puke couldn't get out, her ass was plugged tight, and . . .

"Oh fuckitty, fuckitty, fuck!" she gasped, after Omar finally spurted down her throat then dropped onto the brown couch. She instantly slumped down on Josh's chest and hugged him hard. And now Josh was coming inside her too, she felt his warm spurts of sexual love. And then Roddy was also erupting inside her, emptying himself into her rectum, and that felt like she was an anal bottle being filled to overflowing with dirty love; and suddenly as a result of all that love she was having a final orgasm, and this time, she couldn't help herself, she was kissing Josh and it didn't matter that his breath stank of beer and beer nuts, she just had to share this overwhelming moment with someone.

She rolled off Josh and onto her back. "Oh, fuck, that was beyond incredible!"

Britt said, "Okay, now that you've established your porno credentials beyond all reasonable doubt, can we have our guys back?"

She and Pagan had both been masturbating frantically during Lori's foursome with the guys. She'd come twice; watching Roddy sliding in and out of Lori's ass was just so, so hot!

Now, seeing Josh, Omar, and Roddy all lying there with their faces glazed with deep satisfaction, Britt felt a moment's deep regret. *They're gonna die, these three hunky guys unable to believe their incredible luck at finding three hookers who're miles better than the unreliable slut who'd promised to find them some hot party girls.*

Britt found it odd though. Despite all of Pagan's explanations, she couldn't really get it through her head what was shortly going to happen, largely because Pagan herself didn't really know.

So they'd worked out a plan to rectify that . . .

But that was for later. Now, she grinned as Josh returned to her and once again slid his hardness into her aching wetness. "Oh!" she gushed as her body engulfed his, flinging her legs up and wrapping them tight around his waist.

Across from her, she watched Pagan wrap her lips around Roddy's limp penis. *Hey!* she felt like screaming. *That was just in Lori's butt! Isn't he supposed to wash it first!?* Once it was hard again, Pagan guided the turgid rod between her legs and began moaning too.

Lori looked like the just-concluded foursome had completely knocked all the sex out of her. She lay flat on her back on the floor, one hand up between Omar's thighs and playing languidly with his penis. Omar too, looked out for the count. The black man seemed to be asleep, making only the faintest of murmurs while Lori fondled him, and trying to push her questing fingers away.

Britt concentrated on her own pleasure. They'd agreed to screw till they were all sated before doing 'it.' Britt felt almost there already. One more orgasm and she'd be finished for tonight. God knew her vagina was getting sore. A moment's pure hatred filled her. How she'd love to have been the one doing the foursome instead of Lori, but her ass would never permit it. That was Sin's fault. The mere thought of how painful it had been when she'd been using the toilet earlier in the day (like they were anal eggs, her turds had been speckled with blood) almost knocked her off her sexual flow. But then, thank fuck, she was coming again, and the pleasure was freeing her from her painful memories, and then there was only bliss left.

After one final orgasm Pagan was done too. Roddy was lying on her gasping out, "Fuck, baby, you're the utter best I've ever had."

Pagan's vagina was sated, but there was that other hunger to feed: Avex's evil craving for murder now demanded her full attention. No matter how hard she tried to stem the rushing infernal tide, it shoved its way back up into her. Sex had temporarily quelled Avex's hunger; now the demon's desire for bloodshed had returned with double force.

Josh was still erect though. Now he was on his back, fingers locked behind his head, with Britt riding him hard while grunting and gritting her teeth like she was hurting.

Pagan caught Britt's eye and nodded. *Yeah, let's do this.* Britt grimaced back silently (so yes, maybe *she was* in pain). Pagan looked at Lori, who was staggering to her feet. Lori nodded and retrieved her purse from the angle of the couch.

Omar was just sitting up and reaching for Lori, his brown penis stiffening in his crotch. She giggled, said, "I need to pee," and purse in hand, traipsed off, wagging her buttocks at him.

Pagan wasn't leaving. She did get to her feet though and pulled Roddy up with her to kiss him. The kiss was partly payback—she could still taste Lori's poop in her mouth (Oh, those heat-of-the-moment impulses!) and wanted to share it with him. His stubble pricked her tender cheeks.

She looked over his shoulder, at Britt. The demon was raging in her now, practically screaming inside her ears like acute tinnitus. Her body was trembling as if from passion. She felt like Avex was about rupturing her skin in its bid to impose itself.

Britt, still doing her bump-and-grind on the unsuspecting Josh, was at the same time pulling her carving knife from her handbag. Knife out, she winked at Pagan, then stabbed sideways at Josh's neck.

"Look out!" Omar yelled. But it was too late. Fingers locked behind his head, Josh was defenseless. The knife plunged deep into the left side of his throat. Blood jetted out of him. Britt left the knife in there as the blood spurted. Inside her vagina, Josh's penis jerked as his body did.

Omar was staring wide-eyed at her, the beer in his system preventing him from kicking into military mode.

Roddy tried to turn and see what was happening behind him, but Pagan restrained him with an iron grip, keeping him facing her. (The blood spilling from Josh was providing the final key to let Avex out. Scared now of what she was about doing, Pagan was holding back as hard as she could, but it was useless.)

Fuck! Britt thought as Josh grabbed at the knife in his neck. *This is so much fun!*

Then, like Pagan had warned she and Lori to do, she was up and running for the living room's attached toilet, with Josh's semen streaming down her legs. Behind her she could hear all hell suddenly erupting.

Once she was safe beside Lori in the toilet, they both watched horror unfold before their very eyes.

"Hey, record it!" Britt reminded Lori once she was over her initial shock. This was unbelievable.

"I am, I am!" Lori replied, holding Pagan's cellphone in the crack of the door and catching everything.

Pagan was becoming a monster.

The transformation was still taking place as they watched—a beautiful 21-year-old blonde somehow expanding into a scaly green-skinned creature that seemed more beast than sentient.

The demon-creature was about seven feet tall. Its head was snakelike, yet it had curving ram-like horns. Its mouth, once opened, revealed yellow feline teeth. The monster was horrendously muscular—Pagan's breasts seemed to dissolve into the leaf-colored substance of its chest—and it had huge batwings covered with scaly skin. Tree-trunk legs like a T-Rex's. Its hands and feet were all tipped with long black talons.

The demon looked once in their direction and growled. Its eyes were black slits in its face, marbled with hints of yellow.

Britt and Lori perceived all this in a flash. Too much was happening at once. Both girls were struck speechless.

First to notice Pagan's transformation was Roddy, who'd been entangled with her. He howled and tried to disentangle himself from the demon, but it held him close easily. Then, seeing Omar trying to escape, the demon flung Roddy at him. Both men crashed down onto the couch, all the flight stunned out of them.

The monster now turned its attention to Josh. It surveyed him. He wasn't dead yet, the knife in his neck somehow preventing the outrush of blood that would have totaled him. Besides this was still under a minute after Britt had stabbed him.

The demon grinned at Josh, and it was a horrible sight, all yellow teeth and black throat beyond.

"P-pl-please!" Josh sputtered through bubbles of blood.

The still-grinning demon dipped its head down between his legs and took a bite of what it found there. When it raised its head again, chewing and with blood streaming down over its chin, Josh was quietly howling. He had nothing left between the legs. Not just his genitals were missing, but part of his thighs also and a good section of his groin. The middle of his body was now merely a large bleeding hole from which blood squirted and seeped and inside of which his guts were visible.

Britt whimpered at the sight; it was inconceivable to her that this monster was Pagan. Could they even defend themselves against it if it turned on them? And how? Her gun was over in her purse on the coffee table.

Without realizing it, Lori peed herself from excitement. She however managed to keep recording everything on the cellphone. It seemed impossible not to.

Josh had fainted from the shock of his wounds and was clearly almost dead, but by now the demon was already on its way to attack his two friends. Its wings spread and flapped as if to give it additional speed.

Roddy saw it coming and clambered off Omar, who was still stunned by their joint crash.

The demon grabbed Roddy as he turned to run down the hallway. Holding him by his left shoulder and the left side of his neck, it slowly pulled him apart, tearing him into two down the left side. His startled scream cut out sharply as his chest ripped open in a bloody display of white ribs, beating red heart, and pink lungs. Grinning, the demon reached into Roddy's opened chest and yanked out his heart and a handful of lung and ate them. Then, with Roddy's face showing mortal agony and total befuddlement, it pulled him completely in two and flung the pieces in opposite directions.

Half of him landed in front of the toilet. Britt found herself staring through the crack of the door at half of a human body with the intestines falling out of it. It was the right side of Roddy, his head still attached. There were no genitals; those were still attached to the other half of Roddy, which was draped over the DVD rack and a massive home theater speaker.

Lori bent and filmed the half-corpse. Then, realizing that she might have missed something while doing so, she quickly lifted the cellphone back up to track the transformed witch. A motion on her right made her pause. She looked that way and gaped.

Britt was masturbating fiercely, jamming two fingers up inside her sex and wincing with the pain of it. Her other hand was rubbing her clitoris for all it was worth. Her breathing was fast and ragged and her gaze was riveted on the murderous spectacle in the living room.

Lori smirked. *Dammit, Britt, you're such a hypocrite.* She returned her attention to capturing the butchery happening outside the door.

Omar was trying to run away. The demon stopped him with a hand on his shoulder. Then it dug its other hand deep into his back and yanked hard. Like a white root being unearthed, Omar's entire spine erupted from the brown flesh of his back. Blood splashed the creature's body, painting red the corded green musculature of its broad scaly chest. The black man's eyes bulged, his lips parted wide in a loud scream that somehow had no sound. Without a spinal cord, his body hung limp on the monster's hand.

The demon flung Omar's severed vertebral column across the room in Britt and Lori's direction. Both of its hands then went to work deep inside his body, unreeling his intestines like yarn out of his back. It pulled his liver and kidneys out of his back also and ate them.

"Delicious meat!" it grunted. "Such tasty human flesh! How I desire it!"

Britt was having an orgasm. This was more incredible than she'd ever imagined it would be. True, she was frightened, but it was a thrilling fear, like the worry of being discovered having sex in a public place. The fear simply increased her pleasure.

The demon was meanwhile tearing all three bodies into shreds. Wings beating wildly behind it, it stalked the living room, wading through blood from corpse to corpse and ripping parts off—legs, hands, genitals, viscera—and biting into them, then moving on to tear something else off the next dead body in line. Lori had the clear feeling that this creature—*'Avex' Pagan called it, right?*—was destroying the bodies for the sheer pleasure of doing so. There was more meat than it could eat, and sometimes it vomited up what it had already eaten just so it could gorge itself again. Occasionally it seemed to be talking to itself.

Britt rubbed herself faster and faster. She jabbed her fingers up her sex harder and harder. Finally, she howled, "Holy, holy fuck!" then slumped against Lori.

Lori was relieved that at least the demon-creature wasn't also masturbating. (The demon *was* female—Lori clearly made out the swollen pubic mound and the thin slit beneath between its flexing muscular thighs.) She didn't enjoy monster porn.

Then she noticed that the demon was looking in their direction and grinning its bloody display of yellow teeth. Most of its body other than its wings was covered with blood. The sight of it entranced her. *Wow! It's just so damned powerful!*

Britt had also noticed the demon looking their way. And now it took a step towards the toilet . . . then another.

"Shit!" she gasped in an orgasm-drenched voice. "Lori, we're fucked."

"Yeah, we were fucked. I'm still tingling all over. And this show of Pagan's is quite some afterplay."

"Lori, this isn't a fucking joke. Where's your fucking purse?"

"Behind us. Why?"

Britt didn't reply. She grabbed the purse and desperately rummaged through it till she found what she wanted. Then she hurried back to the door. "Stand back," she whispered hoarsely. Her body, so luxuriously tuned from that last orgasm, now felt like a sweet liability.

"Why?" Lori enquired again. "It's just Pagan—"

"Who isn't herself, still looks hungry as a starved gator, and doesn't recognize us at all. Lori, get your head together—she's going to fucking eat us too!" While speaking, Britt was hard at work drawing crosses on the toilet door in pink lipstick: big crosses, little crosses, swastikas, Maltese crosses; whatever she thought might protect them from the approaching evil.

And the demon was coming closer and closer. There was no doubt that it was headed for them.

"I don't think those crosses are gonna help us much," Lori whispered. "God won't be paying any attention to our pleas. Not after you ran over that mother and child this afternoon."

Lori herself found it horrifying that she was still filming everything. In a corner of her scared mind, it occurred to her that maybe she was just trying to make a record of her death—like in a found-footage movie—for whoever discovered Josh, Omar, and Roddy's corpses; most likely Josh's parents when they got back from wherever.

But I never planned on dying like this. So why then aren't I freaking out like Britt is? Is it because we're together and I'm glad she's with me even if we do die in here?

The demon was now standing right outside the toilet door. It peered through the opening at Britt and Lori's staring faces, opened its mouth as if to say something, then instead looked down at the half of Roddy's body outside the door.

Britt tried to close the toilet door, but found that she couldn't. Lori, who'd moved away from the door to let her draw on it, was now back in place recording and had it wedged open with a foot. Britt decided against forcing the issue: if they did shut the door, the anticipation of waiting for the creature to attack them would almost kill her. Better to keep an eye on the damn thing till the last possible second.

More protection was clearly needed though. She twisted the lipstick tube to get more of it out, then began drawing pink lipstick crosses over her belly, not realizing that drawing from above, she was placing half of them upside-down. Then she remembered Lori and drew some on Lori's back and buttocks too, this time getting them the right way up.

Still grinning broadly, the demon bent and picked up Roddy's right half from the floor. It pulled out some innards and stuffed them into its mouth. Then, like Roddy's meat was off, it spat the guts out, dropped the half-corpse again, and grinned even wider at the two girls trapped in the toilet.

"Fuck!" Britt squealed, kneeling to cover the bottom of the door with lipstick crosses. "Oh, God, help us!" She readied herself to slam the door shut (whatever good that would do them) once the monster took another step towards it.

But she hoped desperately, with everything inside her, that it wouldn't.

Then there was a sudden loud implosion of air, and the bitch-demon 'contracted.' All of its green mass and bulk and batwings somehow repacked themselves into a smaller space, and suddenly it was just Pagan standing there again looking sleepy and confused. She was drenched in blood and her belly was bulging out something awful, but it was just her.

"I-I-I . . .I-I . . ." Pagan stuttered, then collapsed down over the half-corpse on the floor.

Lori pissed herself again. "I think she was about telling us that she's eaten enough," she said as the amber liquid serpent crawled down her right leg.

Speechless, Britt nodded. This had been way too close for comfort.

CHAPTER 33

Kev

In the upstairs bedroom of a two-story house on Sully Road, Honey Maxwell groaned and groaned on top of Kev Parr, shivered a lot in orgasm, then fell flat on him.

Honey liked being on top during sex. With Kev being so fat and herself so thin, it was really the best way for them to fuck. The few times *he'd* been on top, she'd thought he'd flatten her and she'd also had to spread her legs so wide, it felt like they'd rip off her waist. But woman-on-top worked wonders for her. For them both really: she was fitter than a fiddle, and not having to suffer through Kev's huffing and puffing like he was a dying elephant just made sex better.

Beneath Honey, Kev was thinking: Yeah, this was the life. A policeman needed a nice loving woman to come home to after the day's horrors. Most important after the day's work was to eat and replace lost energy. And Honey understood that.

Okay, so she always wanted payment in bed later, but that was okay too, a man was expected to satisfy his woman. Honey was the world's best cook, bar none, and he was lucky she was all his.

"You okay, baby?" Honey asked, raising her head to look down at him. They'd had a completely veggie dinner, with Kev saying he didn't feel up to eating any meat tonight.

He kissed her. "Yeah, I'm okay, darling. It was just the sight of that body in the car at Rudy's—just a complete mess of meat, it was, like if you put someone through a mincer then changed your mind halfway . . . Honey, I ain't never been so scared in my damn life. I almost crapped my pants. I'm sure I would've if Chief Kravitz hadn't been there." Then he laughed. "You know, from the smell of him, Rudy might have shit his drawers though."

Kev had already told Honey about the vanishing girls in Alice's Boutique. Thankfully, she'd not laughed. Her uncle Rafael worked in some creepy west Massachusetts mansion stuffed full of occult relics, and the story he'd told them both the last time he was over here in Raynham was way stranger even than what Kev had seen.

So, yeah, Honey believed him. Just like she believed *in* him.

He stroked her thin face. She had a long sharp nose and thin lips, but her dark eyes had a seductive fire to them. And her black hair was long and thick and glossy. Her breasts were the merest of cupcakes with raisin nipples, and her ribs showed. (It was a joke between them that he had bigger tits than she did.) Still he loved her deeply. Or maybe he just loved her ability in the kitchen? Nah, it was more than that. Honey was good in bed too, but again, it was more than just that.

What he was sure of was that she made him damn happy, and he liked making her happy too; that was to be cherished. Yeah, their wedding bells weren't far off now.

Happy that he was happy with her, Honey lay her head back down on Kev's broad chest.

And then the doorbell rang.

Kev sighed. It was 1 a.m. in the goddamn morning for chrissakes! Who the heck could be ringing his doorbell now? Now, when he'd just come and was feeling sleepy and had to be at work early in the morning so Tina Kravitz didn't rip his heart out and eat it.

But he already knew the answer: his sister.

Honey grudgingly rolled off him. "That's Crystal, ain't it?"

"Has to be." He got up and put on an elephantine bathrobe, then got out his service pistol, just in case it wasn't Crystal.

He nodded at Honey. "Just you relax, baby, I'll see what she wants at this time of night. Most likely a trucker's goldbricked her again."

Detective Kev Parr made his ponderous way downstairs. It was annoying to have an elder sister who was a prostitute. It was even more annoying that Crystal Parr (her real name was Erika; she'd gotten the nickname 'Crystal' from once being addicted to crystal meth) was apparently very good at sinning in men's beds and was greatly in demand.

Most annoying of all, to Kev's mind, was that her being his sister granted her a kind of immunity to offend. Maybe as a joke, maybe just to sadistically cause Kev additional daily agony, Police Chief Tina Kravitz had ordered all her officers to lay off Crystal Parr; they were not to arrest her under any circumstances whatever. So Kev, a dignified and law abiding police officer had to live with the continuous knowledge that his older sibling (if she was younger, he'd long ago have slapped some sense into her noggin) was breaking the law day in, day out. (To Kev's additional chagrin, occasionally—when some of his more duplicitous colleagues pay her visits—she was even screwing the law!)

He got downstairs and got the front door open. Yes, it was his sister: bright blue eyes, ratty pink hair that was definitely a wig (since she was naturally a brunette), white tube top, bright pink lipstick of sufficient quantity to paint a house with, a shop's display worth of bangles and earrings, ripped jeans, and peep-toed boots. Crystal was stacked both front and back, he'd give her that—maybe that was why she was such a hit with the truckers?

Kev instantly understood that something was off with Crystal tonight. Most times when she came over this late, she was either drunk or stoned, often both. (On two occasions she'd had semen running in her hair.) On such nights, Crystal's normal complaint/request was about some jerky trick who'd either lowballed her or balked paying for her services completely. Then she'd demand that Kev come arrest/kick that person's ass/break the asshole's legs for her.

Which was a sick joke. Kev never went and Crystal always called him names then drove off mad.

Tonight though, was different: something had clearly rattled her. Usually her expression was druggy. Now she just looked scared, like she'd had an experience even drugs couldn't gloss over.

She stood there staring at him and shaking her cellphone, like she'd been calling. But she hadn't, had she? Except it had been at that time when Honey had had his dick in her mouth and he'd been lost to the world. Had his phone rung then? He didn't think so.

"Come in," he said warily, conscious of how frightened she looked.

She ducked past his bulk into the house,

Raising his gun, Kev stepped outside and scanned his front yard. The yard was bare of life. Crystal's red Volkswagen Beetle convertible was parked behind his squad car. He squinted. Her car looked empty; and why was he even thinking like this? Would a stalker or attacker wait for a woman to drive up to a cop's house before killing her?

He reentered the house, locked the door behind him, and followed Crystal into the living room.

She was sitting on a chair hugging her knees.

"What happened to you?"

For a while she said nothing, then she said, "You'd never believe me if I told you."

Kev picked out a Snickers bar from a box of them on the coffee table, peeled off the wrap, and bit into it. "Try me. After what I've seen today, you'd be surprised what I'd believe."

"I need a drink."

"You look like you've had one too many already."

"Get me a damn drink, Kev. I frigging need it."

He poured her a glass of wine. She drank it all in two swallows, then winced. "Don't you have anything harder?"

He bit back a retort. "You want another glass?"

"Yeah."

He poured her another glass of wine and she drained that too. Kev refrained from pouring her a third. She was getting a hold of herself now. She wasn't as rattled as when she'd darted through the door. Then she'd behaved like a rat fleeing a cat; no, like a rat fleeing a lion—anywhere would do, so long as it was safe.

Kev ignored Crystal's glance at the wine bottle and capped it again. He finished his Snickers and got himself another one from the box. He sat staring coldly at Crystal. "So, I'm listening, sis, what the hell happened to you? This had better be good. I'll bust your ass if you woke me up just 'cos you're thirsty."

She grimaced. Tapping her cellphone against her thigh as she spoke, she told him:

"I had a contract this evening."

"What kind of contract? You're a hit woman now?"

"Screw you, little brother. An ass-supply contract. Josh Cunningham asked me to find two other girls—nice clean girls—for two friends of his who'd be arriving in town today . . . what time is it? Sorry, I mean yesterday."

Kev nodded.

Crystal went on: "I'd already asked Rosie and Lisa—you know those two, they're normally over at Tony's Bar and Grill."

"Rosie ain't a hooker."

"She needs the money for her son's daycare. She agreed to come tonight; Josh assured me that his two friends were nice guys—college sorts. Lisa was easy to convince: she's apparently been trying to get into Josh's wallet for ages. You know how his folks are loaded."

Kev nodded again. "Sure, go on."

"Can I have some more wine?"

"Sure." He poured her another full glass.

"Thanks. So, I'd got it all set up two days ago. Only, by this evening, Rosie's had a change of heart—she's scared that if the news leaks out that she's prostituted herself, Billy will use it as an excuse to take the kid from her. I can't say that I disagree. But that still leaves me one girl short, right? I've promised Josh three of us and I need to find one more. Do you understand?"

Kev understood that he was getting angry. Now that she had three glasses of wine in her, Crystal suddenly didn't seem in such a hurry to get to what had scared her. "Yes, yes. Go on."

"So I headed over to Lisa's place for a powwow on who to call to make up the slack—I didn't want any of our regulars—and she's got this fantastic weed just in from Mexico. And we get around to smoking it, and time passes us by completely." She shrugged. "So finally I get up and it's midnight."

Kev sighed knowingly. "You messed up the contract."

She nodded. "So yes, here I am thinking what an absolute crap madam I am, and how I need to get over to Rudy's right away and apologize to Josh . . . I mean, Josh has been calling me *like mad*—I've got twenty-six missed calls from him, eight texts, and sixteen voicemails. And I'm thinking how Josh is gonna hate me for showing him up before his cool city friends, and I'm putting on my makeup, and trying to rouse Lisa so we can both get over there. But Lisa is puking everywhere—apparently before I came over she'd already shot some smack—and I have to leave her with her head stuck in the toilet bowl and go."

"And?" Kev prompted, understanding that this was all racing towards a climax.

"And when I get to Rudy's, he tells me that Josh and his friends left about an hour ago with three hookers. New girls. They weren't regulars—he'd never seen them before. The way he described it too, the three of them just *appeared* in the bar and headed right for Josh and his guys."

Now Kev began feeling a tightness constricting his chest. Three new girls who'd . . .

Crystal rushed on: "So now, I'm both relieved that Josh hasn't lost out altogether but also worried about my loss of business. All the other guys in the bar are taken except for that cheapskate Ron Hauser."

Kev knew Ron Hauser. A huge ugly trucker who reputedly hated paying for pussy. All the hookers detested him. "So what'd you do?"

"I left Rudy's and drove over to Jamie Lane, to Josh's place." She grimaced and stared pointedly at the wine bottle. Kev shook his head, so she went on with her tale: "I figured I'd go apologize to him and explain what had happened, and maybe join in the fun. Like, if I give him a freebie this once, he'd give me another procurement contract in the future."

It pained Kev Parr greatly that he, an honest, hardworking American policeman, could be sitting here at 1:30 a.m. discussing his sister's future illegal sexual investments in herself with her. But apparently he had to accompany her along her path of degradation to hear what she'd really come here to tell him. "So? And no more wine till you finish."

She scowled. "Cheapskate." Then she shivered, and he understood, shivering himself, that the reason she'd gone on such a long oral detour was because she was scared of reliving what she'd seen.

"Look, first thing I want you to know is that it wasn't me that killed them. I didn't do it."

"Oh fuck! Josh is dead?" Kev's half-eaten Snicker bar tumbled out of his mouth. He ignored it. "Crystal, why the hell didn't you just say so in the first place?" He began pulling his bulk out of the chair. "Look, I gotta call the Chief—"

"No! Fucking sit down! Don't call anyone until I show you what I recorded on my phone." Now there were tears in her eyes and she looked even more rattled than she had on arriving at his doorstep.

Kev sat, though he didn't like this one damn bit. At this very moment the murderers might be getting away. He momentarily glanced up at the ceiling. Honey was hopefully asleep by now; he didn't want his sister agitating her too.

Crystal said, "I walked up the front steps to the door. I was just about ringing the doorbell when I heard a sound and a scream. It sounded like someone hacking up meat, and the scream . . . it was gurgled, like someone was drinking water and yelling at the same time, if that makes sense to you. Then there was another louder scream, and I decided not to go in until I was sure of what was going on in there . . . one of Josh's friends might have done too much PCP and gone loco, you know?" She seemed now to visibly grow smaller. "So I walked around the side of the house and peeked in the living room windows. The lights were on and it was easy to see and . . ." Words now clearly failed her. She thrust her phone at Kev.

He took a few seconds to understand the controls of the media player she'd called up, then played the video.

Oh, shit! No, this wasn't happening. On the little screen, some kind of monster—it was huge and green and muscular and totally hairless and had wings like a bat—was tearing a naked young man into two as easily as if he were made of paper. Kev looked over at Crystal, who'd now secured the wine bottle for herself and was emptying the last of it into her glass. He looked back at the screen. The monster was biting chunks out of the young man. The camera angle slipped a bit and . . . he rewound the video . . . Oh, holy crap, no! There was Josh Cunningham on the ground, and he was also naked and had a knife stuck in his neck and . . . Kev almost puked . . . nothing but a red hole between his legs—no dick or balls, nothing—shee-it. And the monster was now tackling a black guy. The black guy—this guy was ripped like some goddamn NFL quarterback—was running, his eyes wide with fear, his dick flopping wildly in his crotch, when suddenly he froze and his eyes seemed to turn to glass, and next thing, the monster—or demon, shee-it, it had a snake-face and horns on its head!—was holding up a white thing made of linked bones that it had just pulled out of the black guy's back (*Oh my God, is that his spine!?*) and laughing loudly, and then it flung the vertebrae across the room to hit the wall and the black guy collapsed forward and the demon began yanking his guts out of his back and . . .

The video stopped at that point.

He looked up from the phone to see his sister staring at him. "I got the hell out of there after that," she said, dabbing tears from her eyes.

"I'm impressed that you hung around to record this much. I'd have hightailed it on seeing that first guy torn in two." Then his gaze hardened. "Look, sis, level with me, okay? I know what CGI can do nowadays. True, I see Josh in here, but . . . are you sure this ain't some gag video you downloaded from YouTube?"

Her pink lipstick mouth squeezed tight as a virgin's hymen. "Don't be fucking silly, Kev. Does that look to you like a joke video?"

He frowned. Hell no, it didn't. That was the problem: somehow he'd just watched a *demon* rip three young men to bits.

Crystal said, "So what now? With this evidence, do you still want to call the department?"

He reached for another Snickers bar and peeled off the wrapper, took a big bite, then burped. "I think that'll be a bad idea. It's smarter to just forget you saw anything. This is the kind of Area 52 crap that'll have the national goon squad explaining the supposedly nonexistent Official Secrets Act to you in a locked room."

She nodded. "That's what I thought too. That's why I came over instead of calling 911."

"Crystal, how many cars did you see outside Josh's place?"

"Only two. Josh's and a blue Toyota SUV. Why?"

Kev's fat face crinkled up. "Just that . . . well if the demon did this, where were the other two girls? There were three of them, right?"

Crystal didn't say anything, so Kev explained about the two young women who'd somehow vanished that Monday afternoon, and the dismembered corpse in the car in Rudy's parking lot. (He refrained from also mentioning the pregnant woman who'd been flattened on the Broadway sidewalk with those skid marks from an invisible vehicle on her belly. The memory of that now almost sent him off into puke-zone again.)

"Yeah," Crystal agreed, looking even more scared now, "you're frigging right. We'd both better keep our mouths shut about this."

Kev nodded. "You say Josh's parents are away? I'll find some excuse to drive over there in the morning, then I'll report the crime to the station. Or I might be lucky and someone else would have already called it in." He looked searchingly at his older sister; she looked suddenly fragile, a pretty glass doll about to shatter. "You wanna stay here tonight?"

She nodded. "I'm not going back outside again tonight for nothing. That *thing* might be out there." Then she frowned at him. "Kev, what're we gonna do with this video I recorded? It's evidence, ain't it?"

"I'll keep a copy on my laptop just in case. But forget it: even with sworn testimony that you saw it happen, no one but those Area 52 geeks will ever believe it isn't faked anyway."

After copying the video recording across to his laptop, he showed Crystal to the spare room and went upstairs to join his darling Honey again.

Honey was asleep when Kev climbed back into bed. She stirred groggily, then checked the bedside alarm clock for the time. "You've been gone ages, baby. What did she want?"

He faked aggrieved gaiety. "Oh, just the usual: some trucker gypped her out of her pussy again. She's sleeping off her drunk in the guest room."

He kissed Honey and she went back to sleep. He hated lying to her like this, but Honey was the sort of conscientious citizen who'd *insist* that Crystal show Chief Kravitz the horrible recording she'd made.

Kev lay beside her staring at the ceiling. For an hour afterwards he found it impossible to sleep; his mind refused to dull into a comfortable nothing.

Finally, he quietly got out of bed again and made his way back downstairs to the living room, where turned his laptop back on. While it powered up, Kev made his way into the kitchen and cut himself a big slice of the apple pie which Honey—God bless her soul—had made for their Sunday lunch. To wash the pie down, he got out a 1.5 liter bottle of Dr. Pepper. The Coors Light in the fridge would have been better, but the hangover would be hell in the morning with all the driving he had to do.

Then he settled his bulk in a chair, and in the half-darkness watched the demonic snuff video over and over again. One-and-a-half minutes—that was how long it took—of utterly insane bloodshed.

It never got any easier to view.

Kev was stumped. *What the holy hell in God's name is going on in this Raynham town of ours these last few days?*

Kev was certain that the culprit—the monster in this video—had to be that Satanist chick everyone was looking for. But where the hell was she? And even if they found her, how in the world did you prosecute her for something like this? Get her to transform in court (and eat the judge and jury)? Shee-it!

CHAPTER 34

Pagan

At the exact same time as Kev Parr was reviewing his sister's recording of the massacre on his laptop, Pagan too was watching it on her cellphone.

She sat in a chair beside the motel bed, her fingers in her mouth, staring in horror at what she'd become.

"Shit, am I in so much big fucking trouble," she whispered into the night air, keeping her voice low so as not to wake Britt and Lori, both of whom (now the night's enjoyment/excitement was past) were sound asleep, their gentle breathing mingled with the hum of the air conditioner.

Once Pagan had 'compacted back to normal'—as Lori put it—they'd gathered up their clothes, rushed her back into the car and fled the murder house. Pagan had needed to shower and pee first. She'd been shocked by all the lipstick crosses on their bodies. ("It was *that* bad?" "Just watch the tape.")

Watching her two companions slumber sweetly now like nothing at all was wrong decided Pagan once and for all that both girls were emotionally defective.

I'm utterly horrified and they can't even stay awake.

Then she decided she was being too harsh with them: *Sex is a great body relaxer and we had loads of it tonight.* A smile curved her lips at the memory, then she replayed the video and lost the smile. *What the bloody . . . ? I don't frigging believe this!* Sure, she'd known it'd be pretty bad to view herself like this, but not that it would be *this* bad. But then, what had she expected to see? Herself wearing a dragon costume and playfully slashing at people with latex claws and them playing dead? *Be serious, girl—you've known you were fucked-up since day one in the basement!*

But *this* bad? And there was more: she sensed also that something else was happening here. Something much worse than just her changing skin color and growing more muscles than a gorilla (and wings and horns too) in ten seconds.

And she thought she knew what it was: What bothered Pagan even more than seeing herself bloodily rend three people to messy shreds as easily as if they were sandwich meat, was the 'rightness' she felt about her actions, the pleasant/sweet 'knowledge' that she'd only done the 'right' thing.

Except she forced herself to ethically analyze her actions, she honestly couldn't see what she'd done wrong by killing Josh, Omar, and Roddy.

She felt no guilt whatsoever. Utterly none at all.

I was hungry and I ate . . . and next time I'm hungry I'll eat again and . . .

And then she realized that it was the demon thinking through her. But how? Was it now right inside her mind? Startled, she looked inside herself. What she found alarmed her. She *was* still a separate entity from Avex, but now she felt a definite blending of their two selves, like they were mixing into one being. Now, she'd begun feeling like Avex did, understanding the 'rightness' of its lusts and actions, and how it *must* feed . . . no, how she, Pagan, *must* feed . . . on thousands and thousands . . .

It wants to . . . I want to . . . eat thousands? THOUSANDS!!?? Avex, are you frigging nuts!?? She shook her head violently to the demon's loud assent within. *Oh, frigging hell no! Only over my dead body is that happening, you son-of-a-bitch monster!*

But even as she thought that, she was hit by the sudden clear knowledge—*now* the bastard demon Avex shared it with her—that all choice in her actions were slowly being taken from her; that soon—very soon indeed (the monster within hid details of exactly when)—it and she would fuse and become one and the same person.

And then—it let her know with unmasked delight—the REAL FEEDING would begin. What they'd both done so far wasn't even an appetizer.

Desperately, Pagan connected to the motel's Wi-Fi and checked her email. Nothing.

She was suddenly filled with intense panic. *C'mon, Red Octopus, make up your goddamn minds and come get me! I need help! I'm absolutely losing it here!*

She sat there, leaned forward in the chair, elbows on knees and face cradled in her hands, staring glumly at the brown rug with its dripping of dark lines from when they'd gotten in.

She felt full (her belly was a stuffed hill below her breasts), but also desolate, her soul emptied of her humanity.

Morning couldn't come fast enough for Pagan; she couldn't wait for the new day to dawn and hopefully grant her deliverance from her troubles.

TUESDAY

CHAPTER 35

Joker

Jesus was nailing Joker to His cross again.

This time He was using a nail gun on her. The nails were huge spikes, like for fixing house lumber to a frame.

She was screaming her lungs out. The pain seemed to go on forever and ever. Like eternal life.

"I did warn you, didn't I?" the Savior asked while affixing her right hand to the crosspiece. 'Thunk!' The nail tore through her flesh, shattered her protesting bones, and buried itself in the wood. Her feet were already nailed to the cross upright by two spikes through the top of the left one which was placed over the right, and her blood was flowing freely.

Jesus still looked like Rob Zombie, or maybe it was the other way round, Rob looked like Jesus—the Lord having had a 2,000 year head start on the bearded moody look.

"My daughter, I warned you to get your act together or go to Hell," Jesus said, waving the nail gun at her for emphasis. His face was grim. He wasn't about taking no mess from her.

"I'm sorry," she screamed as He pushed her left forearm down hard on the shaved wood and . . . 'Thunk!' fired two more spikes into her hand. Additional undiluted agony.

He leaned up. "That's almost finished. Just remains the final touches."

This time the barbed wire crown was larger, its barbs so long and sharp that they felt like they were digging right into her brain. Blood ran freely down her face, distinguishable from her red hair only because it was in motion.

He next stood the cross upright so she could look out over the empty landscape. This time she saw no fellow Abyss offenders; it was just herself surrounded by flaming pits.

Her entire world was now a locus of pain. "Why are you doing this to me!?" she yelled down at Him. "You're supposed to be trying to save my soul!"

"I gave up. You need to know how it feels: dying for a planet that doesn't appreciate the gesture."

Joker screamed, not because she'd suddenly appreciated the gesture of the Savior's sacrifice, but because Jesus was now pointing a speargun at her. He pressed it against her left side, just under the ribs. Through her other agonies, she felt the tip of the spear pierce her skin.

He fired. There was simultaneously a loud whoosh of decompressed air and the thud of the spear embedding itself into the wood behind her. There was a magical moment when she never felt the pain of the harpoon having punched a hole all the way through her body, and then she resumed screaming. And louder now, *much* louder.

She glared down at Jesus, suddenly really angry. "Why?"

"Z," He replied, winking at her, then next dipping His hand in the blood gushing from her spear wound and writing the sign of the cross on her naked belly. "Hey, and listen, you little whore: don't you ever dare masturbate to me and my Father and the Holy Spirit again or I'll really—"

Joker woke up, her eyes gaping white. She was drenched in sweat. She lay in the dark motel room gasping for breath, her heart racing. *Another dream? Oh, fuck it! This is the second time since taking this damn—*

With a start, she realized her phone was ringing; that was what had woken her.

She picked it up. It was Nero.

"Hi, man . . . God, you wouldn't believe the nightmare I just had, some kinda freaky Rob Zombie Jesus—"

"Shut up and listen to me, you stupid slut," Nero interrupted her. "We're onto you. We *know*."

The coldness in his voice sent chills down her spine. "What are you talking about?"

"The investigating warlocks discovered that you and Pagan planned this all along. You're meeting her in that damn motel in Raynham."

Joker had now turned pale against the darkness. What the hell was going on? "Nero, I don't know what you're talking about! I really don't." She was practically yelling into the phone now. It didn't matter if the other motel residents could hear her. If the Abyss Club thought she had a hand in Pagan's Avex nonsense, she was screwed: finished, dead, and cremated.

Panicking, she moaned, "Listen, Nero, I really don't know what you're talking about. Honest, I don't. I'm here to do what you asked me to, and—"

"And you just neglected to mention that you and Pagan are both ROC spies."

Oh, unholy shit. "Spies? Me and Pagan? Man, are you crazy? I'm completely loyal to Abyss. You know that!"

"You're a *traitorous* liar, Joker—the worst kind of liar. Anyhow it doesn't matter anymore."

"I'm coming back to Beantown once it's daylight. I don't believe this shit. I can explain . . ." She stopped, confused. What could she explain? There was nothing *to* explain—she was innocent. *It makes no sense: how can anyone believe that I and Pagan planned this nonsense? Someone is clearly setting me up.*

Nero snickered over the line. "Don't bother coming back, traitor bitch. I just called to say goodbye. It's been nice knowing you."

"Goodbye? Nice knowing me!? What do you mean!?"

"You'll shortly find out. Say hello to Mr. Hairy for me."

The phone clicked dead. Joker leapt out of bed and switched on the lights. It was 3 a.m., and a slight breeze moved the window drapes.

The motel room was a void that she tried to fill with her thoughts. *Who the hell is Mr. Hairy?*

Pondering that question while staring at the evening depression she'd left in the bed, she suddenly became aware of a horrible musky smell.

Her eyes widened with shock and fear. *Oh no, they didn't!*

She leapt across the room just as the first massive hoof crashed down through the ceiling, trampling half of the bed into the floor.

Crouched in a corner, she cringed in horror. *A goat!? They sent a fucking goat after me!? But I haven't done anything wrong!*

The massive hairy leg lifted up through the wreckage of the bed and pulled out of the roof. She stared up out of the huge hole it had left in the ceiling. Up there a massive bulk blocked out the sky. Clouds of flies swirled under the bulk. She could feel the goat biding its time, trying to work out where she was, where it should flatten next.

Well, Mr. Hairy, I'm not waiting!

She leapt up, grabbed her clothes off the chair, and dashed across the room to the front door. Then, just before reaching its safety, she stepped on a fragment of the broken bed. The chunk of wood slipped backwards under her, pitching her forward. She landed flat on her belly, three feet from the door.

As she scrabbled desperately up onto her hands and knees, there was a loud shattering above her. Bits of the ceiling rained on her and moments later, she felt the most horrifying pain ever in her lower back.

Confused by her agony, Joker looked back. Her buttocks and legs had disappeared; in their place stood the goat's leg—a four-foot-wide shaggy pillar around which a fog of green blowflies buzzed. The thick stink of the animal's body dazed Joker even more, so it was several seconds before she realized what had happened.

The goat had stamped her lower half into the ground, completely severing her body in two. Except for the blood seeping around where her torso was truncated, she might have been a part of the massive leg now rising from its pit in the motel room floor.

But . . . how am I still alive? Alive or not, her missing lower half seemed to have been replaced by raw pain. Agony ravaged her remaining nerves all the way up to her brain.

She looked forward to the front door. She began clawing her way towards it. As she moved, her innards spilled out from her body. She looked back once and confirmed this: behind her lay a red line of guts leading to the edge of the cloven-hoof-shaped hole in the carpet. She looked up. The goat's leg was just vanishing through the ceiling again.

She had no doubt where it would stomp next.

Then the front door opened and green light spilled into the room.

She winced. Jesus stood there smiling His sadistic Rob Zombie smile at her. She gaped at him.

He laughed His death metal laugh. "My foolish child, this is simply a lesson on how easy it is to separate the sheep from the goats." There was blood dripping through holes in His palms, and that bright green light was shining behind Him, making Him look like a scarecrow in a field of damned souls.

Joker was so entranced by the Savior's divine glory, she almost didn't notice the fall of wood debris over her announcing that the goat was about finishing her off, its massive dirty hoof falling to a crash with her remaining body.

Then she did and she began screaming.

"Oh, you bad, bad goat, Mr. Hairy," Jesus said, and began laughing loudly.

**

Joker woke up again, screaming into the darkness of her motel room. Finally she got a handle on her fear. She sat up in bed, hands clenched in her lap, and shivered.

What kind of horrible dreams am I having? From one, into the next . . . I thought . . . Nero . . . Jesus . . .

Finally her heart stopped racing and her chills warmed. She got out of bed, put on the lights, and walked into the bathroom for a drink of water.

Staring at her face in the bathroom mirror Joker felt spooked. Her eyes were the exact color of the light that had surrounded Jesus in her nightmare, her hair the exact same shade of red as the blood dripping from His hands.

She felt bound to her dream by unseen chains. It had been that vivid.

This isn't any good. Yes, some dreams are Freudian nonsense, our brains making sense of yesterday's problems, but others mean something, even if they're just hazy premonition. What the hell does this one mean?

Still feeling rattled, she walked out of the bathroom again and sat in a chair. Just in case she was still dreaming, she waited for her phone to ring and for Nero to call her a traitor. When that didn't happen, she considered calling him instead and feeling him out to see if he suspected her of anything. Then she realized that doing so would be silly and might even give him the wrong idea about her. Besides which, it was too late to call anyway. If she interrupted him while he was eating Azalea's pussy and the old witch was about to come . . .

And then she thought she knew the interpretation of her dream: *Oh, hell no! The Abyss Club are planning to swindle me out of my reward after I've cleared up their mess. They'd better not dare!*

For a moment she was so angry she could cry. But then, she tried to rationalize things. It was just a dream; she had no proof that Nero wasn't sincere. He'd even been the one who'd told her that the Hollywood job was vacant. She'd not known about that. So maybe she was just getting everything twisted.

Of course, she still had to find Pagan to cash in on the offer. And so far that didn't seem to be happening.

Finally she calmed down enough to go back to bed and fall asleep again.

***

By morning Joker was still rattled, still angry.

She'd slept badly the second time around (though without any more dreams) tossing and turning till dawn. And now this morning, the Jesus/goat nightmare still bothered her. Its vividness had faded, but a patina of dread ringed her brain like a corrupted halo.

The sun was high in the sky; the day had begun without her.

She masturbated once, only getting so far as "Oh my God!" She was wary of getting as far as "Thank you, Jesus!" Maybe that was why He kept torturing her in her sleep?

Afterwards, she dressed and drove into town, stopping at Mel's Diner (which was just down Broadway) for a breakfast of scrambled eggs, home fries, and a grilled English muffin and coffee.

Stepping outside again after finishing her meal, Joker decided to leave her car parked in the diner lot and walk around for a bit. This was partly to stretch her legs, and partly to see if she could find anyone who knew anything about Pagan's whereabouts.

Which she figured would be best done if she eavesdropped on people who couldn't see her.

Joker wasn't nearly as adept as Pagan where casting cloaking spells was concerned. Pagan had a knack for 'looking invisible'; she'd worked out how to magically balance the conflicting energy fields so they cancelled each other out. Joker, on the other hand, found the entire process energy-sapping. She could only hold the cloak in place for an hour or so before the strain became too much for her body to bear; and after that she'd need to eat a large meal fast. (For her, using a cloaking spell was much like smoking pot: afterward she was always so damn hungry.)

Of course, in this case that was the benefit of leaving her car parked by the diner. She'd simply return here once her surveillance was complete, have another breakfast (it'd have to be a takeaway to avoid inquisitive stares), then meet Sin Corbin for their noon appointment at McKinney's farm.

Once she'd rendered herself invisible, Joker properly regarded her surroundings. Mel's Diner was the first shop in a block of five situated between the Center Street and Britton Street corners, and facing the Broadway post office and the Little Flyer's Learning Center to the left of that.

(This Tuesday morning seemed subdued, as though everyone had shared her nightmares. The vehicles passing the diner and their passengers all seemed mirrors of each other. But then, she reasoned, both *were* vehicles of a sort. Cars and trucks carried humans, and humans carried souls in their corporal forms. Which meant humans were corporations of body, mind, and spirit.)

She looked up and down Broadway, debating whether to strike out left or right for her enquiries. In the end she decided to head right.

Immediately next door to Mel's stood a liquor store, outside of which a small group of listeners were currently assembled around an old preacher.

A smirk forming on her face, Joker walked closer to the huddled group.

The preacher looked Mexican, and was probably from Calvary Chapel, the church up the road by the motel. He was dressed simply in a black suit, had a long grey beard, and held a Bible that looked older than he was—its pages were yellow with age and dog-eared.

"Do not be deceived, brethren," he was telling the small group of listeners. "These *are* perilous times. These are times to be sober, not . . ." he flung a fierce gesture back at the liquor store sign, "not times to be *drunken*. These are the prophesized Last Days, when evil shall walk the land in plain view. How else do you explain the recent satanic murder in our once peaceful town? And just yesterday afternoon, that sweet young mother . . ."

Some of his listeners nodded agreement; some smirked knowingly. An old woman swayed on her feet and moaned, "Preach it, Brother!" A bald-shaven young man with gauged ears who was leaning against the liquor store wall and carrying two just-purchased six-packs of beer, whispered, "Damn Jesus Freaks," to his similarly hairless girlfriend, but didn't leave.

Normally Joker would have walked right past the group. She might have spit on the preacher out of personal conviction, but she'd not have messed with him.

But this morning? She was too angry about her nightmare of Jesus torturing her to let the old man go unmolested.

Remembering that no one could see her, she decided to have some fun at the preacher's expense. And who was he to tell people not to drink anyway?

"Believe me, my brothers and sisters, the police cannot help us now! The law is baffled and confused at the current state of affairs! Only GOD can . . . !"

Reaching around him from behind, Joker grabbed a handful of the preacher's beard and yanked down on it. He instantly stopped speaking and gaped down at it, confused. His mouth remained open.

Joker was disappointed. She'd wanted him to cuss, yelp "Shit!" or "Fuck!" or some such like. Not like it seemed the old guy would know any swear words though.

But, oh, she was so going to get him!

She waited.

The preacher smiled apologetically at his listeners and resumed his sermon. "Oh, now, where was I? Yes . . . as it is written in God's word, 'This know also, that in the last days perilous times shall come. For men shall be lovers—'"

Joker slapped him HARD. So hard that though she knew she was invisible, she was still surprised that none of those gathered heard the noise of her hand connecting with his cheek.

They did however see his head jerk sideways and spit fly out of his mouth. Everyone looked at him confused.

The old man stood stunned with his head bent to the left.

"Is anything the matter?" a woman asked. "Your face just . . ."

The preacher slowly straightened up his head. "Get thee behind me, Satan!" he muttered.

Joker laughed at that. *Oh, I am behind you, you old fool! Let's see what your stupid God can do now!*

She wasn't done having her fun. Already she felt better: about the dream and her interpretation of it, about her quest—about everything.

While the preacher collected his thoughts, she crouched behind him, grabbed both his ankles and leapt to her feet again while yanking hard.

The preacher went sprawling. The young bald guy with the gauged ears scrambled out of his way and he hit the ground hard, his Bible landing a yard ahead of him.

"Damn, man!" the young man said, bending over him. "What the heck just happened?"

The old preacher rolled over, and slowly sat up. "There's an evil presence around here. I can sense it."

"You sure you ain't sick, old man?"

"Maybe he's been drinking," someone suggested. There was some laughter, but not much.

The preacher staggered to his feet. "No, I tell you: there is *evil* around us here. I must deal with it . . ."

Joker was laughing her head off. She decided to show him what 'evil' was all about. She'd throw him again, this time hard against the liquor store wall.

She saw the old man's lips moving, but didn't hear what he said.

And then . . .

Next thing Joker knew, something HIT her. She was aware of a force swatting her like a fly. It knocked her off her feet and through the air, flinging her back towards Mel's diner, then over her car and all the way down to the end of the shopping block, where she crashed into the side of the white van parked outside the last store, Mooberry's Frozen Yoghurt.

She hit the van with a resounding 'Wham!' that shifted it sideways.

She fell to the lot floor and sat there stunned while a female shopper rushed out of Mooberry's to investigate. From the woman's confused howls, she'd apparently made a huge dent in the side of the van.

She shook her head clear and looked up to check. It was true, almost like in a superhero movie, her crashing into the van had left an imprint of her body in its metal.

It was ridiculous. *How the hell did that . . . ?*

Forty yards away by the liquor store, the preacher was shouting "Amen, Hallelujah!" and shaking his ratty Bible in the air.

Bruised, and with her ego smarting, Joker got to her feet and stalked back towards him. Now she was *really* angry. She'd show him for real what witches were capable of. What he'd so far experienced was mere child's play. She'd—

Then she saw it: The outline of a HUGE man standing over the preacher. As she continued forward, the figure solidified into full view. (It was somehow both right there and solid and almost transparent at the same time.) The man was massively muscled, was at least ten-feet-tall, and was dressed in a white suit and a white hat. He glowed with a golden light that hurt Joker to look at. Still she made out the cold expression on his face.

She pulled up to a sharp halt and even stepped back two paces. Suddenly she didn't feel like going over there any more.

The HUGE man by the liquor store was cracking his knuckles like he was about punching someone. He pointed a finger at Joker and their eyes met. (Below the giant figure, the old preacher had resumed his sermon like he had no idea what was going on. Likewise, his listeners all had their attention on him. Clearly, as far as they were concerned, nothing strange was happening around them. But then, how could they know something was? Joker and the giant were two *invisible* people.)

"Get lost," the HUGE man told Joker in a voice so deep, she felt it stirring her bone marrow.

Joker nodded, then just to make sure he understood that she'd got the message, she waved her hands at him in a peace gesture. After one last horrified look at the angel, she quickly turned away and hurried back towards Mel's Diner, thinking, *Shit! Shit! Shit! Trust me to pick a live one to fuck with! And on today of all goddamn days! Oh, how I just hate this damn Raynham town!*

She slumped against the diner's brick wall for a moment to collect herself. She was gasping and her ribs hurt. On sober reflection now, it was a miracle that her back wasn't broken. *Okay, that didn't go too well just now. To hell with being invisible. I'd better just buy my second breakfast and head over to see Sin Corbin.*

CHAPTER 36

Pagan

Pagan stared at the phone screen in relief. The message from 'Squidkid' was short, simple, and sweet:

Welcome to Red Octopus, Pagan. We're making arrangements to pick you up later today.

A smile formed on her lips. Tears formed in her eyes and she let them flow freely. Oh, thank God! Thank God! Soon her nightmare would be over.

"Why're you crying?" Lori asked, walking out from the bathroom. "Did someone you love die?"

"Or did you eat them?" Britt sing-songed from the bathroom amidst splashes of water. "Damn, Pagan, I gotta watch that video again. I've never, and I mean frigging *never*, seen anything like that before in my life. I wish *I* could do that."

Lori grinned at Pagan. "Just ignore her," she said. "I've been doing so all my life—it's how we've remained best friends for so long." She reached out a gentle hand and wiped away Pagan's tears, then walked over to the fridge. "Britt, we need to go shopping—we're out of food again!"

"Okay, yeah, but later! It's just ten—I wanna sleep some more first."

Pagan suddenly hated both Britt and Lori. Britt, with her lust for violence, reminded her of the demon in her body. Lori, with her indifference to murder, disgusted her because, well, wasn't everyone supposed to have a conscience? And ethics? You couldn't just decide 'fuck life' and accept whatever came your way, be it good or bad. (From little snippets of conversation between them, she'd gleaned that both girls had been raped; but while Britt was incensed over being

291

sexually abused, Lori couldn't give a shit. In this case, Pagan sided with Britt: you *were* supposed to give a shit about having sex forced on you.)

Wow, there's different grades of sociopath.

She remembered herself. She got off the bed and walked over to look out of the motel room window. Bright sunlight warmed her face. It was a lovely day.

After some consideration, she typed into the phone: *Thanks! What should I do now?*

Thirty seconds later, the reply came in: *What's your specific location in Raynham?*

I'm in Room 9 at the Sun— With a start, she remembered that she'd switched rooms and corrected the text: *I'm in Room 5 at the Sunflower Motel on Carver Street.*

Once she'd sent the message, she heaved a huge sigh of relief. Room 9? It would be criminally pathetic to screw something so simple up now.

The reply soon came in: *Cool. Just stay put there. We'll send a car for you by afternoon. ETA 3 p.m.*

Pagan typed 'Okay' then stood musing to herself, a relaxed feeling blooming in her like spring roses.

She turned from the window to smile at her two companions. Britt was emerging from the bathroom, toweling herself dry.

"You feeling better now?" Britt asked, a crazy glint in her eye.

"Hell yeah."

Lori nodded. "It's important not to let things get you down, you know. Death is just a part of life for all of us. Like it or not, we're all gonna die very soon."

"Yeah," Britt agreed. "We three earlier than most." She dropped the towel over a chair and lay back naked on the bed, then stretched out a hand to Pagan. "Hey, let me have the phone. I want to wank to your evil demon-girl self again."

Pagan considered refusing, then she closed her email and handed the cellphone over. "You're disgusting," she said.

Britt nodded. "Yeah, most likely. I really don't give a shit about opinions anymore; I'm fucking for the moment. Girl, I'm every man's worst nightmare—a vagina without a conscience."

Watching her open the phone's video player app, Pagan was filled with intense revulsion.

"Hey!" Lori called, her face serious. "Remember Kaminski's law: I'm not watching you finger yourself. Go back in the bathroom."

Britt gave Lori the finger, then slinked off, her nude ass wiggling. At the door, she turned back and leered at Lori. "I'm gonna imagine it's you Pagan's eating."

Lori stuck her tongue out. Britt slapped her shaven crotch with a hand and shut the bathroom door.

Pagan gaped at Lori. "Don't you two have any depths of degradation you're not prepared to descend to?"

Lori shrugged. "Stop looking at me like that. Even for me, masturbating to *you* killing people is weird."

Pagan nodded, though she didn't believe Lori. Oh, no, she wasn't telling these two that she was being rescued today. Angry at being abandoned, they might just kill her out of spite before the ROC showed up.

CHAPTER 37

Britt

Sitting on the toilet with her legs braced firmly in front of her, Britt was enjoying herself. One hand held Pagan's cellphone (though its display name was 'Sandy'), the other stroked between her legs, teasing her swollen clitoris and dipping in between her labia. Her eyes were riveted on the killing on the phone's screen.

When the huge green demon ripped out the black guy's spinal cord, Britt came. She shut her eyes, grit her teeth, and shuddered so hard it felt like she was breaking up. She felt like she was going to faint.

When it was over, she instantly felt disgusted with herself—*How can I even be doing this?*—but her self-recrimination soon passed, eased away into one of the many layers of rationalization now comfortably padding her conscience.

Almost before Britt knew what she was doing, she was stroking herself again. Maybe her mind still didn't like it, but her body was telling her conscience to go fuck itself too if it liked.

Oh, yes, pleasuring herself to death like this *was* disgusting, but she simply couldn't stop herself. *Is it that I can't or that I don't want to?* She neither knew nor cared.

She reasoned: maybe this was how men felt watching all those nasty rape scenes in movies—outwardly making pretensions of disgust, while being secretly turned on? *Which ever it is, I've at least dispensed with the masquerade! A plus for female sexual emancipation!*

She dipped her hand deep into her body and pulled more pleasure out of herself. Before she knew it—her eyes focused on Pagan tearing Roddy into two like someone unzipping their fly—she was coming again.

The orgasm now racking her body felt deliciously evil. Oh, so morbidly perverse and perfect. She could die, no—she could *kill* for this feeling. She *would* kill for it. She felt hypersexed, like her vagina extended across the entire USA, like it could contain the entire world if the world was the head of a man's erect cock.

She wanted, desperately needed, a man inside her right now.

But that was the damn problem, wasn't it? If she brought someone here, Pagan was bound to eat him afterwards. Which was good, right? As in, destroying the evidence? Only—and this was another problem—Pagan didn't seem to be able to finish eating anyone. Pagan did monster gourmet-eating, picking out the choice bits of corpse and leaving the kind of mess a lion cub in kindergarten would be proud of.

And speaking of Pagan . . . *What the hell is up with her face this morning? It looks kinda odd, like she's . . . I need to check that out when I get back outside. But first*—the video had looped back to the start and was now showing the green demoness biting out the entirety of Josh's crotch—*first I need to come at least twice more!*

She stood for a moment, grabbed Lori's hairbrush off the glass shelf over the washstand, and sunk its handle deep into her sex. She gasped at the sensation, all the breath rushing out of her as she penetrated herself with the stiff brown plastic.

She sank back down onto the toilet seat. She began thrusting the hairbrush handle in and out of her womanhood, all the nerve endings in her tender wet sexual passage charging up desperately to another violently explosive climax.

CHAPTER 38

Lori

This would be an utterly wonderful day to die, Lori thought.

A pleasant dewy feeling had settled over her as she stood by the window staring out at their blue RAV4, and beyond it, the cars driving in and out of the motel. Beyond the cars, the sparse fringe of bushes and trees that obscured the main road shone bright green in the sun and she imagined she saw frisky squirrels running along their branches. Above the tree line, the sky was a clear blue, the clouds a nice fluffy white, the out-of-view sun unobscured to warm up the world.

A calm, almost drowsy ambience hung over everything, including herself. Lori felt 'settled,' like she'd finally made peace with her personal demons.

Yes this'd be a fucking great day to die, she thought calmly.

Behind her she could hear Britt grunting and moaning through another LOUD orgasm in the bathroom. The erotic noises flew past her like birds. She wasn't disgusted by what her friend was up to.

Lori herself wasn't turned on at the moment. No. Last night with those three guys she'd fulfilled the top fantasy on her bucket list. She'd come up with the list a year ago. It was made up of simple things— she already knew she wasn't going to survive to age twenty-five, so goals like 'Owning my own business' and 'Getting married and having kids' weren't included. There were mainly a number of sexual things that she'd wanted to try out. The top two of those—a threesome with a guy and another girl, and a foursome: herself and a guy filling each of her holes—she'd now accomplished on this road trip. Both experiences had definitely lived up to her expectations, and so now she was ready to depart this cruel world.

She felt suicidal this morning. Not the moody suicidal of being in her Pit, surrounded by black walls of personal isolation roofed by a sky of neglect, but once again her new 'happy suicidal'—the desire to end oneself resulting from the knowledge that one had achieved life's objectives.

But if I'm doing it today, I'd better hurry before I start getting bored and fall back into the Pit again. The problem was, she still hadn't yet figured out how best she'd like to die. That had always been her curse and even now it plagued her still. *Should I throw myself under a truck? Slit my throat? Shoot myself in the head like Lonnie did, and let my brains explode everywhere like the petals of a blossoming pink flower?*

Then, all at once, her longtime fear of the pain before death returned and discouraged further thinking in that direction.

Unsettled by her fears, she looked around the room to distract herself.

Pagan had the TV tuned to the news, but wasn't watching it; she was instead staring at the ceiling with a preoccupied look on her face. Lori wondered how it felt to host a demon in one's body, to have one's flesh as accommodation for a troubled spirit. *Oh, it has to be really cool! Of course Pagan keeps moaning about how horrible it is, but then she would, wouldn't she? But being able to do that kind of mutant superhero transformation . . . muscles and claws and . . . and then there's the fact that she's invisible . . . us too now. No one can see us—we can go on like this forever if we like, spree-killing and kicking ass. Wowee!! But, c'mon, God, I do so seriously want out of this horrible world of yours, and today looks like the perfect day to vacate it. Oh, if only I could figure out an equally perfect way to end my life—*

She was interrupted by a loud burst of moaning from Britt in the bathroom, which had Pagan looking at her and wincing; which put a sudden question in Lori's mind: *Hey—what's the matter with Pagan's face this morning? It looks somehow odd. Is it just her eyes or—*

The bathroom door burst open and Britt staggered out naked, looking drained. She staggered over to the bed and flopped down on it face up. A limp hand floated over Pagan and dropped her phone on her belly. She grinned, said, "Oh fuck! I'll definitely Bluetooth that vid over to my tablet later," then lay limply smiling to herself. Her breasts rose and fell slowly; her nipples were still hard.

Pagan nodded.

Lori hoped Britt wasn't really pissing Pagan off, so that she'd think of ditching them. *It's just great, the two of us lucking onto her—without this invisible thing she does, the cops would have discovered us by now and there'd have been a wild shootout and I'll be on the news, dead and perforated by bullets; a legend before my time, and—*

Then her thoughts were broken up for the second time. This time by loud voices coming from outside.

"Killed, you say? Damn! I gotta tell you, Kev, it sure did strike me as strange that he left town like that, 'cos he still had two days left that he'd paid for. While we were chatting he said he was on his way to Westville for some shoemaker's conference. So someone diced him up like mince?"

Lori peeked out. She instantly recognized the extra-large policeman walking along beside the motel owner—he was the same one who'd chased she and Britt through the shops yesterday. His face was shot through with exertion and he was huffing and puffing and sweating in his filled-out blue uniform. The old man looked concerned but excited at the same time.

Boots crunching the gravel, the two passed the RAV4, heading right, towards Pagan's former room.

"Hey, guys, it's the po-leece!" Lori called back over her shoulders.

Britt and Pagan instantly joined her at the window. Then Pagan opened the door, and they peered out.

The two men now stood outside the door next to Pagan's room, the old man turning a key in the lock. They were talking, but their voices were indistinct.

Pagan said, "You guys wait here, I'll go listen to them."

She stepped out onto the walkway and headed up towards the men.

"She's got to teach us this invisibility trick," Britt said with longing in her voice. "I mean, just look at her go, naked as the day she was born and with her tits out, and no one bats an eyelid?"

CHAPTER 39

Kev & Clint & Pagan & Britt & Lori

For Detective Kev Parr, this hadn't begun as the best of days.

Arriving at the Cunningham house early like he'd planned (he'd left his sister Crystal at home bemoaning her latest hangover to Honey), he'd discovered he didn't need to think up an excuse for visiting the place: the front door was open. And there was blood on it.

He walked in, took one look at the carnage everywhere, then walked right on through, looking for the nearest toilet to throw up in.

The closest toilet was built en-suite to the living room and its door was wide open. Kev walked right in and puked his guts out into the bowl—that was all of last night's apple pie gone for sure. Then he straightened up again, flushed, and rinsed his mouth at the washstand. Staring at his face in the washstand mirror only confirmed to him how scared he was.

Last night, he'd watched that demon-snuff video umpteen times before finally succumbing to sleep's sweet lure, but that still hadn't prepared him for the horror out there in the Cunningham's sitting room.

He was almost too scared to step back out there. Maybe he'd better call the police station from right here inside the toilet. But shit, now he discovered that his damn cellphone was also outside in the car!

Then something here in the toilet caught his eye, and this was even odder than the butchered bodies outside. There was a bright pink smear on the side of the toilet door, which, when he pushed the door shut revealed itself to be . . .

Why the hell are there pink crosses painted all over the inside of the toilet door? His eyes fell on a small abandoned tube. *And . . . they're drawn in lipstick?*

Realizing he'd just solved the mystery of the other two girls the dead young men had picked up (*Shit—they watched it happen?*), he stepped outside again and crossed back to the front door of the house.

While making that return trudge through the living room Kev avoided curious glances left and right. He wasn't interested in seeing more than he already had. He kept his eyes fixed straight ahead, his entire mind intent on escaping the hellish reeking carnage of destroyed flesh that filled the room.

On his way to freedom, however, he stomped something that popped under his foot. Looking down, he discovered he'd just flattened someone's eye. He scraped the goo off his shoe, then hurried outside and sat on the porch to get his wind back.

Then he hurried over to his car and called the station. "Guys, I'm over at the Cunningham house on Jamie Lane! We've got a bad situation here—at least three stiffs! Get your asses out here pronto!"

Now, three hours later, Kev was finally getting around to continuing his investigation on the mangled corpse discovered yesterday in the car outside Rudy's.

It was already clear to Chief of Police Tina Kravitz and everyone else at the station that that crime and last night's massacre were somehow connected. What wasn't clear to anyone, though, was how they'd occurred.

An hour ago Feinstein the medical examiner had delivered his autopsy report on the remains from the car to the Chief. It read in part: 'The wounds to the victim were clearly caused by a large animal; most likely a bear being illegally transported around. And we're likely to discover the same for the three new corpses.'

Kev, who'd been with Tina Kravitz then, had nodded agreement to the coroner's explanation. It was simpler than playing them Crystal's recording.

The State Police Crime Lab were still matching up all the fingerprints taken from the crime scene, including those from inside the toilet.

***

And so now, Kev stared inside Room 10, the dead shoe salesman's room. There was no doubt anymore that the dead man was Kyle

Bennett: the old motel owner remembered the red Dodge because of a peculiar dent on its front bumper.

Together they regarded the empty room. There were no signs of a struggle and the bed was made.

"So you're saying he was killed by a wild animal?" Clint Duggan asked. "But how? And where? And who stuffed him in the trunk?"

"We dunno," Kev replied honestly. He made to step into the motel room. Then he thought better of it; better leave the crime scene for the forensics guys to dust over. He turned back to face the old man. "Clint, when was this room last cleaned, and who did it?"

"My granddaughter-in-law Cherry did it on Saturday. That was before we discovered that Mr. Bennett had gone missing." Then his face turned all sour. "That's what I originally thought you'd come here for—that you had some news of Cherry's whereabouts."

Kev stared at the old man in his denim overalls and plaid shirt. "What're you talking about?"

Clint Duggan wheezed heavily. "Cherry's gone missing, that's what. Me and my grandson—her husband Zak—we filed the missing persons report just this morning. You didn't hear 'bout it?"

Kev shook his head. "No, I was working another case then. We've been so busy with this and that Satanist murder we ain't no got time to look for missing people."

"Shee-it! Kev, you don't think the damn Satanists are the ones who took Cherry, do you?"

"I dunno." Kev thought about it, and hoped they weren't. "Once I get back to the office I'll pull out Cherry's file and get on the case myself." He gestured into Kyle Bennett's room. "Clint, you'd best lock it up again till the lab boys get here. At least now we know for sure that it's Bennett's corpse we've got—he didn't have any ID on him." Then his nose crinkled. "Hey, what's that smell?"

"What smell?"

Kev could smell something bad, like faint traces of a dead dog that had been covered by water. Only it wasn't coming from Bennett's room—it seemed to be coming from the room to its right, Room 9. Yeah, the more Kev sniffed, the stronger the stink grew, like rotting blood . . . like . . . like something had fucking died in there?

He pointed to Room 9's door. "Hey, Clint, who's staying in here?"

The old man mused on the question for a second, stuffing his hands deep into the pockets of his overalls. "No one at the moment.

Yeah, there was this girl . . . lemme see, what was her name again? Susan? No, it was a Sandra something—but she's gone now."

Then all of a sudden, the strange smell from the room vanished. The air was full again of the lovely natural scents of the day, and Kev realized it was a truly lovely day too, birds and trees and beautiful nature everywhere.

Damn, I'm in the wrong business, Kev Parr thought. *This definitely ain't the sort of day to be busting my gut running down monsters and missing men. Nah, I should be out lazing in the sun on a beach somewhere and eating pizza.*

He didn't for one moment consider it odd how quickly he'd forgotten about the bad smell.

"Nah, Kev," old Clint Duggan said, after similarly sniffing the air. "There ain't no weird smell around here. Your work's getting to your nose, kid."

"Yeah, has to be that."

***

Standing there by her former room, Pagan heaved a sigh of relief.

Her hastily pronounced scent spell had worked but—whew!—had that been close! The last thing she needed at the moment was cops crawling all over this place while she was waiting for the ROC to show up.

The big policeman was smiling now, his attention distracted from her previous door.

How did I forget to 'deodorize' the room before packing out of it? Oh yes, it was my fear of Avex's bursting loose if I used magic.

Remembering the results of her using magic yesterday, she quickly checked herself to see if she'd stirred up her demon. She hadn't; Avex seemed almost asleep inside her, though she didn't believe that for a minute. Avex knew she was planning to eject it—that she was planning to join the Red Octopus Corporation who'd likely be able to exorcise it from her—and it had to be desperate now to not let that happen. Despite currently seeming subdued, the demon was clearly biding its time, awaiting an opportunity to take control of her again.

So no more magic; not if she could help it. And she hoped she could. She only had four and a half more hours to wait till freedom.

Freedom!

The cop was now looking into Kyle Bennett's room. The old man was inside checking on something.

"Don't touch anything," the cop warned.

"I won't. Just making sure the water's turned off. Hey, he left his wristwatch!"

"Don't touch it!"

"Alright, son, I heard you the first time!"

Pagan peered back down the walkway at Britt and Lori. Though nominally looking her way, both were engrossed in conversation. She waved to get their attention.

***

"Did you see her face?" Lori was asking Britt. "She looks odd, like . . . like . . ."

"Like last night hasn't completely worn off?"

"Yeah, that right; that's it exactly. Her skin looks weird now, a bit like a snake's. I mean, it's normal, but somehow not really normal, like she's in layers or something."

Britt noticed Pagan waving at them and waved back. "She frigging scares me," she told Lori. "What if she turns on us?"

"She wouldn't do that, she's our friend."

"I don't mean intentionally; I mean like last night."

"Then you'll just have to draw more pink crosses. Keep your lipstick handy."

To avoid strangling Lori, Britt tugged hard on the ends of her newly-black hair. "Stop joking. I'm serious here."

"You're *too* serious. And I'm serious too—I do think the crosses worked last night. Hey, Britt, who do you think is fatter, this cop or my mom?"

"Your mom wins by a mile, and then some."

"And she keeps eating too. That's one reason I've never wanted to grow old, I'm always terrified that I'll look like that some day. So big and—"

"You shouldn't worry about that. Fat women seem to stay more married than thin ones. I mean, your parents are still together—so much for being slim and sexy at forty-five like mine."

"Yeah, but my dad screwed your mom."

"He *did?* She *did!?* How come you never told me that?"

303

"I didn't want to upset you. You know how you always get upset where your mom's concerned, and then—"

"Lori, are you sure of what you're saying?"

"Yeah, I caught him plumbing her on our kitchen counter—he was balls deep in her rear pipe. Our kitchen smelt like your mom had been farting for an hour. Anyway, that's how I got my car: dad bribed me not to tell you or my mom; but especially you."

"But . . . but . . . You're my best friend!"

"Yes I am. We're here together now, aren't we? Besides, your mom was banging everyone else anyway, so I figured it didn't really matter."

Britt realized that they'd veered off the topic of how Pagan might very likely soon kill and eat them both in their sleep. Then she shrugged; they were fated to die somehow anyway.

She realized too, that to her credit, this new revelation of her mother's sexual prowess didn't faze her. She'd had several men of her own over the past four days and she'd really enjoyed the sex, and— she winced—even that single 'forced incident' (thinking of it as 'rape' hurt her pride too much) proved one point: that she was sexually desirable enough for men to want to possess her even against her will.

So her dead mother Joanna could go fuck herself—Britt had laid her ghost to rest.

Meanwhile, she could see the big cop looking their way, and did his eyes just widen in shock? No, they couldn't have. He couldn't see Pagan, could he? And Pagan was standing right next to him. So clearly he couldn't see them either.

She forgot about him. "You know," she told Lori, "what I think we need to do is convince her to teach us her invisible spell. Then, once we can work it, we can ditch her and strike out on our own again, doing as we please like we initially planned. Only now no one will be able to see us and we'll never ever get caught. We'll be America's greatest ever serial killers."

"Now there's a plan," Lori dreamily agreed. She had a dopy grin on her face as if this was the happiest day of her life.

Something in her faraway-sounding voice though told Britt that her BFF was musing on more than just learning magic.

***

Britt was wrong: Detective Kev Parr could see both she and Lori, something he'd just realized now that he'd taken his attention off Kyle Bennett's room for a moment to look down the motel block towards his patrol car, which was parked beside the reception building.

First though, he'd spotted the blue Toyota RAV4. *Hey—now wait a minute . . . Crystal said there was a blue SUV parked outside the Cunningham house.*

That fact, coupled with his knowledge that the corpse stuffed in the red car outside Rudy's had been staying here at the Sunflower, connected the dots: *Yeah, this just might be that same blue SUV.*

That prospect didn't make Kev happy: what if the demon was around too? Then he saw the two girls and . . . Well they looked both familiar and unfamiliar. They were looking his way, pointing at him and giggling. Both were naked too, which was very distracting. It was hard to concentrate on what was different about their faces when their breasts were staring him in the face. And their breasts were quite sumptuous too. The blonde girl, in particular, had a really juicy-looking rack on her. Damn!

Kev finally got a hold of himself. He turned and peered back into Bennett's room, where Clint Duggan was looking into the nook between the left nightstand and the air conditioning unit. "Hey, Clint!"

"Yeah?"

"Who's staying in Room . . . ?" (Kev realized that he didn't know the girls' room number.) "Who's the owner of this blue SUV?"

Clint stepped away from the nightstand and into the doorway. "What blue SUV?"

Kev turned back and pointed. "That blue Toyota over the—"

Then Kev froze in shock. The blue SUV had summarily vanished. There was nothing there in the lot. And the car couldn't have started up and driven off, because then Kev would have heard both its door slamming and the engine start up.

"What car you talking 'bout, Kev? Ain't nothing parked over that way except *your* car."

"B-b-but . . ." Kev sputtered, sweat starting to bead on his forehead, "the SUV was—"

Then he shut up for good. He'd just seen that the two naked girls in the doorway had also vanished. They too could have similarly reentered their room and shut the door, but he didn't think so. Oh no, he didn't. He was sure that if they investigated the girls' room, it would prove to be empty, just like had happened in Alice's Boutique yesterday.

"You sure you alright, Kev? Ain't nobody staying in those rooms at the moment. You said you saw a blue car?"

"Trick of the light or something I ate. I must've imagined it." *Shit! I'm too overweight for my poor ticker to keep having to put up with these kinds of shocks.*

The old man nodded, a concerned look on his face. "Last guests on that side of the block was two sisters from Kentucky—they left Sunday morning. Since then almost all the rooms on this row have been vacant. He pointed down the cement walk. "If you want I can open it up for you."

"No, no, no, that won't be necessary," Kev said quickly. He had no desire to prolong the morning's agony. His head hurt and he thought he now understood why he was seeing strange apparitions: *I'm hungry! That's right: I was in such a rush to get over to the Cunningham's house and cover for Crystal that I skipped breakfast. And the doctors all warn that that's a no-no—breakfast is the most important meal of the day!*

That relieved him somewhat. Yeah, he was just hungry—not enough energy in his brain was making it malfunction, and making him seeing things. In fact, come to think of it, yesterday when those other two girls had vanished (or were they the same ones?), he'd been hungry then too—in fact, he'd interrupted his lunch to chase them, and that exertion must have additionally reduced the energy he'd been charging his brain cells with. But if that was the case, then how come Alice and Tricia had also seen the girls? Maybe they were hungry too. There was that thing called mass hallucination. Yeah, that was what they'd all had: a mass hallucination; there'd never been any girls to start with.

In fact, Kev was convinced of it now. The logical explanation was always the best one.

He stuck his thumbs in his belt, then frowned at old Clint Duggan. "Pops, I'd better get going. First I'll have myself some breakfast, then I'll head over to the office and get to work looking for Cherry. In fact, seeing as I'm already here, how 'bout you filling me in on what you know 'bout her disappearance?"

"Yeah, thanks, kid. It was about noon yesterday when I began wondering where she'd got to. See, she'd normally . . ."

***

Pagan watched the old man and the policeman walk back towards the reception building. Then she sagged against the wall.

Shit! She knew she'd made a big mistake in exerting herself to extend the invisible cloak back to Lori and Britt's room to conceal both girls and the car. But in her haste to overhear the two men's conversation, she'd forgotten that the shield moved as she did, and that this far from the other room, it's effect would likely be neutralized. And once she'd committed that initial oversight, she'd had no choice but to follow through with the rest. With her personal redemption so close at hand, she didn't need half the police vehicles in east Massachusetts swarming in here like roaches.

But . . . she felt it now, stirring inside her—Avex like a swarm of bees seeking exit from their shaken hive. It wasn't nearly as bad as yesterday after she'd done the fire trick, but given time . . .

She made her way back to the other room. As she walked, she shrunk the vision shield that masked them back to its original size. To her relief, this action seemed to block Avex off, as though the wall of invisibility she was pulling back into herself was reforming itself around the demon.

Britt and Lori were staring after the departing men, with Britt making disparaging cracks about the size of the policeman's ass.

Pagan pushed past them into the room and fell face-down on the bed. Her unplanned magic exertion had exhausted her. In seconds she was asleep.

***

For a while, Britt and Lori stood over the bed looking down at the sleeping witch, with Britt silently pointing out suspicious-looking patches of Pagan's skin.

Then Britt nudged Lori and they both walked over to stand in the still-open front door. There they conversed in whispers.

"I told you, it hasn't all worn off. We're in danger now."

"You're right—we are. I think she's more scaly now than when we woke up. That side patch on her butt wasn't there before."

"So?"

"It's like you said: she's our protection, so we can't ditch her yet. We have to wait till we learn the masking spell ourselves."

"She might not agree to teach us. What about if it's only for witches?"

"We'll convince her to."

"I don't wanna be a witch."

"Me neither, though I really like the demon-possession thing—it's just so cool."

"You just wanna go around eating people too."

"Stop it. Look, we'll just have to find a way of making it *necessary* for her to teach us."

"Yes, I get your point. But like what?"

"Hmmm, lemme see. O.K., something like our getting separated from her and getting into grave danger. That'll work."

"Yes, it should. But not today though, so she doesn't suspect anything. Maybe tomorrow or Thursday. Of course, that's assuming she doesn't 'monster up' again."

"You know, 'bout her 'monstering-up' as you put it—we'd better keep our guns handy."

"You think they'll work? She said bullets didn't hurt her."

"No, no, no. What she said was that she didn't remember what happened when she got shot, not that the bullets didn't hurt her. Remember she blacks out when the demon takes her over. She couldn't recall a thing about last night until we played her our recording."

"Alright, I just hope we don't have to find out for ourselves. But still, yeah, you're right. It's way better to be armed than to be disarmed, and I mean that in the literal sense of us losing our arms. Shit, did you see how strong that frigging demon creature was? Holy shit. How the hell can you rip someone in two like that? Even a damn chainsaw wouldn't do that clean a job."

"I could hardly believe my eyes when she did that. It was so cool that I peed myself from excitement."

"Trust me, each time I watch it, I wish it was me tearing up someone like that. It gets me so frigging hot that I just have to touch myself."

"Thanks for mentioning that. You've just reminded me of one last, and *very important,* thing."

"Yeah? What?"

"Girlfriend, we need to keep on her *good* side, so she won't try to ditch us."

"Why're you looking at me like that?"

"Kaminski's law again: you need to cut down on the noisy wanking act. Enough of that already. At least until it's just us two again."

"I hate you."

"That's alright. I hate you even more."

"My hatred is much intenser and greatly superior to yours."

"I've hated you for so long that my hatred's fallen in love with yours. It's why we're still together."

"Yeah, that's right. I think we've hated each other for so long that our dislikes have become soul mates, fallen in love, and gotten married."

"They don't seem to plan on getting divorced either."

Nodding understandingly at each other, they looked back at Pagan, who was now snoring gently. Then they stared out of the door and looked around.

"Hey, the fat cop's driving off."

"Yay! Thank God he's gone—seeing him makes me homesick. But, c'mon, isn't it such a lovely day? Look! Birds and clouds and . . . it's just delightful."

"No, at the moment it's merely a so-so day. Look, we're not doing much. We should be out there killing someone; that'd make this a great day, not this lazing around like we're on serial-killer-holiday."

"Let's wake Pagan up. Time to go shopping."

"I'm not sure she's about waking just yet. If she shows us a mouthful of doggy teeth, that's your damn fault."

"Hey, Pagan! Wakey wakey, let's go have breakfast."

"Arrgh, you evil bitches, lemme sleep!"

"We're hungry."

"Oh, alright, gimme ten more minutes."

"You know, Lori and I have been thinking: Why not teach us your invisible spell? That way, we can go out on our own if we need to and we won't need to bother you like this."

"What? Aw, hell no! The Abyss Club would kill me."

"You're still drowsy. Duh, the club is already trying to kill you?"

"Yeah, you're right—I momentarily forgot. But . . . no, I really shouldn't."

"C'mon, witch—we're your pals! What harm could it possibly do?"

"Well . . . but . . . yeah, why not? O.K. But not today though: I'm too damn weak, not to mention hungry. But how about I teach it to you two tomorrow? That'll be fine. Then if the spell stirs up the demon again, we'll just go out and find us some more hunky guys like last night. How's that sound?"

"Yeah, that's great. Thanks!"

"Thanks, Pagan, you're a real friend."

"Okay, time to go shopping. But just one little thing."

"Yeah? What?"

"Britney Wilson, you dare pull another goddamn hit-and-run act like yesterday's, and I swear by Satan's barbed tail that I'll pull your pussy out through your anus."

"Ouch, that hurts me just thinking about it. Is it even possible to do that?"

"I'm a witch, bitch. I can make it happen."

"Okay . . . yeah . . . okay."

"You're sure?"

"Yeah, I'll be good. I promise."

"Britt, you know what? On second thoughts, *I'm* driving. I still don't like that shit-eating grin on your face. You just might ram someone in a wheelchair instead."

CHAPTER 40

Joker

McKinney's Pig Farm was a large rambling affair. Fields of crops, old and new sheds and barns, and ten long pigpens from which came continuous grunting, honking, and squealing.

The owner, Ed McKinney, could've been the motel owner's twin brother. He was equally aged, gnarled, and bearded, and wore the same sort of denim overalls over a red plaid shirt. McKinney wore a hat too though, a wide-brimmed leather one that looked like he left it outside at the mercy of the elements every night.

McKinney's wife Beth—a woman so fat that Joker wondered how she managed to get through the doors—saw them to the back door but no further. Then, like a she-bear off to hibernate, she re-penetrated the dark depths of the farmhouse.

(On their way over here, Joker and Sin Corbin had run into that fat policeman she'd met yesterday with the Chief—Detective Parr was it? He'd exchanged pleasantries with herself and Sin. He'd been eating from a mega-pack of donuts and also had a big box of Snickers on the front passenger seat along with a 2 liter bottle of Sunkist Strawberry. He'd said he'd missed breakfast, and was working an important missing persons case.

Joker was hazarding a guess that Detective Parr didn't have a partner riding with him simply because there was no space in his cop car for anyone else.

Then she'd driven here with Sin Corbin, easily the most pregnant woman she'd ever met in her life, to meet McKinney's wife, who was equally the fattest woman she'd ever met. And Sin had whispered to her that Beth McKinney was the obese Chief of Police's mother. So large-ladyship clearly ran in their genetic stream.)

At the rear farmhouse door, Ed handed each of his visitors a set of galoshes, then put on a soiled pair of his own, after which he, Joker, and Sin Corbin stepped out into the mud.

Seeing how far in front of her Sin's stomach projected, Joker felt guilty punishing her this way, by making her leave home. But Sin seemed happy enough. "Anything for the Abyss Order," she'd declared.

Joker admired her dedication. Still, to be trudging about in mud with a baby on the way (expected delivery date next week, wasn't it?) seemed a bit too much dedication, even to please Lucifer. Or maybe she was just trying to impress Joker. (If so, it was working: Joker *was* impressed. Sin had to be like fifteen years older than she was but she'd been unerringly deferential since their first meeting.)

They stepped through the door of the third pigpen from the farmhouse. McKinney excused himself and spryly hurried off into the squealing porcine noise and confusion. They watched him pause beside a farrowing stall then gesture across the barn to a farm hand. The hand, a small brawny man, dropped the sack of feed he was carrying and walked over. He and McKinney began picking up the piglets one after the other and examining them.

While they waited, Sin said, "Hey, is it true that at headquarters they . . . I mean, *we* . . . we make animal . . . you know . . . animal pornos?"

"Bestiality movies?" Joker grimaced with memory. "Yeah, it's true alright, though it's mostly used as punishment." She frowned. "Trust me—it works."

"Have you ever . . . ?"

"No, I behave myself." The lie rolled so smoothly off Joker's tongue, she was surprised at herself. She'd been about saying, 'Yes, in fact I had two canine boyfriends just last week.' After all, in Satan's service, the more degraded you were the better; all for the lower good.

"And no one gets off," she warned Sin. "Darlin', it ain't no joke. One pregnant woman who defiantly went to church was forced to fuck a horse till the baby aborted. And everything was recorded in HD."

Sin's eyes widened with fright and she gulped. "F-f-for real?"

Joker nodded. "I saw the punishment video. I puked myself silly on watching it. The expectant mother was tied to a special wheeled frame placed under the horse. She was positioned belly down with her legs wide apart, and the animal's member inserted deep into her from behind. You know how rear-entry is best for deep penetration? Well I doubt she'd ever had it that deep in her life, or ever will again. Then, gripping the wheeled frame, two muscular acolytes slid her back and forth on the horse's dick so she was essentially abusing the animal, not the other way around."

"Ugh!" Sin said, looking sick.

"Yeah," Joker said grimly, aware that she was upsetting her companion, but Sin had asked, hadn't she? Which meant she wanted to know. "It went on for quite a while with the woman screaming blue murder each time the horse's dick slid back in and the two acolytes ramming her back harder and harder on it, till finally she began bleeding from her sex and her waters broke, and the fetus squirted out and plopped on the floor between the horse's legs."

"Then what happened?"

Joker almost laughed: Sin's request for more info was tremulous but insistent, like she really didn't want to know but yet couldn't stop her mouth from asking.

She shrugged. "The mother survived but never dared go near a church again. The fetus—about seven-months-old—was chopped up and fed to the dogs in the animal porn pen.

"Eww," Sin said in a scared little voice, "faithful witch or not, I'd go stark raving nuts if I ever lost a kid that way." She was gripping her bulge tight now, as if to keep from losing it, and her thin pinched face had a determined expression on it that was frightening in its maternal instinct single-mindedness. Joker could well imagine her using an axe on someone who threatened her unborn child.

Damn, Joker thought, remembering her own morning encounter with the preacher, *Nero's right: sometimes serving our boss just doesn't seem worth it.*

Sin was thoughtfully silent. Joker, suddenly maudlin herself, sought to change the burdened conversation.

She pointed down the barn to where old McKinney and his hired help were still disputing over the piglets. "Sin, what on earth did you tell him I needed a piglet for? Why're they taking so damn long with it?"

Sin emerged from her funk with a loud laugh. "Nothing's wrong. I just told Uncle Ed that you're working on a top-secret blood sausage recipe for a Maine grocery franchise, one that requires premium grade piglet blood to make properly, and that you're traveling across the state taking samples from different farms and . . . I don't remember the rest. But he's trying to get you the best pig he can so you'll come back for more."

At long last a satisfactory selection was made and a piglet presented to Joker, a little feisty piebald male that had droplets of milk on its snout like it had been forcefully tugged off a teat.

While McKinney watched with interest, Joker carried the piglet over to a rough-hewn wood table and got three metal-and-glass hypodermic syringes out of her bag. These were extra-large and had been specially dusted inside with a chemical to keep their contents liquid.

"Give me a hand with it," Joker told Sin.

Sin (who was still imagining how nasty it would be to lose one's pregnancy to a horse) didn't react fast enough, so McKinney helped her instead. She stood in the shadow of his old-man smell, all musty like he was withering away right beside her. Then there was all that swine-stink on his clothes.

With McKinney holding the piglet down, Joker stuck each of her three syringe needles in turn into its young neck and filled them with blood. The little fellow at first vigorously protested this metallic intrusion into its flesh, but by the time the second needle was pulled out, its bright newborn eyes had turned all glassy and it was kicking weakly. By the time Joker had filled her third syringe with its red porcine essence, the little piebald pig was dead: she'd drained all the blood from its body.

Joker packed the filled syringes away again with the utmost care. It was essential that their needles not break.

Afterwards, she and Sin Corbin thanked Mr. McKinney. She promised to get back in touch with the results of the 'blood sausage suitability test,' and then she and Sin headed back towards town.

She dropped Sin off at home. Sin said she was expecting her sister's boyfriend Boner in a short while. He was driving her into town for her final round of baby shopping, and also to buy some groceries for dinner. Her sister Ella was at work, and her husband Snake had some business in Attleboro and wouldn't be back till nightfall.

Joker understood that by 'business,' Sin meant that Snake was either buying or delivering dope.

Once again, she politely refused having lunch in Sin's dirty, ramshackle, and rat-infested house. She did, however, accept a slice of shepherd's pie to take away.

After promising to call tomorrow or even later tonight if she could, Joker drove off.

By now, she was feeling quite desperate. It was currently noon. In a couple of hours she'd have been in Raynham for a full day; and she was still no closer now to determining Pagan's whereabouts than on her arrival here.

Where the hell is she? It was a puzzling question. Other than for that single murder that had alerted the Abyss warlocks to her presence here, there'd been no other clues as to Pagan's whereabouts.

"It's that blasted demon she's carrying around," Joker spat out loud as she turned the corner from the Corbin's unnamed street onto the main road. Her cream Lexus SUV rumbled up onto the blacktop, scraping its undercarriage. "That demon is doing its damnable best to stop me moving to California. Well it won't work, Avex, ya hear me!? I'm gonna find you and once I do, you're—"

And then, her cellphone rang. A glance over into the passenger seat—a dancing demon display—confirmed her suspicion that it was Nero calling.

"Shit!" she exploded. "And now he's going to want the progress report."

She picked it up. This was going to be bad. "Sorry, Nero, no sign of her yet. I'm . . ."

"Satan be praised—we've found her," he said. "She's staying at the Sunflower Motel."

"B-b-but that's where *I'm* staying! And I saw no sign of her!" Then, calmer, she said, "So tell me, man, how in the world did you locate her?"

"We didn't."

"You didn't?"

There was a sadistic glee in his voice. "Red Octopus called us thirty minutes ago and told us where she is."

"Why the hell would they do that?" It made very little sense to Joker.

"Pagan contacted the ROC yesterday, saying she wanted to defect to them. They did their research on Avex and their unanimous decision is they want nothing to do with it. My contact Squidkid didn't say as much, but I sensed that those octopus gods they worship would be mad at them too."

Joker mused on that. She found it painfully ironic that Pagan was so dangerous, even the opposition didn't want her.

Like he was reading her mind, Nero said, "It's a lot like the Cold War. Imagine someone back then developing a bomb that could destroy the whole world at a single go and both sides sending assassins after the inventor."

"Are they sending people after her too?"

"No, they're leaving it up to us." There was a slight pause before he added, "Which means you."

"Okay, that's cool. Which room is she in?"

"Room 5. Front block."

"Damn! I've been driving past her on my way in and out then. She might even have seen me. Right, I just got the pig's blood. I'll head over there right now and take her out."

"Don't."

"Why the hell not?"

"'Cos you won't be able to see her, that's why."

"Nero, stop playing games with me. Do you want me to do this or not? How am I supposed to stop Pagan if I can't see or even sense her?"

"Calm down, babe. Don't go there until three this afternoon. That's when the ROC have told her they'll pick her up—they put it that far off in the day so they could contact us first."

"Okay, I'll go at three. But I'll *still* be unable to see her."

"You *will* see her. By then, of necessity, she'll have switched off her invisible shield so the ROC can find her." He laughed coldly. "Of course, she won't be expecting you to show up instead."

"You're as nasty as the ancient emperor you stole your nickname from. We're all just meat-puppets dangling on your strings, aren't we?"

"No, babe. We all are puppets on Lucifer's strings. And I suspect those strings are actually the hairs around his dirty asshole."

CHAPTER 41

Pagan

Oh, no! Pagan decided as she drove them back to the motel. *No way above Hell am I teaching these two any masking spells!*

She was still appalled by the crap that Britt had just pulled. *What the fuck!?*

After 'shopping,' they'd driven into the Shell self-service station on the corner of Broadway and Center for gas.

Britt and Lori had said they'd take care of it. Pagan said 'sure.' All they had to do was slot a card in the machine and pump the damn gas, right?

But next thing Pagan knew, Britt had slit someone's throat.

Right out of the blue like that. The young man—who'd apparently just come back from the restroom after buying gas in his motorbike—had been flirting with the stacked brunette filling up at the next pump, when, grinning like she was demon-possessed, Britt stepped up behind him, pulled out her knife and sliced it deep into the right side of his neck.

The man screamed in pain and vainly started trying to staunch the thick jets of blood.

The brunette he'd been talking to gasped in fright at the sight. Then, leaving the petrol hose stuck in the tank of her red Volkswagen convertible, she turned and fled screaming with her high-heels clattering away loudly across the concrete, clearly terrified that whatever unseen force had miraculously ripped open her friend's neck might do the same to hers also.

Pagan had watched in dismay.

Lori, meanwhile, was slapping her thighs and laughing at the dying man, who'd fallen to his knees and was gurgling blood everywhere.

She pointed to the gasoline now spilling from the runaway brunette's tank. "Too bad we don't have any matches, huh?"

Pagan had almost driven off there and then without them. She'd somehow controlled herself. She'd felt a constraint against deserting them: they were her friends, and all three of them were—for the moment at least—stuck in the same boat. *At least till 3 p.m. this afternoon, and then I'll be glad to see the last of you two!*

So she'd waited while Britt and Lori had gotten back in the car, with Britt saying defensively, though still laughing like mad, "Hey, don't look at me that way; I kept my word." Then she pointed out at the dead man on the ground. "This wasn't a hit-and-run—we're still here! Ha ha ha!"

Lips clenched tightly together, Pagan drove off. *Yes, I'm not actually better than them, and yes, we did scheme and kill those guys last night, but . . . but I was hungry—I mean the demon was, and I needed to feed it.* She began weeping over the steering wheel, again horrified by this seemingly never-ending mess she'd stupidly gotten herself into. *So, I'm a murderer myself, but Britt and Lori here, they're . . .*

She couldn't put into words her revulsion at what Britt had just done to the bike man . . . for fun. Just for the raw thrill of it. And they wanted to learn an 'invisible spell' so they could have more 'fun' of this sort, murdering people all across the country? *Oh frigging no . . . oh shit!*

The bloodshed had stirred Avex in her. Not too much though; she still had a firm lid on the demon. And thankfully, her disgust with her companions seemed to also be tempering its emergence. But she definitely had felt it stir again. That was twice now today.

She wiped her eyes and glared at Britt, who sat all relaxed in the front passenger seat. "Did you have to do that?"

Britt just grinned back. She had that lusty look in her eyes again, as now did Lori too. Pagan winced, realizing it had been a dumb question to ask. Murder was merely entertainment to these two, at best foreplay or an aphrodisiac.

"I'm getting horny again," Britt said finally as confirmation.

Pagan faked gaiety. "Save it till later, darling. We'll go man-hunting again tonight; pick up another set of hunks and bang them silly." What she was really thinking was: *Yeah, you stupid murder-slut, I'll be gone by then, and hopefully the police will be busy arresting you and your dopy friend.* "What I mean is, don't wank first, it'll just take the edge off the sex later; you won't come as good. And I wanna do a threesome too tonight, like Lori yesterday."

"Yeah, that was just awesome, satisfying three men at once," Lori said. "My theory is: the more men you can make ejaculate at the same time, the more female you are, the more of a *real* woman, you know? So maybe I'll try seven next time." She began counting off on her fingers. "Two in my ass—hope it doesn't tear open—one in my pussy, two in my mouth, one in each hand."

Pagan wondered at the dreamy look in her eyes. It wasn't all just sexual excitement like in Britt's case. No, Lori looked like she was tripping on some astral plane.

"Too bad there aren't any dicks small enough to fuck nostrils and ears, right?" Pagan joked.

"Except teeny ones," Lori said. "And those don't count. A *real* woman wants *men* in her, not *little* boys."

Thank God she's not a pedo too, Pagan thought. *Hers is a more reassuring kind of crazy than Britt's.* Then her thoughts locked.

"What the hell?" she blurted out loud, slamming hard on the brake. Lori and Britt (who didn't have the seatbelt on) were pitched forward in their seats.

They'd just reached the Carver street turnoff to the Sunflower Motel. Ahead of them, coming from the opposite direction on Broadway, was a cream Lexus SUV being driven by . . .

Is that frigging Joker? What the hell is she doing here?

It *was* Joker. Pagan would recognize that red hair and pretty face a mile off.

"What's the frigging matter!? What is it!?" Britt and Lori were both yelling. Britt had her gun out and was leaning out of the car window, looking around for the police.

Pagan didn't immediately reply. She watched Joker turn the street corner then drive into the Sunflower and past the front block to the third one. Then she turned to Britt and Lori. "False alarm. I just thought I recognized that chick from somewhere."

"Ex-girlfriend perhaps?" Britt put the gun away. She looked disappointed.

"I don't vacuum carpets," Pagan coldly replied. "She reminds me of the bitch who tried to steal my last boyfriend, that's why I was so damned surprised to see her in her human form."

"You did nasty something to her?" Lori asked.

"I turned her into a frog. She's up in Canada somewhere, still waiting for a prince to come kiss her back to normal."

To Pagan's relief that shut both of them up. She put the car in motion again and drove into the motel. While they unloaded their purchases, her brain boiled with thoughts. *Is Joker here looking for me?*

Then suddenly, it hit her that she needn't bother herself. *Joker drove straight on in back, which means she's been in the motel at least since yesterday. Which also means she has no idea that I'm staying here too. Else the Abyss's goons would have locked this place down by now.*

Still, I'll check on her later, she decided. She looked at her watch. It was 1:30 now. Almost time. She could feel her heart beating stronger than usual, throbbing with the exhilarating pulse of freedom. The delicious anticipation of her release felt like hands massaging her breasts.

She just needed to remember to turn off her cloaking spell before the ROC's guys arrived.

The car emptied, they carried in their purchases into Room 5.

Then, like they were jointly sipping from a pool of communal exhaustion, the three of them lay in bed awhile, not talking to each other.

Pagan found their silence oppressive and ominous. She tried to relax but couldn't. Thoughts of Joker crowded her mind: how the redhead had been smiling knowingly to herself at the wheel, like she knew something that could really hurt Pagan.

Pagan now began to find their joint silence really awkward.

It wasn't actually a strange silence: Britt was flicking through her collection of newly pilfered CDs—Sinatra, Elvis, Harry Connick Jr., Amy Winehouse, and some Carpenters and Barbara Streisand—while Lori was smiling her dreamy smile at the ceiling and humming to herself. To Pagan though, who was tripping partly on anticipation and partly on dread, the silence felt depressed, like demons were eating the wholesomeness out of the air.

The problem was that their quietness gave her mental space in which—like one cultivating lush green cornstalks on a graveyard—to think of everything that could go wrong with her rescue. And she came up with a lot of bad possibilities.

She checked her phone. Yes, they'd agreed for three this afternoon—now only an hour and six minutes away—and there'd been no follow-up text since then, so that arrangement was still good.

She blinked her black eyes at the ceiling worriedly. *Calm down. All I have to do is wait, and try not to kill myself with anxiety before three o'clock.*

Then Lori got to her feet and began gathering up the bath salts and scented candles she'd amassed at Walmart. Then she stripped off and grinned at them both.

"Alright, ladies, I'm off to have the bath of my life. Don't either of you dare bother me. If you need to go, go outside."

"Whatever, bitch," Britt said disinterestedly, flinging her a 'get lost' wave without lifting her eyes from the sleeve inset of her new 'Best of Amy Winehouse' CD.

Pagan, though, nodded to Lori. She noted that Lori's eyes were exceptionally bright, and that she looked slightly more manic than usual, but thought nothing of it. It was likely just spillover excitement from killing that man at the gas station.

At least she was relieved that Lori wasn't about pleasuring herself in there. At least she hoped she wouldn't. At least not loudly. But she doubted that Lori would be masturbating: the lure of another manhunt tonight should make her hold on.

After a final satisfied smirk at them both, Lori vanished into the bathroom and they heard the lock click into place.

Pagan was glad to see her go. That meant that now only she and Britt lay in bed not talking, which was one-third less awkward.

She lay there wrestling with her thoughts. She had to go check on Joker, she just had to. *But, should I? Is it wise? What if . . . ? Yes, what if Joker is being used as bait? What if the Abyss Club suspect that I'm in this area, but don't know exactly where, and they're trying to lure me out to attack her . . . ?*

Then her thoughts became even more oppressive than the awful silence that had both spawned and fertilized them and she got up off the bed.

"Hey," she called down to Britt, who lay on her side facing the far wall and was humming Amy Winehouse melodies. "I'm stepping outside to get some fresh air and clear my head. I'll be back in fifteen minutes tops."

"Yeah, sure," Britt acknowledged, still without looking up. "Have fun. We won't run away."

Pagan shrugged, then opened the door and stepped out. On a reflex, she looked around for the police.

***

The men from the State Police Crime Lab had been and left. They hadn't stayed long. It was clear to them—from comparing the bloody and mangled state of Kyle Bennett's body to the spotless/pristine state of his motel room—that his murder had been committed elsewhere. (In their defense, they also had more pressing work to attend to, sifting for evidence in the mess left at the Cunningham house. Now *that* was a crime scene.)

So the detectives simply half-heartedly dusted for fingerprints, took Kyle's wristwatch away for lab testing, and asked a few questions of old Clint Duggan.

But seeing as the room next to Mr. Bennett's—Room 9—gave off no betraying odors (Pagan's deodorant spell was still working wonders—much better than OdoBan), no one even thought about opening it up for a look. Had they done so, they'd have found one of Kyle Bennett's eye's wedged down between the left nightstand and the wall, and a bathtub crawling with maggots feasting on bits of Cherry Duggan that had blocked the drain. (At that very moment Kev Parr was questioning Zak Duggan about his wife's whereabouts.) And also large clumps of Cherry's hair floating in the toilet bowl around one of Pagan's larger turds that had adamantly resisted flushing.

But the detectives from the State Crime Lab were ignorant of all this, and so the coast was still clear for the three young women.

***

A large black cat was prowling the parking lot. A cold wind was blowing south through the motel. The wind chilled Pagan despite the afternoon sun.

Shivering, she walked back around the motel block.

CHAPTER 42

Lori

She was floating now, just like the mist hovering over the bathwater. The water was hot, almost too hot, but she liked it like that: the heat filled her with drowsiness like she was on a tropical beach, or in an exotic sauna at one of those fat farms her mother kept unsuccessfully visiting to lose weight.

Lori opened her eyes and grinned. This setting—the harem-like ambience of the bathroom now—was just as she wanted it. She felt like a pampered odalisque. She'd turned the lights off and shut the single window, then reversed the darkness with her candles. Yellow and pink, blue and red, black and green, they now burnt everywhere in the bathroom: along the rim of the bath, on the floor, and on both the toilet seat lid and tank cover. Bright flickers like ghosts emerging from enforced solitude, the flames licked the air like it was a lover's sex. The joss sticks stuck in the washstand drain gave out trails of pungent smoke that filtered across the room to her, further exotifying the ambience into that of an Asian temple where the dead were being honored. Additional scent rose on the clouds of smoke from the perfumed bath water.

Yes, Lori thought again, *this is just perfect*.

This was the perfect way on the perfect day to die.

She sank as deeply as she could into the water, till only her nostrils were exposed for the scented air to tickle. She wanted to feel the water entering the pores of her skin, washing away all the sludge of her life. She almost succeeded in this, but there was resistance. She understood what the resistance was: her flesh needed to be cut, to be slit open so that her blood could mingle with the water. Only then could the water enter her and purify her.

323

She lifted her head from the water and regarded the knife she'd smuggled into the bathroom. It lay on her left, on a part of the bathtub rim that she'd left candleless. *Two slashes across my wrists and it'll all be over for good. I mean, completely. No more life, no more lying to myself that I'm good enough to live. Nothing but the blessed extinction of self and my blending into the eternal darkness.*

She was glad that she'd finally found the courage to do it. *It must have been all that sex last night.* Since her foursome, she'd felt incredibly strong, so . . .

Ah, I'm really gonna miss Britt . . .

But everything—even the closest of friendships—had to end.

She stretched water-wrinkled fingers for the knife, then drew them back again. *No, not yet. I like how the water feels.*

This hot bath in this dim room reminded her of the Pit. The Pit: her home for all of her suicidal years. But this was a friendly Pit, not the soul-eating pretentious Pit that she'd been unable to climb out of and join the living no matter how hard she'd tried. No, this hot water around her body was a doorway to freedom, to the new life of nothingness that she'd sought forever. And now, now, now . . . now she'd finally found the courage to end herself.

Feeling a massive burst of triumph swell through her breasts, she grabbed the knife up in her right hand and sliced it across her left wrist . . .

And screamed.

Yes, she screamed for all she was worth. Shit! IT HURT! *Oh, my God, what the hell is this shit?*

She stared at the wet red line across her wrist from which blood was welling, curving around her arm, and dropping into the bath water. It wasn't rushing at all, just trickling out in a miserable line. The red droplets hit the water and fell out of sight, dissolving as they went like they were dying in her place.

Somewhere out of mind she heard loud banging and someone yelling, "Lori, open up! What's going on in there!? Open up, goddammit, you hear me!?" And more banging and yelling. Nothing important. Just a symphony of discouraging noise from the BFF she loved so much and hated to leave behind.

The background noise quieted to concerned knocking, then stopped.

She regarded her slashed uncooperative flesh. Its unwelcome solidity and resistance to her departure threatened to trigger intense distress in her mind.

No, I just did it wrong, she decided. One had to be motivated to die by one's own hands. *And, fuck yes, I'm motivated—death is a blessing!*

She steeled herself and sliced her left wrist again, attempting a deeper, more fatal cut. This time she studied her arm, watching how the knife split the white skin, floating left to right and bouncing over the taut scared tendons.

All she felt was pain again.

She screamed again—much louder this time—and dropped the knife into the hot water. She flailed both hands wildly, knocking candles either side of her into the water and to the floor.

This was just impossible, much worse than she'd expected all along. *Shit! Fuck! I've failed to kill myself again!*

The shame of being too chicken to complete her craved exit hurt Lori worse than her bleeding arm.

The twin red slits in her wrist were demon mouths mocking her cowardice. Horrified by her failure, she screamed again then began weeping, raining salt tears into the scented bath water.

CHAPTER 43

Britt

After the second scream came through the bathroom door, Britt turned herself into a human battering ram and flung herself against it.

Her only thought as she hurled herself at the door was that an intruder had gotten to Lori in there—someone who'd snuck into the motel room while they'd been out shopping—and was busy murdering her.

She hit the door as hard as she could, but it held.

At that same moment Lori screamed again, this third howl a sound of intense anguish that chilled Britt.

Bruised but undeterred, she retreated across the room to the front door, then after a deep intake of breath, charged the bathroom door again.

This time the door gave way and she staggered into a scene like an Oriental temple, candles and incense everywhere, and to one side, Lori sitting up in pink water, weeping profusely, while her left forearm dripped blood to redden the bathwater further.

Britt couldn't see any blades, but from the elaborate sense of ritual evident everywhere she quickly put two and two together.

She stepped up to the bathtub. She was appalled. "Lori, you tried to kill yourself. Tell me that's not true."

"I couldn't even do it right, Britt. I couldn't. It hurt much more than I thought it would. I'm so useless at everything—"

"Lori, how the hell could you do this to me? Tell me! We had a deal!"

Lori peered up at her through grief-reddened eyes. "I'm *sorry*. But today just seemed so right for it . . . Dying should be fun, like with all those people we killed, but not like *this*. This feels like shit, you know?"

Britt lifted her eyes from regarding Lori's slit wrist. The bleeding wasn't extreme, but it was constant, the red dribble showing no signs of abating. Britt didn't know how much blood a human body contained, but she did know that if you let a tap drip, given enough time it would empty whatever reservoir fed it. If she didn't staunch Lori's wounds, Lori just might bleed to death on her.

". . . I think that's what's missing," Lori was saying.

"What the hell are you babbling about?"

Grinning weakly at Britt, Lori fished around in the bathtub, finally producing a knife above the water. (Britt winced. Yeah, it just had to be the same blade they'd cored that guy's butt with.) She waved the knife at Britt. "Britt, you do it, you kill me."

"What?" Now she began getting angry. "Are you crazy, you insane bitch?"

"Britt, you're my best friend, please kill me. Kiss me, then stab me in the heart. I think death works best when you die by the hand of someone you love, that's why I couldn't kill myself. It's not the pain, just that I need—"

She was looking spookily dopey. Britt slapped her hard. Lori's head snapped back, then a semblance of normalcy reentered her gaze. "Lori, shut the fucking fuck up before I drown you in this bath. I'm *not* going to kill you. Listen, you stupid traitorous bitch"—it was hard to keep the tears out of her eyes—"we had a deal that we'd live, fuck, and die together. And what do you go and do? You plan on leaving me, and you don't even say goodbye first."

Now Britt *was* crying. She was hauling Lori up out of the wet water, not caring that it splashed her, then half dragging, half carrying her out of the bathroom into the front room, and laying her in the bed. "How could you fucking do that to me? You're my goddamn best friend, dammit!"

"I'm sorry," Lori said weakly. "Today just felt right, you know?"

Britt was about retorting again, but the weakness in Lori's voice stopped her. Suddenly Britt was filled with an immense sense of dread. Was she even now bleeding to death? The blood still seeped from her wrist. *What the hell do I do about that?*

The fact that Lori might actually die now impressed itself on Britt. She was gripped by a horrible sense of impending desertion, scared-out-of-her-wits-terrified of being left all alone. This was her only true friend, the one person she really cared about, and she seemed to be dying.

Okay, the first thing is, I need to tourniquet her wound.

She used two thongs she'd earlier gotten from the mall. Once knotted excruciatingly tight around Lori's forearm, they seemed to work: the bleeding stopped. But the cuts were still deep and red and horrible to look at.

Where the hell is Pagan? She'll know what to do; maybe she'll even have a healing spell.

But Pagan had gone off walking somewhere unspecified and Britt had no idea when she'd be back. And seeing as Pagan was invisible anyway, it was pointless going into town to look for her. And wanted as she and Lori both were, they couldn't go to any hospital emergency rooms either.

She made up her mind. She began changing from her wet and bloody clothes into dry and clean ones.

Baffled, Lori watched her dress. "Where are you going?" she asked in a voice so weak that Britt almost wet herself with fear.

"I'm driving into town to buy you a first-aid kit and some surgical needles if I can find them. I'll have to stitch you up myself."

"Britt, wait for Pagan to get back. Someone might recognize you."

"Not if I'm alone. They're looking for *two* girls, not one, and I'm no longer a blonde. And I'll wear my red glasses again."

"Okay, but please be careful. I'm really sorry I tried to kill myself; I really am." Tears began spilling from Lori's eyes again.

Britt wiped tears from her own eyes, then bent and kissed Lori on the forehead. "Don't worry—I won't get caught."

Then she grinned. "Hey, Lori, you cowardly little piece of girl-shit, don't you dare frigging die, okay? I swear by God Almighty that if you die before I get back I'll frigging kill you!"

"That's an oxymoron."

"Huh?"

What you just said: you'll kill me if I'm already dead when you get back. It doesn't make sense."

"Just STFU and stay alive, or else . . ."

Leaving the threat dangling, she grabbed the car keys off the top of the fridge and dashed out the door.

CHAPTER 44

Pagan

For the third time in a row Pagan suddenly found herself on the other side of Joker's room.

She skidded to a halt, spun around, then leaned against the wall. The sudden inexplicable transition once again left her feeling nauseous.

She was standing midway down the third motel block, outside Room 38. Joker was in Room 36. That was certain: her cream Lexus SUV was parked in front of it, and loud neurotic strains of black metal fizzed from the window (sounded like Slain Jane again—Joker was a die-hard fan of the band). Which meant she was inside.

And I want to kill her.

Which was proving to be a big problem. Joker—a known savant in magic—had some kind of spirit guard on her room that kept shifting Pagan past it.

Behind her she heard the loud noises of a male-female argument from the room at the far end of the block, outside of which was parked a black Ford sedan. The argument had to do with divorce and who'd get the kids, with "I'll get you for this," threats heavy on both sides.

Pagan tuned the voices out. She had bigger problems of her own.

About Joker? Her wanting to kill the Abyss Club's woman had more to do with malice than with self-preservation. Pagan knew she should just walk away, go back to her own room and patiently wait till 3 p.m. for the ROC (it was now 2:15), but her long-term dislike of the redhead in Room 36 kept niggling at her.

She didn't deny it. She'd find it delightfully ironic (not to mention immensely satisfying) to feed Joker—who'd been there at the beginning of her woes—to Avex just before they ended.

So, for the fourth time, she walked towards the door to Room 36. The first three times she'd rushed at the door. This time, however, she slowed as she reached the boundary pillar, and then . . . she blacked out . . . again.

When she once more regained her senses, she was near the start of the block, two doors further down than she'd intended being.

And, worse still, she felt more nauseated than ever. She leaned over the edge of the walkway and puked on the lot gravel, then straightened up, breathing in great gulps of afternoon air and looking back towards Joker's room.

Suddenly, the door of the last room on the block burst open and a thin brunette in a green dress charged out and ran over to the black Ford. She screamed, "I'll see you in court, you tight asshole, and you can forget about ever seeing Matt and Jenny again!" leapt into the car, fired it up, and sped off in a screech of burning rubber and gray exhaust smoke.

A man ran out after her and began clutching at the air as though trying to catch the departing car. "Hey, Caroline, where the hell you goin'!? Bring back my damn ride!"

The woman drove hard past Pagan, her faced all pinched up and determined.

Pagan once again returned her attention to herself. *Shit, this is maddening. All I need to do is open Joker's door and . . .*

Then she caught herself. This last time before blacking out, she'd felt something . . .

She walked back again, stopping just at the boundary of Joker's room. (Inside the room, Janet Orgasm, Slain Jane's lead singer, was crooning the lyric to the ballad *Dead Ravens*: "I love the way you hate me, I hate the way you love me. I'm gonna hate you, baby, and I need you to hate me too; with all the love I sense in you. I'll never have enough, of this spiteful love; you've got me burning up! Forever, forever, forever, forever!")

And yes, *now* Pagan felt it again, and this time both the nauseous sensation and its source were crystal clear:

Deep inside her Avex had stirred. No, it had more than stirred—the demon was rumbling like a landslide. She suddenly understood that Avex, not Joker, was the one shifting her past Room 36.

And the weird thing was, she could tell that the demon was scared. No, it wasn't just scared, it seemed *terrified*.

Terrified. *Avex is frightened of Joker? No, that's impossible. It wasn't scared of her that first time in the basement, was it? But I don't clearly remember what happened back then, so maybe it's . . .*

Then it hit her: *No, Avex isn't scared of Joker, it's scared of something she's got with her in the room! But what on earth could that be?*

However, it looked like she'd never find out. She stepped into the forbidden zone again and once more found herself two doors down from Joker's room, puking her guts out.

That was it then, she decided. If Avex was stopping her from dealing with Joker, that meant that the redhead was dangerous; and likely to both of them. *I mean, if a Lord of Hell don't wanna tangle with the fire-crotched bitch . . .*

Behind her, from Joker's window, the silence between CD tracks was now filled by a strange sequence of sounds: loud female orgasmic moaning interspersed with yelps of "Thank you, Jesus! Thank you, Jesus!"

Pagan cringed at the noises, but once the next metal tune began, she decided that maybe she'd just imagined them. Why on earth would Joker, a dedicated witch, be gasping those evil words during her sexual climax? Or maybe she was watching a Jesus freak movie?

When Pagan's stomach had settled, she shrugged and kept walking towards the end of the block. She'd circle round to the front row of rooms again. Hopefully Britt and Lori hadn't gotten up to any mischief in her absence.

Then she saw that the man who'd chased after the angry woman was still outside. He was sitting on the edge of the walkway in front of Room 48, feet on the gravel, back against a pillar. He was staring beyond Pagan, in the direction that the black Ford had vanished, with a desolate look on his face. His eyes were bloodshot and he was fumbling open a battered pack of Camels with trembling fingers. Two unlit cigarettes already lay on the gravel between his feet, and while she watched, he confusedly snapped a third in half.

Pagan paused in her walk. The man was good-looking though a bit unkempt. He was unshaven, smelt like he'd been drinking, and his blue cotton shirt was stained with sweat.

Watching him sitting there all sad and woebegone, she suddenly felt very aroused, like his misery was a hand caressing her clitoris. She recognized the signs from her experience with the late Kyle Bennett and the three dead guys—this was Avex's doing, the demon stirring up her flesh.

So now *it was* hungry again.

But, hell no, I'm not about feeding you, you son-of-a-bitch. At least not on this guy who looks like he's just lost everything he ever had in his life.

But that was easier thought than done. She found that she couldn't walk past the sad man (who'd gotten a cigarette up to his lips now and was searching his pockets for his lighter). Her legs felt rooted to the spot and her sex was wetting like crazy. She could feel her juices soaking her panties.

She tried to force her legs into motion, but without success. Avex clearly wanted this man's flesh and wasn't letting her leave until it had had him. (She suddenly realized that she was being rescued just in time: if the demon could now interrupt her at will, and even stall her body, her life would shortly become a total nightmare, an experience not worth having.)

She glanced at her watch. 2:31. *Oh, this is just what I do not need right now.*

She did some quick calculations. On the average, it took her ten to fifteen minutes to reach orgasm if she wasn't pleasuring herself. Even assuming the ROC were late, she'd be cutting it real close if she slept with this guy.

But she had no choice. Now it wasn't just the demon stopping her from leaving: her sex felt so tender and touchworthy, her body so aflame with lust, that even when she felt Avex finally remove its restraint on her motion, she could do nothing else but reveal herself to the seated man.

On seeing a woman suddenly appear before him, the man gave a start and his lit cigarette fell from his mouth.

"Who . . . who're you?"

"I'm the succubus you've been having wet dreams to all your life." She was relieved that he wasn't leaping up and fleeing from her. In her present state of arousal that would have been totally unacceptable. The way she felt, she would melt like wax if he didn't fuck her. She pointed back down the block. "Who was that that just left?"

His misery seemed to overcome his shock at seeing her. He sagged. "My wife Caroline," he replied in a lost voice. "I think we just got divorced. We drove up from Delaware to see her folks and we had a fight this morning and suddenly . . ." The words failed him.

"Forget her," Pagan told him, her vagina now so hot that she found it a wonder her pants weren't burning. "Come inside with me, let's discuss life after marriage." She reached down and pulled him to his feet.

"Caroline's always doing that," he moped. "Then I go plead with her and she comes back to me. But this time I think she means it."

"Come on," Pagan said, taking his hand and impatiently pulling him into the room after her. Fuck! Her sex felt like . . . She had no words to describe her current heat level; she doubted anyone possessed such a vocabulary. "Forget that skanky bitch. I assure you—after me, you'll never need another woman."

Once she had him inside and the door shut behind them, she instantly undid his fly and went down on him. His penis was sweaty and salty and also smelt of vagina, so maybe the couple's divorce argument had begun while they'd been having sex, or right afterwards. She didn't care; what was important here and now was that he stiffened almost immediately he entered her mouth.

Once he was hard enough, she pushed him down on the bed with all his clothes still on. Then she slipped off her pants and underwear and straddled him.

She found that she'd wasted her time worrying about how long it would take her to reach a climax with him. This was like her time with Kyle: she came immediately he entered her, and the orgasms continued in a almost unbroken chain, a cascade of sensations that threatened to drive her out of her mind. Her vagina clenching on his penis flooded her body with pulses of climactic energy that simply refused to stop.

Fuck! Fuck!! Fuck!!! If only this kind of ecstasy came without the violence attachment. I really wouldn't mind being demon-possessed then.

The man was doing his best to keep up with her, squeezing her breasts through the fabric of her shirt. She could feel him thrusting ineffectually under her. His motion was distracting: it upset the rhythm of her enjoyment.

"Don't bother, baby," she gasped through her pleasure, staring deep into his eyes and riding him hard, her hands on his shoulders and her rump bouncing up and down on the hard rod stuck between it. "Relax and let me do the work. All you gotta do, baby, is forget that deserting bitch Caroline and enjoy me instead."

And then, trapped in the throes of yet another mind-flattening orgasm, she saw his face turn all horrified and scared under her. He was looking up at her and gaping in disbelief.

Shit! She knew that look.

She had just time enough to see her hands turn as green as mulberry leaves before blacking out.

CHAPTER 45

Britt

The blind man stood on the sidewalk, by the traffic lights at the turnoff to the Walmart Superstore. He had a cane in his right hand, while his left clutched the leash of a small black guide dog.

Despite her haste, Britt slowed slightly as she neared him, pondering whether to run him over or not. It would incredible to do, and in broad daylight too.

Finally, however, caution won out over the anticipated thrill of the kill. She grudgingly accepted that at the moment, with the blue RAV4 visible to one and all, it wouldn't be a smart thing to do.

And so the blind man lived to cross the road another day. Britt felt an intense sense of regret as she drove past him and turned into the Walmart parking lot. It would have been just delicious to splatter him everywhere, to smear him and his stupid black dog—she wondered how a little mutt like that could look so self-important—all over the sidewalk. To watch his black glasses go flying as she rammed the car into his body.

But soon, oh so soon. Once we've learnt Pagan's spell, everyone had better watch out . . . though they still won't see us coming, ha ha!

Best of all, this blind man's death would have put her on a definite 'up' again after the major downer of Lori's attempted suicide. *I still can't get over it. She was going to abandon me just like that!* It hurt her immensely to think that Lori might have died.

But then, Lori is a major fuck-up anyway. In all the time I've known her, she's never been able to successfully complete anything, so maybe her failure at suicide is just true to type. Or maybe . . . was this one of those 'cry for help' suicide attempts? Did she plan the whole thing just to get my attention? Well if she did, she's definitely got it. I've never been so scared in my damn life!

Then just as Britt parked outside the Walmart Superstore, she remembered that in her haste to leave, she'd forgotten to take any money. That meant driving back to the motel.

But no, thankfully it didn't. Memory flickering in her mind, she opened her purse and came up with Matt Lewis's bank cards and the sheet of paper on which Lori had penned his PIN numbers and ZIP Code.

How lucky, she thought grandly, getting out of the dead man's car and hurrying over to an ATM directly facing her.

People were walking past her, exiting and entering the shopping center. Britt was thinking: *I need a first-aid kit, surgical needles, thread, and bandages. I'll tell them I'm a trainee nurse stocking up my parent's house, just in case . . .*

The ATM spat out twenty-five 20-dollar bills, then refused to pay out any more cash on the Chase Bank card. She switched cards and collected another six hundred dollars.

For a moment she worried about CCTV cameras recording her using the dead man's cards, then decided it didn't matter. There might be a missing persons report out for Matt Lewis by now, but the cops would still be looking south, thinking he'd gotten lost down in Westville. Or that maybe he'd been in a car crash along the way. Or hopefully, like Lori had speculated, his mousy wife was currently imagining he was shacked up with some bimbo somewhere.

An evil smile played over Britt's lips. If only they knew what had really happened to him.

While musing on police activity, she'd collected the money and stuffed it into her purse. She walked towards the nearest store entrance, then froze as stiff as if someone had just emptied ice water over her.

Twenty yards away, a tall thin man was accompanying a small but incredibly pregnant woman towards a yellow Jeep.

Britt's mouth fell open. *That's Sin and Boner!*

On reaching the yellow Jeep, Boner quickly unlocked the front passenger door and gave Sin a hand with getting in. (Britt grimaced at the sight. Damn, Sin made pregnancy look like an affliction, one which she never wanted to suffer. Wow, she was so swollen, Boner had to practically carry her to get her into the Jeep.)

Once he'd gotten Sin comfortably seated, Boner unlocked the rear door and began loading in their shopping bags.

Seeing the hated pair, anger instantly filled Britt. Keeping herself hidden behind intervening trees, she moved closer to their car. Boner was looking away from her and Sin looked tired and out of it, so there was scant chance of her being noticed.

Finally Boner got all the bags loaded. Britt could see that most contained baby stuff like disposable diapers, tiny shoes, and an 'A-B-C'-patterned infant duvet. Two other bags on the far side of the back seat held vegetables.

For Britt, watching them, it felt like they'd just gotten through molesting her again. The intensity of her rage astonished her. Surely the pleasance in-between these two encounters with Boner and Sin should count for something? How could she still be so damn angry?

But she was. Oh, hell yes, she was.

She was concealed five yards from the yellow Jeep now, a curtain of leaves obscuring her body, and could hear everything they were saying. Boner had walked around the Jeep and gotten in beside Sin. Sin was still breathing like she'd just finished a race.

Boner was saying, ". . . Take it easy, girl. It'll be out real soon. You're due next week, ain't cha?"

Sin replied, "Boner, I wish I was due last week, this damn kid is just about killin' me."

He laughed and patted her belly. "C'mon, let's just get you home. Or is there anything else you wanna buy?"

She nodded, then shook her head. "Yeah, but not today. Just take me back to the house. I've gotta get dinner started before Snake gets back."

"C'mon, Sin, let Ella cook for once."

"Boner, I've told you this so many damn times, I just don't get it any more: have all the drugs you do murdered your damn taste buds? My sister can't cook to save her life."

"Aw, stop being so hard on her. She ain't *that bad* a cook. I like her food."

"Boner, stop lying. You prefer eating Ella's pussy to that crap she makes."

He grinned broadly. "Yeah, okay, that's true, but still—hey, it ain't killed me yet."

"Sure, she ain't killed you yet, but keep eating her cooking and you won't make it past forty. I can guarantee you that: eating Ella's crappy food day in, day out was what killed our daddy after our momma died."

"You're kidding, right?"

"Doubt me at your heart and liver's expense. All grease and salt and spices and more cholesterol than a pig . . ." She wheezed heavily and patted her belly. "Look where was I? Okay, so no, no, no—Ella ain't cooking nothing. If I feed Snake any of that slop she makes and calls food, Snake'll be so mad he'll likely kick this damn crumb snatcher outa me."

"Which is what you want, ain't it?"

"Sort of—but I want the kid to come out alive!"

Boner burst out laughing. He started up the Jeep and drove off.

Oh, what a nice lovey scene, Britt thought with deep sarcasm. *Two monsters playing happy family.*

And then it hit her like a rain of hailstones: here was her chance to find out where they lived.

The yellow Jeep was just turning out of the Walmart lot and heading left, back up Broadway. Britt turned and dashed off to her car, started it up, and reversed out of parking. She waited for Boner and Sin to pass her then set off after them.

It was only then that she remembered Lori. *Oh, fuck—I've gotten distracted from what I came here to do in the first place.*

But she didn't panic now. Partly due to the icy spike of anger impaling her through her guts, but mostly due to her new suspicion that Lori might have engineered the whole suicide thing just to get her attention, she considered the situation calmly. She concluded that so long as the thong tourniquet she'd tied remained in place, Lori would keep till she got back.

And besides, this seemed (at least it really felt that way to her) much more important to tackle right now. If she lost them this time, she might never have another opportunity to find out where they lived.

She kept about fifty meters behind the yellow Jeep. She was cautious because they seemed headed out of Raynham and there wasn't much traffic on the road, but even so she wasn't overly bothered about them spotting her. With her red glasses on and her hair now dyed black, she knew she looked completely different.

Even if he noticed her in the rearview mirror, there was scant chance of Boner recognizing the woman tailing him.

As the yellow Jeep turned onto an unfamiliar side road, Britt began grinning to herself. Oh, yes, this *was* her chance to get even.

And she *was* going to get even with these two—no, there were four of the fucking rapists, including the one she hated the most, Snake . . . but oh no, she hated Sin the most!—the preggie bitch had stuck that damn remote control up her butt . . . no, she hated Boner the most for telling her to 'try harder at sex' like he was her stupid dead and unmourned mother. What-the-fuck-ever?

And so it was, that totally unnoticed by either Boner Hewitt or Sin Corbin, Britt followed them all the way home.

Their place was easy to find once you knew the way: Straight up past the Blue Star Memorial Highway, then a dirt road on the left after Raynham Park and Northeast K9 Unlimited (a bit further up than the turnoff to McKinney's Pig Farm and their 'corpse hiding place'). The proverbial boondocks. That final stretch of road to the house was as potholed, bumpy, and uneven as if Snake and Boner had laid its surface themselves. No wonder they needed a four-wheel drive.

Parked out of sight down their road, Britt hung around for three minutes, watching Boner carry the packed shopping bags into the cottage after Sin. While watching, she inhaled her fill of her hatred of both the ramshackle house and its sleazy occupants.

Then, grinning to herself, she turned the blue SUV around and drove back into town to get the first aid kit for Lori.

While casing the house, she'd had a wonderful idea: How about if she just brought Pagan over here tonight for the promised orgy, and let her fuck both Snake and Boner? Then afterwards, have Pagan kill them all?

It would be priceless to watch that green demon eating those four assholes.

By the time she arrived back at Walmart she was laughing loudly.

CHAPTER 46

Pagan / Lori

Once again Pagan returned to awareness of her surroundings, to a nightmare scene of gore. The man she'd just had sex with—she had no idea what his name was—lay in pieces all over his motel room. His torso was in at least four chunks. She could see his ribcage draped over the back of a chair like a hastily discarded shirt, and half of a lung poking out from under the bed. Some of his intestines were piled on the nightstand and most of his pelvis sat on the coffee table. She saw no sign of either his head or his limbs.

Blood lay thick over everything, including herself. Its smell was nauseatingly sweet in her nostrils. She was naked now—the increase in size accompanying her transformation had shredded her bra and shirt. Even her sneakers were trashed beyond redemption, and her wristwatch was no longer on her wrist either.

Her body tingled weakly with the distant memory of an exceptional sexual release.

Once again, she felt no disgust as she became aware of what she'd done. Her lack of revulsion in turn triggered a horror at herself—an intense dread of what she was becoming. Looking down at her body, she made out a faint green hue to her skin; but even as she watched, it faded to rosy pink again.

Her hand was clenched into a fist around some object. Opening up her hand revealed a human eye and some eyebrow.

Standing there covered with blood and swaying in a fading mental haze, she waited for the desire to puke to arrive. It didn't come.

She did however feel drained, like she needed to sleep for a while, and . . . she still felt hungry for more than flesh. Hungry to make more death. Her stomach bulged a little, but not like after past feedings, and it was clear to her that Avex wasn't completely satisfied.

She walked into the bathroom.

The dead man's legs and arms and the rest of his viscera were in the bathtub, with blood smeared all over the wall tiles; and his penis and testicles sat in the washbasin.

She scratched her head and tried to fish up a memory: his liver appeared to be missing; maybe she'd eaten it?

Once again the head was stuffed into the toilet bowl, this time with the cover down over it.

She needed to pee. She lifted the toilet lid and tried to remove the man's head from the bowl, but—*Damn, I really must have shoved the guy's neck down deep!*—it was wedged in tight and wouldn't come free.

So she sat and did her business like that, urinating right on the dead man's brown hair which in turn tickled her shaved pudenda.

She finished and flushed. Then she realized that that was a mistake and winced—the pee-and-blood-tinted water rose and spilled over the toilet rim and flooded the bathroom floor. She padded back before the spillover reached her feet.

Then she remembered her 3 o'clock appointment, and came fully awake. *Shit!—What time is it?*

Thankfully, she didn't have too far to look for the answer. The dead man's watch was on his left wrist, and his left hand was sticking out of the mess of guts in the bathtub.

She wiped the gore off the watch then heaved a sigh of relief. 2:50. *I've still got ten minutes.*

Still, there was no time to waste now. Not bothering to dress (though since she'd taken them off before having sex, her pants and panties were still in one piece), she hurried over to the front door.

Here she faced a dilemma, her feet were wet and red and it was imperative that she not leave any marks on the walkway. Red footprints would certainly alert people to the carnage she'd left inside the motel room. (With the mess inside the bathroom, it seemed impossible to her that she could get her feet clean enough in there to not leave some sort of mark.) Okay, yes, she *could* leap over the walk, but then how would she close the door after her? Particularly as, in that case she'd need to leap from *inside* the room so as not to mark the floor at the entrance.

Aware of the vital seconds ticking away, she retreated back inside the room to think. Thinking was really hard: she was weak and the bed kept calling to her to rest on it.

She finally resolved her problem by first drying her feet with a T-shirt, then wearing two of the dead man's socks on each foot.

She tested the results by placing a foot on the walkway, nodding to herself when she lifted it to find the ground beneath dry. She looked back into the room for a moment and winced. What a damn mess Avex always made of things! Just one more reason why she needed to be rid of it as fast as she could.

Then, framed there in the doorway again and about to flee Room 48, she remembered that she was currently visible to all and sundry.

Shit! Grateful that she'd remembered, and reflecting ruefully that today seemed to be full of such unmindful incidents on her behalf, she 'cloaked' herself again, then shut the door and staggered naked back to the front block.

***

When Pagan arrived back at Room 5, she instantly noticed that the Toyota RAV4 was missing from the parking lot.

The front door was shut. She considered knocking, then whispered a spell to the lock instead so it clicked open. There was no point worrying about triggering Avex anymore, was there?

Almost out on her legs now, she pushed the door wide open and peeked into the room.

Lori was on the phone saying, "No, I like being a celebrity—at least I'm doing something exceptional with my life. . . . Aw, c'mon, mom, stop crying. Don't be like that; you know I *really* love you and dad . . . No, I'm not doing this just to punish you both. Honest, I'm not. . . . No, I'm not handing myself over to the police; they'll have to catch me themselves—that's what the government pays them for." She noticed Pagan sticking her head in the door. "Sorry, mom, I gotta go now, my roommate's just coming in. . . . No, not Britney, another girl—you don't know this one . . . Yeah, I'll call you, but I don't know how soon or from where . . . Okay, I love you too, bye."

She cut the call and grinned up at Pagan. "Yes, don't tell me: I know the cops might have been tracing the call, but I just had to call home. My mom says the Feds think we're east in—"

Then her face twisted up. "Pagan, what the hell happened to you? You're naked and covered in blood. Are you hurt?"

Pagan waved the query off, and pointed outside (she'd left the door open for that purpose). "Our ride's missing."

Lori peered out. "Oh, that. Britt took the car into town."

Pagan shut the door. "Huh? Where'd she go? To look for me?"

"Nah, nah." Lori waved her left arm so Pagan could see her wounds and the rough bindings. "I had an accident and Britt . . ." Then her expression switched suddenly to one of intense horror and fear. "Pagan, why are you staring at me like that? Stop it! Stop it!"

But Pagan *couldn't* stop it. Lori's open wounds were proving a sufficient trigger to activate Avex again. She did her utmost best to hold the demon in, to keep it caged, but failed.

"Run, Lori!" she screamed as her arms turned green.

But even as she blanked out again, Pagan knew that Lori wouldn't run away. All of a sudden Lori's horror and fear had turned to an intense expression of delight and she was reaching out her arms towards Pagan and smiling.

"Come to mama, you beautiful ugly green darling," Lori cooed with an almost sexual urgency in her voice. "Come and give mama what she truly needs. Oh, this is such a lovely day, isn't it?"

CHAPTER 47

Britt

Britt heard the loud noises from Room 5 immediately she got out of the SUV. Medical purchases in hand, she hurried over to unlock the door.

Then she stood there in the doorway paralyzed, letting everything she'd just bought fall from her hands.

What?

Pagan—fully transformed into her demon self—was murdering Lori. The green monster had Lori's guts out in a tangled bloody string and had the end of them in its mouth and was chomping on them with those horrible teeth that were like a tiger's.

It was crouched over Lori facing towards the headboard. Britt watched it spit out Lori's guts, then slash both of her breasts open with its massive black claws, then bend down and bite into them one after the other, and then fling its head back, spitting yellow breast fat everywhere. Then it dug its claws deep into her chest, shredding the muscles and smashing her ribs.

And Lori—stupid, stupid, stupid Lori—was staring at Britt with a crazed excitement in her eyes. "HOLY SHIT!!!!" she moaned like she was coming. "THIS IS FUCKING DAMN AWESOME!!! OH, I LOVE YOU, BRITNEY WILSON, YOU'RE THE BEST DAMN FRIEND EVER!!!"

Then—with a broad and bloody grin on her face—Lori died.

Britt suddenly realized that she was crying. The tears were wet on her cheeks as she stood watching the demon tearing off Lori's arms. It broke each one like they were toothpicks, its immense muscles contracting and relaxing in a disgustingly fluid interplay. Then it started on Lori's legs, ripping those off also.

Britt unfroze. Feeling colder than the North Pole, she walked over past the ravaging monster (not even cringing when she brushed against its wings) to where her loaded revolver lay atop the fridge.

She grabbed the Colt and spun round to face the demon.

"Hey, Pagan, I've got something here for you!"

It didn't reply. So she shot it twice in the back.

Then, with a howl, the monster turned to glare at her. Looking away from her as it had been, she'd been spared the full impact of its horrifying visual aspect. Now she was terrified in full measure. The demon's horned snakelike head dripped with gore; blood and fat dripped from its mouth, and a length of intestine was speared on its right horn. Its entire front (where its ludicrously small breasts looked like nipples perched atop its humongous pectoral muscles) was covered with blood that dripped between its legs.

The monster howled at her.

Trembling with fear and anger, Britt fired again, this time at its face. "Fuck you, asshole!" One, two, three, four, shots that flung it back over the bed; over Lori's body. It lay on its back there as if dead, its legs up on Lori's limbless and excavated torso.

Then the gun clicked empty.

At that ominous metal announcement, Britt looked worriedly over at the demon. *Is it frigging dead? Did I kill it?*

She took a step closer to the bed.

But no, she hadn't killed it. It was sitting up and looking at her. Black blood was spilling from several massive holes in the green monster's face, one of those its destroyed right eye.

It glared at her angrily with its good eye, then said, "Those bullets sting, but they won't kill me. I'm going to eat you, you bitch slut!"

She instantly wet herself. It wasn't so much the words that made her lose control of her bladder as their horrifying sub-octave pitch. Nothing natural could sound that deep; nothing could speak words that one felt inside one's bones.

Shit. She began frantically glancing around for their other pistol, the Ruger. *Where the hell did Lori put it?*

The demon suddenly turned and began fiddling with Lori's body. Britt first thought that it had forgotten her. She prepared to dash past it and out of the open front door (she'd been so stunned by what she'd witnessed on arriving back from town that she'd not even removed the key from the lock), but then it straightened up again and she saw—to her horror—that it had ripped off Lori's head.

It flung the head at her.

She wasn't expecting that. Lori's head hit her flush in the face. The impact felt like she'd been whacked with a sledgehammer. It knocked her back into the bathroom and into the bathtub.

She half-lay, half-sat in there with her brain numb.

Lori's head had come to rest on its side in the doorway, facing into the bathroom. Her eyes were shut now, but her lips were still curved in that final smile of total happiness and peace.

Britt almost felt closure for Lori, but then the demon appeared in the doorway, stomping her head flat. Lori's skull cracking sounded louder than the gunshots, and her brains spurted and splattered all over the bathroom floor.

Britt now realized that she'd lost her gun during her fall. It was empty anyway and so useless. Worse than useless actually: none of the four gunshot wounds that she'd inflicted on the monster's face were still visible—it had completely healed itself.

She began frantically making the sign of the cross at the bitch-demon, but it laughed at her.

"That only works for the holy," it rumbled at her, "and *your* soul is almost as filthy as mine."

It laughed and laughed and laughed at her.

Britt, too stunned at the moment to really appreciate the horror of her situation, nonetheless realized that it was all over for her. Strangely enough, no tears filled her eyes. Also, she found that she didn't regret a thing that she'd done.

At least, this was what she and Lori had planned on—a joint end. To die *together* now at the monster's hands seemed very fitting.

The demon was saying, "And now I'm going to eat you . . ." but then it stopped. It seemed to be having trouble controlling its limbs. It took a step forward towards Britt, then another one back; then forward and back again; then two step sideways to bang against the closets on the far wall; then it clawed at the walls, leaving deep scratches in both door jambs and wide swaths of ripped plasterboard; then it leapt up and down and smashed the washbasin off the wall with a flailing fist. It groped about like it was blind, opening and shutting its mouth rapidly and twisting its head right and left like it was really confused.

Britt gaped at it in equal confusion. Her head was clearing up a bit now and she would have fled, but the green monster was blocking the door.

Finally, the demon creature yelled a loud "NOOOOO!!!!" and compacted back into Pagan again.

Pagan stood there in the doorway for a moment smiling sadly at Britt. "Thank God I controlled it this time . . . I didn't let it eat you like it did Lori . . ."

She sounded weak and tired as hell and was swaying like she'd fall as she stepped backward through the remnants of Lori's splattered head into the front room.

Speechless, Britt watched her retreat out of sight. As her breathing settled, Pagan's voice filtered in to her:

"Shit, it's five past three—I need to turn the spell off . . ." She muttered something, then next yelped in a shocked voice, "Shit! What the hell are *you* doing in here! NOOOOO!!! STOP! PLEASE!"

And then Pagan's voice faded to a horrible gurgling.

Britt hurriedly climbed out of the bathtub and ran into the front room.

Then she froze . . . again.

There was another girl in the room now, this one a six-foot-tall redhead wearing a white pantsuit. The redhead was sticking something in Pagan's neck. Pagan stood frozen rigid at the foot of the bed with her mouth gaping open while the new girl pressed down hard on the object.

When she pulled it back, Britt saw that it was a large hypodermic syringe.

"Stop," she objected hollowly, too confused by this new turn of events to attempt doing more.

The redhead looked at her with a no-nonsense expression. "No, and don't you dare interfere." Then she stabbed Pagan in the other side of her neck with a second syringe, which Britt now determined was full of a red liquid. The girl quickly depressed the plunger, forcing the liquid into Pagan's neck. Pagan's loud gurgling got even louder.

The new arrival looked quickly over at Britt again. "I mean it: don't you even *think* of helping her," she warned. "This is way out of your little-girls psycho league. Yeah, I recognize you from TV." She jerked the second needle out of Pagan's neck, and picked up a third large hypo from an open brown handbag that lay on the bed.

Britt nodded dully. "But what are you doing to her?"

(Pagan looked really horrible now. She still stood in the same spot, at the foot of the bed facing the television. She was staring and her mouth was in continual motion, her lips flapping wildly up and down, while between them, her tongue also moved rapidly back and forth. Her hands flapped at her sides like she was flying. Her legs wobbled and trembled all at once.)

The redhead replied, "I'm injecting her with fresh piglet's blood. Her demon is allergic to the stuff. It's the only way to banish the crazy fucker back to Hell."

She stabbed Pagan in the neck with the third needle, then, with a touch of obvious relish that appeared to border on malice, she depressed the plunger hard.

Pagan gave a LOUD howl of pain. That howl became louder still when the redhead whipped out a knife and, without so much as a flicker of emotion, sliced off both Pagan's left nipple and the area of skin on the left of that breast that had her inverted 'A' tattoo. Her face cold as ice, she dropped both skin and knife into her handbag, then neatly packed the three hypodermic syringes away in there also.

Meanwhile, blood spurted from Pagan's mutilated breast.

Why the hell did she slice her nipple off? That made no sense to Britt. Still she saw poetic justice of a sort in it: Pagan *had* eaten both of Lori's breasts.

Britt stopped staring at the pair and stared at Lori's corpse instead.

All that was left of Lori now was a ruined mortal shell, empty as a bathtub. With her head and limbs removed, she was merely meat—a cow being readied for the freezer.

A jolt of emotional pain hit Britt then, so hard and sharp, it felt like a physical punch.

She turned back to stare at the mess of shattered head smeared across the bathroom floor. She walked over and knelt by it. She touched its clammy wetness, touched the bloody crown of short bleached-blonde hair. She tried to scrape the parts of head together into a pile but they were too mushed and stuck everywhere.

There was a strange smell in the room now, but she paid no heed to it, all she could do was stare down at the horrible, horrible mess that remained of her best friend's brains. Shit! Coming right on the heels of the earlier suicide scare, this was so unexpected that Britt didn't know what to think. All that filled her mind right now were

Lori's final words before she died: 'This is fucking damn awesome. Oh, I love you, Britney Wilson, you're the best damn friend ever.'

At least she died with me there. And she died how she wanted to . . . and happy too. And most important of all—she knew that I LOVED her crazy ass.

The smell in the room was thicker now. Smelt like fire . . . there was smoke in the room now that wasn't just the haze of sorrow in her mind.

She felt a hand on her shoulder.

She looked back at the redhead in the white suit, who now had her brown handbag slung over her shoulder. "What?"

"Pack your stuff and get out fast. She's gonna explode."

Britt gasped. *What?* She got up and turned around.

Pagan lay on her back on the bed now and the smoke in the room was coming from her body, peeling off her nude form in layers like she was evaporating.

Britt looked at the redhead. "For real? She's gonna blow?"

She nodded. "As surely as I'm gonna go to Hell when I die."

That made Britt curious; she decided she might as well ask the question on her mind. This was another bona fide witch here, and there didn't seem to be any other destination except downwards for she herself after death: the green demon monster had assured her of as much.

So she asked, "Hell's a cool joint, right?"

The girl winced at the question. "Are you frigging stoned? Hell's an anus packed full of steaming poop."

"But you and Pagan . . . ?"

"Once you're in with the Devil, it's almost impossible to get out. Alive anyway. So you make the best dinner you can of it; you just use the longest possible spoon you can find."

Frowning, she pointed at Pagan. Through the dark haze slowly filling the room, they could see the skin of Pagan's face peeling off, and beneath it, her skull smoking. Her mouth yawned wide; her lips were stretched taut around her teeth; and her lips, her teeth, her tongue, and her gums all gave off thick trails of smoke. Like a volcano, her mouth poured out dark fumes; like an inferno raged in her throat. The rest of Pagan's body was smoking thick and furious too. And now Britt noted an oddity: this smoke didn't smell like the obscene reek of burning human flesh; it smelt sulfurous, as if the witch was being consumed by flames from a plane beyond the human.

"Pagan was unwise, that's all," the redhead continued. "Me? I'm much smarter." Then she looked coldly at Britt. "I'm warning you: get your things and get out. You've at most a minute more before she explodes. As for me? I'm outa here."

She turned and walked off.

"Hey! Hey—wait a minute!" Britt called after the redhead just as she stepped outside.

She turned with a frown on her face. "Look, I'm not fooling around; we're running out of damn time. I've told you—get your stuff and get the hell out of here."

"Yeah, I'm leaving. But who are you? Who the hell are you?"

The girl laughed then. "Oh that." She winked at Britt. "I'm Joker, baby! The witch who now runs the West Coast. Yoo hoo! Sunny California, here I fucking come!"

And with that she was gone.

Britt hurriedly grabbed up her travel bag and purse and car keys and empty gun and dashed out after her.

Outside, Joker was nowhere to be seen.

Britt jumped into the blue SUV and hurriedly reversed.

The motel room blew up just as she shifted gear into 'Drive.' The door flew off its frame and out across the parking lot and the window seemed to melt from the heat billowing out of the room.

Yeah, it seemed 'hot as hell' in there at that moment. And then additional explosions began inside the room.

Goodbye Lori! I love you too! Britt thought with tears in her eyes.

Then she drove off without looking back.

CHAPTER 48

Kev

"I-I-I swear, that's what I saw . . ." Crystal Parr stuttered.

Raynham Chief of Police Tina Kravitz scrunched up her face and pouted, doing her best to look tough and hide her bewilderment.

Kev Parr sighed. Crystal had been calling him nonstop on his phone and had been waiting for him at the station when he'd gotten back in after a fruitless search for Cherry Duggan. Before he could steer her off somewhere secluded though, the Chief had howled him into her office and Crystal had tagged along behind him.

She'd greeted Tina Kravitz, then, before Kev could safely get rid of her, had sat down and begun getting everything off her large bosom.

Long story short, she'd been buying gas at the Shell filling station on Broadway, and chatting at the same time with Bobby Russell—who occasionally bought pussy from her—when "like a miracle," Bobby's neck had slit open by itself and he'd begun bleeding to death.

Kev believed her. He remembered last night's video and the scene in the Cunningham's house this morning.

Tina Kravitz, though, seemed to be finding it hard to make up her mind whether Crystal was bullshitting or not. With a married woman's instinctive dislike of prostitutes she distrusted Crystal for a start, and additionally now, Crystal reeked of whiskey, which she fiercely insisted she'd drank only after Bobby Russell got killed: "I just turned and ran and ran, 'cos I was scared the evil wind might turn from him and do me too."

She'd been so terrified in fact, that it had been the next customer driving into the self-service, who—seeing a woman running away screaming from a bleeding man on the ground beside the pumps—

had alerted the police. (He'd also had to pull out the nozzle [which was apparently faulty—it was spilling gas everywhere] from the tank of Crystal's Volkswagen and replace it on the pump.)

Tina Kravitz grunted like she was on the toilet and the turds were being adamant about not leaving her behind. Then she got up, placed both plump hands palms down on her desk and stared coldly at Crystal.

"I don't know if I believe you or not. Just be quiet till the lab boys get through with their analysis of the crime scene."

"I told the officers what I saw; they didn't believe me."

Kev shifted on his chair and nodded. After recovering sufficiently, Crystal had gone back for her Volkswagen. Detectives Bonaparte and Reilly—who both knew her—had taken her statement and let her go.

Kev was perplexed over how, with fourteen thousand residents in Raynham, it was his older sister alone who kept encountering this weird shit. (Or was it a family thing, as in genetic? He too *had* seen those vanishing girls . . . No! There were never any vanishing girls— he'd just been hungry, that was all!)

The Chief said, "The boys are checking the station's CCTV footage, and they're getting the bank card details for the last persons who used the pumps before Bobby got killed."

"Tina, I'm telling you there was no one there. Just him and me." She began wiping her eyes again.

"Yeah, yeah, but you could have looked away for a sec and one of those Jap ninja assholes cut him like that."

"Tina, I didn't—"

"Shut up, Crystal." The Chief's fat face pinched together so tight that for a moment she looked like one of her father's pigs. "Listen, just keep your mouth zipped tight. I don't want you going around telling people whatever you did or didn't frigging see. Okay? I know *you* didn't kill Bobby, so just let it go? We've enough crap in town as it is at the moment. Just so you know, the boys are investigating Bobby's death in connection to a pregnant woman's murder yesterday on lower Broadway. There didn't seem to be anyone around then either, but the law doesn't believe in ghosts, okay?"

She kept a cold glare on Crystal till the prostitute nodded meekly, then turned to glare at Kev instead. "Now, kid, let's get down to why I hollered for you."

He unwrapped a candy bar and took a bite. "Yeah, Chief. First of all, I can't find traces of Cherry anywhere. I spoke to both Zak Duggan and that kid Cory Perkins who Zak claims she's seeing on the side. Neither of 'em—"

"Forget Cherry for the moment. The State Crime Lab just rushed in the fingerprint results from Bennett's car, his motel room, and"—her face pinched up again—"the Cunningham house massacre."

"And . . . ?" Kev took another bite of candy and waited. Crystal too was staring at the Chief with interest.

"There were two distinct sets of fingerprints in Bennett's car and motel room. One of course was his. The second set belonged to Pagan Harris—the fugitive witch from Boston."

Kev whistled.

Tina Kravitz drummed her fingers on her desktop, then paced about a little, then settled down in her chair, which creaked in protest. "Most revealingly, the witch's prints were all over the steering wheel, meaning she's the one who dumped the car at Rudy's."

Kev nodded. "How about the Cunningham house?"

"She's all over there too. The lab guys say they're still analyzing the stiffs for DNA evidence, but as far as fingerprints go, we've a definite match . . . which means she was one of the three prostitutes who picked up Josh and his friends from the truck stop last night."

"Hold on, Chief, what about . . . ?"

"The other two hookers with her when she targeted Josh?" She now scowled deepest of all, like she was wrestling to pass the mother-of-all-turds. "You'll never believe this: In the Cunningham house there were these two other sets of prints. They belonged to the Wilson and Kaminski girls."

"Wilson and Kaminski?" Crystal enquired, crossing her legs.

Tina Kravitz sighed. "Those two girls who fled Boston after sawing Wilson's mother's feet off. Christ, Crystal, don't you ever watch the news?"

Crystal looked sick. "Her mom's feet?"

The Chief nodded. "Yeah. Both extremities were found yesterday in Kaminski's car, which they'd abandoned in a cornfield up north along Route 138." She looked back at Kev. "Which unfortunately means that those two young psychotic airheads are still here in Raynham."

"But . . ." Kev said, "didn't the Feds say they picked up their trail west in Michigan?"

The obese police chief grunted and shook her head. "That was just a mix-up. Those two Detroit girls were an interracial lesbian couple who nail-gunned the black girl's grandmother to her rocking chair."

"Nail-gunned?" Crystal asked in horror. Now she looked even sicker. "Why the hell would they do that?"

Tina Kravitz winced. "Yeah, fifty-one six-inchers they shot through the old bird, and all apparently 'cos Gran was religious and insisted that their relationship was of the Devil and tried to break them up." She frowned. "Personally, I don't know if it's just open season on old folk at the moment or if Gran should just have minded her own business and let her granddaughter and the girlfriend hump themselves in peace. Times have changed a whole lot—Bible thumping's a risky endeavor nowadays. Still, that was no justification to do her in like that. Shooting nails into someone's a nasty way to kill them."

The narration was depressing her, so she shrugged it off. "Anyhow, what I was gonna say was: it was the nail gun element that made the FBI at first suspect that Wilson and Kaminski were responsible."

Crystal looked really sick now. Kev hoped she wouldn't puke in here. If she did the Chief would go ballistic.

To change the direction of the conversation, he asked, "The pink lipstick in the Cunningham's toilet—whose fingerprints were on the tube?"

"Wilson's. You know, Kev, that aspect of the case makes no sense at all to me. Why the hell would someone draw crosses inside the toilet like they were trying to keep the devil out?"

Kev said nothing. Just like the chief had said a while earlier, the law didn't believe in spooks. He glanced sharply sideways at his sister. She read his expression and nodded back.

"There's more," the Chief continued, having not noticed the visual exchange between the siblings. "With the benefit of hindsight this all seems planned in advance. All three girls have known themselves for years. Wilson, Kaminski, and Harris all attended Boston's Hyde Park High School. We've also got confirmed reports of Wilson spending a lot of time over at Harris's house several years ago, just after her parent's divorce. So they were close friends. And—"

The door burst open then and Honey Maxwell dashed in, her thin face all creased up worried.

"Girl, you can see I'm busy—can't you knock?"

"Sorry to bother you, Chief," Honey gushed, "but old Mr. Duggan just called in to report several explosions and a fire over at his motel."

"At the Sunflower?" Tina and Kev gaped at each other, Kev's fresh candy bar spilling from his fingers, then both weight-challenged policepersons leapt to their feet and hurried out the door.

Crystal shrugged, then hurried after them.

CHAPTER 49

Joker

Back in her motel room, Joker was exuberant with the thrill of victory.

"Yesss!" she yelped as loud as she could. "I'm in Hollywood!"

Sitting cross-legged in bed, she stared at her vibrator, wondering whether to rub off some celebratory orgasms before starting the drive back to Boston.

Then her phone rang.

She picked it up. "Hi, Nero, I was just about calling you."

"How's the situation over there."

"The powder keg's been neutralized."

The relief in his voice was audible. "Lucifer be praised. Are you sure?"

"Nero, I'm already thinking up titles for the movies I'm gonna produce." Then her dream came back to haunt her, and she asked worriedly, "I still do get the job, don't I? You're not going to gyp me out of this?" It was a valid worry: if the Abyss Club had changed their mind about rewarding her, there was absolutely nothing she could do about it.

He laughed softly. "Not at all. The job is still yours." Then, on the phone, she heard a sudden 'POP!' behind him, an implosion like air filling a vacuum.

He said, "Hold the line a moment."

She waited. Through the phone, she could hear Nero discussing with another voice that sounded like it was being fed through a rack of guitar effect processors. Then it stopped talking and there was another loud 'POP' of imploding sound.

"Okay, he's gone," Nero said.

"Who was that?"

He laughed. "A delighted visitor from the pits of Hell. One of Avex's guards come to inform me that The Ravager is back home in its cell again, and that Satan still doesn't have a clue that it ever went missing in the first place. Needless to say, they're exceedingly grateful." He paused a moment, then added, "So like I was saying, no, we're not going to screw you over—you're in charge . . . shit!"

"What?"

"That demon appearing almost made me forget what I called you for."

"Yeah, man, *I* was supposed to call *you*. Why *did* you call me?"

Once Nero explained why he'd called first, Joker was alarmed. "You guys did *what?* You didn't trust me?"

"We were just covering our bases. Remember how she escaped from both Townsend and Dover? We weren't about letting that happen again."

"Okay, I understand. But I fixed it, didn't I?" She got up off the bed and walked over to pull the window drapes apart. "I can see the smoke from here. Nero, you've got to call that thing off. It might kill someone."

"I can't. You know I don't do spells."

"I mean—get the warlocks to call it off."

"I can't find either of them. Raven took my secretary Sabrina out to lunch and I don't know where the hell Killman's gotten to."

"Oh, shit. When's it supposed to get here?"

"Three-twenty. I made sure you'd have enough time to get out if you weren't dead."

She checked her watch. "That's in just two minutes."

"Just stay away from that block."

"Yeah, definitely. I was about checking out. Now it looks like I'll have to wait till the cops are done asking questions."

CHAPTER 50

Britt

On leaving the Sunflower Motel for the last time, Britt decided to kill herself. Lori was gone and now her life really didn't seem worth living anymore.

Cloaked in a suicidal haze, she drove up towards Rudy's en-route to their secret hideaway opposite McKinney's farm.

Then, just as she reached the truck stop, she changed her mind about the location for her suicide. *I don't want to die and not be found till I'm all rotted away.*

So she drove into Rudy's parking lot and reversed in between two 18-wheelers so she was out of sight of the road.

She picked up the Colt Python revolver—Lonnie's gun. The weapon was still warm from her shooting at Pagan's monster.

After weighing the revolver in her palm for a moment, she broke it open and emptied it of the spent casings. Then she searched through her bag for the box of ammo and slipped a single round into the cylinder.

She'd decided that as a tribute to Lonnie's memory she'd play Russian roulette till she lost, or won. (Ah, meeting Lonnie Young and his death seemed so far off now. Was it really just three days ago that she'd deflowered him, taken his sweet male virginity as her trophy?)

She pushed the cylinder back in place, spun it, and without any hesitation, stuck the gun in her mouth.

'Click.' No luck then. She pulled the barrel out of her mouth, spun the cylinder again, replaced it between her lips and pulled the trigger again.

'Click' again. Then spin-click, spin-click, spin-click . . .

Fifteen tries later, she was still alive with the damn revolver in her mouth, unable to die. She considered just pulling the trigger

358

continuously until she blew her head off, but no, that wasn't the way you played Russian roulette. Lonnie had taught her well: you never screwed yourself over, you gave yourself the best odds possible each time—always 5 to 1 was the bet on your mortality.

Then it hit her: *Holy shit—I must've switched lucks with Lonnie when I fucked him! That's why his luck instantly ran out, while mine . . .*

Britt pulled the pistol out of her mouth and gaped at it, her saliva dripping down its silver muzzle. If she'd deduced correctly, she now had Lonnie's weird luck, and apparently wouldn't be able to win/lose at Russian roulette for years.

She tried again. Spin-click, spin-click, spin-click . . . it was no use. Twenty additional attempts later, her brains were still intact in her head, and her basic depression had passed.

She wiped the Colt's barrel, loaded it up fully again, and shut it away in the glove compartment.

Their ladies riding pillion, a biker gang rode past her into Rudy's on their souped-up Harleys, but they didn't peer into the gap between the trucks.

Watching them wheel by, Britt now realized/remembered that before leaving Raynham she had some business to attend to.

Yeah, she had to pay back Snake and Boner and Sin and Ella.

Once the last motorcycle had rolled past, she started up the blue SUV again, then drove out of Rudy's and back into town, looking for a hardware store.

Just before the Center Street turning, she passed two police cars speeding the other way with their sirens on, one of them driven by that fat policeman.

The fat cop looked across at her. Then his eyes widened like he was seeing a ghost and he quickly looked away again.

Britt laughed and drove on.

CHAPTER 51

Kev

Kev, Crystal, and Tina Kravitz arrived at the Sunflower Motel to see the strangest sight of their lives. The front motel block was crumbling to bits, and apparently of its own accord. It looked like an invisible wrecking ball was demolishing the block, only it was doing so from above, not from the sides.

In anticipation of trouble, Tina Kravitz had ordered another squad car along. Three heavily armed policemen sat in it, ready to kick terrorist ass.

Flagged down by Clint Duggan immediately they drove onto his property, both squad cars parked outside the motel reception and everyone got out.

And began staring.

"Someone or something's got it in for me big time," the motel owner grumbled. "They're trying to put me out of business."

Kev had no reply to that. Even as they spoke the building was continuing its self-demolition act, huge holes appearing at random in its roof like someone was dropping weights on it while at the same time they could see its inner walls crumbling to the floor; and large chunks of the front wall were blowing off and falling into the parking lot like something was knocking them out from inside, and . . . shattered wood beams and shards of steel and broken concrete and sheets of drywall were flying everywhere.

There was a fire truck parked opposite the block near the trees bordering the lot, but the firemen were just staring at the spectacle in confusion. The fire was already out anyway, smothered by deconstruction dust.

"Clint," Kev said worriedly. "This morning you said the front block is currently vacant. Did anyone move in yet?"

"No, thank God. All the rooms are empty, else I'll likely be facing the biggest lawsuit in Massachusetts history."

"Hey, let's move closer," Tina Kravitz said, gesturing to Clint and her men.

"Not you," Kev told his sister as she made to follow them. "This is police business. You stay in the car."

Crystal pouted. "Kev, I wanna see."

"Sis, you've already seen far too much today. Besides you're half-drunk and might get yourself killed. Just watch it from here, please."

"Okay, whatever you say, younger bro." Crystal settled on the hood of Kev's squad car.

He hurried after the others. Clint was explaining to the Chief, ". . . I'd just sat on the toilet when I heard the first loud noise. When I finished and came out, I saw Room 5 burning something fierce, and it looked like something was still blowing up inside there too. So I called you. And then, next thing I know . . ." he gestured at the collapsing building, "just before the fire truck arrived, *this* started. And don't you dare tell me it's a blasted terrorist attack. 'Cos if it's the blasted A-rabs—why would they wanna put me outa business by bombing an empty building?"

No one replied. The spectacle was very impressive.

(Watching a set of brass bath taps blow out through a shattered front window reminded Kev of the story Clint had once told him of how he'd come about the Sunflower's bathtubs. According to Clint, while building the motel he'd run into a Boston plumbing contractor—Kaminski, his name was, same as that runaway girl—who'd found himself stuck with a whole truckload of imported bathroom fittings after a client died, and who, desperate to be rid of the bathtubs in particular, had fitted out the Sunflower at a half-price discount.)

They stood opposite the block and watched. Watched doors flatten and splinter into toothpicks, watched glass crumple to powder, watched the front walls suddenly break up and their parts fly across the parking lot; watched the ceilings crumble and drop onto furniture, beds, TVs, and bathtubs that somehow vanished into the ground; watched the billowing dust clouds; watched the concrete pillars fracture in the middle, breaking like bones in an unfortunate soccer player's leg, their internal steel struts denting at sharp angles like . . .

Like something's kicking them down, Kev thought with a sudden unhappy clarity. It was a stupid illogical thought, but he'd also noticed that the holes appearing in the long rooftop had a gap of about ten or twelve yards between them. And that gap in the wrecking was a constant one—as the front part of the demolition progressed further down the block, the rear assault followed, most of the time pulverizing what the front had already crumbled.

No, he told himself, *there's no giant animal up there, flattening the motel.* But he could smell 'something' in the air: a musk mingled with the cement-and-plaster dust now threatening to choke everyone.

"Chief, do you smell anything odd?"

"Smell? With all this dust in my damn nose? Kev, what the damn hell are you talking about?"

He looked around at his fellow cops. All were just watching entranced. He looked back at his squad car. His sister—her ass perched on the front of the hood—waved back.

He returned his attention to the crumbling building.

"Do something!" Clint was pleading. "Somebody do *something*. I'm goin' outa business here!"

"There's nothing we can do, old man," one of the cops replied. "You got insurance coverage?"

Clint nodded glumly. "Yeah. Still hurts watching it falling down though."

By now a crowd had begun gathering—mostly baffled guests from the rear blocks. And the watchers weren't just on this front side of the motel either. By now, the half of the block towards Clint's reception building was a flattened ruin. Everyone could see clear over the piled rubble to the block behind. An old couple stood there pointing and gaping, their eyes almost as wide open as their mouths.

Kev now became aware of a fresh danger with all these new people about, most of them over at the far end of the motel block where the destruction was still happening.

Admittedly it was a great spectacle. The front lot was by now strewn with rubble—shards of glass, concrete chunks, wood fragments, bits of door and wall, and warped metal projections, all smothered in a layer of dust like brown fog. And from where Kev stood, the back of the building looked exactly the same. One red sedan had half of a wall collapsed on it.

And more stuff was being kicked—*No!* he violently corrected himself. *There's nothing up there!*—was being *knocked* out onto the lot every second.

He nodded to Chief Kravitz, then pointed ahead to where, with a spectator's usual display of nonchalance, a bearded and bald man in Bermuda shorts had just stepped forward and picked up a metal rod from the lot. Then he'd begun examining it, not heeding that he was within range of the still-ongoing building destruction. A skinny woman who had to be his wife was walking towards him, stepping over half of a shattered chair to do so.

"They need to stay out of range of the flying debris," Kev told Tina Kravitz, then set off jogging towards them, huffing and puffing his way across the lot. Shit, this was hard work. He'd need another lunch after this exercise for sure.

Following Kev's lead, two other detectives, Bonaparte and Donnelly, set off for the rear of the block to warn those on that side. Back there (with a crunch that was audible over here) a falling pillar had just totaled someone's Harley Davidson.

"Hey! Hey!" Kev yelled at the couple standing in the rubble as he dashed past the fire truck. "Move back! Get back from there!" A fireman was similarly shouting to the pair, but the noise of the breaking building was louder than bombs.

Kev looked up. The front part of the roof at the end of the block was just coming down, along with half the wall over there. *Damn, this thing really did a number on Clint's building.*

A cloud of dust billowed out at him and he found himself choking for breath. Thankfully, the couple he'd been trying to alert had now realized the danger they'd put themselves in. Coughing, they made their way up to the grass and trees bordering the lot.

Relieved that he could stop his run, Kev made to do the same.

And then it happened: Just after Kev turned, he felt something hit him in the back, simultaneous with a terrible pain in his belly that seemed to go right through his body.

The impact spun him around so he fell on his back. He lay there, his torso a pool of agony.

"Kev! NOOOOO!!!" A female voice screamed. That might have been Crystal screaming, but it sounded more like the Chief.

Kev tried to get up again, but couldn't. He tried to move his legs, but couldn't. His hands worked but not his legs.

He raised himself up on his elbows, enough to look down his body, and then went all pale. He had no belly anymore, just a round hole in his uniform through which he could see the lot floor.

Shee-it! How am I ever gonna eat my lunch now without a stomach? was his inane first thought.

Then there were more screams and pounding feet, and he was surrounded by blue uniforms. And Chief Tina Kravitz was looking down at him and bawling her eyes out.

Kev was surprised. *The Chief likes me that much?* And then Crystal was there too, her makeup already ruined by her tears.

"Hang in there, Kev!" more than one voice was saying. "The ambulance will be here soon."

But it was already too late for Kev. He knew it, and they all knew it too. A flying chunk of pillar had hit him in the back and knocked his guts and spine out through his belly. The severed bits lay in a bloody mess several meters behind him.

Kev already felt like a shadow of himself, like his soul was in the blood pouring from his wound. And it was a lot of blood.

But, as Kev Parr was dying, the sky over the Sunflower Motel seemed to open up like the cover of a book and he saw another layer of the universe. A dark layer like a negative version of reality.

And yes, he saw that he'd been right, there *was* an animal—an immense goat—trampling down the front block. A goat as huge as a star constellation. It was big and black and had massive curved horns. And it stank something awful.

And the huge goat turned to look at him, and it laughed. Yeah, the damn thing laughed, like Kev's death was hilarious to it.

Wow, that animal sure would make a lot of burgers, Kev thought and died.

CHAPTER 52

Britt

Even though the police hadn't stopped her, passing those two squad cars convinced Britt that she was really pushing her luck by driving the blue RAV4 around.

By tomorrow (if it wasn't already on a BOLO list), the SUV would definitely be too hot to drive. (Yeah, the cops might even track the vehicle's onboard navigation system—the fucking GPS. They might be trying to do so already, but then Pagan had blocked everything off. For a moment Britt worried about them tracking Pagan's white Honda too, then remembered it was dead in the woods.)

Tomorrow didn't really matter though. All she needed was the rest of today before someone connected the dots and linked Matt Lewis's non-appearance at the Westville shoe convention to she and Lori.

She intended to ditch the RAV4 immediately after her visit to Snake and Sin's place. But—she grimaced with disgust at herself on realizing exactly how careless she was being—it would be the stupidest thing ever to get apprehended now by the police before she'd even attempted her revenge.

Besides, on further calm consideration, she realized too that she already had everything she needed to carry out that revenge right here with her in the car. She had a gun, a box of ammunition, a carving knife, and some duct tape. And there was also that large clawhammer she'd yesterday noticed in the trunk (sadly there were no nails for it); and also the penlight in the glove compartment.

She had no food though, so she stopped at a Subway restaurant for a takeout sandwich. With her black hair, librarian spectacles, red lipstick, and baseball cap with the peak turned back, no one paid her the least attention. She pouted like her mother always used to do, chewed her lower lip like a porno actress (a mannerism also subconsciously borrowed from the deceased Joanna), and got served.

"No, no cheese please. Yes, oregano would be great, thanks. And, yes, I'd love some pickles . . ."

When the blonde sandwich artist who served her made eye contact, she smirked haughtily like he wasn't good enough for her. Damn, she could almost see his boner through the counter. Still smirking, she paid for her sub and walked off. She was tingling as she strode towards the restaurant entrance; the expression on his face had been like he was psychically fucking her in the ass. She could almost feel how hard he was, feel him inside her, giving pleasure to her flesh with his own.

She looked back after opening the door. He was still staring her way, a longing, almost pleading, look on his face. She winked at him and left. Crossing to her parked car, she imagined him coming in his pants there behind the food counter and getting fired. It was an exciting vision, him getting sacked instead of getting 'that hot slut' in the sack! Oh, the poor guy! He'd definitely remember her and her vehicle if the fuzz came asking, but in a good way. He might even keep his mouth shut.

Armed with the submarine sandwich from Subway, she headed back out of town to the McKinney's Pig Farm turnoff. On her way back she saw the massive commotion of police and citizens at the Sunflower Motel, but drove past without stopping.

That was in her past now, she needed to think ahead.

***

The dirt road to the abandoned farm was as empty as when she and Lori had first discovered it. Driving in here between the overhanging oak boughs, one seemed to have entered another world—the world of the dead.

Britt drove up to the stripped ancient gate and parked beside the tree from which Matt's corpse still hung.

She sat for a while in the car looking around. Pagan's white Honda Accord was still parked where they'd left it, on the opposite side of the road to the dead man's decomposing remains—driven deep under the trees on her right so it wasn't visible from the sky. She could tell its position only because its rear bumper glinted brightly where the sun cut through the greenery.

Her thoughts didn't linger long with the Honda. They'd stripped it of everything useful before ditching it.

Matt's corpse was much more interesting.

She alighted from the RAV4. Staring at the dead body with its rectum clamped over its penis was soothing; it helped her focus, to bypass her personal hurt and look forward to tonight's revenge.

And, oh God, was it so going to be a good one.

She walked over to stand beside the rotting man, the grass compressing like his soul beneath her feet. Helped by the occasional showers of the past two days, the corpse was now quite ripe, the stench of putrefaction thick in the woods. The pentagram carved into Matt's torso teemed with grubs and maggots. His legs had already served as food for some animals—both were largely stripped of flesh below the knees; and something else had either climbed up his body or down the tree to his face and chewed off his nose. Overall, his naked flesh had a saggy look to its off-whiteness, like it was about falling off his bones.

Britt laughed. She felt a definite tingle go through her, a physical memory of how great it had felt to kill him.

Down by the roots of the tree lay the bundle they'd made of the motel cleaning woman, a source of additional reek. The black plastic wrapping had been bitten through in a myriad of places and large holes eaten in her already partitioned flesh. Britt's gaze traced a strand of intestine inward from the tree to its termination amongst the pile of shoeboxes that they'd ditched from the RAV4 on commandeering it. She wondered if maybe she'd startled the creature that had been feeding on the intestine.

Finally, feeling a little disoriented, she walked back to the car and sat in it with the door open. The dashboard clock informed her that it was now 4:30 p.m.

Reaching into the backseat for a bottle of mineral water to accompany her submarine sandwich, she now discovered a 6-pack of Bud Light Lime that they'd apparently forgotten between the seats yesterday.

She got down to eating and drinking. And thinking.

Oddly enough, her thoughts circled not around Lori, but around Pagan. The cold efficiency with which that witch-girl Joker had dispatched Pagan chilled her to the bone.

Her thoughts rewound to yesterday afternoon, when the three of them had been sitting having lunch in the Chipotle Mexican Grill on the New State Highway, and to the conversation they'd had then.

All of a sudden, their girl-talk had turned from which guys in the place had the cutest faces and tightest butts to magic and witchcraft:

"Well, you buy the world with your soul," Pagan had explained. "Sometimes the deal is worth it, sometimes it isn't. Generally though, what one gets out of joining the Abyss Club depends entirely on that acolyte's motives for joining."

"How'd you mean, *motives?* Isn't it all just about a love of the supernatural?"

"Well . . . okay, let me phrase it this way: just be sure that you're becoming a Satanist for the money and the power that goes with it, not because you're pissed off with God because you just got laid off, or because he killed your sister or favorite uncle."

"Why?"

"Well, what happens then if you suddenly get a new job that pays twice as much as the one you lost, or discover two months later that your dead sister had been trying to steal your husband, or that the uncle you were so angry at losing left you a million dollars in his will? Then you're unlikely to still be mad at God, right? But if you've already signed a contract with El Diablo . . ."

"That would be *horribly* ironic."

"'*Hellishly* ironic' is the right expression. And that sort of situation occurs so many damn times you'd be surprised, and it almost always ends badly for those concerned. But see, if you join the Devil's army mainly for personal advancement and the acquisition of supernatural power, well then you know what to expect and you'll happily take what's coming to you both in this world and the next one."

The next one. I might as well check if I'm due there yet.

Britt packed the uneaten half of the sandwich away, ditched her beer can out of the car window, then got the revolver out of the glove compartment. Five plays of Russian roulette assured her that her damned luck was still good—she wasn't about buying the farm yet.

She was drunk enough to laugh at that—particularly as she sat facing a farm that would likely sell for peanuts, if anyone could be conned into buying it.

She drank till 6 p.m., then amidst the fast-lengthening shadows, decided to get some sleep. She set an alarm for midnight if she'd not woken up by then.

There was no real hurry—the early hours of tomorrow morning would best for her attack—she wanted her prey to be both back home and fast asleep before she struck.

***

Britt woke up at 10 p.m., which was much too early.

She looked over at the hanging corpse. Something large and dark was propped up against Matt's legs, jerking its head left and right as it tore the flesh off his thighs. Something else—pale and smaller, with a furry tail—was balanced on his left shoulder, its teeth locked tight on the dead man's left ear.

She considered shining a torch on the creatures to see what sort they were, then she shrugged. They'd likely take to their heels the moment she snapped the light on. Besides, there was no point in disturbing their dinner.

She listened some to oldies on the radio, accidentally catching a news bulletin on Attleboro's Station WARA informing the town's inhabitants that herself, Lori, and Pagan were very likely still on the loose in the eastern part of the state. She laughed at that, then consumed her last can of beer while tapping on the dashboard to ABBA's *Summer Night City.*

She ditched the empty can and stretched. Her top pulling across her nipples made them stiffen and her breasts tingle.

She felt warm, particularly between the thighs.

(She'd grown used to feeling hypersexual since being a fugitive. She drunkenly wondered if maybe Lori was right, if maybe both their bodies, somehow realizing that they were living on borrowed time, were simply trying to cram in as much physical ecstasy as possible before becoming worm food. For what other satisfaction did the human body have except pleasure? While the soul could be satiated by a job well done, or even a compliment, or by the ownership of a lot of things, or (best of all) by love, and the spirit could be satisfied by deity, the body's only reward as its owner paced the earth was sensation, the more enjoyable the better. And what sensation was more delightful than fucking, and fucking as often as one could?)

She unzipped her pants, then slipped her fingers beneath her panty waistband and began stroking her clitoris. It felt good; dirty, but definitely good. Like purging herself from the day's crap, two friends dead in weird ways. As she raised her buttocks off the leather seat and slipped her pants down off her hips, tears filled her eyes on remembering Lori. Then shrugged off her panties too, sat back down and slipped her fingers properly into her wet sex, digging them in deep as a vibrator.

The beer had her relaxed, and her imagination that the dead man on the tree could see her made this instance of Onanism especially surreal.

She reached her free hand up and undid her top, then caressed and squeezed each of her breasts in turn.

But while pleasuring herself here, she had a question: Why did seeing corpses make her so hot now? Was it because she expected to shortly be one herself? Or was something defective in her brain? Or was this one of those things that everyone had but which no one would admit to in a million years—a latent necrophilia? While plunging her fingers into her soaking sex, she thought back, searching her memory to see if she'd ever desired to fuck a dead body. No, she hadn't, honestly not ever. She didn't even like horror movies, her favorite screen viewings were romances, she'd seen *Titanic* at least thirty times and always swooned when Kate Winslet and Leonardo DiCaprio finally had that first kiss.

So why was she now becoming such a monster?

More important, did she even frigging care at her transformation? She asked both herself and Matt Lewis that question, her eyes seeking his eaten face in the darkness. Maybe she was wrong, but it looked like a raccoon or something was sucking out his right eye.

She laughed at the sight. "Sorry, Matt . . . but hey, what do *you* think? Do you think I give a shit that seeing you dead over there gets me as hot as fuck?"

"No, I sure as hell don't," she assured the dead man and herself as her body melted into the pleasures of sexual climax. She rubbed herself as hard as she could, like she wanted to hurt herself, rising as high as she dared, into those soaring heights of physical despair that her body craved.

Oh, fuck, that was just too damn intense, she thought when she finally ceased shuddering. She relaxed back on the seat with her eyes closed. *Oh, Matt, that was just so—*

She fell asleep before finishing the thought.

The next time she awoke, the dashboard clock read 2 a.m. Perfect timing. She ate the rest of her sandwich, then got everything she needed together on the front passenger seat.

She left the car to relieve herself. Thankfully she had toilet paper. Pooping still stung her ass, but thank God she was no longer bleeding back there. The pain of squeezing the turds out simply firmed her resolve to exact vengeance on the bastards and bitches responsible for her hurt.

Once through with her feminine necessities, she got back into the car, started it up, and drove off.

While navigating her way out of the woods to the main road, Britt felt no fear whatsoever. All that filled her thoughts was a pleasant apprehension at the justice she was about to dish out.

Payback's a bitch, she thought with growing excitement, *and I'm the bitch.*

CHAPTER 53

Britt

She parked fifty yards from the isolated cottage and got out.

She'd driven in from the final turnoff with her headlights off, so no one could have seen her approach. Now she got her things out of the car and walked the rest of the way to the house.

She was wearing jeans, a black 'Gypsy Jazz' T-shirt, and her pink sneakers. She carried the revolver in her right hand, and wore the duct-tape reel on her left wrist like a bangle. The hammer and carving knife were stuck in her belt. The knife was to be her primary weapon. She didn't plan on using the revolver except it was unavoidable.

She kept between the trees until they ran out beside the yard. Opposite her now, spread in ominous repose, the ramshackle cottage was a hulking shadow beast, the yellow Jeep its murky offspring. The only lights on were the porch light and a lamp on the right of the yard.

For a moment she felt a twinge of worry—what if this all went wrong? But her hatred of the house's inhabitants convinced her to dare the darkness.

She crossed the yard into the shadows of a neglected flowerbed, then began looking for a way into the house.

Her plan to tape over a window then carefully crack it with the hammer was rendered unnecessary when she found an open rear window.

Two minutes later, she was inside the house.

Okay, she thought, *that's done. Next I need to find out where everyone is.*

But first she paused.

She was in the expected baby's room. Shining her penlight around revealed nursery walls papered with teddy bears frolicking in fields of rainbows and butterflies, laughing frogs, and bright blue skies filled with alphabet and number balloons. The room's color scheme was blue; she guessed that Sin was expecting a boy. There was a baby bed and also a playpen. The floor was thickly carpeted a dark blue. There was also a slight smell of drying paint. She suspected the window had been left open to help the paint dry, and maybe also to keep the room from smelling musty.

This clean room had a happy ambience to it that she found hard to reconcile with her memories of what she'd seen of the rest of the house the night she'd been brought here: the evidence of rats and decay and the dirty smelly evil people who'd abducted then abused her.

For a moment, she considered not wrecking this kid's future, to simply leave now, to leave Raynham, leave Massachusetts, and if her luck held, leave the US . . .

But the lure of her hatred was too strong. Like a hook jammed in her throat it hauled her forward to her violent meeting with the unborn one's parents. So Snake and Sin planned on being good loving parents too, did they? Well, she was gonna show them what she did to loving parents!

Matt Lewis was a doting dad too, as far as I know, and look where that got him. And he didn't even piss me off!

Her heart as hard as stone again, she quietly opened the nursery door and peered out into the dark hallway beyond. The hammer was both heavy and sticking painfully into her side, so she left it just outside the nursery door. She left the duct tape there too.

Then, stuffing the gun in her belt and clasping the knife instead, she left the nursery. She tiptoed along the short hallway to the living room entrance and listened for voices.

Loud snoring from the sofa and the stink of spilled beer alerted her that someone—it sounded like one person—was passed out drunk there.

She padded forward and studied the slumbering figure with her flashlight. She'd hoped that the sleeper was Snake, but it turned out to be Boner. (Once again the old question nagged at her: *What the hell sort of a name is 'Boner?'*) Mouth open—she could practically see the alcohol fumes rising from his throat—he was asleep in his boxers. His penis dangled down one leg, and he was spread over the sofa with purple lipstick smeared all over his chest like liquid bruises.

Grinning broadly, Britt first let the anticipation of the kill build in her. She stood motionless beside the sofa, watching Boner's pigeon chest rise and fall like a pump inflating her anticipation. She snapped off the penlight and pocketed it.

Then, just when it felt like she'd die of her grim expectancy if she didn't murder the son-of-a-bitch right away, she struck like a demoness.

Leaping around the side of the sofa, in a single movement she both covered Boner's mouth with a hand and stabbed the carving knife deep into his throat. Hard, so it went in one side of his neck and came out the other side.

She sat firmly on his chest, pinning him in place as he jerked awake, sputtering blood from his ruined neck. She was aware of his scared eyes searching her face in the darkness, wondering who was murdering him. She considered telling him who she was, then decided the asshole wasn't worth it—let him die in abject confusion. Keeping her hand firmly on his mouth, she yanked the knife from his neck then stabbed it in again (feeling intense delight as his blood stained her hands). Then again, ripping out his throat in the savagery of her retribution. She waited there, thrilling in his death.

He tried to push her body off his, but his efforts to get free were weak and uncoordinated. He'd clearly drunk too much.

In less than a minute it was all over. The knife stuck front-to-back through his neck, Boner lay limper than overcooked noodles beneath her.

Britt got to her feet. Yes, this was exactly what she needed after Lori and Pagan's deaths.

After wiping her hands on her jeans, she got out her penlight again and now properly examined the living room.

There'd definitely been a lot of boozing earlier. Bottles and cans were littered everywhere and little cockroaches frolicked in a puddle of semi-solid puke on the rug. There were also lots of joint butts in an ashtray.

And of course, the hated TV remote unit.

Viewing the mess in the living room, Britt realized that circumstance were playing into her hands. If they'd all gone to bed stoned, the others weren't likely to put up much resistance either. And also, considering the purple lipstick she'd noticed smeared all over Boner's chest before she'd killed him, Ella had apparently been fucked to sleep too, so she should be out for the count.

Avoiding stepping in the blood that had squirted over the rug, Britt pulled her knife out of Boner's neck. She wiped it clean on his boxers then walked back to the mouth of the corridor.

Only three to go now. And dispatching Boner had definitely wetted her appetite for more death.

She now took some time to properly understand the house's layout. The far end of the hallway clearly led out back. Here on her immediate left it opened into the dining room, and beyond that the nursery. On her right were two doors that had to be bedrooms.

She made her way across the living room, to check that way. To the right of the front door as one entered the house (on her left now that she was coming from the hall) was another short corridor that led to two rooms, one of which was open and empty.

She paused her checking and listened for sound, but the night was silent, like she'd killed it along with Boner. Other than for the creepy rustle of rats—she shuddered when one dashed across a tabletop—the house was quiet.

She reentered the hallway and listened at the right-hand doors. Now began the task of working out where the other three were sleeping. Snake and Sin were certain to be together, Ella would be alone. Was Ella here though, or in the room by the front door?

This aspect of her revenge proved easier than expected. As though he was taking over where the dead man had left off, Snake abruptly began snoring too.

That was confirmed then: Snake and Sin were in the second room on the right, the one directly opposite the nursery. Made sense for easy access to Junior.

She padded back towards the living room again. Ella was either in the first room here or in the one by the front door. And it was vitally important that she take out Ella first. If not, the woman might come in to help her sister.

She quietly opened the door next to the living room.

No Ella inside, just an unmade bed, so she stealthily headed across the living room again.

She paused outside the front room to catch her breath, then opened the door. Stepping inside, she shone her penlight on the bed.

Aha! Ella was asleep in here, her body cut by moving blades of moonlight as the drapes shifted. She was naked, her plump form a voluptuous shape on the mattress, her black hair silken shadows on her pillow. Her face was calm and she was smiling.

Britt smirked. *See, bitch? This is what good sex does to you—it makes you susceptible to serial killers breaking into your house.*

Britt used the same tactics as with Boner, covering Ella's mouth and stabbing her repeatedly in the neck and chest till she went limp. Ella spurted blood and flailed and bit her hand to no avail. *You're dying, bitch and that's it,* Britt thought triumphantly as the woman's struggles weakened. Then she stabbed her in the throat some more, ripping it open into a yawning gash.

In this case, however, her eyes locked with Ella's, and in the fluttering spill of moonlight into the room there was a second of horrified recognition before her victim stopped kicking and died.

Only two left now. The two she really wanted. The two deaths she really needed.

At this point she found herself perplexed by a truth: the realization of how easy it was to break into someone's house and murder them. What apparently kept the law-abiding citizen alive and safe was the criminal's fear of prison, not the inability of the angered or aggrieved to reach them.

She left the dead Ella in the widening pool of her blood and returned to the hallway. This time, however, she'd been less-than-careful about getting wet. She was soaked in blood now with her top plastered to her breasts and she left a red trail of footprints in the hallway. But it didn't matter: the odds against Sin coming out now were almost astronomical. And . . . Ella's breath had been almost as alcohol-infused as her boyfriend's, so it was likely that Sin had gone to bed stoned too—not really a great prenatal choice if you're expecting a kid, but the fuck she cared about some dope dealer's certain-to-be-retarded brat.

"Alright, it's hammer time," she muttered under her breath. Then she retrieved the heavy clawhammer from outside the nursery door.

She weighed it in her palm while going over her plan twice in her mind. *Open the door, dash in . . .*

She shifted the hammer to her left hand. She needed the knife first. The pistol remained in her belt, to make its appearance only if Snake woke in time and went for his gun too. She hoped he wouldn't—she wanted to keep her vengeance up close and personal, and for that knives felt best.

Close and personal, huh? Ha ha! She walked back to the living room and returned with the hated remote control stuck in the right back pocket of her jeans.

Holding the hammer and the knife, Britt stood there by the last door for awhile, breathing in Snake's loud snores from within the bedroom and grinning to herself, letting the count-up to their final bloody showdown build up in her like lust. She smiled down at the carving knife she held, its ten-inch blood-besmirched blade a satisfactory testament to her effectiveness as an angel of death.

Then her expectancy peaked like an orgasm, and she clicked open the bedroom door and entered.

She played her penlight over the king-sized bed. Neither spouse stirred. Snake lay on his side on the far side of the bed. He was facing away from her, his snores rumbling his fat hairy frame. He was still fully clothed and had on dirty hole-ridden socks through which his toes poked.

It was on Sin, however, that Britt's gaze was riveted. The skinny woman lay on her back, her huge belly stuffed to bursting with baby. That belly and its fetal content attracted Britt like a magnet. How better to pay Sin back than to . . .

With a howl, she flicked on the bedroom lights. Then, knife raised overhead, she charged the bed.

The knife came down hard right on Sin's navel, dead in the center of her pregnancy. Britt forced the blade in deep, then while Sin jerked awake screaming in agony, she pulled the knife out of the woman's bulge and slammed it in again, this time with all her might.

With Sin's mouth frozen in a scream to rouse the dead, and her knife sunk to its full length in Sin's womb, Britt now turned her attentions to Snake.

He was just sputtering awake and turning around. "Cynthia, for God's sake, what's the—"

Swinging it with both hands, Britt whacked him in the side of the head with the hammer. Snake's mouth had been widening in surprise at seeing that someone else was in the bed with them; now it went slack and his eyes rolled back into his head and he slumped unconscious.

Britt checked to make sure he was still breathing. He was. Good.

Then, that off her mind, she became aware that Sin was still howling her lungs out. Britt was relieved that this house was literally out in the middle of nowhere. Sin was making more noise than a triggered jewelry shop alarm.

She looked over at the pregnant woman, wondering if she'd need to whack her in the head too to shut her up. But now, to her relief, Sin began quieting down a little. Eyes staring wide, she was holding her belly and grunting like she was about to put to bed. Blood bubbled thick and free from her wounds. One hand kept reaching up for the knife stuck deep inside her womb, but each time she touched it she gave a gasp of agony and let go again.

The whole scene was hilarious to watch. *No, it's frigging kill-arious,* Britt thought.

She grinned at Sin. "Hey, bitch, remember me?"

Sin, who'd taken to clawing at the bed in an effort to rouse Snake, now stared at Britt with dawning recognition.

"Oh, I see you do remember my face."

Next, she dug both feet into Sin's side and pushed hard. This action rolled Sin off the bed and onto the floor, where she landed with a loud thump and an even louder howl of agony.

Britt peered down over the edge of the bed and giggled: Sin had landed hard on her belly, which must have driven the knife all the way through the fetus. It looked like the hilt of the knife was now inside her too.

She was mumbling and bleeding and . . . and her pregnancy-expanded backside looked oh so tempting.

Sitting on the edge of the bed, Britt spread Sin's buttocks wide and shoved the TV remote deep into her anus.

She was disappointed at how easily the device slid up Sin's ass—Snake had clearly been travelling up and down his wife's chocolate bar highway a lot.

She glanced over at the husband. Snake was still in never-never land: out cold with a huge purple lump on his forehead.

She returned her attentions to the wife. Sin, propped up on her bulge like some esoteric Japanese sculpture, was howling and sniveling. Britt considered putting her out of her misery with a bullet to the head, but then she reconsidered—her whole intent here was to cause these assholes extreme misery. Let the preggered bitch bleed to death in the pool of the agony of knowing that her fucking baby was already dead and waiting for her in the great beyond.

And from the size of the blood pool spreading under Sin, that mortal exit wouldn't be long in coming.

The remote control seemed about slipping from Sin's ass. Britt first shoved it back in, then she stood up and kicked the projecting inch or so hard. This time the TV remote completely vanished into Sin's body, the victim howling out a muffled scream on its disappearance. This time also, something clearly tore back there, because blood squirted out from Sin's anus.

And blood was now also gushing from between Sin's legs.

Britt laughed aloud at the double-barreled bleeding.

"Have a great miscarriage, bitch," she sniped at the dying mother-to-be (who was by now murmuring incomprehensible gibberish).

Then she rolled Snake off the bed onto the floor. She was very careful about this: she didn't want him to bang his head and die on her.

She dragged him by his feet out of the bedroom and into the dining room. (About time too, she figured: Sin's dying mumbles were starting to grate on her nerves.)

Moving the fat drug dealer was easy work: with four deaths (including the unborn child) to her credit tonight—four people she'd single-handedly reduced to Nothing—Britney Wilson felt supremely powerful.

She felt goddess-like: invincible, invulnerable . . . unstoppable.

Once in the dining room, she soon had Snake set up exactly how she wanted him: stripped naked and bound to a chair facing the door. (The lump on his temple was now the size of a large marble.) Naked, he was even more hairy and lard-laden and repulsive than she remembered. *Ugh, and to think that this pig was actually inside me! I'd sooner screw a dog!*

Impossible as it seemed, her hatred for him ramped up a notch.

Last of all, she duct-taped over Snake's mouth. In addition to the unflushed-toilet reek coming from it (she belatedly thanked God that he'd not tried to kiss her while having his way with her), she didn't want to hear him beg for his life. She wanted him to *want to* speak, to *need to* speak, to have apologies he'd *love to* make, but to be unable to vocalize them.

She had no interest whatsoever in hearing what Snake had to say.

While she worked she could hear Sin moaning out her last moments, an extremely pleasant if distracting sound. *Die, cunt, die!*

Once done, Britt leaned against the dining table and appraised her work, double-checking to ensure that there was no chance whatsoever of Snake somehow freeing himself. Finally, she nodded to herself, satisfied with how thoroughly she'd taped him down. Oh, no, except his middle name was Houdini, Snake wasn't about going anywhere.

She regarded herself too. She was an absolute mess now, so blood-splattered in fact that she looked like a murder victim herself. Most of the blood on her was Ella's, the rest Sin's. Her T-shirt, her jeans, her pink sneakers, all had blood on them. Her hands and arms were red all over and she could feel a second skin of drying wetness on her face. Ugh! The best thing to do once this was over would be to have a long hot shower and put on some of Ella's clothes. If she remembered correctly, she and Ella were about the same height if not the same weight. And while leaving the bedroom after dispatching Ella, she'd noticed a nice denim jacket in the woman's wardrobe.

She laughed. *Yeah, I might as well take it—Ella definitely doesn't need that jacket anymore.*

That minor future detail resolved, she set up another chair facing Snake, then walked on through into the kitchen looking for a drink. On her entrance, two big brown rats deserted the slice of moldy rye loaf they'd been savaging and fled to somewhere behind the counter.

There was a bottle of Wild Turkey on the countertop and beer in the fridge. She got out three beers. The whiskey she'd take away with her; she didn't want to be too drunk to drive.

Back out in the dining room, she placed the drink cans on the long table and sat in the chair facing Snake. From the hallway she heard dead silence. Sin had finally quite her moaning and died, thank God.

She cracked open a beer and shook the can's contents in Snake's face. That only half worked—his head wobbled from side to side and he looked like he was sweet-dreaming. So, seeing as she'd already duct-taped his mouth shut, she pinched shut his nostrils so he couldn't breathe that way either.

In thirty seconds, helped by a second liberal application of beer (this time in his eyes where it would sting), Snake was back in the world of the living.

Slowly he realized that he was bound. Squirming to get free made him realize that he was also helpless.

"Hi, fatso," Britt said brightly with a wickedly wide grin. "Remember me—the girl you poured sperm into? Remember flooding me with semen like I was some barnyard hen?"

His eyes widened in slow recognition, but he kept blinking them because of the alcohol dousing. Tears of irritation were running down his cheeks.

"Well now I'm pregnant with hatred for you. Your damn baby chicken just came home to roost."

"Mmmph, mmmph!" he said behind the gag.

"Don't worry," she said, stroking his hairy face, "I've gotten rid of Sin so we can get married."

"Mmmp!!??" His eyes widened totally in horror. "Mmmhhhh??!!!!"

She realized then that she'd knocked him out before he'd seen how she'd dealt with his stupid wife.

"C'mon, Snake, no need to apologize. Yes, Sin's dead now, so no need for a messy divorce. I'm sorry I killed the kid too—but you know how we women are where offspring rivalry is concerned? Evil stepmother and all that? So I thought it best we start off our marital bliss with a clean sheet."

He was goggling at her in clear disbelief. She put down her beer, then rising slightly, kissed the tape over his lips.

She settled back down again. "So, honey, how about it? We'll just raise my Hatred as our own firstborn. We'll have other kids too: Malice and The Abuse of Women and . . ."

He was staring at her now like she was mad. *She was*—mad with rage at him, that was. He was trembling so much that she expected him to wet himself.

She laughed. She was trembling too, but with arousal.

"Okay, just nod if you agree to be mine forever and ever. Or else I'm gonna kill you."

He nodded quickly. "Hmmph! Mmmph!"

She laughed. This was so much goddamn fun. "Okay, so now I'll let you go and we'll get married."

He was really shivering now.

She faked a frown. "Aw, c'mon now, Snake darling. Relax. I know you're sorry. I also know that you just *had to* fuck me and Lori. I mean, honestly, in your shoes, I'd have done exactly that too. We were both fugitives, and so young and sweet, and just too pretty to pass up. Besides, we were celebrities in our own way, and who doesn't want to fuck the famous chicks, right? You'd have to have been out of your minds to let us go unfucked."

She opened up another beer for herself and took a long gulp. Then she grinned at Snake. "See, I'm laughing. I'm not sore at you and Boner at all. Yeah, sure, my ass still hurts badly when I poop, but that's usual for an anal virgin if the guy's too rough you know—I checked online at Yahoo Answers. Everyone who replied said I'll be good as new in a few days and then you can cornhole me just like you used to do to Sin. Oh, and . . ." she giggled, "I forgot to mention—I killed Boner and Ella too, but not because I'm sore at them. They just both objected to our having our honeymoon on the moon, so—"

Snake gaped at his captor in complete horror, like all the blood splattering her only now took on its true meaning for him. He began crying hard, and these were not tears from irritated eyes, or of terror even, but of his intense horror and sorrow at all the deaths, particularly those of his wife and unborn child.

Britt though, was pissed off that he wasn't pissing himself. She wanted him not just blubbering like a baby, but so terrified of her that he'd lose control of his vital functions. He *was* sweating bullets though, so much so that he looked about to die of dehydration soon.

Okay, she decided, *enough fooling about with this jerk. Time to send him to Hell.*

She leapt up and grabbed her hammer again. "Okay, darling," she told the bound and grief-stricken man. "Now I'll just send you home to inform grandpappy Lucifer about our wedding plans, and then I'll . . ."

She let the sentence hang to confuse him. Snake was still trying to make sense of it when she smashed the clawhammer into his head with both hands. Not the blunt side of it this time, but the sharp cleft end. She'd swung right-to-left; with a sickening crunch, half of the hammer sunk into Snake's head just above his left ear. Without missing a beat, she yanked the hammer out again, pulling it forward as she did, so it ripped away the scalp on that side. The hammer left a jagged hole from which blood spurted.

Snake began jerking in agony, his eyes rolling up to look at her with a pleading expression.

"Stop being such a pussy, darling," Britt sternly chided. "This isn't hurting you at all—I read up that the brain has no nerve endings."

She slammed the hammer down again, now cracking open the front of Snake's forehead. Blood instantly flooded out around the buried metal head. This time, when she yanked the hammer out, it ripped out his left eye also, leaving the orb dangling down on his cheek. Snake jerked wildly in his chair, his good right eye fluttering left and right like it was on optic autopilot.

Impressed with the effect of the dangling and wobbling eye, Britt shifted her focus over to the unruined half of his face to try and duplicate it.

Snake, understanding what she was about doing, began humping the chair up and down to escape from her.

"Hold still, baby!" She slammed the hammer into his right temple and yanked it down and out. This time she had less success: she detached the eye alright, but then its nerve cord sheared off and the eye dropped into Snake's lap.

This turned out not to be as disappointing as she'd expected. Looking down, she saw that Snake was busy pissing himself. Some of the urine splattered her sneakers. She ignored it, she'd ditch the shoes along with her memory of the bastard. Even more satisfying, Snake had shit himself. The fecal stench rose high above and overcame the stink of his sweat and fear.

She looked at his head again and smiled. Yes, she liked the way he looked now: two messy holes where his eyes had been. But no, it didn't look really balanced, so she got her knife and sliced through the left eye's nerve cord. The eye dropped to the floor. Britt grinned at the results. Yes, Snake looked much better eyeless. And he was still wetting himself.

Hmm, too much beer before bedtime is bad for you. You might wet the bed, baby.

Snake wasn't dead though. She considered leaving him like this, blind and fucked-up to the nines for the rest of his life. The hammer had clearly damaged his brain. If he wasn't a vegetable now, he was damn close to being one.

Then she shook her head. For one thing, she hated this bastard way too much for what he'd done to her to allow him any kind of life, however degraded. And secondly . . . well, this was just so much frigging fun. And thirdly, the more she reduced him to nothing, the more she took back from him the self-worth he'd stolen from her on that horrible night.

Smirking at his bloody damaged face and the red lava lakes of his eye sockets, she got to work destroying Snake for good.

Now she made no pretense of being artistic. She swung the clawhammer with all her might over and over again at Snake's head. Blood streamed down the tool's handle and it spun in her grasp; sometimes she hit him with the sharp end, sometimes with the blunt end, sometimes she even smashed the hammer's side into his head. The results were generally the same: Like a forest being defoliated, the scalp and skin stripped off and the bone was revealed. The bone too fragmented and the brain came to light.

After a while of doing this, she dropped the hammer and took a break to drink some beer. She was sweating profusely now.

Then she put the beer down and dipped her hands into the ruin of Snake's skull. She gripped what remained intact of his brain in both her hands and pulped it, digging her fingers deep into the bloody pink meat and squeezing for all she was worth. She intended on getting her abused femininity's worth from his passing. Sure, Snake was long dead by now, but she—Britney 'Definitely Somebody' Wilson—had a lot of anger to work off.

Finally, she pulled her hands out of his head and wiped them off on her chest, unintentionally smearing the dead man's pulped brains over her breasts. Then she realized what she'd inadvertently done and giggled. Would her breasts become assholes too?

Lost in her world of pleasure, she grinned down at Snake's remains. Half of his head was gone—everything above the jaw. His nose and his ears were dangling shelves of meat overhanging his neck. The interior of his head looked like a bomb crater plastered with the mangled corpses of dead civilians.

The sight made her incredibly hot between the legs. Yes, she'd done it the way it was meant to be done. *Hell, yes, I taught this son-of-a-bitch and his stupid family the lesson of their deaths. In another life they'll not mess with me!* Feeling generous, she raised her eyes to the ceiling and grinned. *Hey, Lori, you watching? This one was for you too, even though you never appreciated the value of your pussy. I've paid them back for both of us and—*

Thunk!

Something whacked Britt hard on the back of the head then and she fell forward on Snake.

She was stunned good, but not unconscious. Still, for the moment at least, she'd lost all control of her limbs. She felt hands rolling her sideways off Snake's body, so that she dropped to the floor, then she heard loud gasping and loud weeping.

She'd landed on her back, the hard smack of the impact almost finishing the job of knocking her out. Her limbs still refused to move, and her head felt like it was stuffed with cotton wool padding a blinding migraine. But she forced her eyes open and got her head up enough to see who'd attacked her.

It was Sin. Naked and wet with blood, Sin was bent over Snake's corpse and raining tears on it. That was normal enough, Britt thought blearily. *Let her weep over the bastard. So she's not dead yet? Once I'm back on my feet, I'll send her to join—*

Then she realized that there was something . . . no, *several things* wrong with the scene before her:

Firstly, Sin's belly was now completely flat. She'd birthed the baby. Or had at least miscarried it. That wouldn't have been so bad, but . . .

Secondly, Sin had no stab wounds on her belly. She did have blood on her, but no visible injuries.

But I stabbed her twice, Britt's mind protested. *And afterwards she fell on the knife and . . .*

Then, from her vantage point on the floor, she realized too that Sin hadn't even bothered to sever the umbilical cord after the delivery: the blue/purple flesh-tube hung between her blood-covered legs and was dragging on the floor behind her.

And what was even worse than that?

The baby was still attached to the umbilicus and being dragged along behind its mother. That at least reassured Britt that the brat was dead, or else Sin would definitely first have taken her time to ensure the child's safety.

But then, with Sin still weeping madly over Snake's corpse, and the wool in Britt's head threatening to smother her in welcoming fluffy clouds to dull her splitting headache; and she doggedly forcing herself to look and concentrate, she clearly saw exactly why Sin's baby was dead:

The newborn had no head. And Britt also instantly realized, that no, *she* hadn't done *that*. The child had a deep stab wound on its left leg and its left hand was missing some fingers, but its head had been sliced clean off across the shoulders.

And also, in an island of clean white skin on the dead infant's bloody chest, someone had drawn a pentagram . . . in pink lipstick.

And then Sin stood up from hovering over her dead husband, and Britt saw the seventh and most shocking detail: Drawn just above the new and clearly outraged widow's pubic mound (and clearly previously hidden from view by her pregnancy) was a tattoo—an inverted 'A' tattoo exactly like the one Pagan had had on her left breast.

"Fuck," Britt mumbled almost inaudibly. "You're a witch too?"

The cotton wool in her head was a mental masseuse now, stroking her hurting psyche with soft fingers, telling her sanity to take a rest from the troubles of this new version of reality.

And suddenly, taking that rest didn't seem such a bad idea anymore. Her eyes dropped again from Sin's speechless rage to the spiral lifeline of membrane and blood vessels that dangled from Sin's vagina like an octopus tentacle, and then to the headless child the umbilicus terminated at.

Despite all of Britney Wilson's murderous accomplishments tonight, her second view of that headless baby—now that she understood what its mutilation implied—was somehow so horrifying that she fainted.

Her mental cotton wool smothered her in a bed of unconsciousness.

***

When Britt came to, her mind was clear again. No mental cotton wool. Her head no longer hurt either. Simultaneously, she both opened her eyes and tried to sit up, but discovered she couldn't

Shit! Alarm flooding her mind, she found that she was now both completely naked and tied and taped to the dining table.

Sin wasn't in the room with her.

She was lying on her back. A smelly rope bound her neck, but she could move her head enough to see her whole body.

Now that she was awake, her enforced position was very uncomfortable:

Her arms were stretched out from her sides and firmly secured by ropes that vanished over the edges of the table.

Her legs were arranged differently. She lay with her buttocks near the hallway end of the dining table. Her legs were bent so that her heels rested on the table edge, and her calves were pressed back against her thighs like when she was kneeling. Several circuits of duct-tape around her folded legs kept them in that position. Furthermore, ropes around both of her ankles dropped out of sight over the end of the table.

She tried to move her legs, but found it impossible

One final detail of her bondage alarmed her: her thighs were parted, affording unobstructed access to her shaven sex. (Her crotch itched too—the result of her pubic hair starting to grow again.) She realized now that she'd been arranged in the position one assumed when about to have sex on a pool table (if not bent over it with one's butt stuck out awaiting penetration).

And last time, Sin had used a strap-on on her.

Her alarm fully triggered now, Britt looked around the dining room, her desperate situation dawning on her. *I need to get out of here! I need to escape this place!*

Snake still sat in his death-chair on her right, half his head missing like someone had stuffed a double barreled shotgun in his mouth and pulled both triggers. Looking at him now though only brought Britt horror, a clear realization of what Sin would do to her if she didn't somehow get away.

But how could she escape? She was so tied down at the moment, even a miracle didn't look like it could help.

How the hell didn't I guess that she was a witch? Shit! Shit! Shit!

And on that thought, Britt's eyes locked on a display on a side shelf on her left: five candles arranged around a black circle. She strained her neck and eyes to see better. The candles were arranged at the tips of a pentagram drawn on the shelf wood.

At a noise, she jerked her attention forward again. Sin had just walked into the dining room and dropped something on the floor. Britt hadn't seen what the object was, but it had sounded heavy.

Without the belly protruding in front of her, Snake's widow was a very tiny and bony woman.

Sin had cleaned herself up while Britt had been unconscious. She'd put on a blue dress, and as far as Britt could tell, during that interim had also birthed her dead baby's placenta. Craning her neck up as Sin walked around the side of the table, Britt saw that the woman no longer dangled the umbilical cord between her legs.

For that matter, she wasn't even bleeding down there anymore. Remembering how both of Sin's stab wounds had vanished, Britt no longer knew what to think. This situation was almost too unreal for her to wrap her mind around.

Sin paused at the shelf with the candles set around the pentagram. She lit all five of them, then sprinkled several powders on them that filled the dining room with a nauseating stink. Then she turned to face Britt, a horrible smile playing over her lips. A smile that was as pitying as it was reproachful.

Britt got the meaning of that look and smile and was chilled to her bones. She cringed with dread. If Sin *pitied* her, what was going to happen here was very very bad indeed.

Sin said, "So you finally woke up, you dirty little murderess."

Her voice was as cold as her eyes. And her eyes were full of madness, but it was a rational madness, a controlled madness.

Just like Lori, Britt realized. Just like Lori.

She forced her tongue to say, "Untie me and frigging let me go, will you?" The demand sounded stupid to her but what else could she say?

Sin's smile became a laugh. "Untie you? Really, you little skank? Just like you're a hostage in a terrorist movie and *I'm* the bad guy? You're *really* asking me to let you just leave? Are you frigging stupid?"

"Fucking untie me, you bitch!"

In response, Sin grabbed a handful of Britt's hair and yanked hard on it, so hard that it pulled out by the roots. Britt screamed; she couldn't believe how much that had hurt.

Sin brandished the clump of torn-out hair at Britt. Blood dripped from it like it was the pelt of some animal that she'd skinned.

Britt stared at her, gasping and completely lost for words. The hairless patch on her head was a raw burning hurt. And now, too, her legs had begun playing pins-and-needles with her.

"Listen, you dumb little murdering piece of pig poop, I'm not letting you go anywhere."

"B-b-but—"

"Shut the fuck up." Again Sin's words were cold, her calm smile as she spoke belying the intense rage that visually throbbed through her. "Listen, you can safely put any kind of escape plan out of your head, you damn fool. You just murdered all the people I love in this world and you're asking me to let you leave? Even a total retard like my cousin Gabe can't be that dumb."

Britt racked her brain. "Okay, I'm sorry. Just hand me over to the cops then."

A laugh. "Girl, the cops are too good for shit like you. All they'll do is say you're crazy or you had an abused childhood or an abused teenhood, or you've got PTSD or bipolarity or some other syndrome, and then lock you away in comfort for the rest of your life." She shook her head firmly. "No, girl, I'm dealing with you myself. And you're gonna remember me for the rest of your life, which isn't gonna be very long now."

Then cracks seemed to form in her cool unruffled exterior and tears spilled from her eyes. She stared at Britt like she was seeing her for the first time. "Argh, girl, how could even you do a horrible thing like this? You killed my baby sister and her boyfriend, and my husband too. And my kid too. What the hell justifies you to do that to me?"

Britt figured she had the moral high ground here. "Snake raped me; you did too. You all raped me."

Sin looked confused for a moment. Then she said, "So we had some fun with you. So what? Just 'cos of that you felt you had to kill everyone like you're on TV? Let me tell you about Snake."

"I don't wanna hear it. He was just a fat jerk."

"Listen to me, you little piece of self-righteous murdering shit. You're gonna hear about the man you just killed—the man I loved—whether you damn hell like it or not.

"I was a hooker and a junkie, O.K.? Totally down on my luck and getting the shit beat out of me daily by my bastard pimp. All I lived for was my next fix—sticking that junkie needle in my arm and zoning out from my horrible life, and hoping I hadn't accidentally O.D.'d and killed myself . . . Oh yeah, and trying to survive my fucking pimp so I didn't get beat to death before I got tomorrow's damn fix. Then Snake came along and beat the shit out of my pimp and took me away from that useless life . . . and he got me off the smack too. Okay, so he's a dope dealer himself and I agree he ain't Brad Pitt, but Snake treated me better than any other man I ever met in my whole damn life ever did, and . . ." She shot Britt a look of pure venom, then pointed at Snake's corpse and howled, all pretense of cool momentarily lost, "And you went and did *that* to him!? Oh, hell no, Snake didn't deserve to die like that!"

"He should have kept his stinky hands off me then."

Sin pursed her lips coldly. "You really don't get it, do you? You're so stupid, so intensely dumb in your self-righteousness that you don't get it at all."

"What's there to frigging get?"

"You're a frigging criminal. The criminal world isn't a birthday party—it's a no-holds-barred world. Out here, you take what's coming to you and like it."

"Stupid logic."

"Stupid? Didn't it mean anything to you two idiots that my husband didn't turn your runaway asses over to the cops? Snake was *rooting for you* both to get away—to shit in the eye of the system. He *helped* you. He'd even have helped you flee the damn country if you'd been sensible enough to ask for it. And now you killed him 'cos we stuck it in you. You killed my entire family, you bitch. Would you prefer to be behind bars?"

Britt had no reply to that. Sin just had to be wrong. You couldn't just pluck a woman off the streets and do to her whatever you liked because she was on the run from the police. Particularly not if she was on the run from the police.

Then Sin smiled, a smile that was chilling in its calm Madonna-like beauty. "But yeah, you're right, Britney—getting fucked against your will isn't any kind of a joke. But . . . I can assure you now that it's a whole lot better than what I'm going to do to you for what you've taken from me."

"Hey! Don't you judge me! You're a monster too. You cut off your own son's head."

"That's *also* your fault," Sin explained in a voice as soft as a flowerbed. "Junior was dying anyway—you got the little tyke real good where it mattered. Still, he wasn't fully dead yet, and I was dying too, so I sacrificed him to heal myself." For a moment there were tears in her eyes again. "I'll hate myself for the rest of my life for doing that . . . but I hate you a whole lot more, Britney. I really do."

And now, Britt really became scared. She'd exhausted her deck of argument cards, and her poker face collapsed. She still knew she'd been right to avenge her ordeal at Snake's hands, but this crazy woman was too besotted with her stupid dead husband to realize that.

And now Britt began crying. But she wasn't crying because she was sorry; not in the least. She wasn't sorry for a damn thing that she'd done. *Every single person I fucked up deserved it in some way.* She merely hated this position she was now in—having to beg for her life. Once more—after all her personal growth over the past four days—she'd been reduced to nothing. She was Britney Zero-Person again, elected

Queen of the Nobodies. Being arranged humiliatingly on this table, with her womb spread open to the world, hurt her way more than her bleeding head or the awful cramps in her legs now.

And to cap her fall from glory, now she was having to plead for her life from this stupid hick woman who looked like a stick insect come to life. Witch or no witch, this Sin bitch was just so frigging *ugly*. No wonder Snake was screwing other chicks.

But Britt knew she only had one life, and she decided she'd better plead for it now. Maybe she could touch somewhere merciful inside Sin, mine a previously veiled vein of compassion.

"Please! I'm sorry!! You're right—I was wrong, just hand me over to the police. I really regret all that I've done against you and Snake and everyone else. I promise to spend the rest of my life atoning for it. I'll become a nun in jail, I will. I'll—"

"Oh, there's no need to abstain from sex, girl. In fact, you're about getting a whole damn lot of it right now, trust me. I've got the biggest thrill *ever* planned for you."

Britt quailed. *Oh shit. Sex? Not again!* Remembering the monster black strap-on and the remote control filled her with the horror of even greater psychic reduction.

Then Sin bent, and straining, lifted the object that she'd earlier dropped on the floor on entering the dining room. "Baby, say hello to your new boyfriend—Mr. Andreas Stihl."

Britt's mouth dropped open. What Sin was holding was a chainsaw.

Sin laughed at Britt's expression of total dismay. Now the coldness had left her face, all that remained was the glee of the kill. "Oh yeah, darling, Mr. Stihl here, he just loves vagina. In fact, he don't ever get enough of it. He's gonna eat your little pussy real good. He's gonna go so deep into your hole, you'll be screaming, begging him to stop."

Britt had no words. Despite her desperate attempt to control it, her mind melted into a bubbling morass of fear. This was worse than anything she'd ever imagined happening to anyone in her life. *She's going to chainsaw me in the vagina! She's going to stick that thing . . . !* Her eyes traced the saw's blade along its row of interlocked teeth; she imagined the adamant metal chewing her tender sexual flesh to a million shreds while her screaming nerves fed every second of torment into her brain. *God, please no!*

But then Sin said, "Oh shee-it, silly me. I almost forgot something—that other deal I made with the Devil when I sacrificed my son."

She put the chainsaw down again and returned to stand facing the lit candles on Britt's left. She stood there for a minute, mumbling under her breath with her face and hands both raised.

Britt recognized the sound. It was the same as when Sin had been mumbling after she'd stabbed her in the baby:

She understood that the witch was casting a spell, but a spell for what?

Sin finally turned to face her again. Behind her the five candles now burnt with black flames and the pentagram glowed a bright red.

Britt's eyes flew wide open at the unnatural sight. Her terror instantly doubled. Her mind once again churned up into a whirlpool of fear and dread. *Oh fuck, oh fuck! Oh, Jesus, fucking help me!!!*

Sin returned to her initial position between Britt's legs. She picked up the chainsaw. She curled her bony fingers around the handle of its starting cord.

"Please. Please . . . Have mercy . . ."

"Have mercy on *you*? If you honestly expect that, you're even dumber than I give you credit for." Then she smiled again. "Don't waste your breath begging me. You're gonna need it for screaming. And yes, scream all you want—I'll be sweet country music to my ears. Remember now: there's no need to be shy about crying out—we're well away from any prying ears here. And . . ." that cold pitying smile now played again over her lips, "I'll let you in on a little secret. You want to know what that spell I just cast was for? Sure, I'll share it with you: The spell was so that you're not gonna die properly for at least two hours, no matter how I mutilate you, and you're not going to faint either, Britney. No, you're gonna enjoy every moment of Mr. Stihl fucking your pussy, and I'm certainly gonna enjoy it too, girl."

"Noooooo!"

"Well, I think it's about time you two lovers got properly acquainted, don't'cha agree?"

With that, Sin activated the chainsaw, filling the living room with its metal growl.

As she positioned the whirring metal blade between Britt's legs, Britt began praying fiercely that the tool would malfunction, that it would stop working, or blow up, or . . . anything . . . any death was better than this, any death at all.

But Mr. Stihl didn't stop spinning.

And the next moment its steel teeth and her vagina made contact with each other. A bloody coupling of flesh and steel.

Britt began screaming and screaming and screaming. There were no words—no words at all or even mental concepts—to describe the pain she suddenly found herself in.

And exactly the way Sin had cast her spell, Britt screamed literally non-stop for two full hours on end, while the chainsaw tore her sexual passage into a yawning cavern of gore, then mangled her womb and guts into an indistinguishable sludge of meat.

Blood, skin, and flesh sprayed everywhere, all over the dining room walls, up onto the ceiling, and all over Sin herself. But somehow Britt didn't die, or stop bleeding, or, worst of all, ever stop hurting. During the rare seconds of lucidity that flashed through her indescribable agony, she understood that her body was repairing itself so she could hurt A LOT MORE, sometimes repairing itself even faster than Sin was destroying it.

And worst of all was simply the sheer indignity of having a whirling chainsaw stuck up her vagina.

In between wielding her weapon, Sin took breaks, smoked three joints, and made dirty jokes to a Britt who was too far gone in her terrible agony to even hear her.

Then, refreshed, Sin would resume digging the chainsaw—Mr. Stihl—between Britt's legs again, where the tender vaginal and anal flesh was already miraculously healed and waiting to be ripped asunder afresh.

***

Finally, after two full hours of horrifying, death-defying torture, Britney Wilson expired in an explosion of blood and guts, her torso sawn in two all the way up through her rib cage and into her neck, so that she lay in two separate halves on the dining table. It was to her inexpressible relief that this final time her body didn't pull itself back together again.

She died just as the new day was breaking.

And as Britt gratefully died, she beheld the gates of Hell opening, and a legion of grinning and impatient demons rising to escort her soul down to eternal torment. And then, suddenly, she wasn't so grateful over being released from her destroyed body anymore.

When the devils sank their claws deep into her and began tearing her afresh, she began screaming again, much louder now than she ever had before.

Worst of all, she could feel the heat of the raging sulfurous inferno below waiting to welcome her, heat that incredibly burnt all the way through her like she was being microwaved in the sun.

***

Miles above Britt's damned soul, the blood-splattered Sin Corbin dropped her chainsaw, bent over Snake's body again, and once more began bawling her eyes out.

The End.

ABOUT THE AUTHOR

Wol-vriey is Nigerian, and quite tall.

He currently resides in a state of uneasy stalemate with his threatening-to-thin-beyond-redemption hair, and believes there actually are things that go bump in the night.

Wol-vriey recycles the ridiculous into reasonable reality for the reader.

His WEIRRRD philosophy?

WEIRRRD = Warp/Write Everything into Realistic Ridiculous Readable Distorted Dream Dimension Descriptions.

Wol-vriey blogs at:

http://oddityfarm.wordpress.com

WOL-VRIEY
BIZARRO AND TRANSGRESSIVE FICTION

BOSTON POSH (BUD MALONE #1)

In 2028 AD, the USA is a nation ravaged by hungry dragons and dinosaurs. In Boston, Massachusetts, private eye Bud Malone is hired to rescue a kidnapped heiress. But nothing is as it seems.

Malone works to unravel a tangled web involving Boston Chinatown, a 200-year-old woman with a 9-year-old body, white robots, a human-liver-eating psychopath, a golem, a porcelain dragon, and a snake goddess with a crush on him. There's also a woman obsessed with chicken sex. Then Malone meets Posh Lane, a gorgeous call girl who's desperate to quit her pimp.

Romantic sparks ignite between Posh and Malone, but Posh's past suddenly catches up with her in a BIG way. To save Posh, Malone agrees to run a quest for Earth's new rulers, the Forks. But, Malone has no idea that agreeing to the Fork's odd request will send him on the weirdest trip he's ever been on in his life.

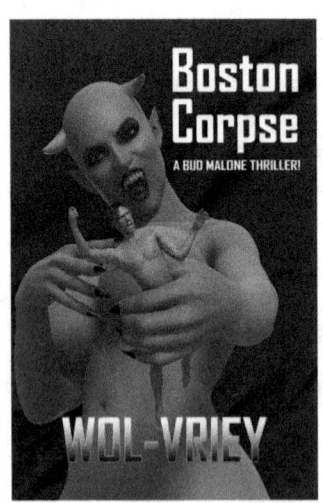

BOSTON CORPSE (BUD MALONE #2)

MAGIC CAN BE MURDER! - Drag queen Lucy Tang is back in Boston, and is hell-bent on settling her vindetta against casino owner Sookie Ling. And suddenly, Bud Malone, PI, has the case of his life to resolve.

When Boston's robot police force are baffled by a mind transfer case, they come to Malone for help. The one person who can likely help Malone out here is the witch Soledad Bathory. But Soledad seems to know a lot more than she's telling him. It's a case not made easier when Malone meets Soledad's beautiful cousin, Josephine 'Slave' Bailey. Slave has her own plans for Malone, most of which involve teaching him BDSM and making him her new Master.

Oh, and Rick Rogers owes Sookie Ling a whole lot of money, a gambling debt that's going to be literally Hell to pay!

BOSTON CORPSE - Not your average detective novel!

Burning Bulb
PUBLISHING

WOL-VRIEY
BIZARRO AND TRANSGRESSIVE FICTION

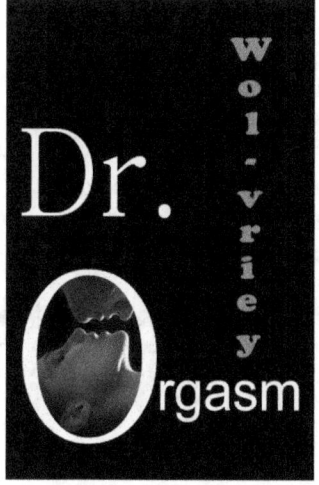

Dr. Orgasm

Courtney Taylor is young, intelligent, beautiful, and successful. She also has a boyfriend who loves her deeply. The problem is, no matter what Courtney does, she can't climax during sex.

When Florence Rigid's communist forces destroy the city of Metaphor, Courtney and her friends Teresa, Highball, Miki, and Heather are cast into the midst of a quest to find the only person able to save the land of Innuendo—Dr. Carol Orgasm, wanted by the communists for developing the O-Pill, a wonder drug that grants women sexual ecstasy on demand.

The communists will do anything to get their hands on the O-Pill and prevent its reaching the millions of Innuendo's women. But Courtney desperately wants that pill too. And so it's now a race between Courtney and the communists to find Dr. Orgasm first.

And Courtney has no choice but to win this race. She must win it: For her own orgasm . . . and for the freedom of female sexuality everywhere.

PUSSY TRANSMISSION

Pussy Transmission were the most decadent Pop Art ensemble of the 90's. Led by the beautiful painter Isis Lynch, the trio revolutionized the art world. Then suddenly, without explanation, Pussy Transmission vanished into historical obscurity. Now, twenty years later, three women come to Lynch Place. Lily and Nina are journalists desperate to interview Isis Lynch. Raven, on the other hand, wants to find her boyfriend, who's gone missing inside Isis's house. Raven's worried—she's heard that Pussy Transmission broke up because Isis began dabbling in black magic . . . with devastating results. All three women will shortly wish they'd never left home. Particularly once the rats in Lynch Place start warning them that they're going to die . . . and Raven meets Betty Butcher, the bouncy supernatural psycho who's intent on chopping her into bits. Pussy Transmission, Baby! Just because . . .

Burning Bulb
PUBLISHING

WOL-VRIEY
BIZARRO AND TRANSGRESSIVE FICTION

VAGINA MUNDI

Rachel Risk is a professional thief with super-strong hair that can stretch like tentacles to manipulate objects. Ashley Status has both a digitally augmented brain, and 'muscle-purses' in her arms and legs in which she stores inflatable objects—cars, guns, rocket launchers, etc.

When Raye is framed as the fall girl in a jewel robbery, the pair flee Chicago's vengeful robot gangsters and take refuge in the Hotel Bizarre, where the gorgeous 'vagina singer,' Femina, is performing for a week.

But the Hotel Bizarre is even stranger than its name suggests, and very soon Raye and Ash are involved in an deadly adventure, a struggle for survival the likes of which they'd never imagined possible—with loads of deviant sex, drugs, music, and violence at every turn. And just what is the old woman in the skin desert really doing with all those cats glued to her walls?

VAGINA MUNDI—a Bizarro Hymn in praise of WOMAN!

VEGAN VAMPIRE VAGINAS

The biggest bank heist in US history. And Tom Palmer can't remember pulling it off. And no, this isn't your standard case of amnesia. After a one-night-stand gone horribly wrong, Boston salesman Tom Palmer wakes up with a vagina implanted in his left hand. Then his day gets worse.

Tom is transported across space-time to a nightmare version of Boston, one where the Bizarro virus has transformed half the population into cannibals. Worst of all, Tom discovers that in this new Boston, he's the infamous gangster Pussypalm, wanted for robbing the Federal Reserve Bank of Boston a year ago. He also learns that the vagina in his hand is prophetic, i.e. it talks . . . after sex.

With 130 people left dead during his bank heist and six billion dollars missing, Tom knows he's living on borrowed time. It is in his best interests not to remember anything. Because once he does . . .

Burning Bulb
PUBLISHING

WOL-VRIEY
BIZARRO AND TRANSGRESSIVE FICTION

VEGAN ZOMBIE APOCALYPSE

In the post-apocalypse worlderness, zombies rule the earth. They're allergic to meat, and brains literally make them explode. Zombies now eat blood potatoes, parasitic tubers grown in the flesh of humancows corralled in maximum security farms. Two fugitives meet in the ancient ruins of Texas. The first is Soil 15-f, a womancow who's escaped her farm a week before she's due to be killed and her blood potato crop harvested. The second fugitive is Able Kane, former head necros food technician, now sentenced to death for heresy. But Soil is no ordinary humancow.

Unknown to herself, she's the vegan zombie agricultural revolution, and the zombies desperately want her back. And the necros equally desperately want Able Kane dead. He's fled with a forbidden discovery which will reshape the world for the worse if used. And Able is just hardheaded/misguided enough to use it.

MELANIE NEMESIS CATCHPOLE

In Springfield, Massachusetts, Melanie Catchpole is hired to fetch back a magic teddy bear worth millions of dollars from a warehouse across town. Problem is, the warehouse is down in Springfield's O-Zone-that totally weird sector of the city where Bizarro fell to Earth. The 'O' is a fairytale land, a place where dreams and nightmares literally live and breathe.

Worse still, the gingers—mutant cannibals—prowl the O. The gingers have already eaten everyone else Melanie's employers sent to get back the magic teddy bear.

Accompanied by the handsome but ruthless Doug Fisher (who she finds sexy but doesn't dare entrust her heart to), Melanie enters the O-Zone. Melanie and Doug are instantly caught up in an adventure they'd never have believed credible even if written as fiction . . . and Melanie's used to experiencing the very weird as the norm.

And now, additionally, there's a mystery to unravel: What does the dark, freezing-cold being called The Fixer want with Mary, the barkeep's daughter?

Burning Bulb
PUBLISHING

WOL-VRIEY
BIZARRO AND TRANSGRESSIVE FICTION

BIG TROUBLE IN LITTLE ASS

From Bizarro master storyteller Wol-vriey comes a truly weird western tale that will leave you awe-struck and on the edge of your seat...

In the town named Little Ass, tight-assed prostitute Rosa overhears a gunslinger's plans to assassinate rancher Edison Bennett. Once the badass Bennett learns of the plot, he ensures there'll be hell to pay for any attempt on his life!

Yes, it's going to take all of gunslinger Jude's shooting prowess, his eclectic collection of strange firearms, a trusty horse that requires an owners' manual, and the help of the lovely and invigorating Nell (who's EXTREMELY odd when the going gets weird), to survive the Bizarro hell that Edison Bennett unleashes in order to hold onto the land that he'd stolen from Madam Zizi.

BIZARRO 101 (A BASIC PRIMER)

Welcome to the strange place:

A collection of 37 flash fiction stories designed to introduce one to the Bizarro/New Weird Genre.

Weird, dreamy, nightmarish, absurd, sad, surreal, humorous . . . this collection of tales is all this and more.

***

"This primer is the very essence of any and all styles and types of Bizarro writing. Wol-vriey collects, distills, and bottles up these 37 tiny stories for your sensory enjoyment. This is an absolute must-read for anyone new to the genre, because it demonstrates the scope of what Bizarro is, and what it can be."
—Teresa Pollack, Bizarro commentator and blogger

Burning Bulb
PUBLISHING

OTHER GREAT TITLES FROM

Burning Bulb

PUBLISHING

WWW.BURNINGBULBPUBLISHING.COM

BELLY TIMBER

From the writers of Darkened Hills, Detour to Armageddon and Night of the Living Dead comes a novel unlike any other...

In the 1800's, ordinary people learned the secret of the Kala and undertook extraordinary measures to rid the earth of this evil. This is their story.

For John McCormick, life on the Indiana frontier held nothing but promise. His settlement along the White River would soon become the crossroads of America. Friends and family from back in Ohio and other points east were all making plans to see what all the fuss was about in the newly-formed city of Indianapolis. Yes, things were good. John had his general store and his friend George Pogue had his blacksmith business. Claims were being staked and relations with the native Indians were amicable. The town was growing and nothing could be better... or so he thought.

In Ohio, an evil was brewing. The Lecky Family, a group of ruthless Mongolian nomads, had made their way to America and were practicing their cannibalistic religion of Kala with reckless abandon. No one was safe, not even John McCormick's family.

Burning Bulb
PUBLISHING

EVERYTHING HERE IS A NIGHTMARE
Collected Works Vol 1.

"Pyles makes it look easy. His characters come instantly alive with the cocksure verve and swagger of rock stars."
- Daniel Knauf, creator of HBO's "Carnivale,"
Executive Producer/Writer, ABC's "The Blacklist."

The critically acclaimed author of Demons, Dolls and Milkshakes returns with fifteen tales of horror and suspense with Everything Here is a Nightmare.

From zombies in the old west, to a young boy tempted by the Devil. From vampires with romantic longing, to an abandoned lighthouse haunted by vengeful spirits. From a serial killer getting unholy justice, to a haunted English race car, Nelson W Pyles invites you to explore a landscape of fear, suspense and horror.

Take his hand and hold on tight. Remember that whatever you find here, whatever you see, no matter what you might think it could be... know this: Everything Here is a Nightmare.

Burning Bulb
PUBLISHING

ANTHOLOGIES
BIZARRO AND TRANSGRESSIVE FICTION

THE BIG BOOK OF BIZARRO

The Big Book of Bizarro brings together the peculiar prose of an international cast of the most grotesquely-gonzo, genre-grinding modern writers who ever put pen to paper (or mouse to pad), including:

NIGHT OF THE LIVING DEAD horror writers John Russo & George Kosana; HUSTLER MAGAZINE erotica contributors Eva Hore, Andrée Lachapelle, & J. Troy Seate and established Bizarro genre authors D. Harlan Wilson, William Pauley III, Wol-vriey, Laird Long, Richard Godwin and so many more!

From Alien abductions to Zombie sex, The Big Book of Bizarro contains OVER FIFTY STORIES of the most outrélandish transgressive fiction that you'll ever lay your capricious and curious hands upon!

WESTWARD HOES

Nine outlaw writers rode into town from obscurity to pen nine tantalizing tales of horror and fantasy, and leaving once they branded their own personal marks on the weird western genre and became living legends of the American Frontier experience.

Like drunken Indian scouts, the writers fervidly tracked down and captured the Western genre, tore off its fashionable veneer and ravished its exposed essence.

So belly up to the bar with your favorite soiled dove and enjoy perusing these thrilling tales of Old West debauchery, danger and desire; compiled by the publisher of The Big Book of Bizarro and featuring the bizarro novella *Big Trouble in Little Ass* by Wol-vriey.

Burning Bulb
PUBLISHING

ANTHOLOGIES
BIZARRO AND TRANSGRESSIVE FICTION

THE BIG BOOK OF BIZARRO SPECIAL KINDLE EDITIONS

OTHER AWESOME COLLECTIONS

DAVID J. FAIRHEAD

"David Fairhead writes compelling stories that offer very human characters and very inhuman monsters. There is no subtlety in Fairhead's imagination - he is simply dying to scare the hell out of you." - Nelson W Pyles author of DEMONS, DOLLS AND MILKSHAKES

THE FALL

Hopelessness... How do you protect your loved ones when Hell itself opens its insidious mouth?

Horror... Nightmarish Creatures invade your world and there is nowhere to hide.

Blood... How long can you hold out before they come for you?

Pain... Where do you run to avoid being eaten alive by monsters with a voracious appetite for your flesh?

Screams... While you selfishly run for your own life.

Questions... Who is to blame? Where did they come from? How many people survived...and how does the human race find the means to fight back?

THE FALL OF TOMORROW is man's last tale of desperation told by those that are striving to salvage some hope against a ravenous bastion of evil beasts bent on ruling our world.

DWELLING IN THE DARK

From David J. Fairhead, author of the FALL OF TOMORROW, comes DWELLING IN THE DARK- A soulful anthology of creeping terror to keep you up in the small hours with horror set in the past, present and future. Overlapping bits of puzzle fitting each other, before and after The Fall of Tomorrow.

A place where three children facing a monstrous foe can only pray that their bloody summer would just come to an end. Go back to the 1960's- THE COMMUNE where overindulging hippies use a mage's diary to control the end of the world, only to see first-hand that their drug induced visions have horrific ramifications. Where a young boy's visit to a haunted house becomes a lesson in RESIDUAL morality. The story, DEEPER- plunges two brothers into a sinkhole only to find they were being hunted by an insidious creature from its depths. Visit the old west as hero Dekker Collins battles evil gunslingers in DEMONEYE.

And so much more...!

Burning Bulb
PUBLISHING

*www.*FairlyDarkProductions*.com*

NIGHT OF THE LIVING DEAD

Why does Night of the Living Dead hit with such chilling impact?

Is it because everyday people in a commonplace house are suddenly the victims of a monstrous invasion? Or is it because the ghouls who surround the house with grasping claws were once ordinary people, too?

Decide for yourself as you read, and the horror grips you.

All the cannibalism, suspense and frenzy of the smash-hit move are here in the novel.

www.TheJohnRusso.com

Burning Bulb
PUBLISHING

GARY LEE VINCENT'S
DARKENED
THE WEST VIRGINIA VAMPIRE SERIES

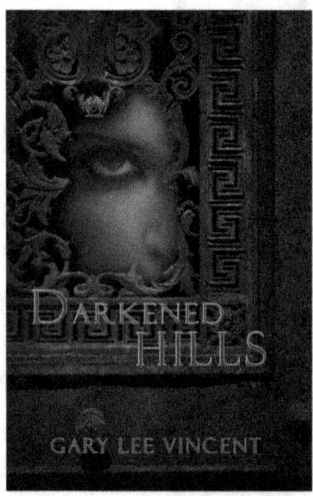

DARKENED HILLS

When evil descends on a small West Virginia town, who will survive?

Jonathan did not start out his life to become a rambler, it justworked out that way. William was a troubled youth with something to hide. Both were from Melas, a small town tucked away in the West Virginia hills... a town where disappearances are happening more and more frequently.

After the suicide of a wanted serial killer, the townsfolk thought the nightmare was over. But when a centuries-old vampire is discovered they find out the hard way it's just getting started. Dark secrets can only stay hidden for so long and when the devil comes to collect, there will be hell to pay. Can Jonathan and William find a way to stop the vampire before it's too late? Find out in *Darkened Hills!*

DARKENED HOLLOWS

In the heart-stopping sequel to the award-winning *Darkened Hills*, Jonathan and William must return to West Virginia to face possible criminal charges stemming from their last visit to the damned town of Melas, where both had narrowly escaped the clutches of a vampire seethe.

And as livestock start mysteriously getting murdered with all of their blood drained, worried farmers are searching for answers - leaving the local Sheriff and his deputy racing against time to learn the cause before a more violent crime is committed.

Burning Bulb
PUBLISHING

WWW.DARKENEDHILLS.COM

GARY LEE VINCENT'S
DARKENED
THE WEST VIRGINIA VAMPIRE SERIES

DARKENED WATERS

When the world goes to hell, the chosen must arise!

As Talman Cane orchestrates a flood of epic proportions in this third installment of the *Darkened* series the towns of Melas and Tarklin are caught completely off guard by the deluge. Hell-bent on finishing what they started, the evil brothers return to the lunatic asylum to take care of the witnesses and add to the ever-growing army of the undead.

Aided by Lucifer himself and the insane vampire demon Legion, the stage is set to channel all of the forces of hell to come forth. In an all-out race to survive, Jonathan, William, and Amanda soon discover they are up against impossible odds as Lucifer opens the Gateway to Hell, ushering in the zombie apocalypse and the End Times.

Find out who will survive this cosmic battle of the ages in *Darkened Waters*!

DARKENED SOULS

Melas and the Madison House are about to be rebuilt.
True evil is about to be reborne!

Young ex-priest and vampire-killer William is drawn back to the West Virginian town that almost killed him, where his vampire arch-enemy Victor Rothenstein still stalks the earth.

The town of Melas lies destroyed after the battle of the End of Days. But why is wealthy Jackie Nixon so eager to rebuild it using the bone dust of murdered souls?

Terrible evil has visited before, but the Gateway to Hell is about to be reopened in a horrific climax. And this time – it's personal.

WWW.DARKENEDHILLS.COM

Burning Bulb
PUBLISHING

WEST VIRGINIA-THEMED HUMORROROTICA
BY RICH BOTTLES JR.

HELLHOLE WEST VIRGINIA

From the heights of Mothman's perch high atop the Silver Bridge in Point Pleasant to the depths of Hellhole Cavern in Pendleton County, evil lurks within the shadows as the sun sets upon the haunted hills and hollows of West Virginia.

Bizarro author Rich Bottles Jr. blows the coffin lid off horror genre clichés with this tour de force cast of Eco-friendly vampires, beach-yearning zombies and sex-starved she-devils.

LUMBERJACKED

If you are easily offended or do not possess a truly depraved sense of humor, this story may not be the light summer reading fare you desire. As for the four feisty female freshmen stranded on top of West Virginia's third highest mountain, they have no choice but to experience the sick, twisted debauchery and perverted mayhem described deep inside the tight unbroken bindings of this horrific missive.

Lumberjacked takes the reader to a nightmarish world where character development and aesthetic integrity are prematurely cut short by the swinging axes of maniacal lumberjacks, who are hell bent on death and destruction in the remote forests of Appalachia. And at the climax, when paranoia crosses over to the paranormal, Lumberjacked makes Deliverance look like a family raft trip down the Lower Gauley.

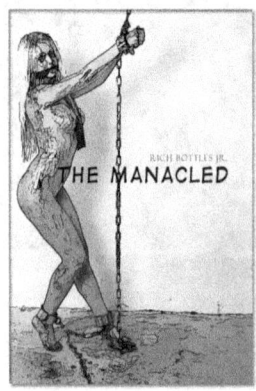

THE MANACLED

What happens when twin brothers lease out the former West Virginia State Penitentiary with the false purpose of filming a documentary on supernatural phenomena, but their true intention is to make a pornographic movie?

Chaos ensues as the disturbed spirits of murdered convicts, along with the reanimated dead from the neighboring Indian Burial Mound, take their vengeance on the unwary and undressed trespassers.

Zombies, ghosts, mobsters and porn collide in this bizarro tale from horror author Rich Bottles Jr.

Burning Bulb
PUBLISHING

THE BOOBY HATCH

With NIGHT OF THE LIVING DEAD, John Russo helped blaze a path in the horror genre that has never been equalled. In this hillarious erotic novel, he blazes a path through the wild, zany Sex Revolution of the 1970s.

Sweet, innocent Cherry Jankowski works for Joyful Novelties, where she tests sex toys ranging from the ridiculous to the sublime. But she can't find love or peace of mind and her efforts are hampered by a Peeping Tom, an exhibitionist, a cross-dressing boyfriend, a quack psychiatrist, and even her own product-testing partner, Marcello Fettucini, who can't get it up anymore and is scared of losing his job!

www.TheJohnRusso.com

Burning Bulb
PUBLISHING

THE TAILSMAN

From the creators of *The Big Book of Bizarro* and *Westward Hoes* comes a new comic unlike anything you have ever seen!

He's hot on the trail, looking for some *tail...*

Sly Franko was a man of the West, a forger of the wild frontier. Like the Country Western song that would be written years after he died, the words, "Faster horses, younger women, and more money," seemed to be the anthem of this horn dog cowboy.

Franko would ride into town on a blazing saddle, find the closest saloon to wet the whistle, belly up to a good card game, and find him a hot-loving hussy to get his cowpoke on with.

However, Sly might have met his match when a visit to bathroom leads to terror and death. Can Sly and his poker buddies solve the mystery before more of the townsfolk are murdered? Find out in this exciting premier issue of *The Tailsman!*

WWW.BURNINGBULBCOMICS.COM

www.ingramcontent.com/pod-product-compliance
Lightning Source LLC
Chambersburg PA
CBHW071221250626
47163CB00001B/61